CW01654602

SECRETS & LIES 1

secrets & LIES

KITTY dB

Cover design by JL Designs

Editing by SophiesProof.com

ISBN 978-1-3999-2183-1

For L

In a world full of seagulls, be a Phoenix and rise from the ashes.

PROLOGUE

Lucie

I'm on my knees; deep in the woods and I can feel the morning dew seeping into my jeans. I remember getting here yet it seems like I'm dreaming. And not for the first time, I question why I am here.

The woods overlook the rear of a massive house that I don't believe I have ever visited but now, somehow it seems so familiar. Have I ever been here? I vaguely knew the road that I parked on to get into these woods but I had to follow the instructions given by Melanie to know where to park and which way to walk. She was specific about me stopping at the clearing, I am now in for the best view.

From my vantage point, all I can see is the back of the house, with its yellow walls that are curved rather than at right angles. It's a beautiful place. The back of the house has a built-up terrace, and the gardens drop away at the end of that patio. Fencing signals the end of the garden and the beginning of these woods.

The house must belong to somebody with money, it's far too palatial to be just anybody's gaff. Melanie's note said I'd find the answers, but it wouldn't bring me happiness. Blunt as ever and more than a little vague. It didn't make any sense when I read it this morning and frankly it still doesn't. She said I wasn't to go to the front of the house. I could only view it from the rear and only from these woods. She also told me to stay out of sight. Blunt and bossy.

So here I am. Hunkered down in the woods looking at somebody's home without any clue as to why. I don't understand what's going on. What is happening? What am I supposed to find here?

The patio leads from a set of French doors and as I sit here wondering what I'm supposed to do next, one of the doors opens.

I squint to see who it is as they exit the building. I don't realise I am crying until I feel my tears drip off my lips.

Suddenly, I feel sick.

PART ONE

ONE

Jack

Six Months Earlier

They say that familiarity breeds contempt. Not today it doesn't. This kind of familiarity means I'm finally home. I've been away for more or less two years. I had a very quick pit stop home just over eight months ago. It seems like forever since I was actually in my own apartment. Funny thing is everything still looks the same. Perhaps it's just me that's changed. I've seen some pretty shitty stuff in the last couple of years and I know it's affected me in more ways than one.

In the last eight months, I've been in the UK and mainland Europe and before that, South America. All over South America. But now I'm home. And I'm tired. Dog fucking tired. So today, familiarity is a welcome and blessed relief.

I open the door to my favourite coffee house and smile as the bell above the door announces new and exiting customers. The aroma hits me hard, soothing my aching body and filling my senses with comfort. I can't complain about the coffee in South America, but the UK? Yeah, that's a whole different story.

'Well, aren't you a sight for sore eyes,' says Cassie, owner of this coffee house and one of the most beautiful women who has ever entered my life. The woman before me is simply gorgeous; head to toe in every conceivable way. Still stunning at 50. If auras exist, hers is golden.

'Hey Cass, good to see you,' I say, smiling up to my eyes. I rarely mean it when I say those words. For Cassie, they're true.

'You too Cowboy, been too long. I was beginning to think my heart would never mend,' I chuckle as she wraps her arms around me in a warm embrace. 'Man, I needed that,' she says loudly with a wink and a wicked smile.

I've known Cassie for nearly 10 years. Whatever she has…it's just got better over time. Garrett, her husband of 30 years thinks so too. G is the closest thing I have ever had to a father figure. I have always thought that they would have made wonderful parents. Watching them together is to see what love truly looks like. Some covet that love; I know I do. Perhaps not whilst I do this job, but in the future, hopefully.

'Back for a while darlin'?' She asks in her southern drawl. Men have died in that voice; I swear to God it's like drowning in honey.

'I hope so Cass, I need my bed,' I smile.

'Cowboy, please don't make me picture you in bed,' she laughs. 'What will you have?'

'Something hot and delicious,' I tell Cass, my eyes gleaming at the possibility of proper coffee. 'Not that shit they serve in England.'

'Watch it cowboy,' warns Cassie, nodding her head in the direction of the barista, 'she'll have you for that comment'.

I look at the barista. I can't see her face, but my instant reaction to her has me christening her 'Little Miss Perky Ass'. Man, I swear it's perfect.

Little Miss Perky Ass is small; 5'2 max. She has to go on her tip toes to reach the cups above the coffee machine. She's bare foot. I'm pretty sure that's a health and safety violation but no way am I telling Cassie that. Now, I love a woman's body and I can't say feet are high on my list of body parts, but she has gorgeous feet. Red painted toes on brown feet, peeping out of rolled up black skinny jeans. As she stretches for the cup so do the muscles in her calves. Now I'm a big guy, 6'5 and built. But right now, looking at Little Miss Perky Ass, my brain is asking if those toned, but little legs, would fit around my hips as I pound her. Jeez…I need to get laid. I can't remember the last time I had a woman in my bed. I haven't even seen her face and yet I'm standing here fantasising about whether her ankles would be able to lock behind my back. I watch her; willing her to turn around. Her hair hangs down her back in glorious tones of summer. Every shade of blonde, long but different lengths and more than enough to wrap my fist around.

Her hand snakes up to reach another cup as the young guy next to me leans on the bar.

'So, gorgeous, when are you going to let me take you out?'

She doesn't even turn to him. Just carries on like she didn't hear him speak.

'Is never good for you?' She says laughing but still not turning his way.

He laughs too. I listen.

'No, not good for me,' he says. 'How about tomorrow night?'

He's persistent. And he's pissing me off. He's practically salivating. I might have to punch him, it's not lost on me that moments ago I was doing the same.

'Never gonna happen sunshine,' she says. I get Cassie's comment now, this girl is British. I don't like their coffee, but the women are a feisty bunch and damn, if I don't like that. She's got attitude and it runs from the bottom of those lush feet right up to her fantastic ass. If you're of a sensitive nature, those British women will stamp all over you. Me? I fucking love it. My cock is twitching and I haven't even seen her face yet. Even so, I know instinctively that she's too good for Dickwad standing next to me. I think I need to just get laid and stop acting like a teenager. But for now, I'll just think about all the things I could do with her glorious ass in my hands.

Turn around. I'm willing her in my mind. Turn around; let's see you.

'I'm gonna try again tomorrow,' says Douchebag.

'Go ahead, it'll just be another day of rejection that you have to face,' she says.

She's laughing to herself. If the rest of her package didn't already have me by the balls, then the laugh just did. Deep and throaty.

'Hey, Ryder, knock it off,' says Cassie. 'Our Lucie doesn't date; do you sweetheart?'

'No, ma'am, I don't,' says the newly christened Lucie.

'Catch you later,' says Douche making his way out of the door. I look at him and give him the stare that covers a thousand words and all of them start with 'fuck off'.

'Not in my lifetime,' says Lucie. Her comment makes me smile. Good girl.

I move into Douche's space and watch her reach for what will be my cup. She doesn't turn around to face me and I can't even see her profile through the hair that falls forward as she reaches for the coffee press.

It's killing me. Not seeing her face is actually killing me. What the fuck is wrong with me? I can get balls deep any time I want and all I want right now is to see her face. I can see Cassie watching me and she looks amused as I stand here staring at her barista. I don't do relationships. I fuck. I fuck then I leave. The job doesn't work for relationships. Not for me or a potential partner. It's too much. Too much leaving at little or no notice. Too much of not knowing when I'll return. Too much of uncertainty which leads to too much insecurity. See? It's just not fair. Better to be in control and nobody gets hurt.

I'm not saying it's not a lonely life. Sometimes the loneliness is a killer. When I'm office based, it's okay. I can go out with my buddies, play pool, shoot some hoops, down a few cold ones after work. I don't even mind when I get invited to dinner with the married friends. Their wives have become my friends too. Admittedly, the constant matchmaking gets tiring, but sometimes, if only for the night, it works out just fine. I don't think I'm an asshole. I try to be a gentleman. Albeit a dirty gentleman.

Now be a good girl and turn the fuck around.

She's turns…finally. HOLY FUCK! Little Miss Perky Ass is… what's a better description than fucking GORGEOUS? Delicious? Not good enough. In-fucking-credible? Words fail me. Are you fucking kidding me, Universe? I'm 29 years old and I've got the beginnings of a hard-on in a coffee shop like some 15 year old kid! She looks up at me beneath her lashes. Fuck me dead. Our eyes meet. And lock.

TWO
Lucie

For the love of God, I wish Ryder would just fuck off. Every day he's here. Every day he asks me out. Every day I turn him down. Enough already! I don't date and even if I did, I wouldn't date Ryder. Don't get me wrong; he's a sweetheart really, just does nothing for me. Nothing. Zero. Nada.

For starters, Ryder and I probably weigh the same. He's taller than me but hey, who isn't? But I don't do thin. No. Just no. And he has those things in his lobes that twist over time to make the hole bigger. Urgh! Makes me want to gag. I imagine him fifty years from now…big holes that his grandkids can watch the sunset through.

Not in a million years' mate. He laughs when I say never. I actually think he just believes I'm playing hard to get. I'm not. I couldn't be less interested. I don't date. Dating means letting somebody into my life. It would involve explaining my story; how I'm here and why. And I just don't feel ready for that. Somebody in my life means I need to let them see into my life and that just ain't gonna happen. I'm here because I can be whoever I choose to be and since leaving home I have chosen to be Lucie Malone. The last thing I need is for my face to appear in some guy's profile photo on a social media site with the words, 'in a relationship with'. But I don't do the casual thing either. I'm really not that girl. I'm like a nun in barista clothing. Do I miss intimacy? Who wouldn't? But part of becoming this 'me' is not without sacrifice. One day, I hope to meet the one. The one I can trust with my story and my heart. But not yet. I like my life. It's simple. Seems perhaps a bit boring from the outside but I'm happy. How many people can say that? Don't get me wrong, I'm no wallflower. I just stick to the people who initially took me under their wing and those friendships give me the space I need to breathe. My sister? My sister I miss. My brothers? Ah not so much. I love them; sure, I do. But you know, brothers eh?

So here I am working with the wonderful Cassie, batting off the persistent affection and advances of Ryder and breathing in the sweet aroma of my beloved coffee. The irony is that I barely drink the stuff anymore. It used to be my go-to drink, no matter what the time. I had a friend once who said that her aunt had worked in the Cadbury factory. When she first started working there she ate chocolate like a demon. Then one day, she just stopped. Said the smell of it every day just meant that out of work, she just didn't want it. I guess that's me and coffee.

I reach up for the next cup. I sniff. Not the most ladylike thing I could do but I do it again. What the fuck is that? All I can ever smell, even after I get home, is coffee. Something delicious is hitting my senses. Citrus? Crisp? Clean? Can I think of any other words beginning with C?

How about Cor? A nice British word. Cor! Mmmmm. I breathe it in.

Coffee made, I turn to pop it on the counter and smile up at the recipient.

I suddenly feel like I'm in the desert, dying of thirst, dying for a drop of water and then boom, I see an oasis. I'm running towards it like a bat out of hell till I finally, get my much-needed drink. The man the other side of the counter is my oasis. And what a mighty fine oasis he is. Man, he's tall. Like really tall. And broad. He looks like he could stop the wind coming in if he stood in the doorway. Dark blue Henley and jeans. Who doesn't love a man in a Henley, right? I'm staring. I know I am. I need to break the stare. I want to turn away but I just can't. Our eyes meet. And lock.

Universe…are you shitting me right now? Seriously? You send him?! Breathe Luce, just breathe. And please God, don't let me dribble. My hand is shaking as I lower the cup. My whole body is shaking…fuck, are we having an earthquake? I shoot a panicked look at Cass to see if she's bracing herself as the earth moves. No. Apparently not. She's just smiling at me. So, it's just me then. Fantastic. Not embarrassing at all. I look into his eyes. My eyes. His eyes. They lock.

He is so very handsome. Dark hair, slight beard and that kind of Hollywood strong jaw. Never really noticed jaws before. And big hands. One is flat on the counter and I notice there is no wedding ring.

'Hey,' I say. I don't think I could string a sentence together right now, so opt for something simple to save further embarrassment. I can feel my face turning heated. Why do I have to be a blusher?

'Hey,' he says back with a smile. Oh, for the love of wet panties, he's got dimples. I want to shout no! Just no…enough. He is the epitome of every horny girl's dream. I swear I can feel the heat between my legs.

'It's okay,' he says with a crooked smile that reaches his eyes, 'I don't date either'.

'That's nice,' I reply. What the fuck am I supposed to say? Inner Lucie is screaming, *'DATE ME!'* Inner Lucie needs to back away from the cookie jar.

He chuckles. Bloody hell, he is mighty fine. I want to lick him…I really do. I want to jump him right now and lick him all over. I'm actually salivating at the thought.

'So, Lucie,' he says nodding at the drink I've just made him, 'you're a British barista'.

Under normal circumstances I really hate it when people state the obvious after hearing my accent. I try not to be rude even though it always seems like such a daft thing to say to me. Perhaps people just need to clarify? Somebody did once ask me if I was Australian. Not sure where that came from.

Instead of delivering my normal half smile with a nod, I hear myself saying, 'yes, have you ever been?' I ask grinning at him.

THREE

Jack

I've read enough in women's magazines (I was on a plane, don't judge) to know that Insta-lust is really a thing. And I want her. Like now. I feel like somebody is standing on my chest and it's kinda hard to breathe. She's beautiful.

'Yeah,' I grin back, 'a few times.'

'And do you like it?' She asks, tucking a stray lock of hair behind her ear. It takes every ounce of strength not to say the words in my head, '*not as much as I'd like to fuck you,*' but instead I say as I lean myself on the bar, 'I do Lucie, I really, really do'.

She blushes. Like really blushes. None of that coy bullshit… it starts at her neck and just keeps rising. I've really never been a fan of blushing. It normally means some kind of inner shyness; being reserved and when you don't have time for conventional relationships, you need the kind of girl that just says what she wants or at least says yes with confidence. Girls who blush like this are - not frigid - that's too strong a word, generally they're just not sassy enough for my tastes. Miss Lucie, however, blushes and right now, I don't give a fuck. She's got the sass in the bag. Cassie taught me all about sassy. Hey, that rhymes.

'So, Miss Lucie, if you don't date. What do you do?' I ask casually, I swear I'm sending her telepathic messages right now, all starting with, '*YOU, I'D DO YOU!*'

Cassie breezes over, 'our Lucie here sings, don't you angel?'

Little Miss Perky Ass looks at her like she wants to die. Then takes what seems like an extraordinarily big breath and says, 'yes, I kinda sing'.

I smile. I want to laugh at how uncomfortable she seems in my presence, but I don't. I'm not cruel. 'Where do you sing Lucie?' If she says in the shower, my brain is going to go into over-drive and I may just come in my pants. Don't visualise her in the shower Jack, too late. Little Jack (a nickname, not a fact) didn't get the memo about not imaging her shower rituals and is now ready to fly.

'Only in The Moon, a few blocks from here,' she says never breaking our eye contact.

I know the place. Cassie and Garrett are pretty much regulars there and I've been a few times with them. The owner, Declan, is a good guy. Solid. Got a daughter working with him but I can't think of her name. I can't seem to do anything but stare at Lucie.

'In fact,' says Cassie, sporting a smile, 'she's on tonight, isn't that right darlin'? Garrett and I are going, why don't you come along Jack?'

'I might just do that Cass. Is that okay with you Miss Lucie?' I'm pulling on the fake southern charm; I think I may need every bit of help.

Lucie looks like she's been caught in the headlights but smiles through her apparent embarrassment. 'Of course, you're free to do as you please. It's not as if they're selling tickets at the door,' she laughs.

'She's underselling herself Jack,' says Cassie. 'If Declan were to sell tickets, he'd sell out in no time. People come from far and wide. Trust me, you don't want to miss out.'

'They do not come from "far and wide",' Lucie says rolling her eyes upwards. 'It's already a popular pub but it's not exactly a stadium. It's not that hard to fill when there are only around 15 tables to start with. You're setting him up for disappointment Cass.'

'Oh, I doubt that very much Miss Lucie. If Cassie says you're bringing in the crowds, I have to believe her.'

Lucie smiles indulgently at Cassie and then retains her smile when turning her head towards me. Cassie slings her arm around Lucie's neck and kisses her cheek. These two obviously have quite a bond. Cassie has always been tactile. For her, affection comes easy.

'And how long have you worked with Cass? I don't remember seeing you the last time I was home,' I say.

'Oh, I've been here just under two years now. Declan - from the pub - introduced us and kind of set the job up for me when I arrived from England.'

'Yeah I know him, good guy'

'Best thing he ever did, darlin',' Cassie says giving Lucie another kiss on the cheek before moving away to serve the customer behind me.

FOUR
Lucie

His name is Jack. He has beautiful teeth and a beautiful smile and I think I'm staring again.

I can't remember the last time I had sex. When was the last time I saw anybody I found even half-way attractive, let alone someone I've met? I can't remember. Since whoever it was, it's just been me and good old Bob. Who needs a boyfriend? Bob is always on hand, never gives me shit, never turns up late and always, always gives me an orgasm. In return I just need to make sure he has working batteries. It's a love affair that has lasted through the years, although we are on Bob version 4.0 now.

Jack takes a sip of the coffee, still standing at the counter, then his eyes lock on mine once again. 'Good coffee Miss Lucie, just another thing I will add to the list of good things about you.'

Oh, I get it. I should have known. You don't look like him without being the stereotypical Mr Player. '*Got a line for everything, mate?*' That's what my sister would say to him if she were here. He is very handsome and I'm sure he really is quite the charmer, but suddenly I find myself not so in awe of this man. What an utter disappointment, but not really a surprise.

If I were a man and looked like him, I'd probably be a player too. Why not? You've got to work with what God gave you. Even so, my disappointment has me offering a small smile and I promptly turn my back and start sorting out my machine. He stays still for a few more moments, clears his throat, then picks up his drink and wanders off to a seat.

Fifteen minutes later, I see him stand and walk over to the counter, cup in hand.

'That was just what I needed, thank you.' Well, at least he's polite.

'Will we see you later sweetheart?' Cassie asks Jack.

'I hope so Cass. I need to see G and it seems that I can catch up with him and catch a show at the same time,' he says looking directly at me, shooting me a wink.

I offer up another small smile but the disappointment in him probably shows in my eyes. He leans over the counter to give Cassie a kiss and heads on out with a wave.

'Ooh he likes you,' Cassie says in her sing-song voice.

'Cass, seriously? If you think I am about to become another notch on that man's bed post, you don't know me at all.'

'Whoa, when did I mention sleeping with him? I just meant that he was attracted to you darlin'. He's a good man, Lucie, a decent man. And those are hard to find. Now I know you're not looking but you've got to date sometime. It's not healthy darlin', never having male company. I worry about you, that's all.'

'There's no need to be worried, I'm perfectly fine. And I could find a date if I wanted to.'

'Like Ryder,' we both say at the same time laughing.

'Well, perhaps not Ryder, but you know what I mean. Please don't try to set me up, Cass.' I plead. 'I'll find someone when I'm ready to and I'm just not there yet. I'm sure he's a lovely guy and you and Garrett are obviously very fond of him. But just leave the matchmaking please?'

'I hear ya darlin'. I won't meddle, I promise.' I wish I believed her.

It's been a tortuous day so far. Ever since Mr Player turned up, my brain and skills decided to up and leave. I finish work at 2pm sharp, give Cassie a quick hug and tell her I'll see her later for my spot at the pub and head off home.

The day is beautiful. Warm and balmy and just what I need after spending so many hours being attacked into cold submission by the air con. I strip out of my uniform back at work and now I'm walking the streets in my shorts and tank vest. I've piled my hair up only because I don't want to have to wash it again for tonight, but I hide behind my sunglasses. I wonder about tonight's gig; I don't believe for one moment Mr Player will turn up. He's probably shagging some bimbo senseless, elevating his ego even more. Lucky bitch.

My apartment is stuffy when I return so I whack on the air con for half an hour as generally that's all I can manage without freezing. People remark all the time that I must love air con, coming from England where it's always cold. Er…hello? Sure, we get a fair amount of rain and some snow but it's England, the land of the damp not Alaska.

Home. I think of my mum. Would I still be at home if Mum

hadn't died? I really don't know the answer to that. Melanie, my sister is still there. As are my two brothers, Chris and David. And of course, the man of the hour, good old Dad. My dad. Best described in a few words like you see on a dating website profile. Male, 56, tall, firm and athletic build, takes no shit, hobbies include fast cars and double-barreled shotguns.

Yep, the old man's job is being a full-time criminal, masquerading as a building contractor. Oh, the absolute joys of being a gangster's daughter. That's gangster not gangsta, two entirely different things. My old man doesn't wear his jeans hanging off his arse nor does he walk around dripping in gold. No, my old man is sharp. A sharp dresser, sharp mind. And when he wants to be, he is the meanest son of a bitch on the planet. I grew up more than a little intimated by him, until I realised that the 'hard man' only really applied during work hours. Unfortunately, in his line of business, it was always quite difficult to get a handle on what those hours were from one day to the next.

So, he's a criminal? It's not like he's a bad criminal. He doesn't murder people. He doesn't hurt the weak or vulnerable. He's more bent than criminal I like to think. Stolen goods, lots and lots of stolen goods. Black market stuff too. Loan shark.

The building firm isn't a front. It's a legit business and a really successful one too. Mainly commercial buildings. Some might think he got lucky but some of us know that getting the contracts have often been about having shit over the right person and using it against them until he got the contract. See? Bent, not criminal.

My brothers 'work' for him. They refer to themselves as businessmen…businessmen who like to partake in bare knuckle fighting. When Mum was alive, they had just started on the fight circuit. Neither of them thought she knew. They must have thought she was born yesterday if they think she didn't know. I would often hear her balling my dad out for allowing it. It made the old man proud that his sons could handle themselves. Mum would go bloody nuts at him but would never say a word to her boys.

Melanie and I grew up knowing what our dad did, knowing that our mum knew and knowing that one day, the boys would follow the old man into the 'other' family business. Who bloody knew that this would also be the career choice that Mel would take? She's a businesswoman, but trust me, if she had to go bare knuckle with somebody, she would. She runs her own business, a boxing club. That's not a front either. Another legit business. It's her night-time activity that takes her into the illegal stuff.

I was always viewed as the fragile child. Mum died when I was still quite young and Dad was always more concerned that I was too small to take care of myself. He'd regularly get the boys to jump me; I'd have to run like I was being attacked. I couldn't do it; I just used to dissolve into fits of laughter. So, the old man sent me to self-defence classes. That lasted two sessions. Dad didn't like me being manhandled by boys. He found me a tutor, a woman who trained with the Israeli army no less. It was pretty much Krav Maga before it actually became a thing. She taught me some invaluable lessons and the best one was that being small was not a disadvantage. Height and weight have nothing to do with being able to defend yourself. She taught me that and I am forever grateful.

When I first moved here, I believed I was safe. I understood that not all neighbourhoods were the same and some were the kind of places you only went once you were dead. Or to die. But I had the smarts to work out what was good and what was bad and as money wasn't much of an issue (bonus to being a gangster's daughter) I managed to get myself a place in an up-and-coming neighbourhood that was more coming than upping. Armed with my self-defence skills I felt okay with that. Ironically, it's Cassie that's worries about my safety. She doesn't know I have skills for days. I have just told her that I did Karate at school and could look after myself.

I love my apartment and the people who are in my neighbourhood have always offered me welcoming smiles. I've made friends in the last couple of years I've been here and working for Cassie has been the best move ever for me. I can sing at night and still get my pin money from work. I never think about the money paying for my apartment as being dirty money. Officially, it's the money my mum left for me but her money was Dad's money so yeah, dirty money. You ignore the unsavoury when it suits you. We all do it.

I'd been living here a few months when the self-defence classes paid off when some prick tried to mug me at 8 o'clock night. 8 o'clock…really? How desperate do you have to be? It wasn't even nearly dark. I don't remember much apart from striking lucky when I kicked him square in the balls. He went down like a sack of shit, so I just kept kicking him. I think, looking back, I may have gone a little over the top as I remember a pair of arms going around my middle, hoisting me the air with the words, '*I think he's had enough of a lesson'*. The cop who lifted me off the mugger laughed as he told me, that if I hadn't been stopped, I'd have been in danger of the mugger pressing charges against me.

I wander into my bathroom to run my tub for step one of my pre-gig ritual. When I found my apartment, it was the tub and shower that swung it for me. A shower big enough for two (ever hopeful) and separate from the bath. A bath big enough for two (always hopeful) that I could sink into. I swear if it had just those two things in it, I still would have taken it. The bath run, my day makeup removed and slipping into the warm bubbles, I close my eyes and remember how I got here.

FIVE

Jack

What the fuck did I say that made Lucie turn cold? Did I actually get her back turned on me? Sassy pants needs to understand I'm a persistent bastard. And I want her. Every inch of her. Preferably underneath, me…naked.

I finish my coffee, which actually is really good and get up. 'May see you tonight then Cassie,' I say, hoping as I haven't included Little Miss Perky Ass in that statement it will make her turn around. It doesn't.

'That would be good Jack, I'll tell Garrett, he'd love to see you.'

'Let's surprise the old buzzard Cass.'

‘Oh yes, that’s a much better idea, Jack. He’s going to be so pleased you’re home darlin’.’

‘Miss Lucie,’ I say before I walk out of the door.

I get a wave, but it’s a wave that doesn’t involve her turning around. At least she didn’t flip me the bird, right?

I make my way home and when I open the door for the second time today, it feels cold in here. I hadn’t even changed since my flight when I went to see Cass this morning. First stop, always. Cassie has been part of my life since the day I left the Academy. Garrett was a senior agent but about a year into my service, he decided to take early retirement after taking yet another bullet and Cassie threatened him that if another one hit him, she’d cut it out of him herself. Garrett knew his woman and knew she’d keep her word.

I acted as his shadow for the first month of my life at the Bureau. He wasn’t exactly a father figure to me, more like a teenager with no fear in a then, 45 year old body. He could still shift it if necessary and still had more knowledge for the job than those younger than him, but Cassie’s coffee shop was doing well, the house was paid for, no kids, so he decided that he’d prefer the golf course to working a desk job.

Garrett has always been the man I seek out when I need some clarity. Whether it be the job or my life. Neither G nor Cassie mention the life I lead outside of work. They know I don’t date in the conventional sense, but they don’t know I get lonely. If I were to tell them I would feel like they would carry that as a burden. Cassie and Garrett, when we talk about me meeting somebody, hum the theme tune to The Littlest Hobo. It makes them laugh. It makes me smile but only because they have a point. Never settling down.

I have no family. No-one. Nada. Zip. Grew up in a foster home after Mom disappeared. She went out one day and just didn’t return. I knew, even as a kid, that she wasn’t like other kids’ moms. She struggled to work and to look after us, but she was a good parent when she was feeling level. I realise now that her issues were depression, perhaps even bi-polar disorder, but at the time, I was a kid, I had no clue she was ill with it. I remember hearing her cry when I was in bed. Her life always seemed too painful for her. Nobody ever found my mom. I still have no idea what happened to her or what made her leave me that day and I don't think I ever will. She left no trace and no body was ever found but I don't believe she is alive. Whatever happened on that day happened and it put me in the care system. The families I was with were good but once I turned eighteen, I was out. As soon as I could, I applied for the Academy and since then the FBI and in turn, Cassie and Garrett have been my family. I've no complaints.

I was lucky. I had the brains and school had been good for me. It gave me something to focus on and a routine. My life with my mom never had any structure, well not in the way other kids knew. I have no idea if my mom gave me my intellect. I never met my dad and Mom never spoke of him. He certainly wasn't named on my birth certificate. That space was always just left blank. I wasn't the only one without a father so I didn't feel that was unusual. I obviously had grandparents at some point but I don't ever remember my mom talking about them and my foster parents told me that the child services would have tried to locate grandparents or other relatives before fostering me out. My mom never mentioned any other family. It was always just me and Mom. She used to tell me we didn't need anybody and nobody needed us. I remember that made me happy. She loved me so much and in return she was my world. When I was placed in my foster home, I felt so alone for the first time in my life. Now I am an adult, I know how much I repressed the feelings of abandonment but I try not to dwell on those times. It won't change anything. It was a long time ago in what feels like a past life. I won't ever forget Mom and I will love her till the day I die. I hope wherever she is, she'd be proud of me.

I start the shower to warm the water through and thank Cassie silently for arranging a cleaner whilst I have been away. Coming home to two years' worth of dust would not have been welcome. As it is; everything is sparkling and clean and I smile as I enter my shower.

The rainfall shower head beats down on me, soothing and calming me instantly. I stand for several minutes with my eyes shut just zoning out. Lucie quickly makes an appearance in my mind. I reach for my stirring cock knowing I need a release and just merely thinking about her gets me hard. I stroke myself back and forth feeling the familiar rise in my balls. I could just make a call and get myself off that way but I'm too selfish to want to have somebody else in my space today. Unless of course that person was Lucie. I continue to stroke myself as I think about peeling her uniform off her, watching her blush rise knowing what comes next. My mind has me pinning her against the wall in this shower, her toned legs do fit round my hips after all but I need to keep one hand under her ass to keep her in position whilst I pound her. Hard and fast. Pushing her further; taking her deeper. My release comes quicker than normal. Fuck, I'm just horny. My mind is laughing behind my back knowing that tonight I will be in that audience as I watch Miss Lucie on stage and fuck, if I'm not really looking forward to seeing her again.

I really could just make a call and get laid, but there's only one woman I want right now and I'll be damned if anybody is going to stop me. The assumption is that I don't date, I'm this no-heart bastard that uses women for my own gain. That's not a total lie but it's not the underlying truth, that is much deeper rooted. I have only seen it a few times but watching a loved one be told that their person isn't coming home again has to be the most heart-wrenching thing to witness. I wouldn't wish that on my worst enemy, let alone somebody I loved. And I love being FBI, therefore, it's a case of lovers rather than loves for me. For the time being at least. Cassie thinks it's funny that I think I can avoid falling in love. You can't do something you don't go near as I have reminded her often but still she insists that one day, Princess Charming is going to ride in and knock all my best laid plans right out the fucking window.

But in the meantime, I need to get my shit together so I can watch Miss Lucie do her thing and try not to embarrass myself with front-tenting my jeans. Drying off, I walk around my place. I have a nice apartment; perhaps not the cosiest nor the sleekest but practical and it has great views. My bags are still on the bed where I left them earlier so chucking them off, I dry myself quickly, pull on some sweats and slip into bed. I know I shouldn't sleep; it's much better to just continue with the day then go to bed tonight at a fairly reasonable time. But I would much rather be up all night than not sleep right now.

As I pull the covers around me and place my hands behind my head, I think about the last few hours and meeting Lucie. She really is beautiful. And she appears to be a sweet girl. I should probably leave her alone; unless I want Cassie to string me up by my balls. I've met a lot of beautiful women but very few are a natural beauty like Lucie. Most are cosmetically enhanced either by makeup or surgery and after a while they all kinda look like each other, all following the same 'recipe'. Lucie, however, was different. Is different. I would say she was cosmetic free, not that I'm an expert, but I saw no obvious makeup. Her hair was naturally a bit unruly but stunning. I wonder what I said that made her suddenly freeze and turn away from me? One minute we were smiling at each other and the next I was ignored.

I can feel my eyes closing and I don't want to fight it. I do however set an alarm. Just a couple of hours sleep will do. I grab the curtain remote and darken my room. And I don't wake up for several hours and some random dreams later.

SIX

Lucie

3 years ago. London. Home.

'Mel, where's my fucking makeup bag?' I scream.

'In your fucking room you blind bitch,' retorts Mel.

'Not where I left it!' I yell.

'So? It's still in there. Stop being so bleeding precious!' I go downstairs ready for battle with her to see her dolled up to the nines.

'Where are you going?' I ask. 'You look like you'd fit in at Pimpsville,' I laugh.

'Oh, ha ha! I'm going with the boys tonight,' she says.

I look at her blankly. The boys? Our boys? For fight night? What the fuck?

'What? Why?' I ask with my eyebrows somewhere up by my hairline.

'Management, chicka,' she says smiling at me.

'Management? I splutter. 'You've got to be fucking kidding me!'

'No. What, you think I can't do it?'

'Mel, I know you can do it babe but why would you want to?'

'Because I love it baby, all that sweat, swagger, hard man shit, I fucking love it and the boys don't want to have to get involved with the bag anymore, so they asked if I wanted in. It's not like I've never been there. I go every time they fight,' she says.

'Mum is spinning in her grave right now, you know that right?' I say shaking my head, giving her the look that screams MORON.

'Oh please, who the fuck do you think took care of the bag for her brother?' She smirks.

No. No way Jose. My mum would not do that. I know she wouldn't. Would she?

'You want this to be your life, Mel? End up with a man like Dad? Tell me you don't hon, please?' My look must be one of pure sadness as she gets up to me and closes her arms around me, kissing the top of my head.

'Each of us are who we are darling, this is me, it's in my blood. I don't want it for you, but I want it for me. I always did. I always wanted to be with Dad and the boys and be in whatever they were. I've never lied about it chicka; you just never chose to listen.'

'So, you want this? Now I have to add YOU to my list of worries? I have to put you in the pile with the rest of my family who may end up banged away?' Tears threaten to roll but I will them back.

'Oh, calm down, you worry too much. Dad hasn't been inside for years. It's coolio chicka. Honest.' She lets me go just enough to

put my face between her palms. 'I love you Chicka and you need to know this is my life and it's what I want.' I do know. I've always known. I just thought she'd change her mind.

'Mel, I need to tell you something,' I start, not letting go of her hands. 'I need to get away from here, I want to travel and live somewhere different, this isn't the life I want.'

'I know bubs. But not for a while eh?' she asks. This time it's Mel's tears that threaten to drop.

'Soon. Very soon. I need to talk to Dad,' I say stating the obvious. God, if I didn't tell him upfront, he'd have the army out looking for me in a day.

I think back to the previous evening when I heard the discussion between my brothers and my dad. Voices were raised, which wasn't unusual in our house, but things were getting slammed too and it didn't feel right. I crept downstairs and listened outside the door. It was hard to understand what was happening as my brothers did have a tendency to talk at the same time. When you're in the room with them, it's actually relatively easy to work out what is being said but away from them, it's damn near on impossible. After a few minutes of listening, my dad shouted for silence. I only heard one complete sentence, delivered by Dad. And it was clearly spoken.

'Of course it wasn't an accident, the only people who ever believed that was the fucking police and your sister.' Even though there are two 'sisters' in this house, I know they're talking about me. The one who only ever gets snippets of information as 'she's too young and too fragile' to be told the truth.

With tears streaming down my face, I remember thinking that he'd just confirmed my inner fear. Mum dying, it wasn't an accident. I instantly felt sick at hearing these words. He knew it wasn't an accident but always said it was? It made no sense. And why was he telling just my brothers? Shouldn't Melanie and I be privy to this information too? Mel was out with friends so I slipped back upstairs before any of them came out the door. I paced my bedroom trying to work out what was going on but kept coming back to the same point. He knew. He didn't want me to know. I felt beside myself with anger, but my dad wasn't somebody I would ever cross and I knew that about myself. There was only one thing to do. I had to get away. Get away from here and get away from him.

Mel brings me back to the present by hugging me. I squeeze her back. She loves me so damn much and the feeling is mutual. But my sister doesn't need me. She doesn't actually need anybody. It was time to leave.

'You ready, boys?' she screams up the stairs. I hear footsteps although it could be a herd of elephants. 'Come on ya lazy fuckers, let's go get some money.'

I find Dad in his office. Home office. Haha, I remember when it used to be the dining room. Then I remember it's where all the stolen goods were stocked. Then I remember it's where the big leather chair and the safe is now. He sits behind the desk, glasses on, nursing a drink with only the table lamp on.

'Pop?' I say quietly

'Hello darling, you okay?' he asks looking up and smiling at me. I think as he looks at me how handsome he still is. In the prime of his life. I don't know if he'll ever meet another woman for a relationship although, God love him, he has more sex than the rest of us! Not that he's ever shared that information, it's just sometimes, he doesn't come home and when he finally does it's with a total spring in his step and a 'just fucked' look on his face. It's almost happy. So, we just don't ask.

'Pops, I've decided to go travelling with some friends. I feel like I need to stretch and learn. I don't want to stay here, this isn't enough for me.'

He listens and nods. Then he smiles. 'You know Mum used to call you her Free Bird. She used to say that you can't keep a Free Bird in a cage. That's you kiddo.' He smiles again indulgently. 'So, is this you asking my permission?'

'No, Dad. I'm not asking permission. But I want you to be okay with it,' I say.

'Can't say that I'm happy about it but I'm okay with it darling. Where are you planning on going?' He asks as he comes around the side of the desk and takes me in his arms.

'Start off in Europe, then onto the States, if possible. My friends only want to do Europe so when they're ready to go back or when I've had enough, I'll go to the States then.'

'You want your old man to sort you out a visa to work?' he asks smiling. I knew he'd offer. He knew I'd say yes. 'Well, you've got a fat bank account from the money Mum left you and I'll make sure it's kept topped up. You okay my darling? You look tired'

'I'm okay, I didn't sleep much,' I feel like a fraud right now. I'm so angry with him but if I show this then he will absolutely stop me from going away. I know that once I am at the airport, I will officially be leaving the UK as Lucie Malone and the previous me will cease to exist. Lucie was the name of our cat when I was little and when Dad asked me to pick a name, that was the first one I could think of. When Mum died and Dad was being a bit freaky, he got us all new passports in fake names, just in case. It's cool. I don't want to go as the real me. I may never want to be found. I used to think Dad was being paranoid but hearing last night's conversation makes me think differently.

Two weeks later and here I am packing my backpack with Mel lounging beside me. She is supposed to help me pack but she's drinking a glass of wine and telling me how much she'll miss me. I'll miss her too, so much, although I am looking forward to never having to find my makeup in her room again, she's like a bloody stealth thief when she wants to be.

'So, Chicka,' she says wiggling her eyebrows, 'men; French or Spanish?'

'Really? That's the choice? There are more than two counties in Europe Mel, you know that, right?'

'Hmmm, fair point and well made. So French, Spanish, or Italian?' she asks laughing.

'You really have got to work on your geography hon; I'm guessing they are the only countries you can think of, right?'

'Nah, just the others would be all quite white and pasty and that my lovely sister is just fucking wrong. Now those olive-skinned Mediterranean men? Hmmmm. You done yet? I want to get plastered with you one last time before you fuck off and leave me forever.'

'Mel, I'm not leaving forever, I just don't know when I'll be back. But you get it right? You understand why I've got to get out of here? I hate being in this house without Mum and I know I've still got you, but this life, the one that took Mum, it's not for me Mel. I don't want to walk down the street anymore and everybody know who I am. You like this life babe, but I don't. And if I get out now, I won't be sucked into it.'

'Jesus kiddo, you make it sound like Alcatraz! It ain't that bad. But I get it, I really do. I have always known this isn't you and so did the Olds. Not that Dad would ever say it but you're his baby and even he gets it. Now, sit down and drink yourself silly with your big sister whilst your big sister still has you here,' she's grinning. She's okay. She gets it. 'Bubs, we need a code; you know that right?' She says looking down.

'We do? What kind of code? What for?' I ask, completely confused with where she is going with this.

'A saying honey; one that tells you if we need you home without having to go into any detail,' she says quietly.

'What? Why? Mel, you're confusing me.'

'Just humour me okay babe?'

We decide on the message that she will send in case of an emergency. I don't say the obvious. Like 'why wouldn't you just call and tell me?'. One thing about my family, they really love a bit of cloak and dagger and who am I to spoil the fun?

The next morning it's time to say goodbye. The boys give me a hug so tight I think one may have broken a rib or six. I get lots of threats from them too. Threats that involve coming to get me if I don't keep in regular contact. I don't say they'd have to find me first.

Mel is openly crying. Not sniffling, but full-on wailing. I'd ask her to give it a rest, but I think that'll just make matters worse. We hug it out instead.

Dad stands quiet and stoic. The tears are threatening to drop. I pray he doesn't start crying too or I will totally lose it. Instead he draws me into his arms and whispers in my ear that he wished Mum was here to say goodbye and watch her bird fly off.

The tears are stinging the back of my eyes. Just hearing those words is so painful. I can't go there. It won't bring her back. Not now. Not ever. Time to put my shit in one sock and get out of here.

Europe lasted 5 months and we had a ball. As I suspected, my friends wanted to go home at the end and I did too. The only difference was that mine was a whistle-stop. I just needed to get the paperwork and a ticket and I would be on my way to the good ole US of A. Dad informed me that he has some distant cousin in Boston who is going to collect me from Logan Airport and I'll stay with him and his daughter, Carmel, on the temporary. Apparently, he has assured Dad that he has a friend who owns an independent coffee shop and he's arranged for me to meet up with her with the view of giving me a job. Thanks to my bank account I don't need to work, but if I can, I will. Even if it's just a little pin money.

The first thing I learn about Boston is that in February it's fucking freezing. Landing at Logan and looking outside to the snow was bad enough but once I met Declan and we left the terminal to find his car, I thought I might just freeze to death. I have never known temperatures like it. In England this amount of snow would grind our country to a stop. Here, everybody just seems to carry on like it's perfectly normal.

Declan seems nice. He looks a fair bit older than my dad and he's kind of round and jolly and warm. He chats non-stop on the way to the bar he owns and lives in. He tells me it's just him and his daughter and how much she is looking forward to meeting me too.

The pub is lovely. Homely, warm, with dark wood and lots of sage green. It's not a dive bar. I don't know what I was expecting but I don't think it was this. Declan shows me to my room as I tell him I'll be out looking for apartments tomorrow after I meet with Cassie, his friend. He tells me that I can stay as long as I want but if I insist then I need to ensure I remain in the same neighbourhood as the bar. Something about a promise to keep me safe. From the little I have seen on the drive here, that wouldn't be so bad. It looked nice. No complaints from me.

The following day, armed with a hand-drawn map courtesy of Carmel, I leave the pub to meet with Cassie. I think about what she might be like. I'm going with kind of sweet and fairly old. You know what they say about assumptions? Yep, I'm the ass in this story because the woman behind the counter looks like a real-life Jessica Rabbit. No shit, she really does. She is probably in her early fifties but she is a SIREN. She might even be a 1940's film star. Whatever she is, she's gorgeous and as I soon discover, warm and totally cool.

'Lucie!' She cries as she rounds the counter heading towards me and envelopes me in her arms with the warmest hug I've had since I

lost Mum. I almost feel like crying knowing I'll never again be held in Mum's arms like this. I think I might have hung in a bit too long but it's so lovely.

'Hello,' I manage to squeak as we part. 'Thank you so much for helping me out, I am so grateful,' I say earnestly.

'Oh nonsense, it's my pleasure darlin', I needed somebody to help me anyway so I guess this is fate, right?' she says smiling.

'Well, I guess we should see how I do first?' I say laughing and not quite believing my luck.

'You'll be fine, I can tell. And the job, well it may not set your world on fire darlin' but you'll be safe and I'm not so bad to work for,' she laughs.

'Thank you so much, I'm really grateful to you. After I leave here, I need to view some apartments so I'm hoping that my luck from this morning will continue for the rest of the day'. I don't plan on telling anybody that I have enough money without having to work. If I didn't get a job, I'd probably never meet anybody new.

The trial goes far better than I could have imagined. I did some waitressing for a Saturday job when I was younger and as I am only a 'trainee' for the foreseeable I can't go too wrong. Cassie is happy to train me. Before I leave, I ask Cassie to help point me in the direction of the first apartment. She seems quite pleased with the address, informing me that it's pretty much smack in the middle of the shop and The Moon, Declan's bar.

I arrive at the address and I immediately fall in love with it. I just do. It's not the largest but it's floor to ceiling white paint and the bath...the bath is HUGE. And the shower is amazing. I have references with me that Declan had thoughtfully provided and the landlord is happy to accept them based on Declan being a local business owner. He informs me I can move in tomorrow. I'm moving in tomorrow! I literally skip back to the bar.

The next morning, I make my way back to the coffee house for 7.30 in the morning as arranged. Cassie is already there but thankfully the door is still locked. It's Sunday and she told me yesterday that she doesn't normally open on a Sunday but is doing so today so we can do some training.

The coffee machine is incredible and slightly intimidating but by 10.30, whilst I might not win any Barista awards any time soon, I can make a decent cappuccino and latte and my hands have finally stopped shaking.

When we close that day at 2pm, my feet are killing me, my bum is numb and I think I'm high from the coffee fumes. Cassie tells me to go home, get cleaned up and to meet her and her husband Garrett at the bar. First, I need to move. Carmel offers to drive me and my suitcase to my new apartment and has given me a bundle of towels, bedding and some other 'starter kit' bits until I have time to do some home shopping.

I am all settled in by 5pm so I take my long lusted after first bath. God, it's glorious. I may stay here forever. But of course, I don't as I have arranged to meet my 'friends' at the pub.

During the course of the evening, I mention to Cassie that I used to gig in local pubs around where I grew up (under the watchful eyes of my brothers and Mel) and also used it as a means to earn an income whilst travelling. She, of course, doesn't keep this information to herself and before I realise what is happening, I have both Declan and Carmel in front of me trying to get me to commit to a gig at the pub.

'Are you actually looking for somebody? I ask.

'Now darling, does it matter?' Declan responds.

The truth is I guess it doesn't, but my mind tells me I should find out as I don't want them to feel obliged and just thinking ahead here, if they hate me then it will be equally hard to tell me to fuck off. This thinking ahead that I do. Total gift.

'To be honest with you, we have been looking for a while to bring in a younger audience here and for that we need somebody younger on stage not the cronies Da' has hanging around the place until kicking out time,' Carmel says nudging Declan.

'Why don't you at least try it out darling, see if you like it, we'll see if we like you and we can go from there if we're all happy. Now how does that sound?' Dec says.

'That sounds good' I respond.

After a really lovely evening in which we sang whilst Dec played the piano, I drank too many pints of the black stuff and even had a game of dominos with one of the old boys who looked like he might be part of the furniture, Garrett and Cassie insist on walking me home on their way and I open the door to my apartment feeling happy and light. Things are going to be okay.

The following day was my first Monday at the coffee house and it was manic, but I loved it. Who knew there were actually so many varieties of coffee and so many bleeding ways to make it? I arrived for 6.30 ready for the business rush to begin at 7am and through to at least 10.30 am the place was bloody mobbed. Cassie was amazing, even when I fucked up orders. She had a permanent smile on her face, the customers loved her and so did I. For the first time in a long while, I felt comfortable, safe, and no longer alone.

SEVEN
Lucie

Lying in a tub made for two my mind once again begins to drift. I'm not thinking about home now, I'm thinking about Jack. Oh my word. How gorgeous was he? Stunning. He was just massive. Taller than my brothers who towered over me at 6'3 and built like a brick shit house. He could literally fill my doorway. His eyes were mesmerising. I wouldn't be surprised to learn that he had hypnotic powers with those peepers. I've never seen that colour eye in my life. I knew eyes could be the bluest of blues, but these were something else. Like those postcards of secret lagoons found off the beaten track in Greece. They made you want to dive straight in. I laugh to myself; twenty dollars says they're coloured contacts. There is no way in hell they're for real.

I'm betting that whatever is in his pants delivers a punch too. And forearms. You know forearms are a bona fide porn thing, right? And I love them. They truly are my kryptonite. It's one of the reasons I don't like the skinny men that all my friends used to love. Forearms should have a smattering of hair and be big. I want to see the veins run right through to big, big hands. Jack has big, big hands and I smirk to myself as I imagine my arse sitting in them. This man has had a ridiculous effect on me. Even though I know what kind of man he is, it doesn't stop the fantasies.

I need to get out of the bath because if I don't, the only thing the customers at the pub tonight will be watching is an empty stage. I get out of the bath and wrap a towel around me before stalking off to the wardrobe to find some clothes. I like to perform in comfortable clothes, but my inner Lucie is screaming, '*GO FOR THE SEXY!*'. I'm not doing this for Jack, obviously. No, I just fancy a change. And if he is there, well, I might want to look a little inviting. Hell yeah. No, I tell myself, he won't be there. Tonight, I have no doubt that he'll be seeing to a stacked bimbo and damn, if I'm not more than a little pissed off at that thought.

I decide on black skinnies, a girl can never get enough of black skinnies and tan high platform wedged peep toe sandals. Hello, extra 5 inches.

I want to show off my arms. I've got good arms. My mother's arms. Slender and toned. A black loose fitting boob tube. I may never win any competitions for being over endowed in the bosom department but by God they're pert! Yep, I'm feeling it tonight. My makeup is beyond simple. Since living here I've acquired a healthy daily glow, gone are the days of full coverage foundation. I never did get a perfect skin tone match anyway. Just a bit of tinted moisturiser, a pop of colour on my cheeks, lashings of a good old mascara and lip gloss. Ta da. I look at myself in the mirror. I'll do. It's The Moon for Christ's sake not Madison Square Garden.

What I love about playing at The Moon is that I can walk there. Guitar slung over my shoulder and my best foot forward. I know that Cassie and Garrett will walk me home as they need to go past my door on their way, worrying like parents that I get home safely. They like a drink and I love that they never drink and drive. My entourage may be small but it's mighty.

The Moon is only a few blocks from my apartment. Whenever I walk there, I always smile that I think of the distance in blocks now. Next thing you know I'll be calling the rubbish *'garbage'*. I love this laid-back city. I never feel unsafe here, despite the attempted mugging, but then I never have, even when my life was anything but. I'm not saying I grew up in a war zone but there were times, a lot of times, when families would go up against each other and fuck, you did not want to be around when it started kicking off. My brothers would take it upon themselves to act as security for me and my sister. The irony was that my sister could take out any bloke that tried it with her. She did on numerous occasions much to my mum's horror. *'Act like a fucking lady'* my mother would scream, you couldn't make that shit up.

Here, I tend to stick to the places I know. Cassie has shown me around the city and the surrounding areas plenty of times, but I don't venture too far on my own. Garrett has warned me that, like anywhere, there are places I shouldn't go but as I told him, I'm not looking to get myself into any trouble so I will be staying close to the nest.

I've made a few friends of my own age since being here. Girls that are regulars at the coffee house have invited me out with them. I've gone a couple of times and had a great time but when I'm not playing at The Moon, I like to stay home and chill. I may not have the most exciting life, but I am happy. Safe and happy. I can't ask for more than that. The girls sometimes come down to the pub and I really appreciate them making that effort. I hang out with them when I have a break from my set. They're all great girls, but I don't have anybody that close to me. I have Cass and I speak to my sister a couple of times a week. And I have Carmel. She hasn't taken over Mel's role, but she is more of a big sister than some far off distant relative. Cassie tries to encourage me to go out more, but I don't feel the need. For the first time ever, my life is completely my own, to do with what I wish. I don't have anybody to answer to so if I want to be a bit of a hermit, I will be.

As I leave my apartment, I say hello to my neighbour, Mrs Dollance and her yappy pug, Maple. Sweet little thing. Barks through the night. I'm sure she drives the other residents crazy, but I like to go to sleep listening to music so it kind of drowns her out. Mrs Dollance is sweet. She always seems to be baking something or other. I regularly find sweet treats outside my door. I know a few other neighbours, they're all friendly and our little apartment block has no trouble.

As I leave my building, the warm air hits me and heats my skin. I love it. I love summer; it's my favourite season. I love seeing the kids in the neighbourhood playing outside, mums sitting on the steps watching them. Everything feels lighter, happier.

I smile with gratitude; my life is good.

EIGHT

Jack

Thank God I managed to get some sleep and now I'm back in the shower having a good wake up. It's only the Irish pub so I settle on my favourite pair of battered jeans and a t-shirt that's at least 10 years old. It fits…just. I have grown in the chest department over the years but what I love about it most is its softness. When I was put into foster care, I never had anything that felt soft. Not clothes, towels, or bed linen. The moment I got my own place I went out and spent nearly a week in department stores looking for the best and softest linen and towels I could find. I still make a mission of it whenever I need new ones. There is a saying that you never miss what you've never had but that's bullshit. You know what's out there. You know luxury even if you've never felt it.

Chucking on a pair of old boots, grabbing my phone and wallet, I'm out the door. Off to see what Little Miss Perky Ass can do. A smile spreads across my face and my cock twitches. Yep, tonight, she's coming home with me.

It's a fair way but I walk to The Moon; it's a nice night and for the first time in so long I don't need to be checking over my shoulder or checking in with somebody. I know it's only a matter of time before I start getting itchy feet to be in the chaos again but for now, I am happy to be home and to just take a break. Breathe a little. Have some fun. Shoot some hoops with my boys. Spend time with Cass and Garrett and get that family feeling that I find comforting.

And let's not forget the added bonus of being friends with Cass, G and…Lucie.

I've never known Cassie and Garrett to be close to anybody like her before, well except me. But that's different. I was forced on G and so our friendship developed from there. Cassie has had girls work for her before, but I've never seen her have the connection she has with Lucie with any of them.

I've never thought of Cassie as being maternal, it just never seemed to be the way she was made. Yeah, she's looked after me for years but only in so much as inviting me to dinner, sorting out the apartment when I've been away from home but that's not being motherly, that's just friendship. But there's definitely something maternal about her when she's with Lucie. I could see the pride in her eyes this morning when she told me about Lucie's gig. The way she slung her arm around Lucie and pecked her cheek with a kiss. It's unusual.

Garrett told me years ago that he and Cassie had made the decision to remain childless after a couple of miscarriages. Garrett couldn't bear to see his beloved wife suffer through another one and

Cassie felt that the miscarriages were for a reason. She said to me one night that there was always the fear there would one day be a knock at the door and she would be told that Garrett wasn't coming home. I think their life had its own level of uncertainty without throwing kids into the mix. The shame is that they would have been amazing parents. Garrett is patient, kind, a man's man. Any kid would have struck lucky to be his. And Cassie would have been an incredible mom. But I guess it was their choice and G has said on more than one occasion that they have no regrets.

I do think that they have always viewed me as some kind of surrogate child. They know my story. They know I have no family. And over the years I've spent Thanksgiving with them numerous times and Christmas too. Just a little gang of three. I think and not for the first time, just how blessed I actually am.

For a kid in the system, I don't think I've done too bad. I like to think that Mom would be proud of me, wherever she is.

NINE

Lucie

I arrive at The Moon to be greeted by Declan. I do love this man. Up until I told Dad I wanted to come to the States, I'd never heard of him. I was actually quite shocked when Dad told me he had a second cousin out here. Declan moved out here when he was nineteen so although there is an American accent there, he still has his Dublin origin present too. His voice always makes me smile. It's warm and welcoming, like the man himself. I love his little odes to his homeland. He has shamrocks on the toilet seats in the Ladies, God only knows what the Gents look like.

'Hello, my wee beautiful girl,' he says with the warmest smile

I know. I have such a soft spot for him. Perhaps it's because he is a connection to my dad. The same dad I have a hard time speaking to. I miss him, of course I do. He's my dad no matter what. But there are lies in our relationship now. He's lied to me about how my mum died and I lied by omission by not saying what I heard that night. Thinking about it too much takes me to a dark place that I don't want to be. Shaking the thoughts from my head, I kiss Declan warmly on the cheek and tell him how lovely it is to see him.

'Would you like a drink, Lucie?'

'Yes, please Declan,' I say with a smile. 'Can I have the good stuff but only a half, and don't give it to me in a boy's glass.'

'Would I?' He says back as he goes to pour my Guinness. My nan used to drink it when I was a little girl and she used to let me have a sip out of every glass. I love it. Mainly because I loved her. Both sets of my grandparents were Irish and somewhere up or down the line, the love of the black stuff was passed to me.

Whilst Declan is waiting for my drink to settle, he gallantly carries my guitar up to the stage area. I get the musicality from my mum. She could play the piano beautifully. She mesmerised me with it. When I grew into my voice and started singing, my mum insisted that I also learn to the play the guitar. She never played it herself, so I did it for her. But now…well it's given me a bit of money when I needed it, so it has become one of my most valuable possession.

'Do you have your backing stuff with you?' Asks Declan. I pass him the CD and he pops it in the machine to test it works.

I won't actually start performing till 9pm tonight but I like to sit in the bar first and chat to people I know. Hopefully, Carmel, Declan's daughter, will be here tonight. She's in her late 30's but we struck it off on the first day of meeting and I just love the energy and warmth she brings wherever she goes. She's very crude, but you would never know it from looking at her. She likes to shock and shock, she does.

Around 8.15 Cassie and Garrett arrive. I spring from my stool at the bar to give them both a hug and a kiss. Garrett, since the day he found out about the mugging incident, has called me Bruiser. I love it. It's the kind of thing Dad would say although Garrett is retired FBI and jeez, there is nothing remotely similar about those two men.

'You look stunning darlin',' Cassie says to me with a smile. 'Just as well if Cowboy is coming,' she winks and Garrett looks confused.

'He's home?' he asks.

'Oh baby, me and my big mouth. I wanted it to be a surprise and as much as he loves you, if he turns up tonight which I strongly suspect he will; I don't think it will be to see you,' she says to Garrett kissing him on the cheek and winding her hands around his waist.

'Really, Cassie? He's not coming and so you can stop it now,' I tell her.

'Did I miss something?' Asks Garrett looking between Cassie and me.

'So, this morning Jack turns up out of the blue and obviously I was delighted to see him, but he took one look at our Lucie and my boy was lost for good,' she stated emphatically, clutching her hands to her chest dramatically.

'Garrett, have you ever known me to go on a date?' I ask him.

He simply ignores my question, shakes his head and then says, 'if this woman, whom I've known for 30 years tells me she lost Jack to you, then angel, I believe her'.

For fucks sake. I turn on my heel and pop myself back on my stool.

9pm rolls around and Declan takes to the stage. He sees himself as a bit of a warm up act and because he's just so lovely the crowd always rolls with him. I'm happy for him to do it. Over the time I've been playing here, he's got into it more and more. There are times when he sounds like he's the guy in the boxing ring, holding the microphone on a high wire, down to his mouth. It wouldn't surprise me if one day he shouts, 'and in the blue corner!'. I'm standing at the bar waiting for Pete the bartender to pass me my water to take with me when I feel a hand, a very large hand, rest on the small of my back. I can smell citrus. I close my eyes momentarily then turn to face him. HOLY FUCK. Here we go again.

I don't want to have this reaction to him. It's mind and body and I don't want it. No good can come of it and yet, as I turn to the look at the handsome bastard all I can think about is straddling him there and riding him like the *'Cowboy'* Cassie insists on calling him.

Dressed in a grey t-shirt, it shows off what my mum would have called *'fucking impressive forearms'* covered in tattoo sleeves. I think I may be drooling. I try to remain calm even though I can hear the blood thundering in my ears. I need to remember to speak like a normal person not a blubbering mess. Anybody got a dark alley they could lend us for half an hour? This really is so unlike me. I don't think I have ever reacted to anybody like this in my life. It's unnerving and I'm not sure if I like it. I can't help but stare at him and in turn he looks at my face with an amused smile. I must look confused as he moves his head downwards and then I notice that it's not just my mind that's having a hard time keeping cool.

'I'm glad I'm not the only one experiencing a reaction Lucie,' he says to me as he leans in and kisses my cheek. It sears my skin. I take a deep breath of calmness and put on a bravado I don't feel. Plastering an amused smile on my face I say hello.

He laughs. His eyes crinkle when he laughs. I want to touch the crinkles but like a moth to a flame, I fear I'll get burnt.

'Hello Miss Lucie,' he says smiling at me, showing his damn fine dimples. They should be illegal. I want to lick those too. He smells so good; too good.

'Er…Lucie? Any chance you can get your skinny arse up on this stage and stop hogging Jacky-boy over there?' Bellows Declan.

I instantly turn red. I could throttle Declan right now. Without another look at Jack, I make my way towards the stage, I might sway my hips and arse slightly as I go.

TEN

Jack

When I arrived at the pub just before 9pm I could hear Declan speaking to the customers from outside. Fuck knows how loud he is in there. During a normal conversation with the guy, he booms rather than speaks to you. He's all hand movements and belly laughs, slaps on the back and loves the banter. I don't think I have ever met such a happy bar owner. The rule is that they're normally miserable bastards who moan about customers, having to keep the prices down and never getting a day off.

They must have broken the mould when they created Declan. He loves the bar, loves the lifestyle and welcomes anyone entering like they are a long lost relative. He drinks too much; a fact that his daughter never fails to remind him of, but he always waves her worries away with his ever-moving hands. The bar should have been called, 'The Jolly Bar Owner'.

As I open the door, I scan the room and within seconds I see her. She's sitting on one of the bar stools near Cassie and G, feet far from the ground, legs swinging. I walk in slowly, watching as she lowers herself to the ground. I place my hand on the small of her back and I feel her take a shuddering breath. After a beat she turns. Christ, she's beautiful. Tonight she is definitely wearing makeup but instead of it taking her natural beauty away; it enhances it. Big blue eyes look up at me under mascara'd lashes. She blinks several times and it just makes her eyes shine more.

As I do a body scan of her, I notice, rather smugly, that she is indeed pleased to see me. I can't stop myself from poking the bear.

'I'm glad I'm not the only one experiencing a reaction Lucie,' I say leaning in and kissing her cheek. Her skin sets my lips on fire.

I've just managed to say hello when Declan's voice echoes through the speaker, before I can turn to listen, I feel an arm go round my neck from behind and a knee is shoved into the back of my leg, making it buckle.

'I have to find out from my wife that you're home? I should kick your ass for that!' Garrett shouts in my ear.

I turn on my heel to face him and embrace him warmly like I would do if this man was actually my dad.

For that I get a slap on the back and a good to see you. The Old Man looks good. It's only really been a few months since I've seen him, but I did fear that retirement would age him. It hasn't at all but I'm pretty sure a lot of that has to do with his wife. Cassie comes round from behind him and gives me a kiss. She's beaming.

'I'm so glad you made it darlin' and just in time too,' she says.

'I told you I'd be here Cass and I am a man of my word, am I not?'

'Oh you are darlin', you are.'

I'm just about to turn around to speak to Lucie again, but she's already on the move, making her way to the little stage that sits in the far-right hand corner of the bar. Her hips are swaying as she walks. She gives me an amused smile over her shoulder. She probably didn't think I'd come.

She gets to the stage just as Dec leans down to grab her hand, pulling her up. There's a stool on the stage with a guitar resting against the legs of it. There's also a piano off to the side and on more than one occasion and a lock in, Declan has given us a few songs. They have always tended to be typical Irish pub songs, with a few of the customers knowing the words and singing along. Not me though. I have no real idea what my origins look like but I'm pretty damn sure they're not Irish.

As I watch Lucie climb onto the stool, I am shocked again by just how small she is. *'Dainty,'* most would call her. I see that blush rising again as she smiles into the crowd who have all turned to face her. She gives a few people an embarrassed wave.

Garrett passes me a beer as Cassie moves between us to take the stool that Lucie had just vacated. G and I stand shoulder to shoulder. He nods towards Lucie.

'She's good, man. I'm kinda shocked nobody has tried to get her to play elsewhere, or ya know, perhaps they have and she turned them down. Don't know. Just know she's damn good.'

Cassie turns to shush us and we both laugh at her.

My focus goes back to Lucie, sitting on her stool. She's perfect; sitting on the stage with her guitar. She takes a deep breath just as the backing track music kicks in. It's not loud, just gently plays along.

Lucie plays the guitar and it's melodic, seamless and fluid. Harmonious and perfect.

I remember when I was little, if a record came on the radio that my mom liked she would take my hand and dance with me in our little kitchen. If she really liked the singer, she'd always say that they *'sung like an angel'*. Lucie sings like an angel. She never once strains her voice, but it ranges from the lightest of whispers to the deep throaty sound she makes when she laughs.

Her eyes keep contact with every member of the crowd, but I feel that she's singing to me. Stolen glances, soft smiles in between versus and never once do I take my eyes off of her.

I want her. It's that simple. More than I can remember wanting anything in such a long time; maybe ever. I feel like a chunk of metal and she's the magnet. Everything about her draws me in. It's more than sexual want. It's more than a physical pull. It's the package; her. I want her but I want more with her. I want it all with her and I don't even know her. Who knows if we could ever go anywhere, but I feel like I've met the other half of my soul. Up until yesterday, I wasn't sure I even had one.

It hits me like a steam train, this really isn't me. I don't need anybody and I haven't for such a long time. But I need her. I need her to wrap her beautiful arms around me, I need her to touch my face, stroke me, wrap her body around me and never let go. It's a craving. I'm craving her touch so badly I feel as if I've stopped breathing.

I want my next breath to flow into her mouth, to mix our breath and become one. The total time I've spent in this girl's vicinity racks up to no more than an hour, but I know what I feel. It's primal but not feral. It's lust but it's nurturing. It's peaceful but also chaotic.

My life is ordered because I don't allow people in. But I want her in. I want to be in her. I want to open up the possibilities with her. She's under my skin. I want to be under hers.

At the break in her set, she winds her way back through the tables to the bar. She's neither looking at us or anybody else; just her feet. She smiles shyly at the pub's customers telling her how much they are enjoying it. The shyness is there front and centre.

A dichotomy, brave enough to sit on a stage singing to the audience but too shy to engage in conversation when finished. Cassie embraces her and tries to offer her stool back, which Lucie waves away. I bring another stool round so she is able to sit next to Cass and pull in another two for me and G.

As she sits down, she accepts the drink that Garrett has lined up for her. Her knees are facing mine and whilst they're not actually touching, they might as well be. I feel the invisible lightning bolt just being close to her. She blushes and I know she feels it too. I lean forward on my thighs, spreading them so that my elbows rest with my hands hanging between my legs.

'Well Miss Lucie, you're quite a songstress,' I say.

She smiles and nods. Cassie and Garrett are now having their own conversation. I need to steal the opportunity to converse with her before she gets back on stage.

'Do you know what I'd really like, Miss Lucie?' I ask.

She crooks one brow and says in a low voice, 'I dread to think,' but the smile on her lips is playful.

'I'd really like to get to know you better. Perhaps walk you home tonight? Or you could come home with me?' No harm in asking, right?

'Wow,' she says with a slightly nervous chuckle, 'whoever said romance was dead'.

'I can give you romance baby, all night long if that will make you say yes.'

'Oh, romance all night? A whole 12 hours of just me and you. Then watch you move on?' She says. 'As tempting as an offer that is and I know, there are probably thousands that would say yes, I'm not one of them. So, either make yourself a booty call or go and have a nice, long wank,' she straightens up and starts up a conversation with Cassie.

Wow Jack. Well done. Could you have fucked that up any better? Now who's the dickwad? My head rages. There's such a distrust in her eyes. I don't know her, I don't know her story, but I'd bet my left nut that there is one. She looks at me like I'm a shark swirling. I don't know what I've done to give her that impression of me. I doubt very much that Cassie has said anything negative about me. That woman loves the bones of me.

'Okay, perhaps that was a bit much, but I'd like to walk you home if you'd let me?' I need to try again.

I look at her as she sips her drink, 'I'll think about it,' she tells me.

'So, you two…' Lucie asks addressing Cassie and Garrett, 'how did you meet the lonesome cowboy here?'

Cassie laughs and pats my knee. 'Garrett was his mentor.'

'At the bureau,' says Garrett. 'Straight from leaving the academy he was posted to my last assignment and we haven't been able to get rid of him since,' he finishes laughing.

ELEVEN

Lucie

Whoa! Back the fuck up! He's FBI? Universe, you utter shit bag. Thanks a fucking bunch. But instead, I smile and say sweetly, 'really? Amazing. I'd better get my arse back on stage before Declan starts singing Danny Boy.' Garrett I can handle; he's ex-FBI, but a serving agent? I can't go there.

I get back on stage. I need to get through it without looking at Jack. He's not making it easy on me; I feel his eyes burning a hole in me. I focus on Cassie. She's making it easy by doing the whoop-whoop thing and yelling like a complete moron. God love her.

Finally, an hour later, my set is over. The crowd are always enthusiastic here and make me feel like a superstar. But once I start packing up, they return to their conversations and drinking. I grab my backing music disc and put my beloved guitar back in its case. I jump down from the stage and weave my way back to the bar to speak with Declan.

'Darling; that was great. Ah, what am I saying? You're always great. The punters love you darling. You know you have something special? You sure you're okay again for tomorrow night?'

'You're very sweet Declan, thank you. And yep, I'll be back tomorrow night, thank you,' I respond sweetly then finish the sentence with, 'now give me my fucking money!'

Declan laughs his nuts off as he opens the till and takes my fee out. I count it out and notice that I'm 10 dollars over. 'Hey Dec, you've given me too much,' I say pushing the 10 dollars across the bar at him.

'Keep it darling,' he says. 'Just remember me when you're famous.' God, what a sweetheart. I take a sip of my drink that Declan has slid in front of me.

He's back. I can sense him. Smell him. The hairs on the back of my neck are acting like a radar system. I know he's close. Then I feel his large hand on the small of my back again. That's obviously his *'go to'* move. His hand is flat and splayed out. He leans in close to my ear and whispers, 'give in baby'.

'Really?' I say as I swivel round on the bar stool to face him. 'Those lines really work for you? You know that makes you sound like Ryder right? Just hotter.' Fuck did I just tell him he's hot? God, I can feel my face flaming with my embarrassing statement. It literally feels like my head may spontaneously combust. I'm mortified that those words came out of my mouth.

But I know I've said them out loud as he blesses me with the *'dimple smile'*. Jesus, I so don't need this. The man has it in spades. He is the single most sexual, hot alpha male I have ever met and I am dying, literally dying of embarrassment. To my utter dismay, I'm also dying to climb him like a tree. I actually think if he looks at me with those eyes and that insane smile one more time I may be done for.

When I was on stage singing tonight, he never took his eyes off me. Every time our eyes connected, I felt hot and bothered. But like a moth drawn to the flame, you know the one that's going to kill it, I couldn't stop it.

My mind and body are at odds with each other. I know what kind of man he is and whilst my body appears to be getting rather infatuated with him, my mind is going to stop me from taking this further. We can't do anything. I work for Cassie and spend a lot of time with her and Garrett. Even a casual hook-up, which is so not me, could make things very awkward.

Cassie had previously mentioned Jack in passing, saying that he was working away but not much more detail than that. Today, she didn't exactly sing like a canary but did give a few more details and because Cassie can't stop her mouth, I am now aware of Jack's dating history. The girls he has dated have one thing in common, they never last. Cassie insists that Jack doesn't lead them on. He just prefers to remain single. She told me that Garrett was a little like that in the beginning of their relationship, apparently when you can be killed, remaining single is advised. But as time went on, Cassie told him that she wasn't interested in keeping it casual and if that was all Garrett was ever going to want, she would go and find herself someone who wanted something serious. Apparently, that made Garrett take the leap from dating on an ad-hoc to asking Cass to marry him.

Jack smells like lemons which, in turn, reminds me of the lemon torte my mum used to make. All citrus and yumminess. I need to stop it. A marching band just started in my panties and I'm having to squeeze my thighs together. I need to turn away from him but he's looking at me like the lion does when he's planning his move to take down a gazelle.

I need to get the fuck out of here.

TWELVE

Jack

Did she just call me hot? Oh yes, score one! Hang on…she also put me in the same bracket as dickwad. Not cool.

'It's just a matter of time Miss Lucie,' I tell her giving her a full-face smile.

'Bringing the dimples out of the arsenal Cowboy? Nice, but you'll have to try a lot harder than that,' she says with a smirk on her face.

'Well, now I know you like it harder,' and with those words I turn and head back to Cassie and Garrett.

Lucie slides off her stool again and tells me that she's heading for the bathroom. Again, I watch those hips sway. Again, I'm mesmerised.

Ten minutes pass by and I turn in my seat to the bar to see what Lucie is up to and she's nowhere to be seen.

'Where did Lucie go?' I ask Cassie.

'Oh, Dec said she left about 5 minutes ago darlin'. She does that. Just slips out. She'll be fine.'

She. Did. Not. Just. Leave.

I'm running. Running like I've got fire in my shoes when actually it feels like I've got a fire going on somewhere else entirely. I see her. Well, I see her back and I know it's her even from a distance because the guitar slung over her shoulder kinda gives her away.

I have no idea why she just left like that. Cassie said it was just what she did, but I knew it was because of me. When she excused herself to go to the can, she didn't look at me. She kept her head low; her hair hiding her face entirely.

My ego tells me I shouldn't be worried. But my ego and brain are not communicating because my brain is telling me I'm a dick, that in the space of a few hours, this girl, with the face and the voice that the angels sent, is suddenly all I want.

THIRTEEN

Lucie

I am marching. Like proper bitch marching. A foot stomping, arm swinging march. My guitar is hanging over my back and I'm almost home. *'Give in baby!'* What the fuck? I'm furious at him and with myself. My body's reaction to him is just ridiculous and annoying.

You might be hotter than bloody Mars mate, but you're FBI. Fuck introducing him to my dad and brothers. Christ, I think even Mel would disown me. Just like oil and water there are people in this world who should not mix. I try to have a moral compass, trust my luck to be the only one in my family to have got that gene. The ethical morality of getting involved with anybody in any kind of law enforcement would be wrong. I guess you could argue that I have already crossed the line with Garrett and perhaps I have but I just don't see it like that. We can make the excuses and twist the truth to make ourselves feel better. I wasn't aware of Garrett's line of work when I met him and Cassie. He had retired by the time they came into my life and it took a while for either of them to mention it. I have always presumed that they didn't know me well enough and chose the moment that fact was released. But the time I found out, I was already working with Cassie and I guess my decision was selfish. I didn't want to walk away from them. Cassie wasn't my mum, she couldn't have been further away from my mum but for somebody who had chosen to not have children, she is a wonderful stand in mum when I need it.

I had come to love Thanksgiving with Cassie and Garrett and their intimate circle but there is also a moral issue here, people. And a huge self-preservation notice on my back. Neither Cassie nor Garrett know about my family and I'd really like to keep it that way, thank you very much. I love them both dearly. I feel that their opinion of me would change and selfishly, I don't want that to happen. I'm happy here. I feel like I have found my place and so I truly can't see me leaving here any time soon. And I certainly don't need an active FBI agent digging around on me to find out the answers I wouldn't offer up. And he looks the sort to try and find out more. Fuck that. I'll just keep walking.

I hear the footsteps pounding down the sidewalk and I know it's him. Muggers don't run before they mug; they do that after. Brace yourself, the Cowboy doesn't like to lose.

I stop walking. What's the point? If he stumbles, he'll only take me down. Now…there's a thought.

'You went without saying anything?' He practically yells in my face.

'What are you? The 'you-can't-go-home-without-telling-me

Police?' I laugh at him.

'Perhaps I wanted to walk you home,' he says like it's the most natural thing in the world.

'Hmmm ever thought that I might not want you to?' I say sweetly. 'Anyway, I'm home now. This is me.' I say pointing at the brownstone that encloses my lovely apartment.

'You could invite me up?' Jack says with a gleam in his eye and the dimples back out of the arsenal.

'I could,' I start, 'but I'm not going to. And do you know why, Cowboy?'

'Why, Miss Lucie?' He smiles. For fucks sake…put the goddamn dimples away!

'You're so sure of yourself. So sure that you think you can talk your way into my pants. Go get yourself that booty call. Because you, my friend,' I say giving him my best smile, 'are a fuck'em and leave'em merchant and I don't give it up to just anybody'.

'You do know every Cowboy needs to ride,' he says smirking. I'm walking up my steps, away from him. It's hard, fuck he's hot. 'You let me know if you need a ride, Cowgirl,' he shouts up at me.

'Oh my god,' I shout back, exasperated by his persistence.

'Yeah, that's one of the things you'll be shouting,' he calls out. My cheeks burn but I don't turn around.

FOURTEEN

Jack

It's not lost on me that I would normally be making a phone call for a hook up versus going to bed alone when I've been away for so long. But tonight, I will be opting for bed alone telling myself that I'm still jet lagged and I wouldn't ever want to underperform. Hey, whatever works for you right?

As I get ready for bed, I'm in the bathroom brushing my teeth looking at my reflection in the mirror and thinking about what it might be like to have someone to come home to. I've never actually had anybody, well, not for a long time anyway. Not for me to keep. And it's suited me.

Until I met Trav. I took up running when I was around fifteen and during that time, I pretty much covered every part of the park near the home I was living in.

That was where I met Travis, in a community basketball cage. He was alone. I'd seen him a few times previously, just him, shooting hoops. One day I entered the court. He was big like me and we eyed up each other, neither of us wanting to make the first move in speaking. We silently shot the hoop and didn't speak to each other for weeks, just 'later' when one of us decided time was up. He turned up one day when I was sporting a black eye given to me by one of the other foster kids. He asked me what happened and I told him that I'd been jumped, as I had supposedly spent too long in the bathroom. He asked where I lived and we just started talking. We talked shit for months and one day I asked him about his parents. He told me his dad was FBI and my interest went into overdrive. Back then I didn't have a clue. It sounded exciting and mysterious at times and it wasn't like anybody was around to give a shit if I didn't come home one day. Whenever we met up, I asked Trav about his dad. Sometimes he'd go into details which I lapped up. Other times, he claimed not to know what he was up to. I get that now. I'm like that with my buddies.

Two years after we met, Travis was shot dead in a case of mistaken identity in a gang war. I didn't know. He just stopped showing up. I waited every night for three solid weeks. Then one day a man in a suit was in the cage alone with a basketball. It looked odd; him in a suit, me in sweats.

I walked into the cage and he nodded. We just started shooting some hoops. He kept looking at me but it just didn't click. We had started to slow when he asked me if I was Jack. Feeling defensive I just stared at him, giving 'the who the fuck wants to know' look I had mastered.

He turned out to be Travis's dad. Possibly the nicest man ever and who turned out to be one of only 3 people ever to give a shit about me. The other two are Cassie and Garrett. I remember so clearly asking where Travis was and immediately tears swam in his eyes. He came to me and put his hand on my shoulder. I was just about to edge backwards when he said the words that stopped my world spinning, 'he's gone buddy; shot by a gang member'. I just stood there for I don't know how long. Feeling numb. 'Sorry kiddo' was all he kept saying. He walked away slowly. His job was done. Only it wasn't. He came by a couple of nights a week to shoot some hoops with me. We talked a lot. I told him about me. Not because I was big on letting people know my life story, but he was good to talk to. Never looking at my pitiful life for what it was. He inspired me to be better. To be the best version of me. He told me he'd been practically the only black kid in a nearly all white neighbourhood and man he'd made his parents proud by joining the FBI. I didn't join to be like him but I wanted to be a good man. A man with principles and who knew right from wrong. When he died of pancreatic cancer 3 years later it damn near broke my heart.

Life does that to you, serves you the stuff you can handle; at least that's what I tell myself.

The next day I'm up bright and early and in need of a coffee. I have a few days' grace before I need to return to the office so I might as well enjoy myself. Walking into the shop my breath hitches. She's laughing about something with Cassie. Really laughing. She keeps putting her hand over her mouth to stop herself from making too much noise. She's beautiful. Really she is. She literally takes the breath right out of me and damn if I don't love it. This girl has me by the balls.

'Morning beautiful,' I say in the general direction of behind the counter.

'Morning handsome,' says Cassie with a knowing smile. Lucie

doesn't turn around but I notice as she reaches for a cup above the machine that her hands are shaking slightly. She's affected. Nice to know it's not just me.

She turns to face me and gives me a heart stopping smile. My cock instantly twitches. What she does to me is insane. Surely there should be a law about women doing that to you. I'm going to look it up.

'So, what will it be, cowboy?' She asks.

'Coffee and dinner?' I reply.

'We don't serve dinner,' she says with a smile. She knows. She knows exactly what I meant. 'But I can make you a coffee.'

'Served in bed?' I ask bringing out my smile.

She blushes. Fuck I want this woman. I am going to do everything I can to get her to go out with me.

She laughs and says, 'we don't do deliveries but I'm sure that one of your millions of women wouldn't mind doing it for you'.

'Hey, why do you think I have a million women?' Admittedly I'm not short of potential coffee makers but I couldn't give a fuck about any of them right now. Her. Just her.

'Ha, whatever sunbeam, whatever,' she says leaning up to grab a cup as my eyes focus solely on her arse and those luscious legs.

'Let me take you to dinner Lucie and in the morning, we'll toss for who makes the coffee,' I say.

She chokes in a kind of snorting way. Then starts coughing. Really coughing. Cassie has to come over and smack her on the back. But it continues. She grabs a glass of water and tries to down it but she's still spluttering.

'Jack! What did you say to her?' Demands Cass.

'Oh my god,' she says her coughing subsiding into laughter. 'You know in England tossing has a whole different meaning, right?'

'I didn't,' I reply, starting to laugh too, even though the joke's on me, 'but it obviously does by your reaction Miss Lucie'. Even though we are all laughing, I heard her rejection.

She said no and not in a *'I'm playing games'* kind of way. More of a no. Just no. Well, even if she doesn't know it yet. She will say yes.

I look at Cassie in a *'help your boy out'* kinda way but she's too busy smiling at me. Her smile says, *'well ain't this a first?'*. I bet she can't wait to go home and spread word of my rejection to Big G. Lucie passes me my coffee and I look down at it then back up at her in confusion.

'Er, you seem to have put my coffee in a to-go cup?' I say. I'm pretty sure I never specified.

'Yep,' she says smiling up at me with laughter in her eyes.

'Oh, to-go cup because you want me to go?' I say, upping my smirking game.

'Yep,' she says again.

'Too much temptation Miss Lucie?'

Lucie glares. Nail. On. The. Head. People, nail on the head.

I grab my coffee, say goodbye to Cass and wink at Lucie. She glares. Again. Fuck she looks hot when she's pissed.

FIFTEEN

Lucie

He's here. Holy fuck! How can somebody look so delectable in sweats? Really? Isn't there a law against that somewhere? How the fuck can I concentrate when Mr Delicious (my new pet name for him…in my head) is in the vicinity? I wonder, for the millionth time, what he'd taste like if I licked him. What is wrong with me? Cassie's all *'hey darlin''* and I'm all mumble, mumble. I just don't trust myself not to say something really stupid. Please God don't let me say something stupid.

He starts with the usual flirting and jumps straight to the asking me out for dinner. I tell him no. I wish he would just accept my answer. He looks at me as though I'm kidding. I'm not. It would be a very dangerous game for me to go out with him. He's not what I need and vice versa, but there is something undeniably sweet about him. I'm so sure he doesn't need me for a date but his persistence is flattering. It's been so long since I have felt this kind of attraction to a man, maybe I never have. He confuses me.

I make his coffee in a to-go cup and thc jokc is not lost on him. He tells me he'll see me later.

I'm playing The Moon again tonight. Sometimes, as much as I love Cassie, I actually want a staple gun to attach itself to her mouth. She thinks the fact that he's coming in every day means he's interested in me. No, the fact that he's coming in every day means that he wants to get laid.

My shift ends at the normal time and I find myself back at my apartment and once again heading for a soak in my lovely tub. I can admit to myself that like last night, I am dressing with extra care. I'm paying a little more attention to my makeup and hair and when I leave for the night, I feel good.

The pub is buzzing when I arrive and so after I stash my stuff, I offer my barmaid services up until my set time. Dec smiles gratefully at me and hands me an apron. Before long, he nudges my hip and tells me I have five minutes. I pop over to the bathroom so I can touch up my lipstick and make my way to the bar.

I see Jack has arrived out of the corner of my eye as I make my way up. I don't normally feel nervous but having Jack here again is making me feel all kinds of fluster. I manage to get through the first number without looking his way. When I do, I see him looking directly at me.

I steal myself for my next song. I hope the words are not lost on him. That he realises through the words of the song that yes, I want him to see me, the real me. But knowing what I know now; that he is FBI, it can never be anything but a fantasy. Our worlds can't collide. Although my family is firmly and securely stationed across the Atlantic, our worlds are just too different. I can't change who I really am for him. He can't change who he really is for me. My world is dirty money and family dug so deep in underworld that sometimes they can't see daylight. His world is what is right and wrong. Black and white. And he is firmly secured on the right side. I don't get involved with anybody…ever. For all the right reasons.

I don't have the backing track but I know the track off by heart. I used to sing it at home when I was 14. I'd fallen in, 'love' with a boy at school. He, for months, was my entire reason to exist. Until I asked my parents if I could bring him home to dinner. My dad had asked for his full name and like a fool I'd given it. Afterwards I cried myself to sleep wishing, just wishing that I hadn't given his surname. As soon as I'd said it, I saw my mum shoot a look to my dad. Dad had stood up and said very loudly, *'over my dead fucking body sweetheart…forget it'*. I asked him why, already crying. He turned his back on us and walked from the room. I looked pleadingly at Mum but she just shook her head and said, *'I'm sorry baby girl, you can't have him here. He can't be in our house; not now, not ever. He belongs elsewhere and this time darling, you're just going to have to wear it.'* She stood, kissed my head and walked away. Later I found out the reason. Two families; mine and his. Enemies. End of story.

This thing with Jack. I like him, he's making it hard not to. He's charming, funny, flirty and so bloody gorgeous, but what's the point? What's the point in starting something that has disaster written all over it? I wish I could just let go and say, *'let's have dinner and see what happens'*. But I can't. I can't take a chance on it. What if it's good? What if it's really good? Then what? No. I can't. I won't encourage him nor will I allow myself to be caught up in something I just can't handle.

My mum was a massive Bee Gees fan and as I start to sing,

'Don't Fall in Love with Me' my eyes focus solely on Jack. I need him to understand what I'm saying, hear the words. Feel my disappointment. My honesty in telling him not to bother, to stop trying right now, that the pursuit won't be worth it. Instead, he starts to smirk and shake his head. It's subtle but it's a definite shake. One that says to me that I'm not getting out of it that easy. I sing it harder and soon I appear to be belting it out but it only makes him smile more. Shit, I'd like to whack that smirk off with the back of my guitar. Sexy bloody bastard. I take my eyes off him and look around the pub. The crowd is as always, mixed. Ages vary from twenty something to sixty something and they are generally a great crowd who always join in. They are really enjoying my upping the tempo right now, we have a few playing imaginary drums and Martha and Clint, two of the regulars, are having an impromptu dance off with another couple. Not sure what they are doing but there appears to be a lot of foot stamping going on. Fuck, I need to finish this song before they go through the floorboards. I finish it and to my utter surprise the crowd go mental. Go figure. They like angry singing. I throw my head back and laugh.

I get off the stage a couple of songs later when I take my break. Jack stands as I approach and asks me what I would like to drink. I thank him and ask for half a Guinness; he responds with raised eyebrows and a smile.

'You don't look like you should be drinking that,' he says laughing. 'You're such a little thing, I'd expect something a bit more dainty.'

'Really? You think because I'm small I can't handle a big boy's drink?' I might sound slightly angry as I say it but really, it's not amusing that he might actually think that.

'I guess so, yeah,' he says openly laughing.

'Oh my god, that's so caveman of you,' but I'm laughing too. I love how his eyes crinkle when he laughs or really smiles. His smile reaches all over his face, making me crave being able to rub my fingers all over his face and beard. People, focus, I said fingers. Although God, my lady parts are doing some kind of cha-cha in my pants right now and I swear he bloody knows it. He really is fucking gorgeous. You know that line about somebody being 'panty melting?' Well it's him. I love that. In England we wear knickers and knickers don't melt. At least the ones my mum used to make us wear wouldn't. Survive the Apocalypse maybe but definitely wouldn't melt. Oh Mum, you should see my knickers these days. If there is something after death, my mum is currently shouting, 'put something on that covers your arse you dirty bint, you'll catch flu at this rate'. Years ago, one of Mel's boyfriends bought her some lingerie. Every time she mentioned it, which was a lot, my mum would yell at her. I can almost hear her now saying, *'lingerie? That's just a posh word meaning clothes for a prozzie.'*

Jack breaks my thoughts by informing me that he'll be walking me home tonight. I smile.

But ten minutes later I tell him that I'm going to sort my stuff out and promptly walk out the back door, with my guitar slung over my shoulder. I'm stealthy like that.

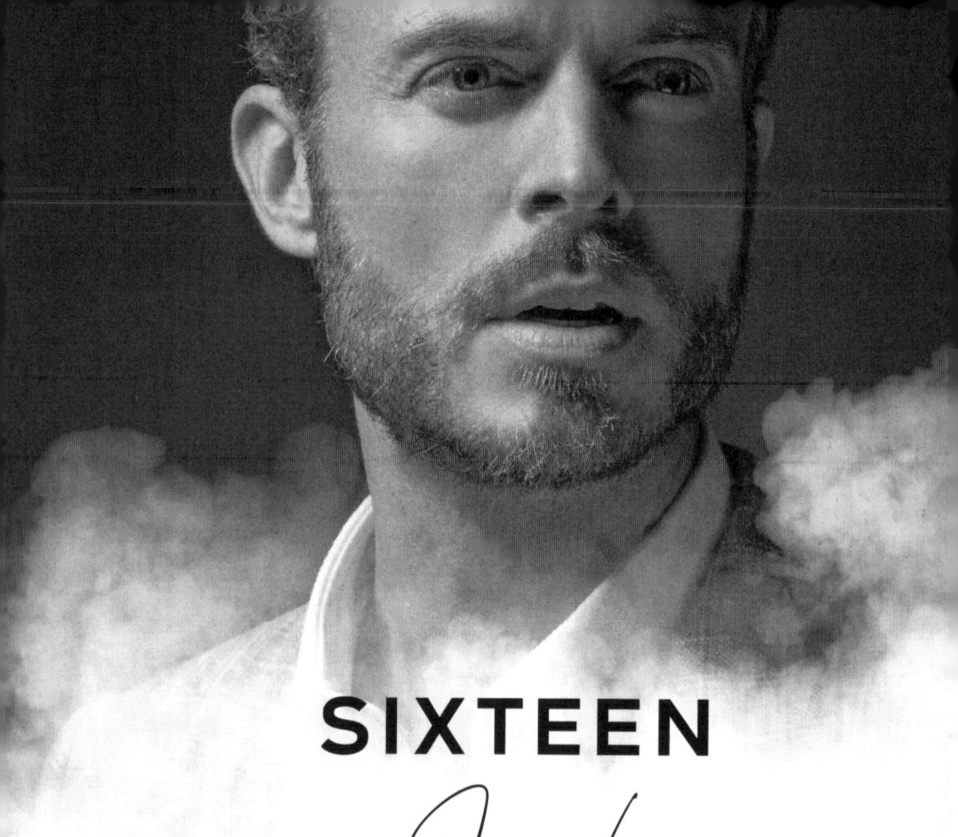

SIXTEEN

Jack

She. Did. Not. Walk. Out. Again. What the fuck is it with this girl? We get on. We even exchange smiles and flirting and I thought whilst she hadn't exactly melted, she was in fact thawing.

Why the fuck am I chasing this girl down the block again? What the fuck is it about her that I just can't get out of my head? I am running after her like a horny teenager which is exactly how she has me feeling. Her whole set was pure torture. My cock was straining against my jeans and it was so fucking tight that I had to put one ankle over my knee so I could scoot down on the chair to alleviate some of the pressure. When I bury myself balls deep inside her pussy, she's going to feel just how tortured she's left me over and over. Fuck, I need her.

I can see her thanks to the fact that I have a damn long running stride. I don't yell at her this time. I just keep running until I am within touching distance, then I raise my arm so my hand can grab hold of her guitar and when I do, she whirls round and practically growls. I growl back.

'Did you just growl at me?' She screams, eyebrows off somewhere in her hairline.

'Are you fucking kidding me with the disappearing act? I said I would be walking you home. What the fuck?' I scream right back at her.

'I…I didn't ask you to and I didn't say yes,' she says but her eyes are telling me something different. I knew the song was to me. I knew it was her telling me to just leave it. But I couldn't. I can't. She must see this attraction we have. When our eyes lock the world fades into darkness leaving just us. I know it. I can feel it. And I know she can too. My need to consume her sets off like the 4th of July. I close the distance between us in one step and pulling her to me by her hips, I take her mouth. She gasps in shock and I lick her lips before sliding my tongue into her mouth. Instinct takes over as her tongue moves against mine and she moans at the same time as I do. I pull her tighter to me so she can feel what she does to me against her tummy. I feel like steel. She feels like heaven. Wrapping a hand around the back of her neck and holding her against my lips, we begin to publicly devour each other. Our mouths continue to dance against each other, her hands are now fisting my t-shirt, dragging my chest to hers. Like the bad girl that I knew was hiding in there, she rubs her tits against me, pushing into my chest.

'No more running, Lucie,' I speak against her lips. She whispers her okay.

Smiling I lean back to look her in the eyes but keep my tight hold of her. 'Come home with me.'

'No,' she says looking down before looking me in the eye. 'You want me to stop running, cowboy? Fine, but you can take me out before you even begin to think about getting in my pants.'

'Baby, my thinking is way past getting in your pants and it's on the page starting with you riding my face,' I respond smiling. Fuck me. She's doing that blushing thing. Fuck, it's so hot on her. As the blush in her cheeks rise once more, I keep my hold steady and firm. Through my body, I implore her to see what she does to me. I know the sex will be off the charts. I can feel that electrical current running into our bodies, mixing and catching alight. But in the far recesses of my mind, I know it, this, us, will be more than just hot fucking. She's a challenge in every way possible. She's the firecracker you find at the bottom of the firework box, the one you don't know if you can be bothered to light but when you do, boom, it turns into the star of the show. That's her. And fuck me if I don't want it all.

'I get it', I tell her, 'it won't be tonight that I push you up against my wall and rub my cock over your covered pussy. Feel your breathing change in my ear. Hear you panting as you become wet for me.' She whimpers when I say 'wet'. I fucking groan at that noise. My girl likes it dirty. She's pushing her hips into me. She fights the need to find some friction out here in the street.

'Tomorrow, after you finish your shift, I'm taking you out. What time are you finishing?' I ask.

'Erm, I'll be done by 2?' She says in the form of a question.

'Is that a guess Lucie or is that the time you want me there?'

'I can meet you later, so that I can get home and change first,' she says.

'No.'

'No? Why?'

'I want to make sure you don't back out so I will come and collect you from the shop and take you home, wait whilst you get ready, then we can go.' I smile at her. She won't win this round.

'Okaaaay…but just so you know, I wasn't going to back out. I don't say one thing but mean another,' she says pouting.

'Well, that's good,' I state, 'because neither do I. And now I'm going to take you home, like I said I would.' I take her hand which goes stiff momentarily before relaxing. I give it a little squeeze and she looks at me, fighting her smile.

'You want me to carry your guitar?'

'No, no need. I'm small but mighty,' she says with a smile.

'I can tell baby, I can tell,' I say with my own smile.

We walk and talk, the conversation not slipping away. Nothing profound or even exploratory just two people chatting. When we reach the steps to her place she stops and starts shuffling her feet. Looking down and around but not at me.

I lift her chin so she has no choice but to look at my face. I rub my thumb along her jaw line and over her bottom lip. When the pad of my finger leaves her lip, she swipes her tongue along it. Tasting my finger. I try really hard not to groan again.

'I'll meet you outside your work tomorrow at two. But right now, I need something from you,' I say as my fingers curl round the back of her neck into her hair.

'What do you need?' She asks, all breath and wide eyes. Fuck, I can't even go there. Right now, I just need a taste. A taste again of her delicious mouth. I just take it because I can't not.

I slip my hand around the back of her neck and gently pull her towards me before slanting my mouth over hers. It's hot and she opens on a groan immediately. Our tongues go straight to each other. I don't know if my tongue is in her mouth or mine. It's not a battle, it's a dance. It's fucking hot. Her taste is intoxicating, I can't stop my tongue probing further into her mouth. It's so much more than a kiss. When we break apart, both of us need to catch our breath as I rest my forehead against hers.

She pulls her face away from mine and smiles up at me through her lashes. I smile down at her. We both know at this moment that whatever this is, it's definitely something.

'You need to go in before I forget that you want a date first because my need for you to be under me, is so fucking strong,' I say with an exhausted sigh.

She turns on her heels and laughs as she goes up the steps to the brownstone apartment. At the door, she turns to face me. She smiles again but shakes her head.

'Why are you shaking your head darling?'

She says nothing but one more smile, opens the door and makes her way in. I wait. I wait until I see a light go on in the first-floor window and see her beautiful face appear there.

SEVENTEEN

Lucie

I am pathetic. Pathetic and weak. What just happened? I wasn't going to say yes. I had it all worked out in my head. Did I not just sing the song? Did I not just tell myself that no matter what I would not be going out with him? I never say one thing but mean another…well I evidently do now.

I'll tell you what happened; that bastard kissed me and I became weak and pathetic and worse still, I agreed to go on a date with him.

As I let myself into my apartment I flick on the light and make my way over to the window facing the street. I look down to see if Jack is still there. I know he is before I even see him. He's on the sidewalk with his hands in his pockets, looking up.

He sees me and smiles. He stays staring up at me for a couple of minutes whilst I stare down at him. Then walks away and I feel disappointed.

I walk back over to my front door to ensure its locked and whilst I'm there I bang my head against the door several times. Why did I say yes?

As I undress I touch my fingers to my lips. They still feel swollen from the hottest kiss of my life. That man looks like a Greek God, kisses like one and in a single moment brought me to my knees.

I need to feel unsexy right now. When I left home Mel packed me, what she lovingly referred to as passion killing pyjamas. As I put them on, I look in the mirror and Daffy Duck stares back at me and makes me smile. Nothing is more unsexy than cartoon pj's on an adult.

I climb into bed and text my sister. This is a routine a couple of nights per week. It's only early evening at home so even if she is 'working' tonight she'll still be home this early in the evening.

Me: *I kissed a boy and I liked it*

Mel: *Well, aren't you a whore*

Me: *Harsh but it may be true. What r u up 2?*

Mel: *You went to public school darling, don't text like a teenager!*

Me: *Soz lol! What are you doing, my darling sister?*

Mel: *That's better. I am putting slap on my face to make myself look EVEN more beautiful…not possible, I know, I know*

Mel: *Who was the boy?*

Me: *I'm a dick. His name is Jack and he's hot as fucking hell*

Mel: *Why are you a dick? Is he a dick? Did he make your knickers fall off? Kevin Brewster made my knickers fall off once round the back of Waitrose in the High Street when I was fifteen. Bastard never did return them to me hahahaha*

Me: *You're a whore too. And no. He's kind of funny and* *charming and fuck, did I mention how hot he was?*

Mel: *You might have but I'm not seeing the issue here kiddo*

Me: *Don't kill me...it's not my fault. Well, not all of it anyway...*

Mel: *I can't kill you...I got a busy night ahead and your demise is not on my to-do list*

Me: *Good. Keep that in mind*

Mel: *You're going to have to spit it out*

Me: *He's FBI*

I can practically count it out and I do aloud. One, two, three...

My phone rings and Mel's name flashes up.

'Hello.'

'Are you actually fucking kidding me right now?' She screams. I pull the phone away from my ear. Christ, she's got a set of lungs on her!

'You can't kill me, you're too busy. You just said,' I whisper.

'Okay, are you trying to fucking kill me then? FBI? Really?' She shouts.

'Look it's just a date, which I wouldn't have said yes to had he not just kissed the life out me.'

'Why did you let him kiss you?'

'I didn't exactly let him, he just kind of took over and it was so good Mel, I couldn't stop it,' I giggle.

'Oh for fucks sake! Have I taught you nothing? Anything to do with the law is out of fucking bounds!'

'I thought that was only at home?' I say laughing. I am, of course, winding her up and the more heated she gets the funnier I have always found it. She's all shouty but she's not losing her shit... yet.

'Listen, you little shit, don't fuck this up for yourself. Who is he? How did you meet? Have you told him anything?' She asks the questions in rapid succession.

‘Hey, no name calling! I have only just met him, he’s a friend of Cassie and Garrett’s and no, of course I haven’t. I’m not stupid. I’m doing a pretty fine job of looking out for myself so don’t talk to me like I’m the village idiot!’ I shout back.

‘Hon, I’m just looking out for you,’ she sounds exasperated with me already. I wish I hadn’t told her now. She’s taken all my happy feelings and stomped on them.

‘I just wanted to tell you and now you’ve made me feel stupid,’ I tell her unable to keep the sulking tone out of my voice.

‘Okay. Sorry darl, tell me about the kiss,’ she says calmly.

‘It was just a kiss Mel. A good kiss. Actually, it was a miiiiighty fine kiss.’

‘Well, at least one of us is getting some action I guess,’ she laughs.

‘Oh, you do okay lady. Don’t act like you don’t.’

‘If only kiddo, if only. Look, I have to go darling, I need to finish getting ready,’ she says.

‘Is Dad okay?’ I manage to slide in before she hangs up.

‘Yeah, he’s fine. Don’t worry about him, we’re all here looking after the old bastard,’ she says laughing again.

‘Okay, that’s good. Speak to you soon. Love you!’ I say.

‘You too kiddo. Take care bubs and for fucks sake, keep your mouth closed around him,’ she says.

‘Even when he wants to put his tongue in there?’ I giggle.

‘Fucks sake, I’m going, love you Bubs,’ and on that note she hangs up.

I hold the phone to my chest, missing my sister, missing my family. Some days I am still so angry with them that I don’t allow myself those thoughts but on other days I see or hear something that I just want to share with them in person.

I put the phone on my bedside just as a text comes through. Opening it up I see it’s from an unknown number.

Unknown: *Kissing you is going to make sleep hard tonight x*

Jack. Now how the fuck did he get my number?

Jack: *You could say it back if you like? x*

That makes me smile. Cocky bastard.

Me: *It was okay :)*

Jack: *I'll work on that. Night beautiful x*

Me: *You do that. Night x*

Once again, I put the phone back onto my nightstand and shut the light off. But I'm smiling.

EIGHTEEN

Jack

I hit the gym like a man possessed. I feel invigorated and I know it's all down to a certain English girl with a kiss that could slay the dragon himself. I push myself and don't stop until I am soaked in my own sweat. On leaving the gym, I sling my backpack on and finish my work out by running home.

My apartment feels too quiet to hang around in today so after showering and getting dressed, I drop a call to G to let him know I'm coming over.

When I arrive, I walk through the unlocked front door and find him bespectacled and sitting at his desk in his home office, looking at paperwork. Yes, G is retired, but he works on odd projects for the Bureau or private companies on a consulting basis. He was never going to just retire so this is a great compromise for him; he gets to 'work' a case but he can still play golf when he wants.

'Hey, old man,' I greet him.

G looks up and smiles. It warms me. He's more than just a father figure for me, he's my best friend. The only true confidant I have had since I lost Travis. I often wonder had he not been killed, if Trav and I would still be friends. I like to think we would be. But had he been around I may not have met his father and the spark of interest in the FBI may not have happened. My mom used to tell me that the universe had a plan for all and opportunity and ideas were sent to us. If they were our purpose, we would find them. I guess based on that theory, I was meant to meet Travis and then his dad. I just can't accept that Travis dying was also part of the plan. No, that was random. He was in the wrong place at the wrong time. Nothing more, nothing less.

'Hey man. Let's go make some coffee, I could use a break,' he says rising from his chair.

Garrett puts the coffee pot on whilst I grab a stool at the kitchen bar.

'So, eyes set on our Lucie eh?' Yep, straight to the point as always G.

'Man, she's something else right? I mean you'd have to be blind not to notice her, or just a very happily married man,' I say, wiggling my brows.

'Don't look at me, my girl is more than enough for me,' he says laughing holding his hands up in surrender. 'But you like her, right?'

'That I do. I told her last night I'd walk her home and she snuck out the door. This you know. But I caught up with her and yeah, I kissed the fuck out of her. She's got me in all sorts of knots man. I practically had to strong-arm her into a date. Told her I'd pick her up from the work at two o'clock today. Didn't give her any room for argument as I could see the no was on her lips,' I tell him rubbing my hand down my face. 'I can't stop thinking about her; can't stop thinking about last night's kiss either. Man, she's hot. Her kiss could kill a man. Sweet, firm, all in. She left me with a hard on that a 15 year old would be proud of.'

'So where are you taking her?' G asks as he pours the coffee and slides one over to me.

'I thought I'd pack a picnic up and drive over to the Edge.'

'Nice, I like it. I think Lucie will too. Look, I know I don't need to teach you how to suck eggs son, but she's gentle in a lot of ways. I know she comes across as a bit feisty but we've never seen her go on a date, always turned any offer she's had down flat. Now neither Cassie nor I know why she doesn't go out with guys but she doesn't. So don't go in all guns blazing, that's all I'm saying,' G tells me.

'I don't get it G. She's young and fucking gorgeous man, she can't have been short of offers although right now I'm glad she turned them down, but why? How much do you know about her?'

'I don't really. Cassie asked me not to look and when my wife tells me not to do something, I don't. Perhaps she's just not the dating type.'

'I like her G. Like, really like. You know I have always stayed away from the dating scene myself, based on your advice actually, but I have and it's served me well. Nobody gets hurt or upset when I have to go away or worse still, worry if I don't come home. But there's something about her. She makes me want to try it. The last couple of years have been lonely. Not that my bed has always been lonely,' I laugh, 'but, even that gets tiring. It might be nice to have something solid for a change. Lucie doesn't appear to need anybody and fuck if that doesn't turn me on.'

G laughs and nods, 'I hear you man. Cassie was just like that. When she told me to shit or get off the pot in our relationship, I had no doubt in my mind that I wanted what we could have. And it's worked. It worked from day one and I have no regrets. I'm as crazy about her as I was all those years ago, maybe more so. She is and always has been my entire world and my only regret is that I can't live this life with her all over again. My wife, well they broke the mould when they made her. Or maybe they didn't, eh? I would love for you to be as lucky as I've been son and so would Cass. She adores you and she adores Lucie. Just don't upset my Lucie because that will upset my Cassie then I will have a problem. We understanding each other here?'

'Sir, yes sir!' I quip as we clink mugs.

A few hours later I am back at my apartment grabbing another quick shower. I love my shower. When I was away, I stayed in many hotels and not one of them matched up to what I have at home. I have the standard rainfall head plus all the side showers and when I'm tired or stressed to fuck, my shower makes my whole world get back into balance.

Dressed and ready to go, I grab my keys and the basket I have made up ready for our picnic. I already have a blanket in the car so all is set when I pull up outside Cassie's store at 2pm sharp. I see Cassie through the window and she waves and signals with her hands that Lucie will be out in two minutes. I nod back and give her the thumbs up.

Lucie walks out of the door a few minutes later looking like a dream. Dressed in a yellow and white sundress and cowboy boots, I find myself adjusting my jeans just looking at her through the window. I hop out quickly so that I can open the car door for her.

'Hey,' she smiles as she climbs in the cab of my truck.

'Hey yourself beautiful,' I smile back closing the door once she is safely seated.

As I climb back into the driver's seat, she asks me where we're going.

'Somewhere beautiful for my beautiful girl,' I tell her.

She laughs. 'I'm not your anything.'

'Yet, beautiful, but you will be,' I tell her taking her hand over the central console and bringing it to my lips so I can kiss it.

'Oh you do have all the moves don't you?' But she's smiling so I smile back and set the car moving.

The drive only takes about 40 minutes so within ten minutes we are out of the city and on roads which cut through fields on either side. I pull off the road when I see the sign I'm so familiar with. This is the place I come to when I need to clear my head. Sometimes I come here if I want to think about Mom. Whatever my reason, it's a stunning place to stop and enjoy the quiet and today, it's my chance to get to know Lucie.

'Wow, this is beautiful,' she says as she jumps out of my cab. She moves too fast for me to get around to open the door; I'll have to tell her in future to stop so that I can do that for her. My momma may not be around to see the finished article but she raised a gentleman. I take her hand in mine and we link fingers. I see her smile out of the corner of my eye and I'm taking that as a good sign.

'I brought a picnic for us. Let me just grab it out of the trunk.'

'You know in England; a trunk is something elephants have. At home we call it the "boot".'

'I know but that makes no sense to me. A boot is something you wear on your feet where I come from,' I say.

'Yeah me too, so it doesn't make a lot of sense to me either.'

We lay the blanket out near the edge, but not too close, so we can look over the valley that stretches out as far as we can see and both sit down.

I start getting the food containers out and Lucie helps with sorting the drinks.

'Wow, you thought of everything. This looks lovely Jack, thank you.'

'My pleasure beautiful,' I say and it is. It will always be my pleasure if she smiles like she is now.

We talk for hours about everything and nothing at all. She tells me that her mom died around eight years ago and I tell her that my mom is still officially MIA. Lucie has siblings whereas I don't, but I am happy to hear her tales of her sister and brothers and laugh along with her as she relays the antics of her brothers.

I ask about her dad and she tells me that he's never gotten over losing her mom and she doubts he ever will. I tell her about Travis and his dad and how I came to meet Garrett and Cassie.

We've eaten the food and are now both lying on our backs in the sunshine. I roll over to my side and prop my head up with my hand as she mirrors me. A lock of hair falls onto her cheek and I brush it back and tuck it behind her ear. As I do, she closes her eyes with a sigh.

I take my opportunity to lean in and brush my lips with hers. She's tastes so sweet. I kiss her again, a little harder this time. I just need more. Her eyes open and in that moment I see it. Us, becoming something more. She leans into me this time and the kiss goes from PG to X-rated in just moments. I'm practically lying on top of her as I ravish her mouth and she gives it straight back to me. Her moan is going to be my downfall. I place my forearms either side of her head as I pull away from kissing her.

'You are the sexiest girl I have ever met,' I tell her honestly.

She smiles up at me and runs her fingertips over my beard then over my lips.

'Jack, I think you own all the sexy right now.' Fuck, the way she looks at me. It sets me on fire. I kiss her lips again then move down her body slightly so I can kiss her neck, then further still so my lips can taste the swell of her breasts. As I kiss her perfect mounds of flesh, she sighs and moans and my cock is screaming at me. I try to move so it's not so obvious but she very subtly lifts her hips. I don't think I have dry humped since I was about sixteen years old but fuck, I'm doing it now.

'Fuck,' I say through gritted teeth. 'I want you so bad baby.'

'Jack, I'm really not a casual hook-up kind of girl. That's not who I am and I won't change just because you are making me feel all sorts of sexy,' she tells me. She's looking at me, her cheeks flushing and she is worrying her lip with her teeth.

'I don't want a night with you Lucie. I want more. We can go as fast or as slow as you want, but this is something. Us. We're something and I just want you to at least give me a chance.'

'You get one chance Jack. You mess me around and this, whatever it is, whatever it becomes, will be over. No second chances.'

'I promise you sweetheart, I won't make you regret taking a chance on us. You have very quickly become my every waking thought and I don't intend to ever fuck that up.'

'Then kiss me again, Cowboy,' she says smiling and placing her hand round the back of my neck to draw me in.

I do as my girl requests. I feel like my body is on fire. I can't get enough of her taste. And I can't stop myself from sliding my hand up her leg towards her panties. As I reach the silky feeling between her legs, Lucie lifts her hips to meet my hand.

I pull away and look at her. 'Lucie, I want to feel you and as beautiful as this spot is, I don't want to get out of control out here where we could end up giving somebody a show. Come home with me Lucie. I know you might feel this is too fast, but this chemistry we have, I want you more than I can articulate.' I rub myself up against her centre again and she moans, closing her eyes.

'Take me home, Jack.'

She laughs as I jump off her and start throwing our picnic into the basket. As she stands, I throw the blanket over one shoulder and her over the other. She's screaming and laughing, smacking my back as I break into a run back to the truck. I deposit her gently back on her feet and open the door. As she climbs in, I watch those beautiful legs swing into the cab. I should just shut the door, but this is Lucie and I can't just do that. I lean in taking her face in my hands and kiss her. Just a simple kiss. I needed another taste.

Heading back to the city, our fingers entwined and with a racing heart, all I can think about is loving her body. Making her feel the way she makes me feel. When we pull into the underground garage of my building and hop out, I'm in a rush. Lucie laughs and has to remind me to grab the picnic basket from the trunk. I couldn't give a shit. It can stay there for eternity for all I care.

The moment the doors of the elevator close, I have her pinned up against the mirrored wall. She links her hands behind my neck as I slide my hands down to her ass and lift her into my arms. Hooking her legs around my waist, she leans back in my arms and looks at me.

'Jack, it's been a while, okay? Just know that,' she says as her signature blush creeps up her face.

'Baby, you're in charge okay?'

'Okay,' she says then leans back in to kiss my lips.

I don't even remember opening the door to my apartment. We are like a tornado bursting through the door and with Lucie still in my arms I power walk my way to my bedroom. When we enter, I slide Lucie down my body slowly. Taking her face in my hands I kiss her deeply. She's on her toes but I've got her in a tight embrace. She lowers herself down and takes a step back. She looks me directly in the eyes as she drops one strap of her dress off her shoulder then does the same on the other. She pulls down the zip that is discreetly tucked into the side of her dress and I watch, my mouth slack, as it falls and pools at her feet.

'Fuck, darling, you've just ruined me,' I say as I trace my fingers over her collarbone and down to her lacy bra. I can clearly see her breasts through the material and the sight makes my mouth water. 'You just keep getting more beautiful baby,' I tell her earnestly.

Lucie takes a step closer to me and pulls my Henley out of the waistband of my shorts, lifting it over my head.

'Wow, I wasn't expecting that,' she says smiling. 'Could you be more buff?' She asks as she places her hands on my chest and begins to rub them all over my torso. Her hands on my body sets me on fire. I slide my hands round her back and unfasten her bra, gently pulling it off and away from her body. I think my mouth falls slack once again.

'Fuck, baby,' is all I can say as I lower my face and take one of her nipples into my mouth, laving it with my tongue and sucking gently. My hands are on her ass and move sideways to her hips where the straps of her panties hug her body. Looping my fingers under them, I pull them down, going to my knees at the same time but keeping her breast in my mouth. Lucie moans out a sound that does nothing but urge me on. As her panties reach her ankles I take each of her feet out of them so she is completely naked in front of my kneeling self. Her hands reach for my hair and rub through it, raking her nails against my scalp. I lean back in to kiss her mound and hipbones. Looking up at her as she looks down at me, I lean further in and swipe my tongue along her centre. It's now my turn to moan but I hear her too.

'Jack,' she moans out my name on a whisper as I take another taste. 'Jack, that feels…oh God, it just…' She doesn't finish her sentence as I slowly take her growing clit into my mouth and suck hard.

'Jack.'

'Fuck baby, get on that bed, I need to bury my face between your legs,' I tell her, pushing her towards the centre of the bed. She climbs into the middle and lays down, opening her legs and inviting me in. I don't need to be asked; my mind, my body and my soul only want to be in one place and as I lower myself between those beautiful legs I feast on all of her taste.

Lucie is so wet and starts to grind against my face. 'Take it baby, take what you want. Come on my tongue sweetheart,' I tell her, lapping at her, sucking on her and as Lucie's thrusts get harder I know she's getting close. Soon her face starts to change and her moaning gets louder and then her taste floods my mouth and I drink it down like a man dying of thirst. Lifting my face, I watch as her chests rises and falls rapidly. Lucie looks at me, a smile on her lips.

'You can do that anytime you want Cowboy,' she laughs. 'Now get up here, find that condom I know you have and let me feel you inside me.'

I laugh as I lean up over her body and open the bedside drawer, finding the condom and ripping it open with my teeth. Sliding it over my cock, I don't dare fist myself as frankly I might just shoot off unexpectedly and that wouldn't be good for me or my girl. Because now, now she is my girl.

I rub the tip of my cock up her slit letting her juices slide over my cock before I gently begin to push at her entrance. Even before I enter her, she feels incredible. Warm, soft and wet. Her legs lift and hook around my back, opening herself up for me. I can't stop my groan of pleasure. I gently start to push inside her heat and my heart damn near stops. 'Baby, you're so tight,' I ground out

Lucie opens her eyes wide. 'I'm sorry,' she whispers.

'No, baby, don't be sorry, it feels incredible. You feel incredible. I love how tight you feel,' I tell her.

Pushing in more, I watch for her reaction. She smiles gently and tells me to continue with her eyes. When I finally bottom out inside her, I know one thing for sure. I'm home. This. Us. This is everything. I have found my everything.

When our lovemaking is finally over, we lie together entwined in each other's arms, her face near my neck as I stroke the beautiful skin on her back. It takes time for both of our breathing to regulate and return to normal.

'I need to get rid of this condom Luce, come join me for a shower?' I feel her nod and as we both leave my bed, now our bed, we make our way to my bathroom holding hands.

As the shower starts up and begins to warm, I kiss my girl again.

'Thank you darling,' I tell her, meaning it from the bottom of my heart.

'Thank you? For what? For giving me glorious and rather incredible orgasms?' She laughs.

'For giving me your body. For giving us this,' I tell her.

'Oh that,' she giggles, 'in that case, you Cowboy are very, very welcome'.

As she moves in front of me to walk into the shower I slap her ass. She yelps, smiling over her shoulder.

'See something you want?' She asks cheekily.

'Damn right I do woman, now come here.'

By the time our shower ends, we have wrinkled skin and smiling faces. I order us in Chinese as we settle down on the couch, wrapped up in each other. I can't get enough of this woman and when we make it back to bed again, this time supposedly to sleep, our passion for each other takes over again before we fall into a sated sleep. Lucie doesn't know it yet but I never want this woman to ever leave this bed.

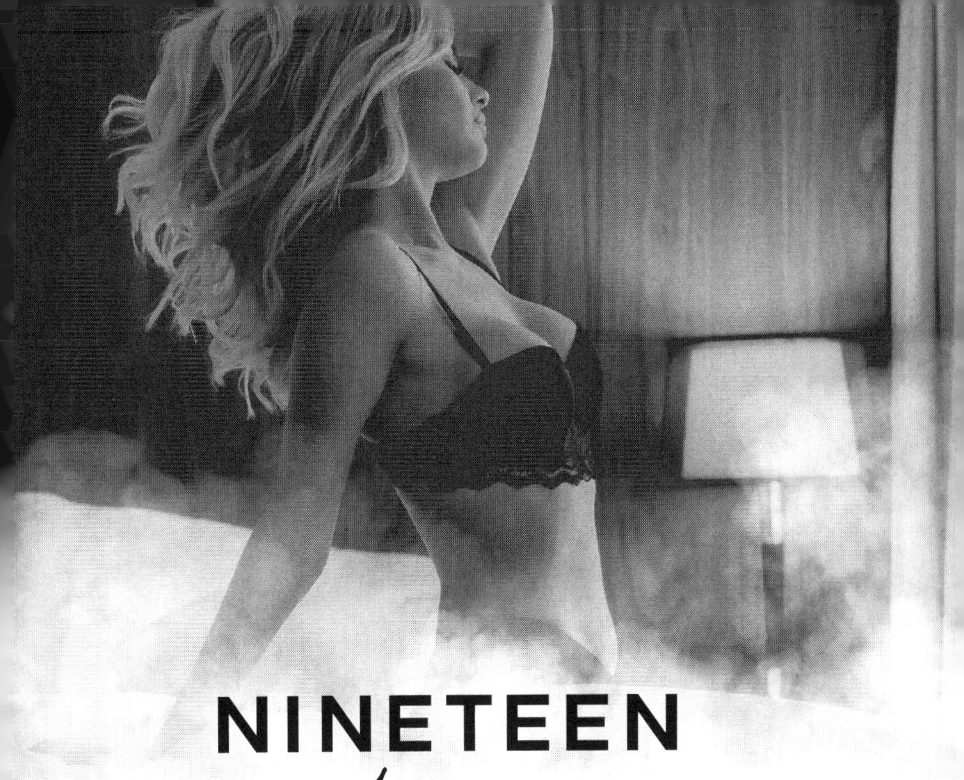

NINETEEN

Lucie

Three weeks. Jack and I have been dating for 3 weeks. Exclusively. Now if that's not an American term, I don't know what is. When you date, when is not exclusive? Well it's a new one for me that's for sure. I was lost for words when we had 'the talk'. Jack had taken me to dinner at a local Italian. A beautiful candlelit bistro where the service was delivered by real Italians and cooked by an authentic Italian chef. It was an amazing dinner and Jack was the perfect gentleman. Up until the point when he whispered in my ear that he would be taking me home to do outrageously dirty things to me. Score another point for Jack. Not the dirty bit, although that didn't knock any points off, but that he just makes me laugh.

He is officially nothing like the man I had made him out to be in my mind. When we arrived back at his apartment he poured me another glass of wine and told me to sit.

'We need to talk,' he said with a very straight face. I was suddenly feeling the fear until he smiled, took my hand and told me not to look so frightened.

'Okay, spill it buddy because if this is the dumping talk, I need to get home and start hitting up Tinder cos you have me all kinds of wound up!'

'Oh wound like a spring is just how I like you. Listen Lucie, we've been seeing each other for a few weeks now and I want you to know that it's exclusive. For me, it's exclusive and I want that from you too.'

'What does that actually mean? I thought we were exclusive. We're dating right?' I asked him, totally perplexed at this conversation.

'Right, yeah, we are but you know, people who date generally date other people too until a time they don't want to date other people,' he fumbles through.

'They do? I don't. I don't really have lots of experience but I'm pretty sure that if you are dating somebody and then date somebody else that makes you a cheating fucker.'

'God woman, I'm going to fall in love with you,' he says lunging for me and dragging me into his lap. Christ this man can kiss like a god. He's my very own Adonis and now, he's kissing me like a man possessed and I have no power or inclination to stop the assault.

'Jack?' I whisper when he pulls away. 'Take me to bed.'

He stands with me in his arms and carries me to his bedroom. I don't know how he manages it but he's like a magician. One minute he is lowering me to the ground and the next my clothes are literally falling to the floor. Have you ever been ravished? It's ridiculously exciting! He just ravishes me and I have no idea what's coming next but I know it's going to be good.

It's nearly three o'clock in the morning when we finish our ravishing and I'm a dead weight on Jack's chest as I feel sleep calling my name. Jack strokes my hair and lays gentle kisses on the top of my head.

'Luce, you awake?' He asks quietly.

'If you want another round buddy you can go fuck the sofa, I'm done.' I tell him keeping my eyes closed. I can feel him laughing, his chest rising under my cheek.

'I meant what I said earlier Luce. I'm going to fall in love with you,' he says.

'How do you know that?' I ask, opening my eyes but not moving to look at him.

'Because it's already started Lucie.'

I don't respond but I do close my eyes again, this time with a smile on my face and the beginning flutterings of love in my own heart.

Waking up a few hours later is another slice of heaven, for I can smell bacon! Is there any better smell in the world than that of cooking bacon? No, I think not. I pull myself out of the veritable cloud that Jack calls his bed and pad my way down to his kitchen where I find the Greek God himself, half naked, cooking my bacon. Be still my beating heart.

'You're killing me Jack, literally killing me. Look at me,' I tell him unbuttoning his shirt I had only put on moments ago. 'You're making my clothes just fall off again.'

'Put that shirt back on witch and sit so I can feed you or I'll make you sorry you started that strip tease,' he retorts laughing.

I do just that because sometimes a girl just needs to eat. This man feeds me a simple breakfast feast of eggs, bacon, and a toasted English muffin and then he removes the shirt so we can properly mess up his kitchen.

'So, what are our plans today?' I ask my Greek God after I am, once again, fully sated.

'Well, my beautiful girl, as I need to be away next week, I thought we would just hit the market and buy food so that we can hole up here for the weekend?' He says stroking my face. I lean into him; I can't get enough of his touch.

'I didn't know you were going away,' I say almost breathless from his touch. I am not, by nature, a jealous person but I feel it rise in me. I think I am simply jealous of anybody who gets time with him if that person isn't me.

'I just need to be away for four nights sweetheart, I will call you each night though so don't think for one minute you can disappear on me,' he states laughing as he gets up to start loading the dishwasher. 'Will you miss me darling?' He asks smiling back over his shoulder at me.

'Oh stop fishing. You know I will. This was your plan after all. Make me addicted to you then leave me wanting.'

He comes back over to where I'm sitting. 'Understand this Lucie, I am not leaving you, not now and if I have my way, not ever. So, get used to it beautiful. And before your mind can start up again, come and take a shower with me and let me show you just how much I'll be missing you next week.'

This man!

TWENTY

Jack

I only left a few days ago and I am feeling at a loss as to just how much I am missing my girl. How, in only a few short weeks, we have become so close, so linked to each other in a way I have never had before, has shocked me to the core. She's everything. People say that the person who is their one is everything they didn't know they were looking for. I understand that now but I know, for me, it's more than that. She is like the missing part to my soul. She doesn't know, can never know, how she has not only plugged but has completely eradicated the void in my heart. Was this void left over from my mom leaving me? Who the fuck knows. But I can state with absolute confidence that she is my person. The one I would go into battle for. The one who is the beginning, middle and end of my life.

After a day working with the field team, I find myself back at my hotel literally hopping on my feet until I speak to her. I am going home in the morning but my need to just connect with her, hearing her voice is like a drug and I need my fix. We've only talked on the phone each night but tonight I plan on Face Timing her. I need to see her face.

The work I have been doing here should have kept my mind fully occupied and it has, except for the moments when my girl enters my head, which are more frequent than I ever would have thought. When it happens, I can feel myself leave whatever place I should be concentrating on and just focusing on her and getting back to feel my girl in my arms again.

She's gigging tonight at The Moon so I have to wait, which doesn't help my pacing. She should be home at 11pm and as the clock in my hotel room hits the magic hour, I start the dial up.

It rings then rings out. I try again. Same damn thing happens, just keeps ringing out. My fingers start getting fidgety as I wait for her to pick up. By 11:15 I'm damn near to losing my mind. I feel worried and frustrated that I can't reach her.

Finally, at 11:50 she answers but by that stage I'm wound up like a tight spring. Before I can stop myself I hear my voice and my tone, exasperated and radiating anger.

'Where the hell have you been?' I practically shout at her.

'What did you just say?' She shouts back, equally loud as I see her in her apartment taking a seat on her couch.

'I said, where the hell have you been? I have been out of my mind with worry. It's well past 11pm, when you said you would be home. Now, I'll ask again, where have you been?'

'Who the hell are you to demand answers from me? You don't

fucking own me Jack so stop acting like you do!' She says, her face contorting with anger.

'Lucie, I'm going to ask you for the last time, where the fuck have you been?'

'YOU don't get to speak to me like that. If I want to stay at the pub and have a drink with some of the regulars after my gig, I fucking well will and I will not ask your permission to do so.'

'Which regulars? Who were you drinking with?' My frustration and anger just keeps rising.

'Why? What does it matter? Are you accusing me of something Jack because if you are you can go to hell!' She screams as I witness a tear rolling down her face. It should stop my tirade but it doesn't.

'Just tell me Lucie. I have been out of my mind with worry. You knew I would be calling. You knew I would be waiting and this is what you do? You just don't care?' I honestly don't know where all this is coming from. I don't know why, now I know she is home and safe, I can't just calm down.

'You know what Jack? Go fuck yourself,' she screams and cuts the call.

I stand there staring at my phone, my chest rising and falling rapidly as I quickly compose myself and redial her number. She doesn't pick up. I keep calling and calling and eventually, when I guess she's just had enough, it goes straight through to voicemail. She's obviously turned her phone off and all that does is make me even more crazy.

I'm not due at the airport until 4am tomorrow but I start chucking things into my travel bag as I know I won't sleep now anyway. Once I'm done, I pour myself a couple fingers of whisky and sip it whilst sitting on the edge of my hotel bed. I place the drink on the floor between my feet as I place my head into my hands and groan. Fuck, she was mad but hell, so was I. Now that I feel a bit calmer, I start working out where the hell my anger came from. It's not like me. I stay calm. If I didn't have the ability to keep it under control then I wouldn't be any good in my job. What the fuck happened?

I can feel it niggling away in the far recesses of my mind, in my memory bank. I think a shrink would call it 'abandonment issues'. I love somebody and I lose them. They walk away and never return. They say goodbye and get killed.

What hits me harder than the realisation that I may have royally fucked up is that I love Lucie. I would never have reacted so badly if I didn't. Before I managed to reach her, I could feel my skin crawling in fear. I know it's not rational but it just took over my mind and my heart. This is what love is. It makes you scared when you can't find your person. It makes you sick that your last goodbye might have literally been your last goodbye.

I don't care how mad she is, I need to make her understand that my reaction, albeit over the top, came from a fear that I had lost her and wasn't there to save her.

I finish my drink, sling my bag onto my shoulder and leave my room. If I leave now I'll be waiting in the airport for the next five hours but I don't give a shit. If I'm there and there is a chance I can get myself onto an earlier flight then I will. If I can't, well I know I'm not going to sleep anyway, so I might as well walk the halls of the airport rather than pace around my hotel room.

At the airport I manage to change my flight to the first leaving this morning as opposed to my later one. I send Lucie a text telling her that I'm sorry, that I'll be home soon to explain, to not be mad until she hears me out.

She doesn't respond but I wasn't expecting her to. I do, however, try calling her again but it's still going direct to voicemail and I guess she is now asleep. Probably plotting my demise but hell, I can do that on my own. I've done a pretty stellar job of that tonight.

When I finally board my flight, I can't even think straight. If I lose her, fuck I don't know what I'll do. I have to get home and make this right.

I can't lose her. I just can't.

TWENTY-ONE

Lucie

Oh God I don't want to get up. Somebody shut that fucking alarm up. Just let me stay here. I'm so comfortable and warm and I want somebody to bring me a cup of coffee in bed. And I want them to run me a bath. And I want them to put me in said bath. I went to bed crying which gave me a headache and it's still there. Fuck Jack. Who the hell does he think he is speaking to me like that? I had done nothing wrong. Nothing. I stayed for a drink with one of the old boys in the pub who was having a drink as his sister back in the 'old country' had died and he wanted everybody to raise a glass to her. I shouldn't have to justify my whereabouts when I was wasn't even an hour later than normal.

God, I need that coffee, but I know that I need to shift my arse out of my bed in order to do that. But first I need to wake up and hope that a bath will help clear my head a little.

Swinging my legs out of bed I literally stumble to the bathroom and turn the taps on. Whilst my bath is running I make my way to my little kitchen to get the coffee started.

I'm so tired, it feels wonderful to be fully ensconced in my tub, relaxing in the heat of the water, coffee in hand. Most people drift off when they have a bath and if I take one in the evening then I feel like that too, but a morning bath wakes me up and I get to put lovely smelly stuff in it that wakes my mind up. Today's little treat is Lemon and Bergamot and it smells divine. I rub it all over me right up to my face, breathing in the perfect aroma whilst thinking about nothing. Until I do.

My mind turns to Jack and immediately I can feel the tears stinging the back of my eyes. Damn him and his shouting at me. I will not get upset again. I will not. But I find that when the first of the tears start to fall, they fall quickly. Before I know what's happening I'm a sobbing mess. I knew this would happen. I knew it! I let him into my perfectly happy life and look where it's got me? Crying in my tub. I rub my chest around the place my heart lies and it hurts. I was falling in love with him. Scrap that, who am I kidding? I am already in love with him. That's why it hurts so much. My dad never spoke to my mum like Jack spoke to me last night. I know I am probably looking at my parents through rose-tinted glasses but I guess that's normal. My mum has gone and will forever be placed on a pedestal for us all to remember her as a perfect person and damn near saint. She wasn't of course but I pity the person who ever tries to knock her off that perch. I know she and my dad argued. We heard them. She had a fiery Irish temper and she wasn't ever going to bow down and play the little woman, but I know that my dad chose his words carefully with her. He would make his point but he always did so calmly, thus ensuring that he got his opinion over without upsetting her.

I briskly wipe the falling tears. That's it. No more crying, he can fuck off out of my life. I'll mend my broken heart on my own. Always on my own.

I rise out of the bath and wrap myself in a towel just in time to hear somebody smacking up my apartment door. I storm to the door ready to give the owner of the pounding fist a piece of my mind and swing the door open.

'Are you fucking kidding me?' Says Jack and owner of the pounding fist.

'What?' I practically shout in his face.

He looks a little red in the face and my body is screaming to brace myself. 'You didn't even check to see who was at the door before opening it! Do you realise that is how people die?' He says bracing his hands of the door architrave.

'Hang on now, it's stupid o'clock, some arsehole is pounding at my door, which frankly sounds wrong at this time of the morning and you have the fucking front to shout at me in my home? Go fuck yourself arsehole,' I scream back slamming the door. It stops dead as he's got his foot in the door stopping it from closing. 'Get your stupid cowboy foot out of my door and take your shouting elsewhere,' I seethe at him.

'Lucie, calm down, I was just stating a fact,' he says like he's so bloody calm.

'No, you were standing at my door, getting redder in the face by the minute, after smacking the door in and then you started shouting at me…ACTUALLY!' I am still shouting but only because he's an arsehole. He grins at me. Oh no he didn't. 'You think this is funny?' I ask, my voice quiet.

'No ma'am, I'm smiling because you are unbelievably hot when you get angry. And now I'm coming in and then I'm going to kiss the fuck out of you,' he says striding into my apartment as I back up matching him footstep for footstep.

'Don't you dare touch me' I shout back, 'you lost that right last night when you spoke to me like a piece of shit. Get out of my apartment, now Jack. I don't want you here. I don't want to see you, speak to you or even think about you. You did what you said you wouldn't do Jack. You fucked up.' I'm now openly crying. 'You said you wouldn't do that and you did. I told you, I told you straight, there would be no second chances.' I can barely get the words out through my tears.

Still Jack advances on me. 'Baby, I'm sorry, just let me explain. I know how I sounded; I know it sounded bad but you've gotta see where my head is at. I'm sorry darling, please, please Lucie, let me explain.'

I walk away and towards the coffee pot, grab myself a mug and pour. I don't offer a Jack a coffee.

'Can I get one of those?' He asks. I shrug at him so he grabs a mug from the counter and pours it himself, taking a sip before he turns to face me. I am now sitting at my little table, my hands round the mug, looking down at the steaming brew.

'Lucie, baby, look at me. Please.' He implores.

I look up and it hurts. It hurts to see his gorgeous face knowing that we are over. I don't want to talk. I just want to go back to bed and for this pain in my chest to go away.

'Listen Luce, I know I fucked up, okay? I knew it at the time but I just couldn't stop. I was so worried. I was just losing my mind not knowing where you were.'

'That doesn't account for how you spoke to me Jack,' I say wiping away the stupid tears that won't stop falling. 'You just started shouting at me, accusing me of God knows what. I didn't even understand what the hell was going on, I still don't. But if you think I'll give you another chance to ever speak to me like that again, you're wrong.'

'After,' he begins whilst rubbing his right hand over his face, 'after you hung up, I just kept trying to call you back. But when you wouldn't answer, I had a chance to calm down. Lucie, you know I don't normally act like that. That's not who I am. But after, when I'd had a chance to think about how I was feeling and what I said, how I spoke to you, I realised what it was.'

He pulls out the chair next to me and sits with his knees almost touching mine. I want to move away; I really do but I can't. He looks so sad. It slays me. Cuts me because I know stupidly I thought I could just cut those feeling I have for him off.

'I don't normally react like that sweetheart; I promise I don't. In that moment, I had been missing you so badly, all I wanted to do was to see your face. I know it was just one more night without you but I was desperate just to look at you. Then you didn't answer and my mind escalated it into something it wasn't. I went from fear to anger in a snap of a moment. I get this is my issue. This is actually my abandonment issue.'

'Abandonment? That's a little strong don't you think, Jack? I was like 50 minutes late. I hadn't disappeared from your life. Fifty minutes, Jack. Your reaction was so unnecessary and so upsetting. You need to explain this to me because I'm not getting it.' I tell him and as those stupid tears continue to fall. He reaches out and brushes the tears off of my cheek and when his hand makes contact with my face, I close my eyes. Is this the last time he will ever touch me?

'Sweetheart, I didn't know until last night that I even had abandonment issues but I know everything I felt last night was how I felt the day that my mom didn't come home to me and just like the day I met Trav's dad at the basketball court and he told me Travis was dead. It was like a flood in my head. All I could see; all I could feel was that you were gone and I lost it. Baby, please, I'm so sorry darling. I never meant to hurt you. I never meant to speak to you so badly. I never meant for it to fuck us up.'

Now it's my turn to wipe the tears from my man's face. And he is my man. Mine. Watching him now, beside himself with fear and desperation, kills me. I reach out to the back of his neck and draw his face closer to mine.

'Jack, listen to me and listen to me good because I am never going to repeat this. You have my body. You have my mind. You have my heart. And I am yours. I will never leave you without explanation. It would take the end of the world for me to do that to you and even then, even then, I'm not sure I would go. Do you understand, Jack? I am not going anywhere,' once again I say it through a torrent of tears.

'Baby, I need to tell you something else,' he begins. I feel my heart stop; please don't make this worse. 'Baby, my reaction last night showed me something I knew but was trying to keep under control but now darling, now I don't care, I need to put it out there. I love you sweetheart. I love you. I love you today darling. I'll love you tomorrow and the next day and the day after that. I just want to spend my life showing you my love.'

Crying, I crawl onto Jack's lap and we wrap our arms around each other. Burying my face in his neck I tell him I love him. He hears me. His embrace around my body gets tighter.

'From now on I need you in my apartment. I want to come home to you each night and I want us wake up to each other every morning. I'm not saying give this place up; I know for you it's important for you to keep your independence but I just want you with me.'

'Okay,' I whisper in return just as Jack stands, still with me in his arms and carries me to my bedroom so we can show each other just how much love we have.

TWENTY-TWO

Lucie

Jack and I have been in a full-on grown-up relationship for the past six months. I still have my apartment but I live with my Jack. We are the first person each of us see in the morning and each night we are the last. Our mornings start with kisses and love and our nights end the same way.

Blissful is an understatement. We spend every moment possible with each other, either just us or with Garrett and Cassie or at The Moon. Our weekends are sometimes crazy busy with hiking, lake swimming, going to the markets for fresh produce, or lazy, where we don't move from our bed or couch, where we watch movies wrapped up in each other's arms, eating junk food and laughing.

It's the laughter that we share that I love the most. There are times it reminds me of my parents. How they would laugh or dance around our kitchen at home, happy, just so happy to be with each other. It breaks my heart to think of my dad, alone now, no more love of his life, no more touching the person he loved more than anything else in this world.

We are going away this weekend and I am so damn excited. We are flying and whilst that makes me nervous - not that I'm afraid of flying – but, you know, fake passport and all that but I am so looking forward to being away with my Jack. Just the two of us, loving each other.

On Friday afternoon Jack collects me from the shop. He has both of our bags and I have quickly changed out of my uniform which my lovely friend Cassie has assured me will be clean and ready on my return. She really is my surrogate mum and I love her for it.

Arriving at the airport I still have no idea where we are going but as we walk hand in hand through the terminal I find myself not caring. That's the moment I realise I would go just about anywhere with this man. I know I love him; he knows I love him. But this is something more. This is trust. I don't think I'm not a trusting person, other than with my family, it has never come up before. I've never really dated, well not as a fully-fledged adult, so have never had my trust broken by a man. I've read enough women's magazine to know it's a big thing out there. If so many women don't trust their other halves I don't understand why they stay in the relationship. What's the point? But I trust Jack, my Jack. He puts me first in absolutely every way and I do the same for him.

As we walk to the check-in I don't care where we are about to fly to. Apparently, we are going to Paradise Island. I've never heard of it but the lady behind the check-in desk has a smile a mile wide as she tells us that it really lives up to its name and exclaims that we are so very lucky. I nod mutely, squeezing Jack's hand, feeling him squeeze mine in return.

Getting to the gate a little while later, Jack puts his arm around my shoulder and asks if I'm excited. I smile up at him with a cocky shrug of my shoulders as I tell him, 'kinda'.

He just laughs and whispers in my ear, 'let's see how you "kinda" enjoy me fucking you from behind in the sea as we watch the sun go down'.

I feel myself shiver at his words and my breasts begin to ache at the thought of him doing that to me, feeling my heartbeat slam in my chest as I picture the scene.

A few hours later and we do indeed land in Paradise. I have never seen anything like it. When we arrive at an exclusive set of private bungalows set on the beach my breath leaves my body. I am in a daze, my mouth hanging open in the most unladylike fashion. Jack leads me to 'our' bungalow, which is yet more in the slice of heaven brochure.

Our bags in the bungalow, Jack wraps me in his arms and tells me it's bikini time and to hop to it. I don't need telling twice, my excitement is ricocheting around the room. I am in my bikini in double-quick time and stop just in time to watch Jack undress. Fuck, this man does something to me. Watching him disrobe is the most erotic thing I have ever witnessed and my heart quickens as every bit of clothing is taken off his body. If he asks me if I see something I like, I'll chuck a flip flop at his head but hell, he wouldn't be wrong.

'You drooling baby?' He asks instead looking over his shoulder at me.

'Damn right I am baby!' I say with an American accent that just makes him throw his head back with laughter.

'Come here gorgeous,' he tells me and I walk to him immediately. 'Fuck woman, you look hot as fuck,' he tells me sliding his large, warm hands down the sides of my body.

His hands move from my sides to slide around to my back and down to my arse. Lifting me into his arms he gives me a heart-stopping kiss. There's no gentle tease, no softness, just rough, demanding and achingly hot. Taking one hand off my arse and onto the back of my head, his fingers tangle and weave inside my hair, slightly fisting it and using it to up the intensity of our kiss. I hear his moans just as mine releases from me. I feel him shifting us and presume he's getting ready to lay me on the bed. But then I feel his naked cock pushing against the material covering my core. Another moan comes from me without warning. I feel his fingers pushing my bikini bottom to the side and the tip of his cock beginning to rub against my wetness. Jack slides me lower down his body until I feel him push inside me. My head wants to fall backward but this man, he is so in control. He holds my head securely so he can continue to kiss me until he is fully seated inside my body.

We moan in unison, our love and bodies connecting on every level, making us one. Feeling Jack's hands lifting and lowering my body, in rhythm with his thrusts has my eyes rolling in the back of my head.

'Fuck, Lucie, you're so tight, so snug, I fucking love being inside you baby.'

'Jack, don't stop, please just don't stop,' I beg him.

I feel him push my back up against a wall and as soon as my flesh makes contact with it, Jack starts to fuck me harder. When we both come, we stay as we are, both with our eyes wide open, panting, breathing in each other's breath. Looking at each other and knowing this love is everything.

Getting cleaned up is fun too, curtesy of a secluded outdoor shower where Jack insists on washing my body, lathering and worshipping it simultaneously. My turn is just as much fun as there is little more I enjoy in life than running my hands all over Jack's delicious body.

Finally, clean and back in our swim stuff, we head off hand in hand towards the beach. The white sand and turquoise water. As we walk into the softly lapping water, our real life feels a million miles away. Jack lets go of my hand and moves to stand behind me, his arms encircling me.

'Happy?' He asks

'I am Jack, I really, really am. It's so beautiful here. Thank you for bringing me,' I tell him sincerely.

'There is nobody else I would rather be with sweetheart. Just you and me. Today and always,' he says kissing my bare shoulder.

'I love you Jack,' I say, tears springing to my eyes.

'Baby, I fucking love you too. With every part of my soul,' he tells me.

We swim out just a short distance, deep water really isn't my thing. But Jack is with me and he would never let anything happen to me. He also doesn't push my limit of fear. When I tell him I want to turn back around towards the beach, he doesn't hesitate. He doesn't make me feel less for not being adventurous in the water's depth, takes no glory in watching me be frightened just so he can act like the hero. He would never belittle my feelings or my fears. And that's because he's a real man.

The evening comes quickly and we dine alone at our bungalow. A luxurious four-course dinner is delivered and devoured and as soon as we finish we pop ourselves back into our swimsuits and walk back into the sea where Jack fills me from behind, as promised, as we watch the sunset on our beautiful day. The weekend passes quickly but the memory of our time there will be burned in my mind forever more.

The evening we return home we unpack and take a shower together, continuing our love. As we lay in bed that night we speak in whispers as we talk about our future. I know it's time. I need to tell him everything. How can I love him like I do and not tell him? But I can't tonight. I don't want to spoil our time. I don't want to see the disgust in his eyes when I tell him what my dad is. Jack is on the right side of the law; it's ingrained in him. No matter if it's petty or serious crime, a criminal is a criminal. I love my dad, I don't want him to be judged, but I am caught at the crossroads between my love for Dad and my love for Jack. If I want Jack to be my future, he deserves to know the truth about me, who I am, what my real life looked like before arriving here and who my family is.

Tomorrow. Tomorrow I will tell him everything.

I smile to myself as I fall asleep on my man's chest knowing that come tomorrow night, there will be no secrets. And I hope that Jack will still love me.

BOOK 2

Lucie

I'm on my knees; deep in the woods and I can feel the morning dew seeping into my jeans. I remember getting here yet it seems like I'm in a dream.

The woods overlook the rear of a massive house that I don't believe I have ever visited but now, somehow, it seems so familiar. Have I ever been here? I vaguely knew the road that I parked on to get into these woods but I had to follow the instructions given by Melanie to know where to park and which way to walk. She was specific about me stopping at the clearing I am now in for the best view.

From my vantage point, all I can see is the back of the house, with its yellow walls that are curved rather than at right angles. It is a beautiful place. The back of the house has a built-up terrace, and the gardens drop away at the end of that patio. Fencing signals, the end of the garden and the beginning of these woods.

The house must belong to somebody with money, it's far too palatial to be just anybody's gaff. Melanie's note said I'd find the answers, but it wouldn't bring me happiness. It didn't make any sense when I read it this morning and frankly, it still doesn't. She said I wasn't to go to the front of the house. I could only view it from the rear, and only from these woods. She also told me to stay out of sight.

So here I am. Hunkered down in the woods looking at somebody's home without any clue as to why. I don't understand what's going on. What is happening? What am I supposed to find here?

The patio leads from a set of French doors and as I sit here wondering what I'm supposed to do next, one of the doors opens.

I squint to see who it is as they exit the building. I don't realise I am crying until I feel my tears drip off my lips.

Suddenly, I feel sick.

PART TWO

ONE

Jack

ENGLAND

Jesus, the sun might be shining but it's not warm. These woods are damp and boggy and I feel like my head is going to explode. Bloody jet lag will do that to you every time. I'm with the firearms division on the task force I spent part of the last year working with before returning home. They're good men and women on this team. I'm not saying they're hesitant but you can always tell when people haven't grown up with guns. They are serious but not comfortable. Focused. Understanding that to fire may result in the death of somebody, even if that somebody doesn't deserve to live.

When I got the call to come back to England, it was just twenty-four hours after Lucie had disappeared on me that night. I'd spent those first hours trying desperately to track her down but unable to find any answers. Even in that short space of time, I discovered things I am still trying to get my head around. None of it makes sense. We loved each other; I know we did. I know it was real, but I was starting to feel like my Lucie was a ghost. Lucie Malone wasn't her real name. She was travelling and living on falsified documents and I didn't know; hell, I didn't even suspect. Everything was set up for her on arrival in the States but none of the details were genuine. Somebody has the answers but just when I was getting close I got the call to come back here and 'no' wasn't an option. Saying, 'sorry, I'm trying to find my girl. She disappeared into thin air one night after we'd spent the night making love, making plans, building a future together.' I was always aware that I didn't know everything about her, that there were things she was holding back, but I had felt confident that in time she would talk to me and fully let me in. I put it down to the fact that there were unsavoury things in her past and she had needed more time before opening up. I felt we would get there and didn't feel this had made our relationship any less real. Perhaps I was wrong, but I've always had great instinct and my instinct tells me I wasn't wrong about her.

Now however, is not the time to focus on my girl. Now is the time to be in charge of a 16-man firearm unit, guns and binoculars focused on the house at the end of the woods. We know who we think is in there but our informant wasn't as specific as we'd have liked him to be. We know that Ronnie McDowell is in that house. We know that Ronnie left home and is currently classified as missing by his family. Not that they have reported it to the police but we have good intel that this is the case. We know he is our key to getting the Langfords and the team felt confident that it was only a matter of time before they could get Ronnie to talk to us about Billy Langford. Billy, the Kingpin of everything we despise in this world.

Billy Langford is a legend and like in history, not all legends are good. Billy, his blood and extended family of thugs run the drugs through this part of England. They also traffic people; specifically, girls who end up in sex clubs in Europe. He's linked to the Russians and the Italians and everybody in between. He orders hits on those he sees as rivals to his business and sometimes, we know, has done the deed himself. Not one to avoid getting his hands dirty when he wants to.

The base team have been working on getting Billy for over 8 years. They've infiltrated the gang several times and in the process, lost 3 good men. Falling out of favour with Billy and his sons seems as easy as a walk in the park but less expected. Like my girl, they're ghosts and as such, informants are scarce.

We know that Billy had a sister whom he was estranged from for 15 years. We know she died 8 years ago in a car crash that ended in a ball of flames. There was nothing left, but she had been seen driving the car all day, had just been into a store to do the family grocery shopping before driving back home. Only she didn't make it. She had last been seen in the car not five minutes before the crash. The police investigation concluded that there could only have been one person driving the car prior to the accident and that was Maree. Maree McDowell née Langford.

Several informants, who incidentally are now in witness protection, told the investigation that it was a 'hit' by Billy as a final punishment for marrying a McDowell, whilst showing Ronnie that no matter what he did, Billy was in charge of his future. Killing your own flesh and blood takes a special kind of psychopath and Billy is that person. There was no evidence to suggest that it was anything other than a car crash except the connection to Billy, but this wasn't obvious to the officers in charge of the incident on that day. No dots were connected until much later. There were skid marks on the road where the crash happened. The front of the car was totalled in the crash but it seems extreme that the car would go up in a ball of flames. By the time the fire brigade arrived the car was all burnt out on a country road that rarely ever saw traffic. Ronnie, at the time, claimed he couldn't understand why his wife would have taken that route home. Standing here now, it feels clearer. The road where Maree crashed and died is a few minutes' walk from the house now in our viewing range.

At the time, the family held a memorial in lieu of the normal funeral and the reason was given that there just wasn't enough left of Maree to put in a coffin.

Maree had been 45 at the time of her death, leaving behind Ronnie and four children, the eldest of which was Melanie at 22 years old, 'Irish twin' boys of 17 and 18 and a 15 year old second daughter, Polly.

Turns out the eldest is a bit of a force to be reckoned with. Melanie is present at every underground fighting ring in the South of England. She runs the bag for her brothers as well as running her own boxing club. The club itself is legit and unlike her other less savoury activities, the boxing seems to be the only business running out of there.

Her night-time activities are a whole different matter. Running the bag takes a fearless person in some of these clubs. The fighting rings are illegal bare-knuckle affairs. It's not unknown for the loser to not just end up beaten, but dead too. The money running through those clubs is increasing year on year and the level of violence is rising along with it. The fighting is not even the most obvious concern. It's the networking that goes on there. The businessmen might wear suits but they are not gentlemen.

Melanie is certainly a chip off her mother's block. The late Maree started her dubious career as the bag holder for her brother Billy.

Everything we have learnt since about Maree has built a picture of a formidable woman, feared by many, but revered by others. She was a little out of place in the fight club world being old school glamour. She turned into a loyal wife and loving mother. On meeting Ronnie, she wanted out from her life being Billy's right hand. We have been told that leaving that life was with Billy's consent. According to those who knew the couple, Ronnie and Maree were devoted to each other and to their children. Ronnie has a legitimate business now but he is and always will be a career criminal. He seems to have quietened down since Maree's death but that's not to say that he has no links to illegal activities. It seems Maree was determined that her children be educated and educated well. All four of the kids went to private school and whilst Melanie and Polly excelled at their studies, the boys were hell bent on causing chaos which resulted in expulsion for both. Polly was only fifteen at the time of her mother's death and was removed from the school whilst the family grieved, only to be shipped back just two months later.

Since the moment Ronnie became a widower he pretty much became a recluse and handed the on-site running of the building contractor business to his sons, taking a backseat and working from his office at home. They seem to have been constant, even if their methods have been less than polite. Stories have emerged of them threatening developers and competitors to get business and however unsavoury it seems, their methods have worked. The business is thriving with a solid workforce.

We have only secured images of Polly up until the age of 10 and have found no footprint for her since. We've been told that she left the family home to go travelling in Europe and to our knowledge hasn't returned since. We have found no evidence to suggest that this story isn't true but given the family history and capabilities, we're still looking into finding her. Unfortunately, mainland Europe is vast and the resources aren't available, so we have relied on contacts who knew her to keep us informed if any word on her whereabouts is mentioned. She was a kid when all this happened; she's not involved in the family business nor in the fighting ring so she has never been marked as a person of huge interest.

So here we are in the woods, waiting to catch a glimpse of Ronnie who apparently has gone missing. Our informant told us that the heat from the Langfords was getting too much and he felt it safer for his children to disappear for a while. We have yet to ascertain what this 'heat' looked like. There doesn't appear to have been a meeting between either the two men or anybody on Billy's side making any connection with Ronnie. Again, all we can go on is hearsay as to why he has gone underground, but if we can get to him, our hope is that it will give us some concrete leads to Billy and his activities.

We know that the house at the end of the woods was once owned by Ronnie's uncle on his mother's side and is currently owned by Ronnie's company, left to him in part inheritance. For years the firm rented it out to travelling businessmen and their families, sometimes for a few weeks or at times, much longer. Scoping it out last night, we discovered that the house is guarded by a security team around the clock. High security is not unknown for high powered businesspeople or those with great wealth. Often, they have bodyguards, so this hasn't raised any alarm bells. There are no cars in the driveway but there is a triple garage that we haven't managed to access yet.

My thought process is interrupted by Gillingham, the unit's base leader onsite with us here today. He is busy signaling something to the right of us. From my location I can see a body which looks like a person squatting down, keeping still but with eyes on the house. So we aren't the only ones interested on the goings on here? This is an interesting development. This place is off the beaten track. There is no footpath. Anybody else here, like us, is here for a reason.

Gillingham is viewing the interloper through binoculars as I make my way over to him.

'There's a girl watching the house. She's tucked down low so we can't see her face only the profile. I think we should watch her for a while, see what she does,' he suggests.

Taking the binoculars from him to view the subject I feel like I'm about to have a heart attack.

I know that profile.

That's my girl.

My feet are moving before I am consciously aware of my actions. Shouting into the radio to keep back, just stay the fuck back. I gotta get to my girl.

I'm running like I never have before, hitting trees and ground brambles on route. Just as I get within touching distance she doubles over and throws up. She just keeps hurling and coughing, screaming in-between her convulsions. I get to her and fall to my knees wrapping my arms around her, holding her close, holding like I've needed to since she's been gone.

'Baby, it's me, its Jack, I got you baby, I got you,' are the only words I can find to utter as I hold her, rubbing her back, pushing her hair back, God anything just to touch my love.

She raises her head till her eyes meet mine. She looks like she hasn't slept since leaving, she has her own vomit down her chin and I don't care as I wipe it away with my fingers.

She lifts her hand and touches my face, closing her eyes and leaning back into my embrace.

'Luce, baby, why are you here?' I ask as gently as I can muster.

'My…my…oh god Jack, they lied to me, to us. They lied,' she cries and clings to me harder.

'Who lied, Darling?' I'm not getting it. She's in a bad way but she is desperate to convey what she needs to.

'My parents, Jack, they lied. My mum… my mum is alive. I've

just seen her walk out of that door down there.' She says pointing in the direction of the house.

In my haste to get to her, I missed the moment of exit.

'Wait…what? Your parents?'

'My parents are both down there Jack, don't you see? They lied. They told me my mum was dead. She died, Jack. In a car crash when I was fifteen, but they lied, she's not dead, I just saw her.' Her sobs once again take over.

'You're Polly?'

'Oh god, oh god, Jack I'm sorry,' she cries. 'I had to lie, Jack, I had to. I had to be somebody else to be able to get away, to be free of this fucking shit that my life was, I had no choice Jack, you must see that?'

'Baby, we gotta get you out of here. Lucie, do you understand me?' The sobbing has taken over again and I'm not sure she can hear what I need her to. 'We've got to get you out of here. There's a team just behind me in the distance and they can see you, can see us. They're here watching the house, now watching your parents and when they come over here, they'll have questions and they won't be satisfied that you don't know anything. Do you know anything Luce? You have to tell me if you know anything. Baby, you gotta trust me, I can't protect you if you don't tell me,' I implore.

'Jack, I don't know what's going on! I've just found out that the mum I have spent the last eight years grieving over isn't fucking dead! She's not dead Jack! Oh god, I need to be sick again. Jack, help me. Please, I need to get out of here. Please Jack, get me out of here.' Lucie is doubled over again, crying uncontrollably and it's breaking me. My girl's heart is in pieces and I'm at a loss as to how to help her, other than keeping her tight in my arms. To protect her. And I swear to God, I will until my dying breath.

I hear footsteps coming towards us and take a quick look over my shoulder. Gillingham is making his way through the undergrowth towards us.

'Lucie, listen to me, you need to go…now. I can't come with you. I can't protect you if they find out your relationship with me. Baby, I love you and making you get the fuck out of here is my best way of protecting you. Go home. Lay low. No matter what I'll find you darling, but I can't do anything if you don't do what I say now. Lucie, go, run and get out of here.'

Lucie looks at me; her heartbreak evident, tears rolling down her face. 'I love you Jack, I never lied about that.' She gently rubs her fingers up and down my beard.

'I know baby, I know. Now go, I'll come for you, I promise.'

Common sense and survival instinct kick in for her and within seconds she's running. Branches and shrubbery hitting her body as she runs. She doesn't look back and I'm glad. I really can't let anybody know that she's my girl.

'Who the fuck was that?' Gillingham bellows as he finally reaches where I am standing.

'Some poor girl, one-night stand and doing the walk of shame home. Thought this wood would lead her where she needed to get home and got lost. She started freaking out and last night's booze came up too. Nothing like some random girl hurling at ya feet eh?' My words come out in one sentence. Lying on your feet is standard FBI work. I'm pretty sure I'm believable too.

Gillingham smiles in a way I want to knock his teeth out. Leary. And then he says it.

'I could only see the outline but if I'd have fucked her last night, I'd have stopped her from fucking leaving,' he laughs.

Gillingham isn't a bad guy; in fact, up until this moment he has always made my stay in the UK bearable. Right now, I could happily get him in a head lock and pound the motherfucker till he cried. But the truth is, despite what I feel, I can't do that. I look at him, do that chin raise thing and just say 'right'. Even that one word makes me feel like I'm betraying my girl. I can't even begin to get my head round that my Lucie is actually Polly McDowell. I thought I was good, but I never saw that one coming. She no longer resembles the girl that appeared in our photo file. That kid was just that, a kid. I could kick my own ass but I truly saw no connection and frankly, I still don't. If she came running back and told me it was a joke, I think I'd believe her. I wish she would as I know this is about to get seriously complicated and the thought of Lucie being anywhere near this situation is going to make me lose my mind.

'So where did she go?' Gillingham asks me.

'I told her to get the hell out of here, told her there were poachers in the area and she would likely get shot if she stayed,' more lies fall easily out my mouth. Whilst not a quality most would like, given my career, I am an accomplished liar and to date, I don't remember ever being called out on one.

'Well I enjoy a pretty girl as much as the next man, but I reckon you did her a favour. Fuck knows what's going on but we've just seen Ronnie McDowell's dead wife, Maree, exit out of the back doors with him. That woman apparently died eight years ago so unless she has a perfect double, I'd say this unexpected turn might twist this shit up some more, don't you?'

I nod absently, my mind solely focused on Lucie and where she is right now. Did she make it out of the woods without being seen? We've left a few guys out by the roadside entrance to the wood but as there are no actual footpaths through the woods she could have taken a hundred different routes. We didn't note any other cars parked up when we arrived so my best hope is that she parked out of sight and can get out without being clocked by anybody. Not that I think anyone would recognise her as the youngest daughter but hey, stranger things have happened.

'Are you even listening to me?' Asks Gillingham.

'Yeah, sorry, I was thinking how a dead woman can look so

alive and what that could mean,' I state with as much conviction as I can muster.

'Only one way to find out,' says Gillingham, stomping back the way we both came.

I follow behind, all the while thinking how I need to start making sure I cover my tracks carefully when I go looking for Lucie. I know we have McDowell's address. If 'home' is where Lucie is headed then I need to watch my back. I need to slip under both the unit and Langford's possible radar.

We both reach the others more or less at the same time. I can hear my earpiece coming to life with questions from some of the guys. Gillingham looks at me expectantly.

'First things first,' I begin. 'We need to ascertain how Maree is alive and why she has been underground, presumed dead, for nearly a decade. I don't think it takes a genius to work out that it's something significant. Rarely do people fake their own death but when there are children, then it's really fucking unusual. It's got to be something to do with her brother. We know they were estranged shortly before her death. All our informants have said the same thing; family disagreement, Maree flew off the handle and they never made up. Now that might be true but we know Billy. You'd have to be a fucking mad man to pick a fight with him whether you are family or not. We need to get the intel on the real reason for them going separate ways. And if we can do that, then maybe we can find out why Maree came back from the dead.'

'Sir, sorry, bit confused here. Why do we need to look into the McDowells? We want Billy and his gang. If Mrs McDowell has been dead to the world for all these years, she won't know anything about his current business dealings and we know that Ronnie has pretty much kept his nose clean. Shouldn't we be looking into those who are still connected to Billy?' Asks one of the guys.

'In principle,' I tell him. 'I agree, but we had word that around five weeks ago Melanie was threatened whilst collecting the money. She sustained a black eye and a cut mouth. Now that's not an unusual incident to happen at any underground fight club but our informant heard her being threatened verbally before they smacked her about. He said and I quote, "tell your old man we're coming for him and his missus. Nobody makes a mug out of Billy. Not even family." Within days of that incident, Ronnie flies the nest and hasn't been seen since, well, at least not until today. I think it's safe to assume that Billy is aware that his sister isn't dead. I could understand it if she faked it to get away from the husband. It would make sense to cut herself off from her children as well as everybody else. But every person we've asked has said the same thing and that's that Ronnie and Maree were absolutely devoted to each other and we have seen nothing to contradict those statements. The file on the McDowells is one of a happy family, a devoted and loyal mother and wife. So, we have to assume that her running away was with her husband's knowledge and consent.'

'We need to know who knows what, for how long and why Billy is suddenly sending his boys in to scare his niece, or is that just a convenient coincidence? Nobody is going to approach Ronnie or Maree until I say so. I want this house watched night and day. I want to know if and when Ronnie leaves, where he goes and does Maree ever leave? Nearly a decade in hiding, she's gotta get out of the house sometimes. Does she have groceries delivered? If so, we need to find out which company brings them and make one of our guys the next delivery guy. We also need to know if there are ever any visitors to the house. They used to rent it out; we need to make enquiries as to whether that is still an option, if not, find out how long ago that status changed.'

My mind is back to reeling, going into overdrive. Has Lucie got out without being noticed? The answer must be yes as we've had no radio contact from the roadside guys. Surely Lucie wouldn't come back here to confront them? God, I hope not. I've just given the order that the house needs to be under constant surveillance but anything else wouldn't make sense to the team and I don't want them to be suspicious. Fuck, I wish I knew that Lucie was away and safe from here. For the moment, I'll have to just keep my worries very close to my chest and hope there are no more surprises in store for me.

'Gills, you have anything else you want to add?' I ask looking at him.

'Here's how we're going to split this,' he states. 'Tom, your team, spread out and stay down, eyes on the back of the house. If anything is seen, radio in immediately. Chris, I want your guys to come back with us to base, let's start on the tactics of how we can infiltrate the premises when we're ready. The guys on the roadside can stay there to cover your backs but be alert. Billy has eyes and ears everywhere. Right, Tom, contact base and confirm who you have here and place your markers. Radio that in. I ain't losing any more men. The rest of you, back to base now.'

Gillingham starts off in the direction we came in through and it's not lost on me as we walk back that it's just that a direction. The woods are so overgrown that it's near impossible to recognise any previous routes taken by us or anybody else.

TWO

Lucie

I'm running. Running for my car like my feet are on fire. Jack. My Jack is here and I have no idea what the fuck is going on with my life. Looking back to the night I left Jack in bed; I want to throw up again. We had spent the night together, locked physically and mentally together, in sex, intimacy and in words. We spoke at length that night about us, about our future, about creating a family together and I can remember clearly thinking that I needed to tell him the truth. Who I really was, my family, why I had to leave home and why I never wanted to go back. I mean I would have come home at some point, God I could never not see my dad again but I didn't want to have to stay.

I had created a new life for myself with Cassie and the pub and I loved it. I loved the freedom of new life. I had no ghost of Christmas or any other season's past hanging over my head.

Even when I reached the States, it had only been six years since Mum died and I was still very much wrapped up in grief. I knew in reality that would never go away, but in a new place, with new people, making new memories, it was getting easier to block it out and pretend I just couldn't see her at the moment. Pretend she wasn't dead. Then when I met Jack, the void in my heart became full of him. It had already had some filling from Cassie and Garrett and the guys at the pub, but Jack, oh god, Jack gave me something I never wanted to give back; he gave me his heart.

One minute I was lying in his arms and the next I watched my phone flash to life. It wasn't unusual for that to happen. A time difference when you live away from your family will make that occurrence commonplace. I slid the bar sideways to look at the message. The name flashed up, my sister, Mel. The message was just one sentence, 'our bird of love has flown'. Innocuous and deliberately vague; I knew immediately what she had meant. Dad had gone and I need to get home. I'd slipped silently out of Jack's bed, soon to be permanently our bed after all our plan-making that night, got dressed and left. On racing back to my apartment, I knew immediately that somehow he would try to find me. And so I did it on purpose. It was the only clue I could possibly leave that would indicate something wasn't right; I left my guitar.

From my apartment, I'd grabbed my passport and nothing else. I didn't need anything. I had a wardrobe full of clothes at my home in London and nothing I had here was suitable to wear there anyway.

Within 30 minutes I was at the airport where I knew a ticket would be waiting for me. Mel and I had discussed an event such as this happening prior to my leaving home. We had devised a 'coded' message, which wasn't coded as such, just a bit odd, but would mean she could send it and if anybody were to read it, it would mean nothing to them.

The plane journey home was the longest time alone I have ever experienced with a stop-over I didn't want. I didn't sleep at all; just stared aimlessly at whatever movie was playing. The stewardess kept asking if I wanted a drink and even though I said no, I wanted one desperately. I wanted the drink to numb the pain I was feeling in my heart and the pounding of my head. I don't remember thinking once about my family on that flight, just Jack. Jack waking up and not finding me next to him. Jack wandering around his apartment calling my name. Jack realising that I had gone and then trying to call me. He wouldn't have been awake until I was well in the air and my phone had been off. Did he call Cassie immediately or did he run straight over to my apartment only to not find me there either? Did he get angry or upset or did confusion mask those emotions? By the time I landed hours later and turned on my phone whilst waiting in the passport clearance line, I had racked up forty missed calls from him and currently had 15 text messages, each one getting more and more desperate. The first voice messages were mere curiosity and had then become more emotional. Where was I? Was I okay? Lots of words about loving me, about how our life together was just beginning, had he done something wrong? I stopped listening after the first 10 voice calls, leaving the remaining messages in cyberspace. With tears rolling down my cheeks, I cleared passport control and went to look for Mel.

What had I done? Should I have woken him up? Perhaps I wouldn't have had to explain; just said I needed to go home, that my family needed me. But I knew instinctively he would ask questions, fuck, who wouldn't? And I know that I wouldn't have been able to give him any credible answers.

I couldn't do that, as to date, I hadn't told him anything about my family of any great worth. The basics only. Mum dead. Dad and siblings at home running the family business. I knew that given time, I would have shared my story with him but it hadn't seemed important and I guess my sister and brothers' extra circular activities just seemed a bit shady in comparison to the life I was now living. I have never been ashamed of my family. He doesn't even know my real name. Or that my dad is one of those 'businessmen', the type that spends part of their kid's childhood inside a cell. Not wanting to be part of the fighting scene means I didn't approve of what they did. I just wasn't interested and at times, couldn't understand how my sweet and nurturing sister could love it so much. But she did and although the boxing club is fully legit and gave the local teenagers a positive place to be, what happened after dark was, at best, repulsive and nauseating.

My mum used to say I didn't have the stomach for anything other than roses. If any of my siblings got sick, I would go to my nanny's house until my mum gave me the all clear. One of my brothers was responsible for my vomit phobia. Mel had been sick during the night when I was around five years old and my brother chased me across the landing of our house with a bucket of puke. He didn't actually throw it at me but he did, albeit through his laughter, try to dunk my head in it. My dad caught him and whooped his arse, whilst I silently threw up in the downstairs toilet.

I'm pretty much the same way about blood, just another reason why I stayed away from the boxing and subsequent fight nights. If you have ever seen two men go at each other like animals, no head-guard, no mouthguard and bare-knuckles, the brutality of it can take your breath away. Once. I went once. I lasted two rounds before I ran out crying and hurled behind my brother's car.

Landing at Heathrow had my stomach in knots. I only had hand luggage so could bypass the bag carousel but still, I dragged my feet knowing the moment I exited the terminal, the reality of the situation would strike and my courage may leave me. My fear was a definite ten but I know my sister would not have called me back from my self-imposed isolation if she didn't need to. All I had when I boarded my flight was the text, 'our bird of love has flown'. The message was clear. Come home. I didn't, of course, know what I was coming home to, but I knew that once I stepped out of the airport doors I would have the answer. I knew Mel would be waiting and whilst I loved my sister, I knew whatever it was, it was going to be serious. The fear building inside me wasn't just about what I was walking into but what I may have to walk away from permanently. The life that I had built for myself across the Atlantic. The life that I loved. The peacefulness and comfort that I was missing already. I liked being anonymous; it gave me safety and the independence that I could never have had if I stayed home. It wasn't being the youngest in the family that had clipped my wings when I was younger and would eventually make leave. No, it was the suffocation of everybody knowing who I was, watching, waiting to gain points by giving titbits of information to my family. And worse than that were the lies my family had fed me, deliberately keeping me out of the inner loop. My life had never really been my own. Whilst I had been able to make my own friends at high school, even that had still felt rather contrived. Get in with her and you'll be protected. Be friends with her and nobody is going to bother you. Get in with her and they'll think you're untouchable. God, what a fucking joke. Of course, I did have true friends but they had been formed out of family connections. The friendships had been written by our families when we were born. It wasn't that my mates and I hadn't loved and cared for each other or that we would have given them up, but we were all aware that we had been put together. Cassie and Garrett and the guys at The Moon were my choice. People I wanted to be with, wanted in my life, knowing nothing of who I was, where I came from - apart from Declan - not that he and I even spoken of our familial connection. For the first time ever, I had forged friendships that were truly mine. The ache in my heart was already painful, not knowing when or even if, I would get back to the States. Not knowing if yesterday would be the last time I would see 'my people'.

And then Jack. Leaving him asleep last night had brought me to my knees. I wanted to scream, wake him, beg him to stop me from leaving. Take the choice away from me. Closing the door behind me I knew that left in that room, lying next to Jack in the dark, was a piece of my heart that would never be returned unless I went back for it. And at this moment in time, I didn't know if it would be missing forever. He looked so peaceful, so content, so goddam sexy. My perfect man. He is, was, totally unexpected in every way. I certainly never intended letting any man into my heart; least of all Jack who had turned out to be my soulmate. I truly believed when I met him that his attention span in me would be short, that his interest would wane fast. I was wrong. So very wrong. My Jack turned out to be loving, attentive, protective, and a good man with a beautiful heart and soul. The pain in my chest, which during my flight home I had attributed to fear was now actually far scarier. The thought of never seeing Jack again, never touching his beautiful face or ever feeling his arms around me when I woke is the epicentre of the pain. It was actually the pain of my heart. For the millionth time since boarding the plane last night, I could feel the tears beginning to burn at the back of my eyes. My unshed tears making them burn. I fought back a sob. I didn't cry. If those flood gates are opened I know I will never close them again. As I wandered slowly through the terminal, I wondered again about what he thought when he woke up? Did he reach for me like he always did or did he instinctively know that I was gone? Was he angry at me or just confused? Did he think I had just gone but would be back soon, perhaps with breakfast pastries like either one of us had done so many times previously? Had he found my note?

I guess my biggest fear was if he wouldn't just take it and come to look for me. I want him to but don't want him to. I don't know what I am walking into. I don't want my love to be part of that. I don't want him to see my ugly. Thankfully, as he doesn't know my real name or any real details of my home, he wouldn't know where to start, but I think I'm just kidding myself really. I left the note but I also left my clothes and guitar. He knows I take my guitar everywhere with me, would never leave it. Via his job, he has access and resources to find anybody in the world, but everything he knows about me is my 'passport' name. I have no social media accounts or activity so there was a certain level of protection there but Jack, my Jack, was a resourceful man and persistent. Part of my heart is begging him silently to come and find me. To track me down and take me back with him. To give me no choices but to fall into the safety of his arms and our life back in the States. All I left him was a note.

Please Jack, if you love me, don't come for me.
If I can find my way back to you I promise I will. But don't wait for me.

Don't wait for me, I didn't mean that. I want him to wait for me. I'd wait forever for him. But how can you ask that of somebody, despite loving them with all your heart? It's wrong and morally unethical. But I want it despite how wrong it might be.

Two days ago, at Heathrow, I find Mel leaning against her car, smoking a cigarette. She throws it in the gutter the moment she sees me and we run to each other and hold on in a tight embrace. Mel places kisses on my head over and over.

'I'm sorry bubs, I had to do it, I need you here,' she says holding

my face in her hands looking at me. Her thumbs wipe the silent tears finally tracking down my face. I just couldn't hold them back any longer.

'Come on, let's get home,' she says taking my hand and pulling me along to her car.

On the drive back to our childhood home, we are both silent. It's an awkward silence at best. I'm tired, distraught and confused. Mel looks like she's carrying the weight of the world on her shoulders. As we turn the last corner into our road, Mel reaches across and squeezes my hand.

'I won't ask you if you're happy to be home Pol, but for what it's worth, I'm glad to see you.'

She releases my hand to pull onto our drive. The house looks exactly the same as the day I left. Not that I was expecting anything else but still, it feels odd that nothing has changed here but my whole life has in the time since I left.

As we exit the car, the front door opens and my brothers appear. Chris walks up to me first and wraps me in his arms kissing the top of my head and then my cheek.

David follows suit but lifts me off the ground with his hug. As we enter the house, the first thing that I notice is the smell. It smells like Mum. She was always a little bit heavy handed with her perfume, I guess some of it got stuck in the furniture and walls. The door to Dad's office is closed so I ask Mel if he's home.

'No darling, that's why we called you back. Dads gone. Not dead, oh god, Pol I don't mean he's dead, fuck at least I hope he ain't,' she says in one breath.

'Come on Pols, let's make a cuppa and we can talk,' David says slinging his arm around my shoulders.

'Where is he?' I ask my siblings.

They just look at each other awkwardly, rather than answering and it quickly becomes apparent that they haven't discussed what they were going to say to me once I arrived. I can see it clearly in their faces, avoidance.

'Listen Pol, have a cuppa, then get to bed. We will all talk in the morning. Nothing is going to change tonight, so let's just shelve it until you've had some sleep. We've both been working tonight,' Chris says pointing between himself and David, 'and we're knackered too. Let's just start this back up in the morning, okay?'

I am tired. So bloody tired. I just nod numbly. For once, I actually appreciate that Chris is trying to look after me. Chris places the mugs, milk and sugar on the table and fills the teapot with boiling water.

Mel takes the lead and plays 'Mum', adding milk to my tea. We all sit and talk for about half an hour before my eyes start to droop. My brother's regale me with stories of their antics with Mel chipping in, typically with her sarcastic put downs. I see them through outsider's eyes, my siblings. They are what people around here would call 'wrong-uns' and that's not exactly untrue but within their less than conventional ways, good hearts still beat. The boys and my sister are definitely the type to settle disputes with their fists but like the old-fashioned gentleman gangster, they don't pick on the innocent. If a fight does ensue then you can be sure it is because somewhere there has a valid score to settle. I get that they sound like confusing people and I guess they are, but ultimately, like the saying goes, they're still my family and I love them. Not wanting to stay here wasn't because I didn't love them, I think I felt like the feeling wasn't mutual. They kept things from me and although I know they believe they did it to protect me, it still hurt. It still hurts. But, I am too tired to go down that road. I just want to crawl into bed and sleep my headache and heartache off.

'Guys, I'm going to hit the sack. You're right, I am so tired, I can't think straight,' I tell them.

'Your bed is exactly where you left it Bubs,' says Mel, standing

and kissing my face.

I, in turn, kiss the tops of both of my brothers' heads and say goodnight.

As I walk up the stairs of the house I could still walk around with my eyes closed, I walk past my parents' bedroom. I stop at the door, my hand on the handle. 'Just one look,' I tell myself. Opening the door, an involuntary sob gets caught in my throat as I look around the room. It hasn't changed since the day she never came home. It smells like her and Dad. The bed is neatly made and still sports the duvet covers she bought one day when I was out shopping with her.

I crawl onto the bed and lay my head down on the pillow that would have been my mum's.

'Hi Mum,' I whisper in the darkness of the room, 'I miss you every day,' I tell her.

I must have fallen into the deepest of sleeps as it is daylight when I wake up. I am surprised to find myself in their bed, under the covers but still fully dressed in the clothes I arrived home in. Jetlag and a migraine are my only companions.

As I stretch into the morning, I reach for my phone and notice that it's just before 8am. I didn't sleep as much as I thought I would, or for as long, but I get up and head downstairs in search of a cup of tea.

The house is quiet, my brothers are no doubt still asleep and Mel probably is too.

I wander into the kitchen and put the kettle on, find my old Justin Bieber mug and make my very English morning brew. Now this I have missed. Neither the milk nor the water taste the same in the US and thankfully, Mel sends me over regular supplies of proper tea bags.

Tea made I take it to the kitchen table and go in search of something for my headache. After knocking back some tablets, I sit back down at the table and find a note from Mel. Frowning I read the message.

Morning darling, it was an early start for us and we didn't want to wake you. You will find the answers by going to the road below. DO NOT GO TO THE FRONT OF THE HOUSE! Stay in the woods that lead from the back of the house ONLY. I love you, we all love you. Please call me when the answers come to you. I can't say it will bring you happiness but at least you'll know. Mel xx

Why was I born into such a 'cloak and dagger' family? They live for this shit. I just want it straight but I guess for now at least, I'll just follow directions of the note.

I finish my tea and head off for a long-awaited and much needed shower. Neither help my jetlag nor my headache clear and so I decide to go back to bed; my bed this time. My room no longer smells familiar, like Mum and Dad's did but it's still my little haven. Crawling under the covers, I start to drift almost immediately. When I wake, it's dark outside but I can't even bring myself to check the time. I can't move. I just lie in bed, staring at the ceiling picturing Jack. I stay that way until I start to feel the onset of tears. Instead of giving into them, I get up and go in search of my siblings. I can hear them from up here. Good to know somethings never change! As I enter the room, David is the first to pipe up,

'Fuck me, it's the night of the living dead,' he shouts whilst the other two instantly crack up.

'People in glass houses shouldn't throw stones Davey-boy,' I say back ruffling his hair and kissing the top of it as I walk past. 'Anybody going to make this dead person a cuppa?' Don't ask, don't get and all that.

'I'll make you one Bubs,' says Mel putting her arms around me and kissing the side of my head. 'Are you hungry? Dinner is nearly ready. We've having stew in honour of the baby being home.'

'Is there crusty bread?' I ask as I take a seat at the table.

'Course! What kind of establishment do you think this is?' Chris answers, taking my hand and kissing it gently.

"I'm starved,' I tell them. 'I did try to get up this morning but my head was banging so I went back to bed. I hope I can sleep again tonight; I've lost the whole day. And thank you all for not breaking my Bieber mug,' I say as Mel hands it to me full of tea.

'You're most welcome but it was more luck than judgement, damn thing won't break. Believe me, these two idiots have tried!' She says laughing.

'So, your note,' I say. The words hang in the air as they all look at each other.

'Let's talk about it later babe, let's just have dinner all together and a catch up,' says Chris.

I should object, I should at least question it after all. Whatever is going on, brought me home, but I can't. Selfishly, I just want a bit of happy time with my siblings before it all goes to shit. Because I know it's going to. Mel wouldn't get me to come home over Dad just going off on a wander. So I nod and spend time with them. Tomorrow. I'll tackle it with them tomorrow.

Only when I wake the following day, the house is empty. There is no one to question. So I take the note Mel left yesterday, unhook Nanny's car keys from the hallway wall and pause to smile as I think of getting back in the old banger for a drive. It's odd, since I have been away I haven't driven at all. I don't have a car so if I can't walk it, I take the bus. I don't even Uber it. I like the bus, it suits me.

Getting in the car all I can smell is stale smoke. My nanny smoked like a freaking chimney and it's obviously ingrained in the fabric of the car. How did I never notice that before?

The car starts first time, even though the car looks ready for the junkyard, it never not starts. It's so old it only has a radio in it but I don't bother turning it on. I need to concentrate after not being behind the wheel for so long. The car has no power steering either so it feels like you're driving a tank.

On reaching the road Mel has directed me to, I park up off road by a green housing unit that contains electrical boxes.

Getting out, I wish I had worn a coat. The morning air is still chilly and as I move further into the woods, the damp and cold don't take long to seep into my bones.

It's not long before I see the back of the house that Mel described and familiarity hits me out of nowhere.

At least I thought ahead and brought a flask of hot tea with me. I don't know what the answer to all of this is going to be, hell, I don't even know the question. The only thing I know is that I am going to be here for quite a while. I sit down on the ground and pour myself a cup, just to keep warm. Half a cup at a time, the contents of the flask may have to last longer than I initially thought.

THREE

Jack

We've been walking back in silence for a few minutes when we hear gunfire. Everybody falls to the ground and our earpieces spring to life.

'This is Cross, Sir. Man down, roadside, repeat, man down,' comes the information. Gillingham scrambles on his legs and belly to reach me.

'What the fuck is going on?' He shouts to the roadside crew but all we can hear is running then painful moaning.

'Somebody give me an update now,' he bellows.

'Sir, Mac is down, repeat, Mac is down, blue Mercedes, partial plate taken, two men and a woman, one of them was the shooter, took fire out of passenger side window. FUCK, MAC, SPEAK TO ME MAC!' Shouts Cross.

Everybody is on their feet in an instant and off running towards the road. As we exit the woods and hit the concrete, we can see Mac on the ground. Cross has his hands over the shot that Mac's taken to his groin area. My first though is that sustaining a shot to the femoral artery rarely ends well.

Racing towards Mac, my gut is screaming at my head. A woman. A woman in the car. Is that woman my woman? I can't think about it right now. We need to deal with this moment first. As we reach Mac, we can hear the siren of the ambulance coming our way. It pulls to a halt, blue lights flashing, men jump out and run straight to Mac and Cross. Cross backs away so they can do their work. Within minutes they have Mac on the stretcher and are on their way to the hospital. Cross is still on his knees, leaning back on his heels., Mac's blood covering his hands. Drawing in deep breaths, eyes shut.

'Cross! What the fuck happened?' Gillingham shouts at him.

'Sir, there hasn't been another vehicle on this road since we arrived, but ten minutes ago we heard a woman's scream,' Cross says.

Instantly, I feel my blood run cold. No cars since we arrived, the only other person other than our crew to be seen was Lucie, a woman's scream, then a car with a shooter.

'So, we heard the woman scream and ran towards it. We had no idea what we would find. One of the guys had his hands on the woman, dragging her to their car, the Merc and they saw us. We continued running to them but they reached their car before we could, Mac was still running towards it even though the car was heading directly at him. The car swung out but at that moment the passenger took aim at Mac and hit him directly in the groin. I don't know if Mac is going to make it Sir, he was bleeding out.'

‘Did you get eyes on either the shooter or the driver?’ Gills asks.

‘Yes Sir, but not anybody we’ve seen in any of our files.’

‘Right, get back to base, work with the sketcher whilst the faces are still fresh in your mind. You got a partial plate?’ He asks and Cross nods.

‘Let’s go. Everybody back to base NOW before anything else fucking happens,’ Gillingham shouts turning in a circle, rubbing his chest.

‘Cross, what about the woman, did you get a clear look at her? You say she was being dragged to the car, if you haven’t seen another car, how did she get here?’ I ask.

‘Rafferty said there is another car, about a mile down the road, half on the road and the front end in the start of the woods. Said it was an old banger, but the driver’s door was open and we can only assume that it belonged to the woman. It would seem that the Merc stopped by that car and grabbed her before she could drive away. She’s young, early twenties, looked like she had blonde hair, was screaming in the back seat.’

My heart is pounding so hard I can hear it. I know I need to get back to base with Gillingham and the others but fuck if I don’t want to get to my girl more. My head is screaming. I need intel now so the other way I can help her is to get a clear picture of who the men were that took her and try to work out from there where they could have taken her. There is no doubt in my mind that it was Lucie in the back of that Merc. Even if my gut wasn’t telling me I’m right, on this deserted road, there is just no other possible or viable alternative.

We pile into our vehicles and Gillingham and Cross are talking at speed but my brain just can’t process it. I need to clear my mind. I need to become detached from what is going on around me. I need to focus so I can feel Lucie in my arms again. If I can find her then I am willing to give up and walk away from everything I have worked towards for so long and slip off the face of the planet if I have her with me.

Anything. Right now, I would sell my soul to the devil to spend the rest of my life with her in my world.

FOUR

Melanie

Having my Polly home is both a blessing and a curse. It's wonderful to have her back under the same roof and just to be able to see her in the flesh but the feelings of guilt are overwhelming. What have I got her back for? More pain than what she's already had to endure. I need to shut those feelings off. We've been lied to by our parents and I can't be complicit in those lies if I don't give her a chance to discover the truth. Before I even arrived at the gym this morning, I haven't been able to shake this sense of doom I feel in the pit of my stomach. Should I have gone with Polly? I think now that I should have, but I was scared to. Scared she'd hate me for knowing about this shit show before her. For not telling her the truth the moment we found out.

I was being a coward. In truth I didn't want to see her pain. I can cope with her anger because she is going to be so fucking angry when she gets home, but I can deal with it because it's not like I've always known. And believe me, when it comes to my parents, I have enough anger going on for the pair of us.

How any mother could do this to her children is beyond me, but my heart breaks most for Polly. She was so young when Mum 'died' and before we could even get through the grieving process, Dad shipped her back off to boarding school.

I'd begged him not to but he didn't listen. He never listens to reason, it's his way or the highway. In hindsight, I know why he did it. Polly has always been his weakness and it was obviously just too hard to keep her around. Whereas before I would have believed it to be out of love, I'm pretty sure it was because seeing her pain every day would have made him feel guilty. As for Mum, I just don't know what to think.

On one hand I know it must have been bad to go to the lengths of faking her own death, but my head is telling me that there must have been a better solution. Surely, we could have left home, all of us and started again elsewhere?

I just can't get my head around any mother allowing her children to grieve for her when she herself is safe and well. I can feel my breathing getting heavy as I begin to get more and more stressed out by my thoughts.

It reaches boiling point and I grab the first thing my hand gets to, the stapler and chuck it hard against my closed office door.

'Fuckers!' I scream out.

Nobody is here. Nobody comes to check I'm okay.

I take my seat at my desk, waiting for my phone to ring. Waiting for Polly.

FIVE

Jack

As we drive back to base, the discussion in the vehicle is fast paced but all I hear is noise. My thoughts are solely on Lucie. Where is she? Who took her? What do they want and will they demand a ransom? What's the deal with her abduction and her parents? Is the obvious Billy Langford connection too much of a coincidence? I can't clear my mind for even a second to think rationally.

'Yo! Jackie-boy, are you listening?' Gill turns to me, obviously waiting for an answer.

'Sorry man, thinking about this girl they took,' I reply as nonchalantly as possible.

‘I was saying, do with think the girl in the woods was lying? It can’t be just some other random woman taken. That road is barely used and the morning we find one other person in the woods with us, not twenty minutes later, screams are heard, a woman is taken and Mac gets shot.’ He is looking at me but I can tell he hasn’t finished speaking. ‘She said she was doing the walk of shame right?’ He asks as I nod my acquiesce.

‘Yeah, that’s all she said. She was trying to make her way home after a one-night stand, thought the woods would be a short cut to where she was going and found herself lost, hungover then started throwing up.’

‘So where was home?’ Says Gill.

‘I didn’t ask man, fucks sake, she was hurling all over my feet, I just needed to get her the fuck out of there,’ I state, making my voice sound exasperated.

‘Okay, well, I think it’s safe to say that vomit-girl is full of shit. We have to think from this moment on that she is the woman who was taken and you’ll need to work with the sketcher to try and identify her. If we can find her then we might get a connection between her and either the McDowell’s or Langford himself. Perhaps she’s fucking old man McDowell?’

I nearly choke on thin air as I think of my Lucie fucking another man, not even the fact that Gill thinks it might be Ronnie. Her father. But he doesn’t know who she is. When I woke up this morning, I didn’t know who she was and so I am hoping that with the lack of a grown-up photo of Lucie, it won’t be possible for them to match the dots. I’m no artist but I could draw my girl with my eyes shut in finite detail, but I am fucked if I am going to give them a good enough description whereby an identification of her is possible.

I know that I am going to be working on finding her on my own. I need to ensure that I don’t draw attention to it or to her. She’s mine. My responsibility to find and if, if I can’t do it on my own, I’ll bring in Garrett. He is the only other person that I trust with Lucie's life and I know how much Cassie and Garrett love that girl. She's the daughter they never had and I know G would rather go down in a hail of bullets than let anyone take her.

I need to calm down, I feel like I'm gonna have a heart attack. I have never known fear like how I'm feeling now. I have never been that agent who didn't value their own life and never once have I taken the gift of life for granted. There's an irony to that the day you walk into Quantico that death on the job is a very real possibility. That's not to say you disregard the value of life, whether it be yours or somebody else's. You are trained to do everything in your power to stay alive because in a lot of situations you are on your own in the job.

Right now, I have to think of this as a solo job and if I need help then it'll be G that I call.

A few minutes later we arrive back at the base. The crew pile out of various vehicles and as we enter the building we are met by Jenkins, today's base unit leader who Cross called to update about the Mac situation when we got in the car.

'You got an update on Mac?' Asks Cross.

Jenkins walks in with us and confirms yes, with a nod. 'He is still in surgery, trying to get the bleeding to stop. Femoral artery damage. Told us we wouldn't hear any more for a couple of hours. His wife has been collected and taken to the hospital and we have two guys on security with her.' Jenkins informs us as we get inside the unit's team kitchen. Some of the guys collapse onto the chairs and sofas in the room, others head straight for the three coffee machines lined up and ready to be destroyed and emptied in seconds.

'Grab a drink guys, then everybody into the briefing room. We need to get everything down,' I say, back in control, at least on the outside.

As we enter the briefing room I can see Cross already sitting down and he's talking to Taylor, our police sketch artist. Taylor isn't drawing just listening, but you can see his mind taking notes.

'Okay, listen up,' starts Gill. 'Today we got the unexpected three times; firstly, we saw Maree McDowell, supposedly dead for nearly a decade and I think we can all agree that she looked far from skeletal.' Rumbles of agreement ferry around the room. 'Secondly, we have on our hands an unknown woman found by Jack in the woods who claims to have been lost after a night out. Thirdly, we have an abduction and it doesn't take a genius to work out the woman taken was the girl in the woods. Question is, was she in the wrong place at the wrong time or was it a targeted kidnap? Jack will work on getting an e-fit of the girl and when Mac gets out of surgery we can get him to do the same. He would have been the only other person who could identify her but right now, we don't know if he even got a clear look at her. So whilst we wait for Mac, Jack you get started with Taylor then you and I are going to pay Melanie McDowell a little visit to see what she knows about her mother being alive and well.'

I feel sick. I know in my heart it was my girl. I renegade on my own deal that I won't give every last detail of Lucie to the sketcher. I realise I can't be selfish if I want to protect her. I know now that I have to do the e-fit correctly to help find her but God damn it, I want to do this on my own. I don't need these fucking idiots to find my woman. I need G.

In the meantime, I sit down with Taylor to give my description of the girl I can see in my mind without ever having to close my eyes.

When he has finished I see almost my girl looking back at me. Anybody who knows Lucie would recognise her from the drawing but I know her face intimately. There are tweaks to be made but it's not necessary. We'll be taking a copy of the drawing with us when we pay a visit to Melanie and she will, undoubtedly, recognise her sister too.

Just as we are making our way out of the unit, we're stopped by one of the guys who informs us that the 'getaway' car is in the possession of a Dimitri Kasovolovnic. He tells us that the vehicle isn't registered to him but informants have confirmed he is the 'owner'. Twenty-eight years old, born in Albania.

Gillingham tells them to throw everything at checking who he is, who he is linked to and finding an address or just somewhere he hangs out.

As we get in the car, Gill slams his hands on the steering wheel and swears. 'Fucking Kasovolovnics!'

'You know of him?' I ask turning in my seat to face him.

'I have ears, don't I? Fucking half of Europe knows them,' he tells me.

What he doesn't know is that I know exactly who the Kasovolovnic family are. I know what they are too. They're traffickers. And they're really good at not being found. If they are the ones who have my Lucie, then I need to get hold of Garrett sooner rather than later.

We arrive at Melanie's gym and from the outside it certainly looks legit. Smart signage, clean and tidy from the outside, not the run-down establishment I had it painted in my mind as. When we were younger, Trav and I joined a boxing club as something to do. Neither of us really liked it. Even in those days it was full of meatheads and only a few guys our own age. Shooting hoops was our thing and we stuck with that until Trav's death. The club we'd gone to was a run-down, back street establishment with peeling walls on the outside and damp coming through on the inside and the stale smell of sweat circled you the moment you entered.

In comparison, Melanie's club looks like a five-star hotel. As we walk into the lobby a female receptionist greets us with a smile.

'Gentleman, how can I help you?' She asks.

Gillingham flashes his badge and her smile fades. 'We'd like to see Melanie McDowell' he tells her.

'Of course, let me just see if she's available,' she responds picking up the phone and quietly speaking into the handset. 'She'll be with you in a moment, if you'd like to take a seat,' she says then looks back to whatever she was working on prior to our arrival.

'Gentleman,' Melanie McDowell says as she walks through a set of double doors to the right of the reception area.

'Ms McDowell?' Gillingham asks, knowing full well who she is but needing confirmation from her.

'Yes. How can I help you?'

Again, Gillingham flashes his badge and tells her that we'd like to speak with her in private. Her smile doesn't falter once as she tells us to follow her.

We walk through the body of the gym, busy with guys on equipment that surround two rings. A young-looking lad jabs and weaves against a partner in one ring whilst an older, tired looking guy spars solo in the other.

Melanie leads us into what is obviously her office. Sparse and functional is the best way to describe it. It's almost clinical. A desk, computer, phone and a filing cabinet plus chairs make up the entire furniture. Melanie asks us to take a seat as she moves behind the desk to take hers.

'So, gentleman, to what do I owe the honour?' Melanie asks warmly.

She bears a passing resemblance to my Lucie, but there are parts that are frighteningly similar. Her voice is harder than Lucie's in tone but the accent is the same. Her eyes are completely different but her nose is the same. She's an attractive woman for sure, but with her harder features she doesn't possess a tenth of Lucie's beauty or femininity.

'Firstly, do you recognise this woman?' Gill says handing over the e-fit image.

The smile on Melanie's face vanishes the instant she takes a look at the image.

'That,' she says, her worded hesitant, 'that is my little sister, Polly. Why do you have this? Is she in trouble? Because if you think she is, then I can tell you, whatever you think she's done, you're wrong. Our Polly is a good girl. The best girl. She would never do anything illegal,' Melanie says in a firm voice.

'We believe the woman in this image, who you have just confirmed is Polly McDowell, was abducted early this morning from the woods on Old Kent Road.'

Melanie's cool demeanor drops immediately. Instantly, tears well in her eyes and she lowers her face to her hands. Her shoulders begin to shake.

When she looks up, her distraught face is hard to take. We remain silent whilst she tries, but fails, to compose herself.

'How do you know it was her?' She asks through her tears, her hands shaking violently.

'My colleague here,' Gill says, motioning to me, 'spoke to her after seeing her in the woods, whilst we were in the area. She claimed to be on her way home after a night out and had got lost on what she thought was a shortcut. The men who we believe abducted her, shot one of our officers and whilst he is still in surgery and therefore yet to confirm this was the woman taken, we can only assume it was the same girl as there were no other people or cars in the vicinity. In fact, the only other car we saw was the one she was trying to get into when she was grabbed.'

'She's only been home a matter of days!' Melanie yells at us.

'Where has she been, Ms McDowell?' Gillingham asks.

'Living in the States. She's a good girl, the best. She's soft and gentle and would never hurt a flea. I don't understand how this could have happened. If you were there, why did you let them take her?' She shouts, clearly, her upset is now turning to anger and I can't say I blame her.

'Why did she return?' I ask, not being about to keep the one question that has gone through my mind over and over since I saw her this morning. Melanie pauses before answering. 'Ms McDowell, why did your sister return?' I ask again, impatient to know.

'Because I asked her to,' she says quietly, the anger in her voice now completely gone as she looks out of her office window and stares into space.

'And why did you ask her?' Gill asks.

'Because we wanted to see her,' she says. Her eyes tell me she's lying. I know in my heart she's lying because what Melanie doesn't know is that night, the night before she fled, we were happy. We were making plans and no fucking way would she have just upped and left without a word if her family 'just wanted to see her'.

'Why now?' Gillingham asks, not an unreasonable question.

'For fucks sake, we all know that you know who we are, who our dad is, who our uncle is, so why don't you just ask the one question I know you're dying to?' Melanie shouts.

'Okay then. Are you aware Ms McDowell that your mother is alive?'

There is no surprise on her face. She couldn't deny it now even if she tried.

'Yes, yes I am,' she says quietly.

'Well perhaps you'd like to tell us then why your mother faked her death?' Gillingham enquires.

'Because her children were threatened. Listen, I really don't care what you think of my family but my mum did what she had to do to protect her kids. We make no apology for that. It was simple; either us or her and for my parents there was no contest. As to why Pol would be kidnapped, I don't know. Do you know where she's been taken? Are you even out there fucking looking for her?' Melanie challenges.

'Ms McDowell, we don't know why she was taken and until the officer who was shot is out of surgery we are not one hundred percent sure it was even her. Is it the most likely scenario? Yes, but we need our officer's confirmation that the woman he saw abducted was indeed your sister. As to your question regarding locating her whereabouts I can personally assure you that we are looking into every lead to locate the car we believe took your sister as well as the occupants. Now, Ms McDowell, would you please explain how long you have known that your mother is alive? Your parents are together. When was the last time you saw your father? Did he say something that would ask your sister to return home?' Gillingham states with an urgency to his voice.

Melanie explains that her father had told her that he was sick of living a lie, sick of living without his beloved wife, he told Melanie and her brothers that he would be leaving to join Maree but as soon as they could, they would both return home and in the meantime, by any means necessary, she was to get Polly home.

Well, I guess now I have my answer. Had it been Melanie's first version, that she just called her home, Lucie would never have left me under the cover of darkness and she would not have been in the terrible state she was when I found her in the woods this morning.

'Ms McDowell, was your sister aware that your mother was alive?' I ask.

Melanie has the good grace to at least appear ashamed as she looks me square in the eye and tells me no.

'And are your brothers aware that your mom is alive?' I ask.

She merely nods her acquiesce.

'Can you tell me why only three out of four siblings knew? Why was Polly kept in the dark?' I ask. Using the name Polly for Lucie feels so alien to me. I understand they are one and the same, but to me, she will never be Polly.

'Because she's not like us. She never has been. She's fragile, I guess,' she says.

Again, this makes no sense. My Lucie is not fragile. Far from it. Feisty, forthright, unafraid. Never fragile except in our alone moments when speaking about her mom.

'Fragile? How so?' Enquires Gillingham

'She suffered badly when Mum died. We, myself and my brothers, didn't know it was all fake at the time. And Polly unraveled so quickly. She was the baby of our family. My mum's baby. She was still at school and Dad was obviously worried about her. When he told us that Mum was alive and the circumstances surrounding it, like why they did it, we made a decision not to tell her. Well, he made the decision but as I said earlier, it's his way or the highway, so we went along with it. We all saw how bad she was; how her grief consumed her. How were we then supposed to tell her that it was a planned and fake death? Dad was worried she would go off the rails, so we agreed to keep it from her.'

'And how were you going to explain her mother coming back from the dead to her? You think that was going to be better for her than finding out years ago?' I ask, not even bothering to hide the disgust I feel in my tone.

'That was never the plan. Well, not until about a week ago when Dad told us he was going away but would be returning with Mum at some point. My brothers and I discussed it and we all felt that we should just get her to come home and rather than tell her, direct her to the woods that would view the house and hopefully, she would find out. Then we would pick up the pieces. It wasn't the best of plans but we didn't fucking start this.' She pauses for a second. 'Listen, you may not believe this but I love my sister, we are close, we speak every week. Was I happy being a coward and not having to tell her myself? No, I wasn't, but neither could I be the one who would break her all over again.'

'I have to inform you, Ms McDowell, that your explanation would appear rather at odds with somebody who claims to want to protect your sister from further pain,' Gillingham tells her.

'I don't give a fuck what you think of me or my family. We don't answer to you,' Melanie says, clearly not liking criticism of the choice her and her siblings have made.

They stare at each other, neither one wanting to back down.

My mind in the meantime is backed up, running and thinking how my girl is even going to begin to process this information.

But first, I need to find her.

SIX

Billy

'Make sure somebody stays with her at all times, am I making myself clear? She doesn't get hurt or touched. Get her ready. I will be over at some point next week. In the meantime, Dimitri, spread her legs and lift her skirt up, I need to send a photo to her family.'

God, my darling Maree is going to freak the fuck out when the photo arrives but I have warned her and Ronnie that it's the only way.

Things are most definitely not what they seem. This 'kidnapping' is a planned event but it's all part of a greater plan. I 'agreed' to this with the Albanians as part of a deal I have made.

Eight years my darling sister has been in hiding. It has torn her family apart in ways they, her kids, don't even realise, but it was the only way. The threat was that her children would all be killed and she would rather 'sacrifice' herself than put them in any danger.

Her kids and Ronnie are her everything and when the three of us, Maree, Ronnie and myself formulated this plan, she jumped at it. Ronnie took much longer to convince but ultimately he agreed because Maree insisted.

There was one flaw in our plan. We never had an end mark. We knew it was going to be long-haul but who knew that eight years later, Interpol still wouldn't have enough on those fucking Albanians to shut it down.

As I reach my car I brace myself to call my sister on the burner phone my boy recently picked up for me. Kieran is waiting by the car and nods at me as I walk towards him.

'Everything go okay Dad?' He asks.

'Yeah boy, all according to plan. Can't say I'm looking forward to the next part but gotta do it. Got the phone, boy?'

Kieran reaches into his pocket and passes the burner phone to me. I quickly take it and hit up the only number stored on it.

Maree answers in one ring. 'Is it done? Is she okay Bill?' Asks my very tearful sister.

'It is darling and I promise you on Mum's grave babe, no harm will come to her. I promise,' I tell her.

'Okay' she whispers down the phone.

'Can you put me on speaker so I can talk to you both babe?'

'Okay Bill we're both here,' says Ronnie.

'Right, after this call, you know I am calling you back on my usual number. You know the script, so make sure you stick to it. If they're listening in, which is almost a certainty, we can't afford to slip up. Are you both ready?' I ask.

'Yep, do it Bill,' says Ronnie. I hear my sister quietly crying in the background and it damn near breaks my heart.

We hang up and get my own phone out of my pocket. Taking a deep breath, I call Ronnie's number as planned. Again, it only rings once before Ron picks up.

'What the fuck do you want Billy?' He shouts down the line.

'Oh Ronnic, is that anyway to answer the phone to your brother?' I ask, laughing.

'You ain't no brother of mine, fucker. What do you want?'

'What I want is to talk to my sister,' I tell him calmly.

'Are you having a fucking laugh Bill? Were you not around eight years ago when you had her killed?' He screams.

'Oh Ronnie, we both know that you're standing with her right now. So do us both a favour, drop the facade and PUT HER ON THE FUCKING PHONE!' I bellow.

I hear Ronnie sigh and mumble 'fucker' as per the plan.

'Hello Billy,' I hear my sister's voice.

'Well, well, well...if you ain't back from the dead, Sis.'

'What do you want Billy?' She asks me, no longer teary but that fight back in her voice. God, my sister has always been able to pull it out of the bag when needed. That's why for so many years she was my 'right hand man', never had to school her, she was a natural.

'Gonna tell you a little story babe, but first I'm just sending you a little family photo. Let me know when you get it.' I send the photo a wait for it.

Within a few minutes my sister is screaming and crying and Ronnie is shouting just about every obscenity known to man.

'Do you like it?' I ask, laughing down the line. 'Did you really think that once I found out you weren't dead I'd take it lying down, Mar? Who the fuck do you think you are playing with, ya silly bitch? Eight years. Eight fucking years I mourned you and for what? For you to make a mug out of me? You think that you and that weak piece of shit you're married to can humiliate me? Let's see how you like the humiliation of knowing your precious baby is going to spend her time entertaining men not of her choosing.' I all but scream.

'You fucker, I'm going to fucking kill you Billy. If one hair on my girl's head is harmed, I'll rip you apart with my bare hands,' shouts Ronnie whilst Maree cries hysterically in the background.

'Oh Ronnie, it would be too easy to kill her. I'm not an animal. I don't need her dead. I need her to inflict the kind of pain that her mother has inflicted on me.'

'What do you want from us Billy?' My sister says. It sounds so genuine.

'If you think the pain is bad now then I would strongly suggest that you brace yourselves. You'll be hearing from me you pair of fucking idiots,' I tell them then hang up.

The script was kept to, each of us playing our parts as practised. I know they are both genuinely worried; you can't fake fear, but I made a promise that Polly wouldn't be hurt and I intend to keep it. I am a man of my word.

If those Albanians don't keep to their end of the bargain, I will take them off one by one because unlike the Police or Interpol, I know exactly where to find them.

SEVEN

Jack

We're still asking Melanie questions when her phone beeps with a message.

Mel looks down and although she regains control immediately, I see her body stiffen and her eyebrows raise slightly.

'Who is it?' I ask.

'It's a message from my dad.'

'Read it out loud,' Gillingham instructs her.

Mel takes a laboured breath and opens the message. As if in slow motion, she gasps and drops the phone on her desk so that she can bury her face in her hands.

I grab the phone in an instant to view the message. It simply reads 'just received this photo from Billy Langford. What the fuck is going on? Where is Polly? Has she been in touch? Call me now!'

A photo follows the text. It's an image of Lucie sitting on what looks like a plane. She appears to be asleep; her head is lolling to the side, but her arms are awkward in the way they are positioned on her lap. Zooming in, I can see that her eyes are slightly open and I instantly know that she has been drugged. What really makes me want to punch something is that her skirt is up, showing her underwear and her legs are parted. I'm in danger of losing my mind any second. What the fuck am I doing sitting here listening to this shit, when I should be out there trying to find Lucie?

Gill takes the phone from my hands and looks at the image. 'That's definitely the girl from the woods today. I fucking knew she was tied up in this. It never did make any sense that she was taking a shortcut through the woods. The roadside is in the arse end of nowhere and she wasn't dressed like she had spent the evening out. Ring your father please Ms McDowell,' requests Gill.

She lifts her head and eyes me through her falling tears. 'You fucking ring him! It's obviously their fault somebody has Polly. Presumably my uncle as he sent the photo. Right now, I don't know who I want to kill more, Billy or my parents.' She screams at me.

Gillingham scrolls through Melanie's contacts till he reaches the number assigned to Dad and hits call.

'Mel? Mel, what the fuck is going on? Where's Pol? Have you heard from her?' Ronnie is shouting but through it we can hear the sobs of a woman, presumably Maree in the background.

'Ronnie McDowell, this is DCI Gillingham, we're here with your daughter Melanie regarding the abduction this morning of a young woman who we believe is your youngest daughter Polly,' Gill begins but Ronnie immediately starts to shout over him.

'Mel, what the fuck is he talking about? Pol is in the States!

Mel?'

'Dad, they have seen the photo you have just sent me. They know that it's from Uncle Billy. You can stop the pretense.'

The other end of the line goes silent even though it's still connected.

Mel breaks the silence. 'Dad, we called her back, like you told us to. You told us to fucking call her home and now because of your selfish fucking actions, my sister has been abducted!' She screams at her father.

'Oi! Watch your mouth girl, remember who the fuck you are talking to!'

'Are you shitting me Dad? Where's Mum?' The sobbing of Maree behind Ronnie gets louder. We can hear her mumbling, 'I'm sorry baby' over and over.

'Listen Mel, there are things you don't know and can't possibly understand but know this. We did what we had to do, to protect your mum and to protect you, your sister and your brothers. Fucking fat lot of good that's done us now though,' Ronnie sighs.

'You told me to get her to come home so don't you dare try to fucking pin this on me! Unlike you two, I give a shit about my sister, I would never knowingly put her in danger. This is your fault!' Melanie is standing and screaming down at the phone. Tears are falling thick and fast and her face is glowing red.

'I'm not pinning it on you darling,' Ronnie says softly.

'You just left us Dad,' Melanie sobs. 'You told us you would be back with Mum and I was to get Polly home. Then you just fucked off when we weren't around. Your computer was left up and running, there was half a cup of coffee left on your desk, the newspaper was on the floor. Do you know what that looked like? It looked like you had disappeared into thin air. It was either you had left in a hurry or somebody had taken you. So, we did what you wanted us to do; got Polly home. Always what you want eh? And now we get a photo of

Pol, looking like she's half dead. Haven't you two already caused enough damage? Do you remember how bad Polly was when Mum died? Do you understand grief, Mum? Do you understand what it's like to be a kid and to lose your mum? You would never think that pain could never be replicated, wouldn't you? But guess what? The pain of finding out you are alive and well and left us, obviously on purpose? That pain is so much worse. I will never forgive you Mum. And if anything happens to Polly, as far as I'm concerned, you two are to blame and it will be her blood on your hands.' Mel slumps to her chair and once again puts her head in her hands, her body wracking with sobs.

'Mr McDowell, Ronnie, we know where you both are.' Gill tells him, 'and you should expect a visit from us very soon. Do not leave the house. We have men watching it from all sides so we will know if you try to go anywhere. That applies to both of you.'

'I'm not fucking stupid,' Ronnie seethes. 'The moment my wife steps out of the door, she is a dead woman.'

'You are such a selfish bastard! My sister is out there, possibly, fighting for her life and all you're concerned about is yourself and Mum. What about trying save your own child? What kind of fucking parents are you?'

There is an audible sigh on the end of the phone along with Maree's continued crying.

'I just don't know how we can do this Mel,' Ronnie states.

'Just tell the police everything you know; anything that can help them find her.'

Ronnie says yes and Maree in the background echoes with a yes.

'Okay, we'll see you at some point today.' Gillingham tells him.

I'm sitting here seething. I can't believe that their first thought was for themselves and not Lucie. Mel is right; they are beyond selfish.

'Right,' says Gill. 'We are going back to headquarters. Melanie, this is my card, if you hear anything please contact me immediately.'

'Yes, of course. What about my brothers? Should I call them now? I feel it's only right that they know what has happened.'

'Call them and tell them that they should return to the family home, if they are not already there. Please ensure that your brothers don't start running around town asking questions. That most certainly will not help your sister,' I tell her.

'Jack, I need to make a call then we'll go okay? Gill asks me.

'Yeah, fine,' I say, avoiding eye contact but looking directly at Mel.

As soon as Gill steps out of the room I address Mel.

'Melanie, listen to me, I don't know what, if anything, Polly has told you about her life in the States, but to me, Polly is Lucie and Lucie is the love of my life. I need you to be my ears. I will find her. I'm here on an advisory level but I'm FBI. You need to keep me informed of everything you hear. This is my cell number,' I say handing her my card. 'Mel, you can't tell anybody that we've had this conversation, you can't tell anybody that I know Lucie. Polly. Is that clear?' I rush out in one breath.

Mel's looking at me through shocked eyes. 'You're Polly's Jack?'

'She told you about me?' I know my girl loves me, I know it. Even when she left in the middle of the night, I never believed that for one second it had anything to do with us. I don't know if she said it or I perhaps I dreamt it but I remember that night, feeling her loose hair on my face, hearing her words to me, 'saying goodbye will forever be my most painful memory'. I hear those words over and over again in my head and now, more than ever. I know she spoke those words to me before slipping out the door in the middle of the night.

'Yes, she said she'd fallen in love. She told me your name was

Jack and that she had never felt happier, safer or more loved. It was amazing to hear; no matter how much I missed her, all I ever wanted was for her to be happy, Jack. I wish to God I had never called her home. What did I do?' She asks, her tears once again making an appearance.

'You weren't to know this would happen Mel. Now we just need to find her; I need to find her. This lot will just spend endless hours pushing paperwork around. I can't do that which is why I need you to feed me any new information you might get before you speak to anybody else and that includes him,' I say pointing in Gills direction. 'Every piece of information is going to help me, no matter how small or insignificant it may seem. Do you understand what I need from you Mel? Here, put your number in my phone.'

Melanie takes my cell and puts her number in. I ring her phone so she now has my number too.

'Promise me you'll find her Jack? I don't know my Uncle Billy; we haven't seen him since we were kids. I know about him though and what I know isn't good. Is it true that he's involved in trafficking people? Well, girls? Oh god, is that why he's got Pol? I heard that a couple of years ago in a pub we used to go to sometimes, but I don't know if it was just rumour or fact. My brothers have had a few run-ins with his sons, our cousins, a few times over the years but nothing to write home about. Just general mouthing off, acting like the big men but then again, that could also be said of my brothers so I'm not sure what to think. I met the eldest, Kieran, about a year ago. I didn't know who he was but he came right up to me and started giving me shit, telling me that my family were all dead anyway, some shit about my mum having killed her own mother and Billy covering for her and that my family owed his dad as he covered for her. Perhaps that's true and this is why he's doing it? I had no idea what he was talking about, I still don't. It was nothing I had ever heard of before. I asked my mum when I was little why I didn't have a Granny on her side and she said that she'd got ill and died before I was born. She didn't say what of and I was too young to question her about it, but she did have a large photo of my Granny in the house, it's still in the hallway at home, which she put flowers under every Sunday. Even when Mum "died",' she says using her hands to show quotation marks, 'we continued to put the flowers there. Right now, Jack, I'm still reeling at finding out that Mum is alive.'

'Lucie, sorry - habit - Polly, told me so very little about her family. You are probably the only one she ever spoke about and even then, it was just to relay a story rather than any information about you. She was always very vague about family information and it always seemed obvious there was more behind the of lack of information she gave, but I never pushed her for more. I knew she would confide in me when she was ready. I kinda presumed that she'd been through something, although I had no idea what and she wasn't ready to face it yet. Nothing, and I mean nothing, would have stopped me from loving her, wanting her, fuck, needing her with me and when she disappeared suddenly, it was just so confusing. It just made no sense. The night she left we had spent making plans. Plans about our future. She was going to move in with me. She doesn't know this, but I bought a ring. I actually bought the ring long before we started the discussion about where we were going or her moving into my place. I knew that I wanted her for life, in every way possible. I know she feels the same. I'm not blaming you Mel, but if you hadn't called her that night or sent a message, whatever, she would never have left me. I know that in my bones.'

'I know that too, Jack. I spoke to her about a month ago and fuck, she was just so happy. It was like I could feel the good vibrations over Skype. She looked so healthy, smiley, and totally loved up.'

I think back to the day that Lucie had told me she'd had a Skype call with Melanie. That's the moment I have gone back to over and over. I'd got home and found her already at my apartment, sitting outside the front door even though I had given her a key to use. She didn't care, she was just camped out leaning against the door playing on her phone. As I'd walked out of the elevator and saw her, she'd looked up at me and blessed me with her most beautiful smile whilst pushing herself upright, telling Melanie she had to go. Ending the call, she'd flung her arms around my neck and I had lifted her off the ground so that I could kiss my gorgeous girl. That moment. That moment is what convinced me that everything she told me about loving me and building a future with me, had to be true. The following day, with Lucie gone, I'd found out that my Lucie didn't exist. Not in the States anyway. There was a paper trail to Lucie but that stopped quickly. She had a social security number, a visa to be living and working, everything checked out until it came to tracing her back to the UK. Then I'd reached a dead end. I was determined to find out what was going on when my superiors called me in to inform me that I was coming back to the UK and Gillingham's team as they were closing the net on Langford. What had initially started out a couple of years ago with the Bureau doing an exchange of personnel, quickly turned to my being part of the team and the request for me to come back. It wasn't a request in reality as there was no choice. So, no matter what my personal circumstances were, I had to return. But before I left, I had spoken to Garrett.

The day of Lucie's disappearance.

I arrive at Cassie and Garrett's door, but it swings open before I can knock.

'Heard you pull up son,' Garrett says putting his arm around my shoulders, with a tight grip. This man means more to me than any man has ever done. Never having had a dad in my life, I didn't know what I was missing. Until Garrett. He has always been more than my mentor. He knows it too.

'Come on through to the kitchen, Cassie's waiting.'

We enter the kitchen as Cassie walks towards me. She loves Lucie; I have never seen Cassie have a relationship with a person outside of her marriage that means so much to her. She is devastated that Lucie has gone. She comes towards me with tears welling up in her eyes and wraps her arms around me.

'How ya doing Darlin'?' She asks quietly.

I wrap her up in my arms and whisper in her ear. 'I'm doing okay but I need to speak with you both.'

We all take a seat at the centre island and Cassie hands me a beer, even though I don't normally drink this time of day. I take a long pull and place it carefully on the counter, much due to the slight shake of my hands. I feel wired and exhausted and my day is far from over.

'Listen guys, I've been pulled back to the UK. I have no idea how long I'll be gone but I need you to keep your ears to the ground for any signs of Lucie. I have found some stuff out this morning and I'm going to share it with you now but at the moment, I can't piece it together and as of tonight I won't be here so don't have my normal resources. Although I'm at least heading logistically in the right direction to track who she really is.'

'What do you mean who she really is?' Cassie chokes out.

'What the fuck man?' Is all G can say.

'I tracked all the information I knew about her. I had her social security number, spoke with the landlord who had a copy of her passport and visa on file, ran everything and it all checked out. It all checked out from the moment she arrived here from London, but go back to the start point at Heathrow and that's where the trail ends. There is no record of a passport in the name of Lucie Malone. There is no Lucie Malone that matches the date of birth on her passport. Whilst nobody picked up on it, preliminary checks indicated that her passport was a forgery. A very sophisticated one but still a fake. She,

or at least somebody on her behalf, went to an awful lot of trouble to make sure she could leave the UK and start again here under an assumed name.

'Jack, I don't understand, why would Lucie lie? Surely, there's been a mistake? Lucie wouldn't do that. She's no criminal,' Cassie says getting upset. Garrett reaches across the counter to take her hand. She grips his tightly and then places her other hand over their joined ones.

'I don't know why she would lie Cass. I always knew, no that's not right, I had a feeling that Lucie was holding back on details about her life. Nothing big, just stuff with say perhaps her family etc. I just kinda figured, in time, she'd speak to me about it. I didn't think it was anything that would affect us and our relationship so I just let it go. But then time went on and we were happy, I know we were both happy. Lucie would have hated me to get all FBI over her so I didn't. I respected her silence. I knew she must have a good reason and I just thought we'd deal with it when it came around. I don't believe Lucie deliberately lied to us; even though the evidence now suggests she did, but I refuse to accept that she did it with any malice. I'm inclined to believe that she was first and foremost trying to protect herself and that she just wasn't ready to deal with it with us. Cassie, she adores you. You know she does. And you too, G. And no matter what, I know she loves me as much as I love her. Something is wrong. I'm not saying she's hurt or anything sinister but the only explanation is that something has happened with her family? What do you think G?'

'Given the information you've just told us, then yeah, I'm inclined to go with that than to believe she was deliberately deceptive with us. I don't see that as Lucie's MO. My worry is not that we can't find out who she really is but how long it will take us to find out. We don't have any knowledge of what's going on so have no way of knowing if she's in any danger.' Garrett says as Cassie lets out a sob she's been

holding in. 'Cass, baby, we'll find her, okay? I promise.'

Cassie nods sadly.

'I've compiled this file. It's just notes really; it's everything I've just told you,' I say handing it over. 'I've put my UK cell phone number at the top of the file so that you can contact me. Once I arrive in England and get checked into the Unit, I'll call you. You may need to call in some favours at the Bureau, man. I don't know how you want to go about it, I'm confident to leave it with you if you're happy to continue with trying to work this shit out.'

'Of course, I'm happy to do it. She means the world to Cassie and to me, but Jack you know that when some people disappear without a trace it's usually because they don't want to be found? You understand that whilst everything we know about Lucie says she's not that girl; it's a possibility. You get that, right?' He asks me, taking glances at Cassie as he says the words I have thought to myself but never said out loud.

'I do G, I really do. But my heart man, my heart knows that she didn't leave meaning to be gone for good. Her guitar. If she was leaving without the intention of never returning she wouldn't have left that. Which means that she left it here on purpose. That she left it knowing either me or Cassie would find it. It was either a clue or a statement that she planned to return at some point. She would never leave that thing. Even if what she told us about it once belonging to her mom isn't true, we know that she loved it and she'd never leave it behind. She made no plans with the landlord. Her rent is paid up for another six months; a payment that she only made last month. I could find no paper trail of where the money came from. She didn't live like she had money. Declan paid her in cash as far as I know. When I called him this morning to ask if he'd heard from her, he hadn't and he sounded genuinely shocked that she'd just upped and left with no word to any of us. He's got her booked in on an on-going weekly rolling booking.'

'She told me once that Declan was some kind of relation to her dad,' Cassie says.

'What? When? When did she tell you this?' I shout.

'That was how I met her initially. Declan contacted me saying a distant cousin of his had a daughter coming to the area and would I be able to offer her work. I thought you knew this Jack?' Cassie says.

'I knew that's how you met and how she came to end up working for you but I never knew there was any kind of connection between Declan and her family. Neither of them have ever mentioned it to me. Never said a fucking word. Even this morning when I told him she'd just left, why would he withhold that from me?'

'Perhaps he thought you already knew, man. Did you mention to him that Lucie wasn't her real name?' G asks me,

'No,' I say, shaking my head even though the damn thing is banging. 'No, I didn't because at the time, I wasn't aware that Lucie Malone wasn't her real name. Look guys, I'm going to go over there now and speak with him and I'll let you know how I get on. If she is a relation, no matter how distant, he will absolutely know what her real name is.' I get up from the stool, ready to say my goodbyes. 'I don't know when I'll be back but I'll speak to you later before my flight takes off, okay?'

Cassie walks around the island to give me a hug. 'Bring her back,' she whispers.

Garrett and I shake hands and share a quick hug then I'm out the door, heading to the pub.

I know I'm over the speed limit on my way, but my mind is whirling and I just need to fucking get there and speak with him. Arriving at the bar, it looks all locked up. It should be open; it's always open. I get out of the car and start banging on the front door shouting for Declan to open up.

'Stop banging,' I hear Carmel shout from the upstairs window.

'Where is he Carmel?'

'Da's in the hospital Jack, had a fecking heart attack not more than a few hours ago. I'm just home collecting some stuff for him. Give me two minutes and I'll be down, okay?' She says slamming the window down again.

Five minutes or so have passed and I'm pacing when the door opens and Carmel comes out.

'What happened? Which hospital is he in?' I ask.

'Firstly, if this is how you're going to be with him, I'm not telling you shit. The man had a heart attack! You go in there shouting and screaming and you'll give him another one. So, tell me, why do you want to see him and what the fuck has got you so fired up?'

'You know that Lucie's gone?' I say to her knowing that she does. When I called Declan this morning, I could hear Carmel talking to a delivery guy in the background. Declan then turned the phone off speaker so she obviously overheard our conversation. 'What I want to know is why your dad, why neither of you, thought it important to mention that you're both related to Lucie? I want answers Carmel and if you're not going to tell me, I'll go down to the hospital and knock it out of your father.'

'You listen to me Jacky-boy, you go near my dad right now and I'll take you out cold myself. You don't fucking frighten me. Why didn't we tell you? Because Lucie made us promise that we weren't to. Good enough for you?' She spits out.

'Why? Why couldn't I know?'

'I don't know Jack. Lucie had her reasons and I didn't question them. My dad was happy to go along with it. Listen, I don't know my dad's family okay? I was born here, never even been to Ireland. She has her reasons Jack and we weren't about to betray her confidence.'

'What's her name, Carmel?' I ask.

'Her name is Lucie. What a stupid question Jack,' she laughs

out.

'Her real name isn't Lucie. Tell me what it is.'

'I, I don't know Jack. I'd never even heard of her before she came here and I was never told she was anybody other than Lucie. I want to help Jack but right now, getting my Da well is my top priority. I'm sorry she's gone Jack, I really am. You know I love her, but I don't know anything Jack, I swear I don't,' she says. I believe her. She's being truthful.

'Okay, so you don't know. How did Declan explain the connection between them to you? Try to remember everything he said Carm.'

'He brought her to the bar as he'd collected her from the airport. Said he was going to be collecting the daughter of a distant cousin of his and that she'd be staying here at the bar with us temporarily. Da got her back here, made the introduction and we got Lucie settled. A couple of nights later he told me that Lucie was going to do a set for us and if all went well, then she'd do it on the regular. He told me that he'd already spoken to Cassie, like before Lucie got here and that Cassie was going to see if she was suitable for a job with her. You could tell straight away that her and Cassie had this instant connection. She got the job immediately and Cassie and Garrett always came to watch her perform. Whenever she played, she would just sit with them afterwards and talk. You know what the pair of them are like Jack. Look, Jack, I don't know who this distant cousin of my dad's is. He's got six brothers and four sisters. His immediate family is enormous. When he said distant cousin, I kinda lost interest. Fuck, it's not like I was ever going to meet them, so I didn't bother to question it.'

'So, this mystery relative arrives and you don't question who her parents are?' I ask.

'No. I'm sorry Jack. For your sake. For hers too, I wish now that I had but it was just so irrelevant. Even after you called this morning to ask if we'd seen her and to tell us she'd gone, my da just

said, "it was obviously what she needed to do" then he made a joke out of her being a "traveller".'

I believe what Carmel tells me and I don't want to upset her further when frankly, she has enough going on. Nor do I want to make matters worse for Declan by barging into the hospital given what she'd told me. I decide instead to ring G on my way to the airport to update him about Dec's heart attack and my subsequent conversation with Carmel. He will get to the bottom of it and if there's something there of concern, he'll let me know.

Five minutes later Gill re-enters the room and tells me we are leaving. I thank Mel professionally for her help and say we will see her later. I need to speak with Garrett and start my plan to find Lucie.

EIGHT

Jack

Fuck me, how did life get so confusing? As we walk back to the car, Gill tells me that he's got an update. I nod and try to act cool even though my heart is back to pounding through my chest.

'So, our man is out of surgery and out of the woods, if you'll excuse the pun,' he says chuckling at his own joke.

'I have sent a couple of men to the hospital as guards and they will alert us when he wakes up. We need to know what and who he saw. The sketcher will go over there too so we can see if yours and his e-fits match. I think at this stage it's a forgone conclusion but we need to cross all the T's. I say we get back and try to work some of this shit out whilst we wait for the confirmation.'

Gill starts the car and puts it in gear before pulling out onto the main road.

'Can we drive round to the McDowells before heading back?' I ask.

'Why? He ain't there. The house will be empty. Whilst we've been here I've had a couple of guys go round there to check the house is empty and they have confirmed to me that it is. What do you think you'll find?'

Call it paranoia or just plain exhaustion but the way Gill asks the questions, makes me feel like he's looking for something in my thoughts. I need to shut that shit down immediately. I can find the address myself and go look on my own and I need to do that without Gill or anybody else in the unit knowing.

'Just thinking out loud man. If you've already had somebody go out there then yeah, no point in revisiting a dead end,' I say and Gill nods, obviously satisfied with my answer.

I don't dislike Gill, but I wouldn't choose him to be a buddy of mine. There is something likeable and unlikeable about him in equal measure and whilst he has never been anything but professional with me, aside from the comments he made about Lucie this morning, I just don't get a good read on him. The world over you will find dirty cops. That's just how it is. I don't think that Gill is dirty per se, but I'm not sure he wouldn't bend the rules to suit his own needs either. I don't know, I think I'm so fucking exhausted and out of my mind with worry, I'm starting to see things that aren't really there.

We arrive back at base a short time later and we all gather once again in the briefing room.

My mom had a saying about men who commanded attention through being loud, she used to say they were like a 'dog with two cocks'. Watching Gill enter the room, shouting to the guys, telling them he needed a run down on what we know to date, has me thinking about that saying. Gill definitely is like a dog with two cocks.

'Brief me,' he shouts to nobody in particular.

A guy called Anderson stands and makes his way to the front of the room where Gill and I are leaning up against a desk. He stands next to a white board which has a rough timeline drawn on it.

'We've managed to establish that the Blue Merc seen at the scene is riding on stolen plates. However, a couple of our informants have told us that it is currently being driven around by two Albanian brothers, Dimitri and Bogdan Kasovolovnic, twenty-five and twenty-eight respectively. They have a flat on Old Palmer Road, but neighbours have said they rarely see them and even then, it's only ever at night. Apparently, these two are a pair of psychos and whilst they have never been picked up they are known by the Home Office. They work for the family-run operation, somewhere out of the Balkans and the head of the family is Sokol Kasovolovnic, said to be in his sixties. According to the Home Office, he has never been to the UK although Interpol reference him travelling in mainland Europe. The family are mixed up in everything from guns to trafficking girls and Interpol apparently has eyes on one of his clubs at the moment. They declined to tell us where. Stands to reason that they don't want 'local' law stepping in anywhere and messing it up for them.'

'I don't give a fuck. We've got a shot officer and an abduction 'locally' and until we are told otherwise this is our case and ours to investigate. Anything else?'

Anderson looks down at his notes then back up to Gill. 'We haven't had a chance to speak to Mac yet about what he saw, but when he does wake then we can get confirmation on the ID of the Kasovolovnic brothers and the girl taken.'

'Here's what we do know,' begins Gill. 'We know that Maree McDowell isn't dead, therefore the family faked her death.' Not all the family I think, remembering my girl's reaction to seeing her ‘dead’ mother.

‘According to the eldest, Melanie McDowell, she at least knew that her mother was in hiding rather than deceased. A phone call took place in our presence confirming that fact. She has confirmed that she would be contacting her brothers and arranging for them to return to the family home and wait for her there. When we’ve finished up here, Jack and I will be visiting Mr and Mrs McDowell. Question is how exactly is Billy Langford involved in any of this? We know he sent a photo of the girl to her parents, with the obvious intention of letting them know that he either has her himself or knows who does. We are assuming right now that the abducted girl and Polly McDowell are one and the same. But the question remains, why was she taken? I don’t fucking believe in coincidences so don’t bother giving me that rot. Don’t believe it for a second. She was a target so another of our priorities is to find out where. Whoever is behind this has had plenty of opportunity to take the elder McDowell daughter. And we need to find out where this Polly McDowell has been all this time. Where has she been living, what did she do, who did she mix with? Friends, lovers, the fucking works. I want a complete picture of her life from the moment she left till when she returned a few days ago.’

‘Good luck buddy,’ is all I can think. Lucie’s footprint is non-existent and I know that the backwards trail only goes back to landing at Logan Airport. It means that any trace of her from when she arrived on US soil will be a stonewall. Polly ceased to exist in London and re-emerged as Lucie at Logan.

There’s no fucking way these idiots will be able to trace Lucie to me, Cassie, Garrett or Declan and Carmel. I decide that my next call will be to G to brief him about today’s events and it hurts to know that I will break their hearts with the news I have to deliver. I feel like my own heart has been ripped apart but for now, I need to keep my shit together.

Cross walks into the room, 'Guv, Mac's awake. Groggy but awake. You want me and Taylor to go over there?'

'Yeah, do that now and call me once you've spoken to him.'

Cross nods and leaves the room. I know there is no other outcome than the confirmed identification of Lucie but part of me wishes I had more time to try to figure this shit out before Gill starts putting the pieces together.

I inform Gill that I need to call the Bureau which he accepts without question. He's seen me do this before so I am not exhibiting any unusual behaviour. I excuse myself and walk outside, away from any possible eyes and ears.

It's the early hours of the morning for G and Cassie, but I need to talk to them and I know they won't care about me waking them.

It barely rings twice before Garrett answers. 'Jack, you okay man?' Are his first words.

'G, sorry to wake you, is Cassie there too? Put me on speaker phone, save me repeating,' I tell him.

'No can do Jack. My woman is a mess. She barely sleeps as it is. She convinced herself that Lucie has been harmed and she just can't seem to switch off. She's not in a good way, boy.' I can hear his voice; it's like mine, fraught and full of worry.

'Well then this call is definitely what she doesn't need to hear,' I tell him quietly.

'Tell me what you know.'

I proceed to do just that. Every once in a while Garrett stops me, making notes as I speak and I know these notes will be his map to finding out as much as he can and use them as instructions for anybody else he wants to bring in on it.

'I have to tell you son, I'm obviously alarmed by the information you have shared but more so that Interpol and the UK Home Office are aware of these people. On the plus side if Interpol are involved we can possibly secure more information than the Unit you're working with.'

'Are you going to tell Cassie?' I ask, internally worrying how she will take the news.

'The abridged version, Jack. Right now, I just don't know how much more she can handle. She's closed the shop Jack, did I tell you that?' He doesn't wait for my answer, which would have been no. 'She doesn't want to be there without her girl and she's not in the right mind to handle the day to day. She's spent a lot of time with Carmel and between them they are nursing Declan back to health. He has been hit really hard by all of this. I have spoken to him at length to see what, if anything, he knows, but it really hasn't led anywhere that will help, but he did have some intel on Lucie's parents. Ronnie, her dad, really is a distant cousin of his. They met once but only when they were kids and Ronnie and his parents were visiting family in Ireland. He hasn't seen him since but apparently, there is a cousin who works in between them, a sort of middle man as you will, or in this case a middle woman. She set it up that Declan would be able to look after Lucie when she first arrived, following Ronnie requesting help Stateside. Apparently, Lucie's dad didn't mind his daughter going to America but it was under controlled circumstances. She could go, but she needed to go to Boston and that was it. What would have happened if Lucie hadn't found some happiness? I don't know and neither does Declan, but I guess it's not worth speculating over as that wasn't the case. He said that he and Lucie had never really spoken about her family other than kind of surface information right up until the point of her mother's death. Although we now know that there was no death. So, what are your thoughts on that particular point?' He asks me.

'Man, I don't fucking know,' I tell him honestly. 'It makes no sense at this juncture. Lucie, on the rare occasion spoke about her mother, was obviously still devastated by her loss. Why would they do that to her? To her siblings too? Melanie said that she only found out about her mother being alive a few weeks ago and that it had knocked her on her ass. She certainly didn't know that when she called Lucie back home, on the instruction of her father, that it would put Lucie in any danger. She's beside herself with worry and given that we were witness to the phone call between Melanie and her parents, she wasn't holding back her anger with them. What I can't seem to understand that from the outside this is a close-knit family and yet, it's full of deception and lies.'

'That's not different from most families Jack. I know it's not your experience but it's true. You yourself have many unanswered questions about what happened to your mom and you know how much that has plagued you throughout the years. I don't think it takes a genius to work out that Lucie's dad was happy for her to go away and probably for a variety of reasons; all starting with the lies that he has told his family. Lucie was still young and still living with the grief so perhaps her dad thought he was actually doing the right thing by her, even if that meant continuing the lie.'

'So G, what's your next move given the info?'

'First thing will be to call a buddy of mine who has eyes and ears in Europe. Whatever is going on with Interpol and this Kasovolovnic family, he'll find out and when he does I'll let you know. But you gotta know man, trafficking is so far underground it won't be easy to find out where they have taken Lucie, but we will man, we will,' he says emphatically.

'Wherever she is G, I want to be the one on the ground to find her. I need to be the one to find her and I know our girl; she'll be expecting me to find her. Garrett I don't give a fuck how much this costs, money is no object man. Pay what you need to. There is no price on this one. I just want her found and safe.'

'I know that son, you don't need to tell me, but the best way to do this is through favours owed rather than cold cash. I've never asked anybody for any help so I am owed all over the place and I intend to pull in every one of those deeds that have helped others. We will find her son; you need to believe me. In the meantime, I need to speak with Cassie. She's going to be devastated Jack so I'm going to water the information down a bit, just to save more pain.'

'Garrett, you will not water down anything for me,' suddenly I hear Cassie's voice over the phone and wince. Her voice betrays nothing.

'Cass, baby, listen to me,' I hear G tell her, 'let me finish up this call and we'll talk'.

'I want to talk to Jack first,' she says then she's on the line and in my ear.

'Jack,' her voice is not her own. My Cassie is strong and confident. This Cassie is broken.

'Cass, I wish this was a good news call but it's not. I need to let Garrett tell you everything that's happened but I promise you, I promise you I won't come home alone. Lucie is my life Cass and I will not live without her.' I state with more confidence than I feel right now, but Cassie doesn't need to know that. She needs to focus on the positive before Garrett delivers the news which we both know will break her further.

'Make sure you do Jack, just bring her home,' Cassie whispers. I can't take the pain in her voice. Not for the first time, I wonder if I had done the right thing, waiting on Lucie to tell me her secrets. Perhaps if I had pushed her for those parts of her life she hadn't told me, we wouldn't find ourselves in this position now. Perhaps that would have meant that instead of slipping out of our bed in the dead of night, she would have woken me up. I would have gone with her. I would follow her anywhere and for whatever reason.

But we didn't have that luxury. Not that I am angry with her, I'm not. I get that she has secrets from me and I don't believe that her not telling me was through lack of trust. No, she was caught because I work on the right side of the law and her family is firmly on the other side.

Again, not for the first time, I wonder if she didn't tell me to protect me or to protect herself. I hate the thought that she might have been thinking that I would turn my back on her, turn my back on us because of the deeds of her family. I would never have done that. I wouldn't have 'loved' it, but I know that Lucie was not the sum of her roots.

I end the call with me promising to be in touch and Garrett doing the same. I know the next move is for me and Gill to go and pay a visit to Ronnie and Maree and I know that I have to tamper down the anger I currently feel towards Lucie's parents. I just need to rein it in and get it over with.

NINE

Melanie

I watch them get into their car and leave before I let the breath that I'm holding out. When I do, I feel my legs give way and I land on my chair with a thud. My chest feels tight and my head is spinning. Never, ever in my wildest dreams did I think that my Polly would be harmed when I sent her to the woods. Fuck, I didn't even know if she'd be there long enough to see Mum and Dad walk out the back of the house; but that was how they wanted it. They wanted her to know. Why after all these years I don't know, but I just thought that she would return home and I would once again be the person to pick up the pieces of a broken Polly.

I can't stand the thought of anything happening to my beautiful sister and if one hair on her head is harmed, I will never forgive either of my parents. This was not part of the plan. She was just supposed to see them and return home to me.

For the record, I didn't know any of this shit until three weeks ago, when the old man called me into his office at home. I'm not sure what he was expecting but it wasn't my anger.

'Sit down Mel,' my dad says to me after I knock on his office door. I do as he requests.

'What's this about Dad? You look so serious,' I tell him laughing.

'Mel, darling, what I'm about to tell you will shock you and will no doubt have repercussions for our family, but I need you to keep your head girl, alright?'

'So, I'll ask again, what's this about Dad?' I suddenly feel the oppression of worry hit me. Whatever he is about to tell me, I know deep in me, that it's not going to be good.

'There's no easy way to say this sweetheart so please forgive my bluntness. Your mum. Your mum isn't dead.'

I just laugh. What the fuck am I supposed to say to that?

'I'm not kidding Mel. This isn't a joke so I'd appreciate you not laughing,' he says sternly.

I feel it happening. I feel my blood beginning to boil. All we have endured; missing her, being without her, Polly's eighteenth birthday, the grief. The grief that crippled me. Crippled us. I feel the heat in my body rise and within moments I reach the point of anger which won't easily be tampered down.

'Who the fuck did we cremate then?' I all but scream at him.

'Watch your mouth girl. I don't give a fuck how upset you are right now; you will not speak to me like that!' He bellows.

'Why? What the fuck are you going to do? It's not like you can tell Mum...oh hang on...isn't this fucking awkward,' I shout back,

equally as loudly. 'You've got to be winding me up and if you are, it's fucking sick. And if you're not, that's even worse!' I scream, the tears that were moments ago burning the back of my eyes are now streaming down my face.

Dad stands up from behind his desk and walks towards me. I stand too.

'Come here darling,' he says opening his arms. Does he actually think I'm going to let him embrace me? I want to fucking kill him! Rip him limb from limb. Instantaneously, I hate him and I fucking hate her for doing this to us.

'Don't touch me!' I scream moving around to the back of the chair I was sitting in, putting a barrier between us.

'Listen to me lady, I know it's a shock and I know you're angry but you need to fucking listen to me.'

'You know I'm angry?' I ask, mimicking him. 'You have no fucking idea how angry I am right now! You two tore us apart. My sister moved across the Atlantic because she couldn't get past her grief and you stand here now telling me that you know I'm angry? How dare you? How dare you think that you can just tell me this and I'm just going to sit here and listen to you. How could you? How could she? We're your kids and you do this to us? Well, fuck you and fuck Mum!' I shout then turn on my heel and walk blindly through the house, barely able to see through my tears and devastation.

I can hear him calling to me but I walk on. I walk up the stairs into Polly's bedroom. I all but throw myself onto her bed as the sobs wrack through my body. I hear him walk up the stairs and I swear to God, if he comes in here, I'll go for him.

The door opens but I don't get up and attack him like I thought I would. My face is turned away from him, from the door and I can't turn around even when I feel the bed dip as he sits on the side. I feel his hand land on my back, rubbing in circles. A soothing motion that my mum used to do when we were unwell. Oh the fucking irony.

'Darling, I just need to talk okay? Just listen to me. It won't make this easier for you but it might explain the rationale behind our actions. It's not just a case of doing this blindly without thought or consequence. We just never thought the day would come where we would have to tell you. You have to know that your mum loves you and will love you all until her dying breath.'

I turn to face him. 'Will that dying breath be a lie too, Dad?' I ask, noting that the fight in my voice has gone. He ignores that comment.

'As you know, our family has never been whiter than white in the way other people are, but it wasn't all grey areas. Eight years ago, some people who did business with your Uncle Billy and me, made some threats. Serious threats. Billy got word and we spoke to Mum, who damn near lost her mind. The threat was against her and you and your sister and brothers and Mum...well, Mum wasn't about to let anything happen to her babies. The choice was simple Mel; we either took a chance on your lives or we staged it that Mum 'died'. What were we supposed to do? Lose one of our own kids? That was never going to happen. Mum would never, ever have taken that option. We had no choice.'

'I don't understand, Dad. They, whoever they are, they wanted one of us dead...how did Mum dying in a car crash balance that out?'

'Uncle Billy had a man on the payroll, an old friend, who worked with these people. Simple as that. Our inside man volunteered to do their dirty work and set it up with us that Mum would be at a certain place at a certain time. As you know, this went ahead and the people believed the debt had been paid and we got Mum out of there and into hiding.

'And that meant that from that moment we were all safe?' I ask, knowing the answer.

'Yes, darling. You were all safe. We arranged for Mum to live

in the house that we used to rent out through the company. Do you remember the house?' He doesn't wait for my answer. 'Well, anyway, that's irrelevant. We still continue to rent it out occasionally, just to keep up appearances and if somebody does stay, then as far as they are concerned, Mum is the housekeeper. Renting it out has always been a legit business and because I own the company which owns the house, there was also no reason why I shouldn't go there from time to time, which of course, meant I could spend time with Mum. Bubs, if it helps, this heartache that you are feeling now, your mum has lived with it every day for the past eight years. Don't think for one moment that she hasn't suffered. Not seeing her children has near enough killed her; it's broken her heart but not as much as if something had happened to one of you.'

I sit up, wiping my tears and look at him. He holds out his hand to me and I take it in my mine.

'Dad, what's changed? Why are you telling me now?'

'Ah yeah, why now eh kiddo?' He stands up and paces the tiny floor space with his hands in his pockets. Stopping in front of me he runs one hand over his face. 'Well, our man on the inside? To put it simply, he fucked up. Told the wrong person that he had been involved in Mum's fake death is the short version, but it goes further back than that. Let's go and have a cuppa so that we can talk this through eh?'

He holds out his hand to me and I take it allowing him to pull me up from the bed and we walk downstairs together to the kitchen. We make our teas and sit down and over the next hour I am blown away by my father's words. He tells me that about 3 days before my mum's 'death' there was a 'public' falling out between her and my Uncle Billy to ensure that when she died, people who were in my dad and uncle's world would know it was something to do with Billy getting us or him into trouble. 'It would therefore be logical that I would break all ties with him and we could keep the façade that we were estranged from each other and my family was left alone to grieve' he says. He goes on to explain that it's why we never saw Uncle Billy after that, but that he and Billy still talk each week and occasionally in the dead of night, Billy will go to the safe house to spend time with Mum.

'Okay, this is so confusing but is kind of making sense, but now I need you to clarify the situation as it stands today,' I tell him.

'Right, well, I'm getting to that. Listen darling, I know this all seems a bit far-fetched but it was a business deal that went wrong. Billy and I stole from the wrong guy. It was a mistake; turns out to be the biggest mistake of our lives. They were bad people Mel, really bad. The likes of which neither Billy nor I had ever had dealings with before and had we known? Well, that wouldn't even be a question. We would never have mixed with these people; they were so out of our league and we definitely wouldn't have stolen their cargo. Anyway, they made threats and these people? They didn't say anything they didn't mean. The old man was the lowest of the low, would kill his own Granny for a slice of cake. They threatened me and Billy by threatening to kill one of those we loved. Now, you know, as did everybody, that Bill was estranged from his own boys for most of their lives so it wasn't going to be them, which left Mum or any one of you kids. Mum damn near lost her mind at the thought of anything happening to her babies so the only way this would end would be to finish it ourselves. Billy told them to fuck off for one very good reason. Charlie Brooks, our inside guy had grown up with Mum and Billy and had been playing with the big boys for a long time but he and Billy were tight. Bill spoke to him and he told Billy that he'd 'volunteer' to kill Mum so the debt would be settled. He was in with the Stanfords, that's who these people were Mel, the fucking Stanfords.' He pauses to look at me, to take a breath and a mouthful of tea whilst I stare at him with wild eyes.

'The Stanfords? You stole from the Stanfords, Dad? How can

you not have known?' I ask, shocked that either Dad or Billy could ever be that dumb.

'Mel, it was a container at the docks. We lifted the wrong fucking container. We certainly didn't plan on messing with them. By the time word got out it was theirs, we had to offload it fast and then it was just too late. We could hardly go around asking for the contents back, most of it was already up the noses of the Mayfair crowd by then anyway.'

I hang my head and take a deep breath. My temples are pounding. Despite the headache I need something stronger than tea. I go to the cabinet and pull out a bottle of whisky and turn back to the table with the bottle and two glasses.

'Really darling, this time of the day?'

'Dad, are you shitting me right now? You pretend my mum is dead for 8 years and you're getting shitty with me for having a drink this early in the day?' I scream.

'Alright, I was just saying. Just calm down darling,' he says placing his hand on my arm. I snatch away from him, my anger palpable.

'Right, so we fucked up and they wanted one of us, well you lot really, dead as punishment and Charlie was the man these people turned to when they wanted to get shot of somebody for good. Charlie and Billy set everything up to make it look like an accident to the police. It was all perfect. Mum was safe, you were all safe and as much as I missed having Mum here with me, the alternative was not something any of us could stomach,' he says casting his eyes down.

'So how did this all go so wrong Dad?'

'It seems that Charlie is having some kind of mid-life crisis and got himself a younger girlfriend. Guess he was showing off and filling her in with his past exploits when he told her that he used to do jobs for the Stanfords and that one he got paid for was actually a set up. Anyway, turns out his bird is mates with or she's a sister to,

I don't fucking know, one of the Stanfords boys. Old man Stanford is dead and his two shithead sons run the business now, but now they're in bed with the Albanians. Now Billy knows the Albies and whilst they ain't friends, it's cordial. The Stanford boys are looking to get into a clean business. They, therefore, don't want to get their hands dirty but now they are looking at getting back the debt owed to them. So what do they do? They sell the debt to the Albanians knowing that the Albies want Billy to work with them thereby forcing Billy's hand. So now the Albanians have given Billy three months to pay back the value of what we stole.'

'Why are you telling me this now? Do the boys know?' Instinctively I know that Polly has no clue. She suffered in her grief worse than any of us. She was just so lost.

'Because now I need you to call your sister home and I need you to do as I ask without questions.'

TEN

Ronnie

What the fuck have we done? This is bad. We believed Billy when he said he had it under control but watching my beloved wife right now, doubled over, her body convulsing in fear, the dread that we may have misplaced our trust in his words hits me hard.

Life used to be simple. Hard but simple. When Billy approached us all those years ago and told us about the threats and how we were going to deal with it I wasn't happy. Maree was convinced immediately. I trusted Maree's judgement against my own. I'm not blaming her; I would never blame her. She loved her kids. Loves

OUR kids. The woman would throw herself in front of a moving train to protect them. She thought the plan was the best way, the only way, to protect our children.

I bend over to wrap my arms around the only woman I have ever loved; could ever love. Her pain is my pain. Her tears are my tears and the pain that is ripping through her right now, I feel it in my very soul. What the fuck have we done?

I move her in my arms, towards a chair so I can get her sat down. Once she sits she slumps forward whilst I get on my knees in front of her. Her crying is hysterical. Making sounds like only a mother in pain can feel. It's unbearable to watch somebody you love in so much pain.

'Mar, darling, look at me,' I implore. 'Maree, Maree look at me.' I hear my voice getting sterner in tone, but I need to get through to her, need her attention on me to calm her.

She lifts her head slowly and as her eyes connect with mine, the pain, I see in them slays me. Not for the first or probably the last time, I ask myself once again, what the fuck have we done?

'Ronnie, promise me, promise me they won't kill my baby? Promise me Ronnie, I need to hear the words, I need to believe them because if I don't hear them from you, I have nothing. Nothing. I will die from this. Polly. My baby, Ronnie. Our baby.'

How do I respond to that? I have no idea. I don't understand what the fuck is going on, what went on to get us to this point. Billy assured me this was only ever going to be smoke and mirrors. An illusion of the facts. Now suddenly, the illusion has gone wrong and our child is God knows where and her mother is going to die from the pain of losing her.

But promise her I will. Anything. I will say anything to bring my Maree back from the edge she is teetering on.

'I promise darling, on my heart, I promise she will be okay. We'll get her back safe and sound darling, I promise you sweetheart.

You hear me Mar? I promise.' I tell her with as much conviction as I can muster as I gently wrap my arms around her and hold her tight.

ELEVEN

Lucie

I'm so cold. I can't open my eyes. I don't want to open my eyes. I can hear crying around me and immediately remember seeing the other girls on the plane. I try to sit up but my body feels heavy. I try again but my back and shoulders just can't do it. Whatever I am lying on feels too soft and I can smell damp.

'Up!' A voice out of nowhere shouts. I immediately open my eyes and turn my head left, towards the voice. It takes around ten seconds for my eyes to focus, they feel so heavy and gritty.

I see the woman from the car who got on the plane standing in the middle of the room. She's looking directly at me. She is one hard looking bitch.

'You girl, get up, you have slept enough today,' she says pointing at me. I try to swing my legs off of whatever I am lying on but end up falling on my knees on the floor. She lets out a laugh. I turn my head to stare at her and before I can stop myself my mouth opens.

'Fucking bitch!' I scream at her.

She takes four or five steps before she's standing directly at my side. She bends down slightly, yanks my head to the side by grabbing my hair and spits in my face.

'You belong to me little girl, so when I say get up, you get up.' I'm trying to pull back but she just holds my hair harder. As she leans in closer, she moves to the side of my head and gently whispers in my ear, 'Polly, I'll get you out of here, I promise'. I look her in the eye, shocked by her words. She barely nods but I see it. I don't know who or what she is, but somehow, someone just sent me a guardian angel.

She stands to loom over me. I look around me to the other girls who look as petrified as I feel. They are all fairly young, like me, no more than their mid-twenties. A few are huddled together, hands interlocked. Along with the damp, I can also smell the fear in the room. I'm not sure if I look the same to them but I certainly feel it.

'Girls, in a moment, two at a time, I will take you to get showered and dressed. You will not speak to me and you will not speak to each other. Do you all understand me?' She doesn't wait for them to answer although most of them nod their acquiesce. 'Once you are cleaned and dressed I will take you into another room so that you can understand why you are here. Do not try to fight back, if you do, the guards will kill you. Understood?' Once again, she doesn't wait for a reply and doesn't look to see if anybody gives it.

'You two in the corner, get up and come with me,' she says pointing at two blondes huddled together. They rise to their feet unsteadily and follow her to the door. The door opens from the other side and when I look I can see a man there with a gun slung over his shoulder. Dead eyes stare back at me. Once they leave a few of the girls start to cry. I get up and go over to them as they all move so that everyone is together.

One of the girls who is shaking violently asks the question we are all feeling and thinking. 'Why are we here? What do they want with us?' She has an accent, European and her English isn't good.

'How did you end up here?' I ask her.

More tears flow as she tells me and everybody else that she's been living in England for around five years having been trafficked from her home in Croatia. A few of the girls nod as she speaks so I presume that their stories are similar to hers. She continues her story telling us that she wanted to come to England to make a better life for herself and was offered transport by a man who came to her town and spoke to her whilst she was working in a bar. She said that although she'd hated her life back home, the one she was forced into in England was worse. She was sent to live in a house with fourteen other girls and had been forced into prostitution. She was twenty-three years old and since arriving in the UK had only been out of the house once. She and another girl had attempted to try to escape only to be caught and beaten. The other girl didn't make it and from that moment on, she tried to just zone out of her life. Her day-to-day existence was one of sex and drugs. Her addiction to drugs, she said, was the only thing that kept her going. It was the only thing she lived for now.

A few days ago, a man came to the house and picked her up. They went into her usual room where she expected to have sex with him. Instead, he offered to inject her with something he said would 'take the edge off' and she agreed. She laughed gently as she told us this with tears streaming down her face.

'I remember being taken somewhere in a vehicle then onto the plane but my legs wouldn't work properly and I couldn't talk and now we are here. I want to die.' She crumpled forward and I held out my arms to catch her, holding her whilst she sobbed.

I look around at the other girls. 'Is that the same story for each of you' I ask.

All but one girl nods at me. I focus on her. 'What about you?' I ask gently.

'I'm English like you but I've been working the streets since I was a 14 year old runaway. I don't know what happened but one minute I was getting into a car with a John then like you all, I was on the plane.'

'Did you recognise the man who picked you up?' I ask.

'Nah, never seen him before. He was a mountain of a man. I got in the car not realising there was another man in the back seat and I just remember feeling the stab of a needle in my neck. Now, I'm here. Was I picked on purpose or just in the wrong place at the wrong time? I have a boyfriend, he's going to look for me, I know he is.'

We all just stare at each other. It seems clear to me that there is only one possible explanation as to why we are here. I can't get my head around why me. The other girls are all, whether their choice or not, sex workers.

I'm not. I don't know why I am here but I know it has something to do with my uncle. I know that I was 'hand-picked' for a reason but I don't know what that could be. Whoever those men who abducted me are, they knew where to find me, this I am sure of. How was that even possible when I didn't even know I would be going there until I woke up that day? And Jack. Jack was there and he told me to go home and he would find me. How is he going to find me now? And who is the woman? How does she know my name?

Startled, we hear the door open and the woman comes back in. She points to another two girls and they duly follow her. This pattern goes on for some time but I don't know how long, the concept of time has gone. The room has no windows. I imagine it is a basement but could simply be a room with no windows. Soon I am the only one left in the room. I sit with my head in my hands. I really need Jack. I squeeze my eyes shut thinking that in my moment of deepest need, it's Jack I pray for, not my family. My family of liars. My family who have betrayed me. The moment I saw my parents exit the back of that house I knew my life would never be the same again. And the one person that truly loves me, was the one person that arrived just at that moment when my family's betrayal came full circle on me. He held me. He knew that no matter that I had left him in the dead of the night, we would always be us. That we were each other's true twin flame that would burn for eternity.

No matter what happens now, no matter how bad it gets, I know in my heart that Jack will find me. That Jack will save me. I believe that. I have to believe that.

The door opens, for what will be one last time and the woman re-enters. She shuts the door behind her.

'Polly, we only have a moment so don't speak. I am going to take you to get cleaned up and as far as everybody and I mean everybody, is concerned you are just like all the other girls. I am law enforcement, it is not necessary for you to know who or why, but you were taken for a reason, I am sure you have already worked that out. Your uncle set this up but he is not the man you think he is. He has been working with us. We are close to the end and you are our ticket to finally getting the men we want and thereby stopping their business. Your treatment here will be different to that of the other girls. The other girls will ask why but there will be no answers for them. The deal your uncle has made is about humiliating your family. It doesn't matter why; what matters is that you don't do anything stupid to put yourself or me in danger. No one must know of our conversation. Do you understand that Polly? If you put me in danger of exposure, I will kill you myself. Now, we need to go and

I need you to be strong even if you feel like you are falling apart. Just be strong,' she says to me hauling me to my feet and pushing me towards the closed door. As she opens it to allow us through the same man as before is there. He puts his hand out and places his index finger under my chin. I quickly try to turn my face but as I try to twist away his fingers lock around my chin. He laughs as me and gives me what I can only describe as a leery smile. Fucker.

The woman pulls me by my arm and tells me to behave myself. We enter a bathroom, in its simplest form. There is just a toilet, wash basin and shower, like a very basic wet room. Basic in its purest form.

As we enter the bathroom, she starts the shower up immediately.

'Shower, Polly, then clean your teeth. The clothes you must wear will be in here by the time you finish. Wash your hair. You have to look your best and we need to ensure nobody suspects anything. Do not try to talk to me about anything we have discussed or what will happen next. I will speak to you only when I consider it safe to do so. Do you understand?'

I nod my understanding and start to undress. Even in this environment and in my state of fear, I actually do want to get clean. I feel disgusting and my head is so foggy. I am hoping the shower will clear my thinking somewhat so I can have more of my wits about me.

As I step under the running water, the tears begin to slide down my face. I won't let anybody, not even my so-called 'guardian angel' see me cry. One thing the old man taught me was to never let anybody see you weak. The shower is far from luxurious but God, it feels good as I scrub myself clean and wash my hair. When I turn the shower off, she's standing there ready with a towel. As I dry I stop myself asking the questions that are running through my head. I want to know how long I will be here, where the fuck is 'here', why have I been taken, does she know stuff about me, about my family?

But the biggest has to be, who is coming to get me? My thoughts return once again to Jack. I know without a doubt that if he can find me, he will. My heart belongs to him and I know his is all mine. But then the fear once again creeps in. How is he going to find me? Does he know who has taken me and why?

The clothes that I am passed to put on are cheap and frankly, fucking nasty. If I get anywhere near a naked flame I'm definitely going to light up the skies.

'Why do I need to wear this?' I shout whisper to the woman.

'Because you need to look like the other girls and although the other girls are here for a different reason to you, you are to at least look the same. It will be easier for you too for the time you are here.'

I simply nod as I put the clothes on and try not to think about what will happen next. As soon as I am dressed and my hair is brushed through, she turns me and plaits my hair. I see no reason for her doing this but it feels nice to have it out of the way. She tells me to leave my own clothes where they are as we leave the confines of the bathroom.

She leads me down the concrete corridor; it looks more like a tunnel really. At the end we go through a metal door into a room where I can see all the other girls I arrived here with. It looks like a club. There's a stage off to the left and a bar on the wall opposite the door. When I say 'club', it looks like a dingy strip joint and I'm pretty sure that's what it is. The girls sit on chairs in front of the stage in various stages of fear, some of them are crying. The woman pushes me to a vacant chair where I sit without question as she walks up and onto the stage. I expect her to start speaking but she just stands there expectantly. A man walks onto the stage to join her. He looks to be mid-thirties and is dressed in a badly fitted suit. His jet-black hair is slicked back and his olive skin is shiny with sweat. He says something to the woman and she smiles at him. I don't know if the other girls see what I see or if it's because of my conversations with her, but her smile is far from genuine. He laughs but it's more of a sneer. I am instantly repulsed by him.

'Ladies, welcome to my club. I trust Olga has made you comfortable?' He asks, obviously not caring for the answer. His English is quite good but with a heavy European accent. 'Today you will be under the instruction of Blerta, you will meet her in a moment. She will instruct you on your new job and what is expected of you. Let me take this opportunity to make myself clear. You belong to me. Your life belongs to me. You do what you are told from now on. I don't allow you to ask questions. Don't fuck with me ladies or I will, extinguish you.'

Extinguish? It seems an odd choice of words but I don't think it's a mistake. Some of the girls begin to whisper to each other.

'Silence!' He bellows. 'I did not say you were allowed to talk. As I was saying, you do what you are told to do or you will lose your life. I can find many women to take your place. They would want to take your place. Your life is of no consequence to me. You are inconsequential. This is your only choice. Do not make the mistake of crossing me. You will not enjoy the result.' With those final words, he leaves the stage as a woman takes his place next to Olga.

'I am Blerta, welcome ladies. Let's get started,' she says. Blerta looks to be in her twenties but she is so overly and hideously made up, it's hard to tell. Her clothes are provocative in an ugly, obvious way that is probably meant to appeal but in reality, just makes her look like a comedy stripper. I notice something on her arms which I think are track marks but I can't be sure. If they are, I have to wonder why her arms aren't covered?

The next several hours don't fly by. It is indeed a strip club but the girls are also expected to 'service' the customers when requested to do so. There are several poles on stage and those girls who have stripping experience with poles are pushed over to the left of the stage whilst those, including myself, without experience of stripping are moved over to the right. We are told that we will 'dance' on the stage and if we are lucky enough (are you fucking shitting me?) to get 'picked' by a customer then we may leave the stage for that purpose. Otherwise, we are to stay up there 'looking pretty'. There are only 4 of us who need to dance and 'look pretty'. After what seems like forever, we are told to leave the stage for food. I'm not expecting a banquet but in fairness the food isn't bad. It resembles and is laid out like a Greek meze and lots of it. The girls and myself are hungry, I can't remember the last time I ate and they probably can't either. Some of them push others out of the way in their desperation to get food onto their plates. The room is silent whilst we all eat. I keep trying to catch the eye of Olga but it's obvious she is avoiding eye contact with me.

Blerta claps her hands to get our attention. 'When food ends, we will go back to work. When I tell you day is over you, go to your new accommodation.' She begins in broken English. 'In room there are clothes for you. You will undress and put those on. You must hang the lovely clothes are you wearing now ready for tomorrow night when you begin work. Hurry with your food, I will be back soon,' and with that she ups and leaves. As soon as she is out of the room the girls start speaking to each other in whispers. It doesn't last long as a big lump of a man comes to stand next to the food table. He folds his arms over his chest and if he's intention is to look intimidating, it's working for him. The table quietens down immediately apart from a small blonde girl sandwiched between two others. Her head hangs low as she sobs. The girl to her left is holding her hand whilst the other puts a supportive arm around her.

When I was growing up I knew a lot of men like the dude standing looking over us. He might frighten them but I've seen worse. I can feel my anger starting to boil but I know I have to reel it in or else I could blow getting the fuck out of here. I know it before it happens so when he shouts 'silence', I am the only one at the table who doesn't jump or gasp. No, fuck him, I look straight into his eyes. He raises a brow at me. I raise one back. I know I'm playing with fire but I just can't seem to stop myself. My brother used to throw the Shakespeare quote at me 'though she be little, she is fierce' and fucking right I am.

The fear in the room with the thug standing over us is palpable. I have no idea the backgrounds to these girls and whether they will be able to weather this storm we find ourselves in. As I start to get lost in my own head, Blerta re-enters the room.

She claps her hands together to get our attention in the way a teacher would. Personally, I think she is more Nurse Ratched than educator, but I'll keep my mouth shut on my opinion of her.

She separates us again and as I go to join the other girls, the 'thug' grabs my arm and pulls me away and out of the room.

I pull my arm out of his grasp. 'I can walk by myself; I don't need you to drag me,' I say to him. He levels me with a stare but I cross my arms over my chest. I hope this isn't my last act of defiance.

He opens a door off to the left of the dark corridor and pushes me through it. In the room is a large desk with the 'boss' sitting in the chair and Olga standing to his right shoulder. Her eyes are hard and I understand immediately why.

'Welcome Polly, I trust you have enjoyed your lunch?'

'Well, I can honestly say it was vile but better than nothing,' I retort.

He barks out a laugh and tells me that I'm 'feisty'. Prick.

'So, you are quite unusual in my wonderful establishment. You are here not to work as such, at least not like the other girls, but you will be out on stage nightly and you will do as you are told. Insolence will not be tolerated. Are you understanding this?'

'If I'm not "working",' I say using quotation marks. 'What am I expected to do on stage?'

'Well, it's really quite interesting. Please take a seat and I will explain. You are here to dance but you may not service my clientele, even if you want to.'

I gag at the thought. All I can think of is those girls in the other rooms, expected to fuck some weirdo.

'I have reached an agreement with your uncle. You are not to have sex as that would probably be pleasurable for you,' he tells me with a salacious smile of his ugly face. 'You will be on stage of course, but you may only dance. I assume you can dance?'

Fuck him. Fuck my uncle. 'No, actually I can't,' I tell him with a defiant stare. His face transforms from smug amusement to a blistering stare. I have always had a knack of not shutting up when I should. This is one of those moments.

'Well, I suggest you fucking learn fast and if you ever talk like that to me again, I will ignore your uncles request to leave you unharmed. I hope I am making myself clear but just in case you don't understand, I will show you. Olga, bring me a girl.'

Olga levels with me a deadly stare as she exits the room. A few minutes later she returns with one of the young girls. The man instructs the girl to come round to his side of the desk. As she complies he stands and without warning backhands her round her face, knocking her off her feet and causing her lip to split. The girl cries out at the same time as I do.

'That was your fault. Don't fucking test me!' He screams in my direction.

Olga helps the girl to her feet and takes her from the room. I'm stunned by what has just happened, not to mention sickened. That was my fault.

'I understand,' I tell him quietly.

'Good, now get back out there with the other girls and don't cause me any trouble.'

I leave the room followed by a man who had been standing in

the corner of the room. As we exit the room, the man grips my bicep and says something in whatever language they are speaking to the man behind the desk. The arsehole laughs but I keep my eyes on the floor.

When the door shuts, the man leans down to whisper in my ear. Although he is at the side of my head, I can smell his stale breath. It's vile.

'If you need someone to fuck, for your pleasure, it will be me.'

TWELVE

Jack

Gill and I get back in the car and head out to the house where the McDowells' are hiding.

'Gill, how do you want to play this?' I ask him, looking out of the passenger window.

'Well, given what these people are and that we now seem to be dealing with two cases instead of one, although they are now linked. I'm thinking a case of Good Cop, Bad Cop is probably the best way to go,' he says laughing. If only he knew how badly I wanted to go in bad cop.

'I'm happy to be bad cop unless you have a preference?' I tell him. Any excuse to vent some of the anger I feel towards Lucie's family.

'Works for me man,' he says in some kind of American accent which I don't appreciate right now.

Pulling up at the house, we can see that Melanie has beaten us to it, even though that wasn't the arrangement we made with her. After the phone call back at the gym, I can't say I'm surprised she's here. As we walk towards the front door, we can hear them screaming at each other. I put my hand on Gill's arm, signaling him to wait. Experience says you tend to hear more when you are eavesdropping on private conversations than when you are asking questions. Melanie's voice is high, her screaming words taking no punches. We've obviously started listening mid-way through their shouting match but we get the gist fast.

'…what's owed to them from the debt or Polly dies,' we hear Ronnie say. My body tenses, the crushing pain in my chest is back.

I want to stay and listen to more from where we are but now I can't. I want to storm the place and kill Lucie's fucking father for putting her in danger. The door is open and we enter the house, walking towards where the shouting is coming from. Melanie is crying hysterically, screaming in pain like an injured animal.

As we enter the kitchen, Ronnie stands and walks around the table attempting to put his hands around Melanie. She's having none of it, pulling away from him.

'Stay the fuck away from me!' She screams, spit flying out of her mouth.

'Watch how you talk to me lady. Show some bloody respect,' Ronnie shouts back.

She laughs in his face. 'Respect? You want to talk about respect old man?' Mel screams and attempts to hit out at him. He moves fast, grabbing her wrists and restraining her.

'Ronnie don't touch her!' Maree screams.

Maree is not what I was expecting but she's familiar too. Of course, I've seen photos of her, but in the flesh, I can see that Lucie looks like her mother. Maree is old school glamour. She's a looker for sure, even with her red-rimmed eyes and unruly hair.

They haven't even noticed us standing in the doorway of the kitchen.

'You have allowed my sister to be killed. If she dies, it's her blood on yours and Mum's hands and I will never forgive you. Ever. And neither will the boys. You will both be dead to us. Well in Mum's case dead AGAIN!'

'Seems like we arrived at the right moment,' says Gill as all three turn to us in shock. Maree slumps in her seat and Melanie looks directly at me.

'Good luck trying to make these two take any responsibility,' Melanie says. 'I'm not needed here and I don't want to be here a moment longer. Please do not put me in the same bracket as my parents. I love my sister; there is nothing I won't do to bring her home safely and that includes throwing these two plus my uncle under the bus if necessary,' she says with tears streaming down her face as she walks in between Gill and me in the doorway and leaves the house.

Turning back to look at the McDowells, Maree is sitting with her head in her hands.

'And who the fuck are you two clowns? Police? You think you are going to crack this crime? You haven't got a fucking Scooby!'

I have no idea what a Scooby is and right now I don't care. I want to put my hands round his throat and choke the truth out of him. I'm not averse to doing it either.

'I don't actually think you have room to comment right now Mr McDowell. We spoke earlier when you were on the phone to your daughter. Your eldest daughter, you know the one that hasn't been abducted. So why don't we all take a seat and you can tell us what you do know,' Gill says calmly taking a seat at the table.

‘Let’s start with the basics, shall we? Do you know who has abducted Polly McDowell?’ I ask them. Calling Lucie ‘Polly’ feels like acid on my tongue. She’s not and never will be Polly to me. I feel disloyal using her given name. Even though the name she has been using with us, those who love her Stateside, is a lie, she is still Lucie to us and always will be. Even when this nightmare is over, when she is back in my arms and home with us, I will never call her Polly. That name will forever be synonymous with what is happening right now and I will never let my girl re-live this nightmare.

‘I’m not telling you shit,’ Ronnie starts but Maree puts her hand on her husband’s arm and levels him with a look.

Ronnie takes a deep breath and exhales slowly, sinking into the chair next to his wife. Running his hand down his face he looks at her, using his fingers to wipe her tears away.

‘Ronnie,’ Maree says, ‘tell them everything. We started this and now we need to finish it if we ever hope to get Polpol back to us safely.’

I want to scream at her to shut up with the intimate nickname she obviously uses as a term of endearment for her daughter. How fucking dare she sit here like the grieving mother? How dare she look forlorn and broken when she’s played such an integral part in her daughter’s kidnapping. Disgust fills my soul.

‘We made a mistake, a long time ago and now we are paying the price. Is that not enough?’ He asks his wife.

‘No Ron, it’s not enough. If we don’t give them the pieces of the puzzle, how will the jigsaw ever be complete again? Please Ron, I don’t care what happens to us, or to Billy, I just want her to be safe. Please, for me, for Polly, just tell them. This lie that we started could be what takes her from us forever. Melanie is right; if she dies, it’s her blood that will be on our hands forever.’

‘Fucks sake Mar,’ Ronnie says hanging his head and staring at his hands. Looking up and focusing on us, he fills in the gaps we don't know, which right now is plenty. 'Not long before we faked Maree's death, Billy and I were working together and we had a job to nick a container that had just arrived from Europe. Long story short, the wrong container was taken and the contents, which we didn't know about until after we took it, contained almost three million pounds worth of cocaine. We were laughing all the way. We'd never been involved in drugs previously and actually we haven't since, but why look a gift horse in the mouth, eh? Anyway, suffice to say we got rid of it, got rich from it, then we got word that it belonged to the Stanfords. Heard of them?' He asks.

'Yep. Bad move Ronnie,' says Gill. I on the other hand have no idea who the Stanfords are and all I'm interested in is the punch line to understand how we get to the point of Lucie's abduction.

'So, then what?' I ask. 'You find out whatever you stole belonged to these Stanfords and what happened next?'

'Well, as I'm sure you can imagine, when you steal a Christmas payday, people are understandably pissed,' he says with a shrug of his shoulders. 'Especially when it's stuffed to the gills with coke. You've got to know, we never touched drugs, not of any suggestion. Had we have known it was coke in there, we wouldn't have touched it with a ten-foot pole. But we didn't and yeah, we took the wrong fucking container. Total mistake. Anyway, we had a man who did jobs with people like the Stanfords, a guy who was trusted by many to sort shit out. This guy grew up with Billy and Maree, was as good as family. He was the guy who was going to sort the debt out for the Stanfords and as we didn't have the product or the money it was worth, they wanted paying back in blood. Back then, all the kids, ours and Billy's were a lot younger. Billy's boys lived with their mum, bleeding miles away and to be honest, he didn't have a relationship with them then so that was a dead end, if you will. So that left our kids on the tightrope. We couldn't let that happen and Maree offered to be the sacrificial lamb.'

I scoff, not being able to help myself.

Ronnie levels me with a look. 'Something amusing you son?' He asks with a sneer.

'Just thinking it's kinda ironic that the sacrificial lamb is safe and well and yet your youngest daughter, innocent I might add, has become the lamb after all.'

'Fuck you, you piece of shit,' Maree screams. And that ladies and gentlemen is where the similarity between Lucie and this bitch ends for me. I can hardly tell her that Lucie is the oxygen that runs through my body, keeps me alive and vital. Neither of them deserves to know what Lucie means to me. But when this is over, when I have Lucie back with me, then they'll know. In the meantime, I need to not give them any reason to hold out on us.

'My apologies, Mrs McDowell, that was out of line,' I tell her with as much sincerity as I can muster up, even though saying the words feels like chewing on cement.

'Ronnie, continue, please,' Maree tells her husband.

'We decided, me, Billy and Maree, that the only way we could protect our kids was for it to be Mar who would die. Now obviously, no way in hell were we about to let that happen for real so Charlie…'

'Charlie who?' Interrupts Gill.

'Brooks. Charlie Brooks, that's the guy who grew up with Maree and Billy. Gets paid handsomely for dealing with the shit that the arseholes of this world don't want to do themselves. Pay for it, sure, but not actually get their own hands dirty. So, that was what we did. Set it up on a specific day that the Stanfords chose and it was ready for Charlie to carry out the job. Only, we also had it set up that Maree would get out safely before the moment of impact.'

'And the body in the car that day? Who was that?' I ask.

'Just some geezer Charlie lifted out of a morgue that his brother-in-law worked at. Same guy who identified it as Maree and performed the autopsy. Chuck enough money at a situation, you can buy just about anything. The police at the time were satisfied it was an accident and along with the identification of the body, closed the case as an accident which resulted in the death of Mrs Maree McDowell. I know you think it seems callous, that we would mislead our kids like that and believe me, there were times when we wish we could have just turned the clock back. Watching your kids grieve and knowing that they would forever feel the loss of their mother, it's hard, to say the least. But it was necessary and keeping our kids safe was not something we were ever going to regret. Well until today, of course. You can't imagine how much pain this is causing my wife, us.'

'Right, enough of the family profile. Ronnie, explain to us what's changed. And why now? I'm sure you can appreciate, for the sake of your daughter, time is crucial to the investigation,' Gill tells them, clearly getting fed up with being given the run around.

'For fucks sake! You people want the inside out of a duck's arse!' Ronnie shouts. I almost laugh. I have never heard that said before so what could I do but raise my brows to Gill. I hear him sigh.

Ronnie continues 'Unfortunately, for us, the Stanfords got pally with some Albanians. Now those fuckers are mad. The Stanford sons sold our debt onto the Albanians after finding out that we duped them. It's not quite as simple as just selling a debt. It doesn't work like other business. Billy has had dealings with the Albanians in the last few years and more recently, they've been putting the pressure on him to help them run girls to Europe.'

'Run girls to Europe?' Gill asks, knowing full well what he means but needing confirmation.

'Yeah, you know girls. Prostitutes to work in clubs, their clubs in Europe,' Ronnie says not looking at either of us.

'Sex-trafficking. It's called sex-trafficking Mr McDowell,' I say to the room.

'They're prostitutes! What fucking difference does it make?'

Ronnie shouts.

'What, apart from them being someone's daughter you mean? Apart from being taken against their will?' Gill shouts back. I actually want to clap him on the back.

'Yeah, it's unfortunate I agree. They started trying to get heavy with us, trying to take over our business, getting land that was marked as ours, trying to ruin us. The only way to stop your enemies is to sometimes get in bed with them, whether you hate them or not.'

People never cease to amaze me. How the hell can this man stand here and justify his actions that have led to the abduction of his own daughter because they were losing business? I stand, needing space away from looking at this man. This man is adored by Lucie, who speaks of him in a way that only a child who truly loves their parent can.

'You need to break this down for us Mr McDowell as I can't see the connection between pissing off the Albanians and the abduction of your daughter, who you now believe is in danger, even though you or Billy appear to have set this up,' Gill says in his tell-tale annoyed voice.

'They let us know that they knew, as did the Stanfords, that Maree was alive. They also told us that they now owned the original Stanfords debt. Billy and I discussed it, at length and just as we were trying to figure out a way of sorting it. Well, we started doing business with them not knowing that the Stanfords had sold on the debt. Billy managed to make it seem like it was all on me and Maree. We went out of our way at the time of Maree's death to make the falling out between Billy and me as public as possible and we did that in front of 300 witnesses on the day of Maree's funeral. I blamed him, he said one day he'd get revenge, the usual shizzle. Of course, it was an act. Billy sees Maree at least once a week and has done for the past eight years,' Ronnie reveals.

'Backtrack a moment Ronnie. Why did the Stanfords sell the

debt? Why didn't they just come after you themselves? They have a formidable reputation; well, up until a few years back but that kind of rep sticks forever, does it not?' Gill questions.

'Old man Stanford died a few years back and the sons wanted to clean the business. Don't get me wrong; they're still fuckers, but they wanted their business clean. After the old man died, the sons set about clearing house and at that point, found out that Charlie had fixed the job. Just so you know, don't bother looking for Charlie Brooks. He is nowhere to be found. We hope he just did a bunk, but he could be six-foot under himself by now, who knows. Now apparently, Old Man Stanford was mates with these Albanians and when he died and the Stanfords boys wanted to clean up their act, they spoke with the Albies. There must have been a conversation between them at the time where Billy's name had come up and so they bought the debt. They sold the debt we owed to them to the Albies and here we are. They want payment. Because Billy already had dealings with them, it wasn't like we could hide. We owe them three million and we have three months to come up with the cash. It's not easy, nobody has that kind of money lying around. So, they wanted a deposit,' he shrugs.

'And your daughter was the deposit?' I question. This has to be some sort of fucking joke.

'Bad choice of words but yeah. She's safe. Billy has an agreement with them and they won't renegade on that. They will just keep her there until we pay them off, which is happening. We're getting the money fast.'

'Where is "there"?' asks Gill.

At this question Maree starts to cry again. 'We don't know exactly,' Ronnie confesses.

'But there's more to this story, right Ronnie?' Gill says, standing and walking to the sink to grab some water.

'Yeah. Billy has, is, working with Interpol.'

I'm lost for words. Interpol. That's my way in. G knows some agents. I almost sigh in relief.

'Look, Billy was approached by Interpol. Now, how the fuck Interpol knew about Billy was beyond us, but it gave us a ray of hope. They wanted Billy to "get in bed with the Albies" and Billy would be able to inform on them. The Albies we are dealing with arc wanted by Interpol and somehow, I don't fucking know, Interpol found out about our debt and approached Billy. We lead them to the Albies, Interpol does their thing and our debt is cleared.'

'And your daughter? Is she just going to be collateral damage? These people don't mess around Ronnie; we both know that. They might just pop your daughter for the hell of it,' Gill says running his hand down his face. We, me and Gill, both know this is far above his pay grade and him and the team are far, far out of their league.

'We, well, Interpol, obviously have somebody on the inside. A woman. I only know her as Olga. Never met her but I think Bill has. We don't know if that's her real name but I fucking doubt it. Anyway, she will keep Polly safe,' he says, taking Maree's hand and squeezing it. She looks at him like he's just walked on water as opposed to sentencing his daughter to death.

Gill barks out a laugh. A deep, condescending laugh. 'You think they give a shit Ronnie? If you do, then you're delusional mate,' he tells him.

Maree removes her hand from Ronnie's grasp, stands and puts her hands to her face. I consider myself a decent human being, I know I would normally feel sorry for these people. I wish I could feel some ounce of sympathy for her, but I don't. They knowingly sent their daughter into a lion's den and for that, I will make sure that neither of us ever forgive them. Hell, they don't deserve our forgiveness. My mind is spinning again. I need to get hold of Garrett. He's worked with Interpol, a long time ago, but he will know somebody or know somebody who knows somebody. Whatever the fuck he knows, he's the man to get intel on Lucie.

'I'm going to level with you Ronnie,' Gill begins as he stands then takes his seat again, his eyes are directly levelled with Ronnie's. 'As much as we sympathise, this is way above us now, so I will be relaying this conversation to my superiors and I fully expect them to move forward from New Scotland Yard in conjunction with Interpol.' I feel nothing but relief at his words. I will find a way to get 'pulled back' home but instead I can travel to Europe. Melanie will be my link to Billy and the McDowells. She's angry at them right now and rightly so, but she won't keep herself out of the loop as she seems to be the only one who genuinely cares what happens to her sister. How fucked up is that?

I fist my hands under the table. What I want is to slam them into Ronnie's face but I can't let my guard down. I can't show my hand and I won't until I have Lucie back with me then only God will be able to help them.

'I strongly advise you both not to leave this house, for your own safety.'

When we get in the doorway, Gill turns back to face them. 'I have to say, you two are pretty special. I have a daughter and the thought of using her as a pawn in any game, is sickening. I don't know Polly but having met Melanie, I can say without a doubt, you don't deserve her. No child deserves parents who would sell her out in the way you have.' And then we leave.

'Unfuckingbelievable right?' Gill asks when we get in the car.

'Yeah, unbelievable,' I say back, staring out the window.

My head is in planning mode. Get back to base, make my excuses and get Garrett to pull some strings to get me back 'home'. Then I can make my way to Europe and find my girl.

THIRTEEN

Lucie

I wake with a start, simultaneously dripping in sweat and freezing. I had been dreaming of Jack; all my dreams comprise of him, whether they're night time dreams or when I drift off inside my head when I'm awake. My heart physically aches not knowing when I will see him next. But I know that along with my wits, I need to keep my optimism up. I know him. He knows me. I know that he is my only hope and I pray that his love for me is strong enough. That he didn't give up on me, that he knows I need him.

I squeeze my eyes shut, tears welling up. 'Please save me Jack,' I send up into the universe.

I can't sleep. Fuck who could sleep here in this hell-hole? It's not exactly the Ritz. I have Olga 'looking after me' but she's pretty damn scary.

My thoughts drift to my parents, like they have done many times over the past 24 hours. Why did they lie? How could they lie about Mum dying? My dad saw my grief firsthand. I was inconsolable when my mum died; what child wouldn't be. The loss of any parent is not something you just get on and deal with. I was sixteen and I needed her so badly. And now knowing it was a lie? It makes me feel sick. I feel hate burning up inside me. I don't know if I will ever be able to forgive them. Can love and hate co-exist?

I feel so consumed right now with hate for them. It's not a feeling I am used to. I have put my mum on a pedestal since her death, making her almost saint-like in death. Whatever flaws once existed, I deleted from my memory. How do I even begin to process it? Will I ever be able to understand what has happened? Lying here on this hard, cold bed, I don't know what to think. I just want to go home. Actually, I just want to get out of here alive. These people here? Yeah, they're not the kind you cross and live to tell the tale.

My stomach hurts but I don't know if that's fear eating away at me or if it's the remnants of the drug that was injected into me. I roll over and look around the sparse room and wonder, not for the first time, if I am the only one with my own room. I haven't yet asked the other girls; worrying that if they all share and find out I don't, they will think something is amiss.

There are no personal belongings with me, I have no idea where my phone is so it's just a rail with some clothes hanging on it. Melanie would call it a 'TV hooker wardrobe' and frankly, she wouldn't be far off the mark. Gaudy and cheap is probably the nicest description I can muster at the moment. Also, somebody has left me hideous shoes to wear. I fucking hope nobody expects me to wear them, I'm not sure I could walk in those if I tried. Balance has never been a strong point for me. I almost laugh. Almost.

I swing my legs off the bed and place my feet on the floor, which is hard and cold. Jack would laugh that I haven't got my Uggs on my feet. They are my home footwear of choice and right now I would do just about anything to slide my feet into them.

I need to think. I need to plan a way to get out of this place. To date, I haven't seen a front door. This bloody prison must have one but I don't even know where to start. The window in my 'room' is high and long and the bed I sleep on is fixed to the floor so I can't even drag it over to look out of the window. I'm too bloody short to jump up and reach the sill. I have to find a way.

I'm sitting here thinking about it when the door opens and Olga walks in. I don't say hello or morning and neither does she. Instead she stands in the middle of the room just staring at me. I break the silence first.

'If it isn't my fairy godmother,' I say.

'Don't act like a child Polly. I neither have the time nor the energy to deal with it. Our moments away from ears will be short so I need you to listen and do as I say. I can't protect you if you choose to not listen. Do you understand me Polly? Because I have to say right now, you are nothing but a complication to my job.'

'And what exactly is your job Olga?' I ask her. She is so self-assured and looks comfortable in her role as what? Madam? I guess that's what she is.

Olga sits on the bed next to me. 'Polly, you know I work in law enforcement. My role here has been to gather intel on these people. They are not good men Polly. I have seen things in the last year that I never want to see again in my life but my role here is not to intervene. If I did that, they would know I wasn't who I say I am.'

'And what is that? What do they think you are?'

'To them, I am a fixer. To them my history is running a brothel in Austria. My résumé was very thorough. I have won the trust of these people and I can't have you messing it up. But now you are here and I have to ensure your safety too. Your uncle, Mr Langford, is working with my people and my tasks here have now been complicated by your presence. You are a lucky girl,' she informs me.

I laugh. How can I not? 'Lucky? Are you shitting me? I was abducted, drugged, flown on a plane to God knows where and I seem to be living in a sex club. That is not what I would call lucky!' I tell her in a whisper shout.

'Keep it down. Listen to me. You are lucky. Firstly, I will do everything in my power to keep you safe, that's a damn sight more than any of the other girls here. Secondly, you are not to be used for sex. Count yourself very lucky little girl.'

'Then what am I doing here if not to be the same as the other girls?' I ask here, totally confused.

'You my dear are a deposit on a debt,' she tells me.

I stare at her, unable to comprehend her words. 'A deposit on a debt?' I ask. 'What does that even mean?'

'It means that you are only here up until the debt is paid.'

'What debt? Whose debt?' But my gut knows the answer. I know what she's going to say. I want to be sick. I feel the heat rising up in my body, flooding my head, making my ears burn and the acid in the back of my throat begin to burn my tongue.

'Billy Langford's and your father's.'

'Did, did….my dad and uncle know I would be kidnapped?' I can feel my hands trembling.

'Yes, they did. They set the whole thing up but the people who run this place, the ones you don't want to cross, don't know who your uncle is working with. If they did, you wouldn't be sitting here talking to me now. So, keep yourself together and do what I tell you, exactly what I tell you, so I can keep you safe.'

I can't think right now. My dad set this up? With my uncle? The same uncle that he hasn't had any involvement with since my mum died? My dad has blamed my uncle for my mum's death since her funeral. There was a big falling out that day. A massive argument in front of everybody. It almost came to blows but my brothers managed to restrain my dad. Why would he have been working with my uncle? It makes no sense to me. But then neither does my mother faking her own death and I can't even begin to get my head around the fact that she is actually very much alive and kicking.

'What do they want with me? I'm not their fucking plaything. I'm not going to sit here and be abused by these people. If anybody touches me, I swear, I'm going to fight for my life. And those bastards can go fuck themselves,' I tell her, the quiver in my voice betraying my fear.

'You are a deposit and we can only hope they will keep their end of the bargain but I haven't yet been given any details. But I am warning you, don't talk back to them, don't think you can use clever words with them. They won't like it and I can't help you if choose to make this harder on yourself than it needs to be. I can't keep you safe, unless you control yourself,' she tells me sternly. 'Now get some clothes on and follow me,' she says.

'I haven't… can't I have a shower?' I ask. 'At least, can I clean my teeth?'

'Later you can but for now, get some clothes on and hurry up.'

I find the least offending outfit and put it on. I try to walk out with her barefooted but she points and the shoes and tells me to put them on.

As I could have predicted, I experience immediate and immense trouble balancing and walking in them. I have to walk down the corridor with my hand sliding along the wall so to stop myself from falling over.

We reach the end of the corridor and walk into the main room of the club where the other girls are already in attendance and by the look of it, their training is continuing. One of the girls is currently being shouted at by some middle-aged redhead. The girl looks terrified. My instinct is to go over there and protect her but I heed Olga's warning. It's not in my nature to watch a person being treated like that and not intervene but I want out of here so badly and I am scared that if I do try to get involved, I will be the one who is punished.

The redhead eyes me as we walk in. She looks at me with utter contempt and I can't stop myself from giving her the same level of interest back.

'You,' she says loudly pointing at me. I startle as I feel Olga's hand on the small of my back urging me towards the woman.

'You, come here. I have work for you,' the redhead says clicking her fingers in the air.

Any other moment in time, I'd tell her to fuck off. But I'm not exactly in the strongest of positions right now. I walk towards her, unsteady in the laughable shoes provided for me.

'Tonight, you will serve drinks,' she informs me as I step up in front of her.

'In these heels?' I ask before I can stop myself. It's just an automatic reaction but looking at her stern face which seems to have become sterner, I need to keep those reactions in check.

'Sorry,' I murmur, hoping that will go some way to appease her.

'Yes, in your shoes. Listen to me child, I don't care if you break neck,' she says in broken English. 'I tell you to work, you work, you understand?'

'Yes, I understand,' I say.

'Yes, I understand Mistress,' she volleys back to me.

I look down at my feet. Everything I am is telling me to chuck something back at her, but I know I can't. I make a promise to myself here and now. I will not get myself in trouble.

'Yes, I understand Mistress.' My sister would desert me if she could hear me now. She backs down to no one and if she thought I was, she'd be slapping me around too.

'Good. Now go to bar. Speak to man and he tell you what you do. Now go!'

I'm walking the very best I can towards the bar, trying to keep my focus on the barman whilst trying not to break my neck in these fucking clown shoes.

'Can you walk with a tray?' He asks as I approach the bar. He's an Aussie. I couldn't be more shocked.

He's another big guy. Burly, my mother would have called him. Black shirt fitted tightly across his chest. Melanie and I would be laughing right now if she was here, 'think he does weights?' one of us would say. How his shirt is not ripping on his bulging muscles like the Hulk when he loses his shit, I don't know.

'I've waitressed before, so I can wait tables; I'm just finding it difficult to walk in these shoes,' I tell him. Right now, I have no idea if he is a friend or foe and until I can find out, I'm just going to jump every time he tells me to.

'Well, little suggestion for you doll. Learn. And fast. You will start work at 4.30 taking drink orders and delivering them. Your shift with me will end when I say. Now take these drinks over to the table where the Boss is sitting at. Don't talk to him, just smile,' he informs me solemnly. I nod in acceptance of his instructions.

Making my way over to the table in the ridiculous heels I can feel my heart hammering inside my chest walls. My legs feel like they are barely keeping me upright but I will not let it show.

As I near the table I lower the tray holding the drinks and place them on the table with as much of a smile as I can muster.

I turn to walk away when the 'Boss' grabs my wrist, spinning me back round.

'Nothing to say little girl?' His sleazy look repulses me.

I say nothing. Looking instead down at my feet.

'I heard you were a fiery one? Is that not correct?'

'No,' is the only answer I give him.

'Well, little girl, we'll have to see how you respond to a little poke, no?'

I want to spit in his face, his words crawling over my skin make nausea rise in my throat.

'Go,' he says pushing me away by the hip. I don't need to be told twice.

My shift makes for a long night. But around 11pm Liam, the barman, informs me that my work is over for tonight. I can't explain the relief. My feet are literally killing me and my back is aching like a bitch. I walk towards the door that I came through initially when I was accosted by Olga.

'Where are you going?' She asks.

'Liam, he said I've finished for the night'.

'You don't walk through that door,' indicating to the one I was heading for, 'go through the door behind the stage, it will take you to your living quarters.'

I nod and start the walk towards the stage but as I am just about to reach it, Boss man grabs my wrist.

'Are you going to dance girl?' He asks in his leery way.

'No, er, my shift waitressing has finished and they said I could go,' I tell him.

'You don't finish work unless I say so. Do you understand me little girl?'

He's taunting me, I know this and all I want to do is get away from him.

'So, dance for me girlie.'

'But, but I can't dance. I mean I'm not a dancer,' I splutter.

'Well tonight you are, so go do it,' he tells me as he stands to his full height, towering above me, even in these heels.

'I don't know what to do,' I say meekly, hoping with everything in me that he'll take pity on me. But no such luck.

'Blerta will show you how,' he says, once again shoving me but this time in the direction of Blerta.

They have a conversation in their own language whilst I stand there. He laughs and so does she. It's not a nice laugh that emits from either of them. It can only be defined as a sinister laugh that makes my hairs stand on end. Instinctively, I know this isn't going to be good.

'Come,' says Blerta grabbing me by the wrist. I don't even bother trying to fight her off. I need to pick my battles. My dad always told me that.

She drags me along behind her until we reach the area behind the stage where the girls who are 'dancing' are waiting.

'Please don't make me do this,' I implore to her better nature even though I know deep down she doesn't have one.

She approaches me with lipstick, a vivid scarlet. It's so predictable. Blerta is obviously intent on doing this herself as she grabs me by the chin, forcing my face towards her and proceeds to put my lipstick on. It's feels heavy and sticky and smells disgusting.

Once again, she grabs my wrist and pulls me to just behind the curtain of the stage.

'So, you can't dance little girl?' She asks with a smirk.

'No, I've never done this before,' I tell her.

'Good. Tonight, you just need to move your hips and let me make this very, very clear to you. If you don't, if you make a fuss, if you don't satisfy us, your punishment will be quick and simple. Would you like to know what it will be?'

'Yes,' I tell her even though I don't want to know, at all.

'You will be whipped,' she says smiling like she just told me that Santa would be coming tomorrow.

'Whipped? You can't be serious?' I ask.

'Carla! Carla!' She shouts as a girl with long black hair

approaches. 'Carla, show our new girl here your back.'

Carla duly turns around and slides her dress off of her shoulders so it pools around her waist.

I cannot stop the gasp that leaves my mouth nor the hand that flies up to it. The whipping that Carla obviously endured is evident in ugly red welts. Too many to count. It's horrific. There is no other way to describe it.

'Carla, go,' Blerta tells her and Carla slides away. Tears prick the back of my eyes. Fear grips my heart and my head is pounding with the flow of my blood.

The stage is cut into two sections. One section, the place I am in, is curtained off whilst the other is on display to the club. I have witnessed tonight that one curtain raises as the other lowers and vice versa.

Blerta drags me towards a pole just behind the counter and tells me to put my hands on either side and link my fingers together. I do as she asks; my fear is eating away at me.

From out of nowhere she produces a set of handcuffs. My eyes must show my horror as she gives one of her sinister smiles as she clips them around my wrists so that I'm attached to the pole.

'These will help you, no? Keep you steady,' she tells me as if it were some kind of aid for me. 'When the curtain moves, you dance girl,' is all she says then walks away.

I stare at her as she walks away. Another girl comes up to me. 'Just do it honey, it's not worth the fight,' is all she says before the curtain in front of me lifts.

FOURTEEN

Jack

We pull back into base just as my phone goes off. I'd managed to shoot a quick text to G knowing he would read and act on it immediately.

'Excuse me,' I tell Gill getting out of the car but staying close enough that he'll be aware of the conversation as he gets out.

'Sir?'

'Son, it's G. Okay, I've sorted it this end, you just need to play the part on your side,' he tells me.

'Yes, Sir. I'll be back as soon as I can arrange my flight, Sir.'

'Call me when you're free Jack and we can go through the set up. Be careful, speak to no one,' he says.

'Yes, Sir. Thank you, Sir.' I say.

'Problem?' Gill asks.

'I've been called back. Gotta arrange a flight and I'm out of here. Let's catch up with everybody and then I need to leave.'

'That's a shame Jack, I feel like I could really do with your experience on this one. You'll be missed but totally get it,' he says moving towards me to shake my hand.

I almost feel bad for leaving so quickly but this is no time to get caught up in those feelings. G has a plan and I need to be in the right place to execute it. Then I need to get Melanie onboard. I don't know what I will need her for yet until I speak with Garrett but I know that she, like me, will do anything she can to help ensure Lucie's safe return.

As Gillingham and I head back into the office, he calls out for everybody to come into the briefing room so we can be updated and in turn relay our information.

Once everybody is in the room, Gill and I move to the front and perch on the desk to face everyone.

'First things first, give me an update on Mac,' instructs Gill.

Jenkins stands to address us. 'Cross is at the hospital Sir and Mac is out of surgery. The doctors say he will make a full recovery in time but it was pretty touch and go for a while. The bullet just missed the main artery but the damage was still extensive. He hasn't woken up yet so Cross will stay there until he does so he can get the details of what went down and what Mac saw,' he says taking his seat once again.

'Good, that's good. We need to know everything he can remember ASAP. We've been to see Mr McDowell and the late Mrs McDowell who, as we all know, is no longer deceased.' Gill tells the guys with more than a hint of sarcasm in his voice. 'Melanie McDowell was the one who requested that her sister return from the States, under instruction from Ronnie and it was also Melanie who set her sister up to go to this morning's location. I understand that we haven't, as of yet, been able to get a positive ID from Mac, but if it walks like a duck? Melanie McDowell was obviously very distressed to learn of her sister's abduction and we have no reason to believe, at this stage, that Melanie knew anything untoward would happen to her. She sent her there, on the pretense of finding answers. The answer being that her mother was alive. It appears, on the surface at least, that the sisters are close and Melanie didn't want to have to inform her little sister that their mother had faked her death. Therefore, arranged that at a certain time, with Polly McDowell in situ in the woods at the rear of the property, her parents would walk out into the garden in full view of Polly McDowell. All seems rather cowardly, but who are we to judge eh?, As I say, Melanie McDowell was extremely distressed to hear of her sister's fate this morning and I can tell you from first-hand experience that I believe her. Later, when we arrived at the property where Ronnie and Maree McDowell are holed up, Melanie was already there and we walked in whilst she was given them what for.' He then gives the team a rundown of our meeting with Ronnie and Maree. He also informs them that my time with the team is over and I will be leaving after this briefing.

When all of the information has been shared, Gill dismisses the team and he and I are left in the briefing room alone.

'So, what's your next move Gill?' I ask, needing to know before I head off.

'Going to call the Yard then wait for Mac to wake up and tell us what he knows. I'm surprised that neither Ronnie nor Billy could come up with the three million in cash.'

'I guess it's just tied up. They own property and land but that's not to say they are cash rich,' I say standing. 'Listen Gill, I need to head out man. It's been a pleasure working alongside you and I hope we can do this once again one day. In the meantime, good luck with all of this,' I tell him as we shake hands.

'You too, Jack. Thank you for all your efforts.'

As I walk out into the main office, I grab my bag and the jacket I have here and say my goodbyes. It all takes less than ten minutes before I am out of there and getting into my car. I pull away and drive for about 15 mins until I reach the place I have been staying in. Making myself a cup of coffee, I dial Garrett who picks up immediately.

'Hey Son, you all done there?' Are his first words to me.

'Yep, all done man. You have a plan right G?' Please God, let him have a plan.

'Okay, first things first, within the next hour there will be a package delivered to your door. I need you to be packed and ready to go the minute it lands. In the package is your burner phone with enough credit on it to last a lifetime. There's a new passport in there so you can travel and new identification papers. The package will be delivered by a driver who will take you directly to the airport where you will collect your tickets. Everything you need to know is in the package including where you need to meet my contact when you arrive.'

'Where am I flying to G?'

'As I said, everything you need to know is in the package. On the burner there are three numbers pre-set. One is mine; I'm sure you'll be able to figure out which one. Jack, son, I need you to understand that whilst everything is set up to move forward the outcome is unknown. I trust you son; I believe in you. But you have to understand me when I say, sometimes… sometimes life can take an unexpected twist, even when you expect it to and whatever happens, you have to believe you have done everything possible to secure Lucie's safety.'

'Polly,' I state flatly.

‘Polly is Lucie. Once she is back with us safely, then she returns to being just Lucie. How she is referred to in the meantime is of no consequence to our mission.’

‘How much does Cassie know G?’ I need to ask. I can only imagine that Cass is going out of her mind with worry. Like a mother would. Cassie has always been a ‘motherly’ figure to me without being a surrogate mom but I know her relationship with Lucie is different to mine. Lucie and her share a mother-daughter bond, the kind you would expect from her real mother if she wasn’t such a piece of useless shit and hadn’t dibbed out when Lucie needed her most. Fuck knows what Lucie will say or feel when she finds out the truth. And yes, call me an asshole but I will be telling her the truth because her parents? Yeah, her parents are never getting within ten feet of my girl ever again.

‘She’s going out of her mind Jack. Her heart is broken and she’s scared. I’ve set her some stuff to do for Lucie’s return which, well, I hope, it’s helping. Busy hands and all that. It’s hard for her without the shop, she’s not used to not being in her routine. Not that she gives a shit. She wasn’t coping being there or being without Lucie so it’s a good thing to walk away at the moment.’

‘I hear you. How’s Dec recovering?’ Again, I need to ask because our Lucie loves Declan and he loves her, as does Carmel.

‘He’s doing good; out of the hospital and now back at the pub. Carmel is handling the day to day running so he can rest but as you can imagine, his version of resting is sitting on a chair at the end of the bar telling Carm what to do. Cass and I went over there to see him as he was desperate for any news on Lucie. I’ll go back and see him tomorrow and give him the update he needs to relax.’

‘Seems like you’ve pulled some magic out of the bag old man,’ I say with a wry smile.

‘Once you get on the road, call me from the burner,’ he says and hangs up.

It takes me less than ten minutes to throw my stuff together in a holdall. I am happy to leave everything else here, just take what I need if I'm going to be travelling. I change out of my current clothes and into my jeans and a Henley then pop a jacket on and wait for my ride.

I'm not waiting long when I hear a package drop through the letterbox. A quick peek out of the window confirms there's a car outside, waiting on me.

Opening the package, I find the phone, a passport plus my ID papers. There's also a credit card and Euros in cash. Also, in the package is a photograph of a man, in his fifties. He looks different to the last time I saw him which must have been around five, maybe seven years ago. He's an old buddy of Garrett's but not FBI. No, Frank Myers is pure CIA. I guess it's Frank I will be meeting first. I don't need to be told protocol here so I move to the sink, grab the lighter from the drawer and set fire to the photograph. Once it's sufficiently burned where the face can no longer be recognised, I grab my bag and head on out to the car.

The driver says nothing to me as I get in and I say nothing to him, merely nod and he puts the car in drive and we are on our way to the airport. After fastening my seatbelt, I turn the phone on and go directly into the contact option. Three names with numbers are in there like G said and yes, I know immediately which one is G. I hit on the name that reads 'Big Man' and wait for him to answer.

'See you knew which one was mine?' He chuckles down the phone.

'Always G, always. I'm meeting with Frank?' I ask even though the answer is already known to me.

'Yeah, he'll be at the airport to collect you. Just go straight out to the arrivals area and he will find you. Once the meet is done, Frank will go through everything else.'

'Okay. In the meantime, I need you to get hold of Melanie.

Unlike the fucking idiots who are Lucie's parents, Melanie does give a shit and she will want to be onboard. I'm going to text her number now to your personal cell. Like the parents, Melanie will be being watched, of that I have no doubt, but that will take time to set up so I need you to get her out of the country sooner rather than later.'

'And we trust her, Jack?' Garrett questions.

'Yeah man, she's nothing like Lucie, but she's a good person. She's angry though and I think she's ready to kill her parents over what has happened. There are two brothers too. I don't know what she has told them, if anything, or what they may already know. It might be that they were in on the plan. Who the fuck knows?' I remark, feeling my own anger boil up again at what her parents have done.

'I'll deal with it Jack, just get yourself to the airport and meet Frank. Talk soon son. Be careful,' and with that he promptly hangs up again.

It takes less than an hour to arrive at the airport and once we arrive I head straight for the airline quoted in the notes and collect my ticket.

Less than two hours later, I am on a flight bound for Lyon, France.

As my bag is only carry-on I'm out in the arrivals hall in less than 40 minutes. Before I even get a chance to look around, I feel a hand on my shoulder and turning, I find Frank Myers. THE Frank Myers. CIA legend, if there is such a thing. This guy, to my knowledge, retired some years ago but looking at him now, I'm not sure if that's true or he will always just be CIA. Trust me when I tell you they're not easy to spot but if you know an agent, they just have this way about them.

'Jack,' he says grasping my hand in a firm handshake.

'Frank, good to see you.' I tell him earnestly. One thing that's going to make this plan work will undoubtably be Frank. He's not a legend for nothing.

'Let's go,' he says to me walking away and I duly follow.

In the parking lot is black Lexus with a driver. 'You don't drive over here Frank?' I ask as we get in the back seats.

'No, son. The French are crazy bastards driving; this old man can't be doing with all that. Let a local drive and deal with the road rage,' he says laughing. I watch his eyes crinkle as he does. He looks older, hell he is, but you can see there's everything still going on in his brain.

'I have a secured office in the city. We can talk once we get there,' he tells me then turns away to look out of the window.

If my mind wasn't running at a million miles per hour, I would probably take in the scenery. I'm sure it's beautiful but I can't function right now on a relaxed level and so I close my eyes and don't open them again until Frank touches my arm and tells me that we've arrived at the destination.

Getting into the office that Frank has is pretty extensive, like a mini Fort Knox. His Fort Knox includes, amongst other security procedures, retina eye scan.

'You know who is based here in Lyon, Jack?'

'Interpol I believe?'

'Yep, about 10 minutes from here. It's handy you know?' He says laughing as he makes towards a coffee machine. He holds up an empty cup indicating the question of if I want one.

'Yeah, please. Just straight up black.' I need caffeine. My head hurts from the last 24 hours and I need to hit the reset button if I am going to do any good.

'Jack, I know you don't want to hear this right now, but I am telling you. Before we start you off, I need you to get some sleep. I'm not saying a straight 12 hours but you need to have some energy in the bank. I suggest we drink the coffee, go over the plan, eat a decent meal, then you get some shut eye. We can't meet with Thierry until tomorrow morning anyhow,' he says passing my coffee over to me.

'Thierry?'

'Thierry Artus. Interpol. He's a good man. I've known him nearly thirty years. We can trust him. May not always like his methods but he'll help and we need him. By God, Jack, do we need him.' He tells me emphatically.

'Okay. I hear you Frank, although I'm not sure I am going to be sleeping all that well you know?' He nods as he takes a seat opposite me.

Sipping his coffee eyeing me over the top of the mug, he briefly shuts his eyes. 'Jack, you will thank me later for the sleep you are going to have.'

I run my hands through my hair trying to relax. Garrett and Frank have a plan. I need to trust in that and listen. I nod and Frank begins with the outline of how this is going to happen.

'Tomorrow we will meet with Thierry. He is in charge of an agent called Guillaume Clermont. Clermont is Olga's handler and Olga is Interpol's woman where Lucie is being held.'

'You know where she is Frank? Why the fuck are we sitting here when we could just go and get her if we know where they have her?' I shout at him, raging inside.

'We extract according to Interpol. They have been working on finally nailing this family for a long time. If we go in, all guns blaring, not only are they likely to lose their agent Olga, but there's a chance it could blow their whole plan to pieces and I have made assurances that we won't do that. We have to play it their way Jack, or this deal? This plan? It's off.'

'Where is she Frank? Here? In France?' My heart is beating out of my chest. I can't believe they know where she is.

'No Jack, not here. I don't know exactly but I do know it's in

Albania. So, tomorrow we meet with Thierry and then the next stage is to get you to Albania to meet with Guillaume.'

'Is he there alone?'

'No man, there's fucking hundreds of agents from Interpol and other agencies all over the Balkans, so no matter what, you're never alone. I believe that Guillaume has a team of 14 but he is Olga's official handler. Thierry has arranged for you to get to Albania and to meet with Guillaume. He will take the lead in your girl's extraction and will arrange for the both of you to get out of the country when it happens. You will fly to the Netherlands. From there you will be back in my vicinity and I will be arranging for your transfer back to the States with Garrett. Now finish your cup of Joe and let's go eat so you can sleep,' he says standing up to place his cup in the kitchenette.

I can't remember the last time I ate and although I don't feel hungry, I'm not going to argue with him when I know I have no hope in winning.

FIFTEEN

Melanie

I didn’t go back home after the showdown with my parents. I just couldn’t face the boys yet. They’re probably climbing the walls whilst they wait for my return but they won’t go against me. They won’t go out there looking for information and bringing trouble to the door.

Ever feel like you are having an out of body experience or somebody is playing some elaborate joke on you? It’s kind of how I feel right now as I sit at my desk in my office with my head in my hands. The anger that is burning in me is in danger of catching fire, coursing through my veins like lava.

‘When this is over,’ I say to myself out loud, ‘when this is over, I will no longer have any parents. I will think of myself as an orphan. Fuck them and if my brothers side with them, then fuck them too.'

I need an outlet to alleviate me of this fury before it takes over.

I head to the door and see Sammy Dean working up a sweat against a bag. I didn't even bother to say hello when I got back but I knew he was here and I'm pretty sure he saw me.

I can't think of any other way to clear my mind, even if it will only be short-term and so I step out of my office and make my way to him.

'Hey Sammy, you got five minutes?' I ask casually, not wanting to speak out here in front of people.

'Sure,' Sammy responds with a knowing smile, wiping his hands on the towel that is hung around his neck.

We make our way back over to my office and as soon as I am over the threshold I head to the only window, the one facing the car park entrance and drop the blind.

I hear Sammy chuckle behind me. Turning on my heel, I look at him quizzically to see what's funny and watch him as he smiles over at me whilst reaching behind himself to lock my office door.

'You feeling angry Mel?' He asks.

'What makes you say that?' I counter.

'Well, princess, you walk out there, a woman on a mission to collect me. Come in here and the first thing you do is drop the blind. I know I'm in for a good fuck Mel and I know you're at your best when you're angry,' he says walking towards me.

He's not wrong. I do fuck him when I'm angry; only ever him. He never makes me feel fragile or weak. He gets off on my strength and he just angry fucks me back. Two peas and all that.

'If you're not up to it Sammy, I can find someone else,' I tell him as I back up against the wall by my desk. I fucking love watching him in his advance towards me. He's a big guy but he's actually quite graceful; like most pro boxers. He doesn't swagger, he doesn't need to. He knows he's hot, to me at least. I like to pretend he's nothing to me, but I know he sees through that lie, even if he doesn't acknowledge it. But the truth is, angry or not, he's the only man that I have sex with. Not that I've told him that. Fuck, he lets me get away with being the one who always chooses when we have sex but I'm not letting him know he is the only one I choose to share my body with. But fuck, he's so good and right now, I need him.

'Fuck the anger out of me Sammy,' I ask of him as he places one hand on my hip and his other slides into my hair at the back of my head and grips it hard.

His mouth slams onto mine. There's no warning, no warm-up, no gentle coaxing as his tongue plunges into my mouth and we immediately begin our battle.

The hand on my hip travels lower, bunching my skirt in his fist as he yanks it further up my thighs. Instantly, we're a mess, we're on fire for each other. I'm tugging at the waistband of his shorts as he pushes my panties aside so he can push his fingers inside of me. Rage or not, nothing can stop me riding his magical hand. Not for the first time, I wonder how he manages to turn me on so much with just his fingers. All the while, he's licking, sucking and biting at my neck and clavicle.

'Fuck Mel, why do you always have to feel so good? Spread your legs babe, I've got to taste you,' he says, falling to his knees. I don't get time to mourn the loss of his hand before his mouth is on me.

I lose my train of thought and I couldn't care less. He is simply magical. He is the unicorn. Jeez, no wonder I never have sex with anybody else.

'Sammy, get inside me, I need to feel you inside me,' I whine.

Rising from his knees he goes straight back to my mouth with his kisses. His left hand lifts my leg under my knee whilst his other positions himself at my entrance. No sweet talk. No coating himself, just thrusts right in and damn, if I don't love it. Our 'lovemaking' is frantic, hard and like always, fucking glorious. When we both finally come, hard and loudly, Sammy holds me. In our messy state of undress, he just holds me and I let him.

A sob lodges in my throat. I don't cry, I am NOT a crier but in this moment, when I am filled with fear and sorrow, I give myself permission to break down. And I do. And just when I think my crying is going to lead to some sort of panic attack, Sammy begins to brush the hair away from my face, kissing my tears, instantly calming me.

'Whatever it is, I'm here darling. I'm always just going to be here, waiting for you to come to me, not with anger in your eyes but with the chance to see how good we might actually be together,' he says quietly. I am about to answer when he speaks again. 'Don't say it Mel, don't shoot me down again. Just know that I don't just love the Melanie with a fire in her belly but I also love the Mel that's soft and giving. I want both of those Mels. All you've got to do is say the word and I'm there. For the record Mel, I don't fuck around with other women. There's only you and it's been that way for so long, I'm in danger of losing my man-card.'

I hiccup a laugh as I look up at him. I know he means his words. I know that inside the big, muscular exterior is a sweetheart. He doesn't know that I did some digging around about him when he first registered with my gym and long before we started having sex. I know he's handy in the ring, I know that he takes no prisoners, but I also know that he's loyal, hard-working and a dog dad; who doesn't love a dog dad? I've seen him running around Lexton Park with his stupid retriever and have walked away with a smile on my face.

'I know Sammy, I just need time,' I tell him, buttoning up the blouse I didn't even know was undone as he puts himself back into his pants.

Gently, he kisses me on the forehead. 'Just let me know when you're ready beautiful,' he says quietly then calmly makes his way to the door and steps out of my office.

On shaking legs, I sit back down at my desk just as my phone lights up with an unknown number. As a rule, I have no issue answering calls from unknown or withheld numbers, happens all the time, but when I answer I thank my lucky stars that I do.

'Is this Melanie?' Asks the voice. Male, American.

'Yes, who is calling?'

'Melanie, my name is Garrett. I am a close friend of your sister; she works with my wife Cassie.'

'Hello Garrett, I know who you are. Polly talks about you both often. What can I do for you?' I have no idea why he could be calling me or how he would have got my number.

'Jack gave me your contact details. I'll be flying to the Netherlands within the next 48 hours and I'd like us to meet up. Is that doable for you?' He questions.

'Yes, that's doable. How long will I be there for?' I will need to make arrangements for the gym so I need at least a little guidance.

'I'd like to be specific honey but I can't say. Could be days, could be a week or so,' he's not giving much away but it's the vagueness that is more comforting that anything else. He doesn't know how long, so I can only hope that means one thing: at some point, the Netherlands is where my sister will be.

'Should I book somewhere to stay Garrett?'

'No, I will text you the address of where you are staying and the arrangement is live now so get there as soon as is convenient with you. But Melanie?' He starts.

'Yes, I know. I know what you are going to say. I will make sure I go undetected.'

'Good girl. See you there,' he says before clicking off. I stare at the phone in my hand taking a few deep breaths.

I shout Jimmy to come into my office. He's my number two here and the only person I would trust with my business.

'Yeah Boss,' he says with a flirty grin as he walks into my office.

'Jimmy, I've got to go away for a while, maybe a week or even a bit longer,' I tell him as I gather everything I need and pop the items in my bag.

'Where ya going?'

'Oh, an old friend needs me. She doesn't have anybody else and could do with a friend right now so I said I'd go to her. She's in Edinburgh,' I tell him looking down in case he catches me in my lie.

'Oh right. That's fine. I'll keep it all ticking over. Anything in particular I need to know before you go?' He inquires.

'No, not that I can think of,' I tell him. I genuinely can't think of anything but I'm sure even if something springs on him, Jimmy will be fine.

'Right, sorry for the short notice but I'm out of here. See you soon Jimmy,' I tell him making my way out of the door towards my car outside. I hear a 'see ya' on my way and wave my hand behind me so he knows I heard him. I don't look in Sammy's direction as I leave, but I know he'll be watching me.

I need to run home and collect my passport. Not my real passport but the one that Dad got me a few years ago. He called it an 'insurance policy'. As much as I fucking hate him right now, I am grateful that he did that. I've never used it until now, why would I? At the time, I'd laughed but I'm not laughing anymore. Travelling under a false name is perfect and it's not like the old man is in any position to dob me in for using it. Although given the last few hours, I would no longer put it past him if it meant getting his way.

I have the passport and a week's worth of clothing thrown into a bag and I am back out of the door within half an hour.

I book an Uber to collect me and take me to the airport and an hour and a half later I'm there, I have my ticket and the address for where I am to meet with Garrett and I'm on my way.

Grabbing a cab at Schiphol airport I head to the address I have been given on Oudezijds Voorburgwal, which is apparently a bit closer to the Red Light district than I would prefer but it's not like I'm going to be playing tourist during my stay.

As we pull up to the house number I have, I exit the car with my bag and look out over the canal thinking how incredible it would be to live here and wake up to this view each day.

I ring the doorbell once and a lady opens it with a smile.

'Melanie?' She asks.

I return her smile and confirm that yes, I am Melanie.

She takes me up a narrow flight of stairs to a bright red door and opens it up to allow me to walk through. The apartment is beautiful, huge windows, almost floor to ceiling. Wooden floors and industrial I make for a truly spectacular place to stay.

'The fridge is fully stocked and I have popped my number on the counter in the kitchen so if you need anything else, please call me.'

I thank her and close the door as she leaves. I walk around the apartment and note that there are two bedrooms both with en-suites. I'm not sure how long I will be here on my own but I have my phone, if Garrett contacts me again and so I quickly hang my clothes up in the wardrobe of the bedroom I have picked and walk back into the kitchen to see what I can find to drink. I'm glad I managed to remember to pack my iPad so I can at least while away the hours whilst I am waiting on Garrett to arrive. I have no desire to leave this place and go anywhere so I log onto my email to check for any new messages.

Nothing in particular needs my attention right now but I note that now that my phone has connected to whatever network is running here, messages are popping up on my screen.

Messages from my parents.

Messages from each of my brothers.

I can't bring myself to read them right now and instead log into my Netflix app to watch a film.

I wake up a few hours later realising it's now dark outside and I haven't eaten, or that's what the rumble in my stomach is telling me even if my heart wants no part of it. Looking in the fridge I see there is cheese and start opening cupboards because if there's cheese there must also be some kind of crackers here too.

Once I've eaten, I decide to change into my pj's and open the doors to the Juliet balcony which is in the lounge area. There's a bottle of red wine on the counter and fuck it, I need a drink I think pouring myself a large one.

I haven't smoked since I was twenty-two but I picked up a pack when I was at the airport because for the first time in forever, I know the only thing that will calm me down is a smoke.

Standing looking out to the canal, I can't keep my thoughts off of my baby sister. I speak to the universe and ask for her total protection. I hope it's listening.

Some hours later I find myself waking up on the sofa again when I hear the door being opened. I am up on my feet instantly with my heart beating rapidly.

An older man walks into the apartment and gives me a warm smile.

'Hey Melanie,' he says.

Garrett. I instantly calm and walk toward him as we both hold out our hands to shake them in introduction.

'Would you like a coffee?' I ask him, knowing that he must be exhausted after a long flight here.

'That would be great,' he tells me as he dumps his bags on the floor and puts his hand luggage bag on one of the chairs at the little dining table.

Getting the coffee is easy and I make a mental note to invest in a

Nespresso when I get home. Passing Garrett his drink, he asks how I'm doing.

'Well I slept, which I didn't think I'd be able to but now, I guess I just need to know what's going on and why I needed to meet you here.'

'Okay, let's get down to business,' he says pulling a note pad and laptop from his bag. 'Let's discuss the plan for Lucie's safe return.'

'Your Lucie, my Polly,' I tell him with a sad smile.

'Yes, indeed,' he confirms, with a sad smile of his own. 'Jack is now in Europe too. He met with an old buddy of mine, who has contacts all over the place including Interpol. The men that took your sister are very much wanted by the authorities so whilst I don't know exactly where they have her held, they, Interpol, plus other law agencies, will do. Jack will make his way across to Albania where he will meet with my contact's guy. It's important for you to understand Melanie, that much to Jack's annoyance and mine to a certain extent, we can't just turn up there all guns blaring and get Lucie ourselves. They have people working undercover in these groups and we can't risk playing with their lives so that means that, however frustrating it might feel, we have to follow their lead and do this their way,' he tells me. I nod. I get it, of course I do. Yes, I want nothing more than my sister safe and returned to me as soon as possible, but equally, I do see, or at least I try to understand, that we need to play by a different set of rules.

'The contact that is meeting with Jack is the handler for an agent on the inside. The agent, a woman, knows about your sister and is tasked with protecting her. I don't know these people, nor do I know this agent, obviously and I can only hope that she can give Lucie all the protection she needs until we reach the point of extraction.'

'Firstly, thank you,' I tell him sincerely. 'Thank you for helping and using your contacts. My sister means everything to me and yeah, it's frustrating but I don't want you to think I'm ungrateful. What can I do? I presume you called me here to do something?' I ask him, almost hopefully. I've never been a twiddling my thumbs kind of girl so I would rather do something.

'That's not actually why I asked you to meet here,' Garrett stops and looks me directly in the eyes. 'When Jack and the contact he is going to be working with extract Lucie, they will make their way back here. Melanie,' he begins, looking down at his hands on the table then back up to me with a sigh. 'Melanie, as I said before, I don't know how long it will take to get your sister. Until the point of her extraction, I can tell you nothing of what is happening. I swear I wish I could know myself. Therefore, I can offer you no guarantee of how she will have been treated, what sort of condition we will find her in, or if, please God she won't be, but if she has been hurt in any way. We have no way of knowing any of those things as of yet. What I can say is that when Interpol set this whole thing in motion with your uncle, he apparently made it clear to the Albanians that Lucie/Polly was not to be hurt in any way. We can only pray that they keep to their word. The reason I asked for you to be here is that your sister is going to need you. Jack will return with her, of that I'm sure, but she is going to need you too. I hope you don't feel like I have called you here on false pretenses, it's not like either of us have much to do other than wait,' he explains.

'No, I don't feel like that. Do I wish there was something I could do? Of course. But you're right, I want to be here when Polly is returned. And just so you know, I will absolutely support and encourage, if necessary, but I don't think that's going to be needed, her return to the States. I don't want her going to home, I mean to England. I wish to fucking God Garrett, that I'd gone against my dad's request in telling her to come home. This is beyond my worst nightmare and I know I will feel the same guilt I feel today, for the rest of my life. How can I ever not feel like I made this happen?' My throat gets so tight, I can no longer form words. I just want to close my eyes and wake up with this nightmare over. Even then, even when I shut my eyes briefly, all I see is Polly. Polly crying. Polly being held against her will. I don't close my eyes for long as the images become too much for me to handle. I pray my imagination conjures up untrue pictures of her. I pray she is safe and stays that way until Jack can reach her.

I don't know Jack but I do know what Polly has told me about him and this means all I can do is put my full trust in somebody who I barely know but, at the very least, loves my sister enough to go into battle for her.

'Can Jack do this? Can he really find her?'

'Honestly, I wish I could tell you that this will be over soon, but I can't. What I can tell you is that if anybody can find her, Jack will. I suggest we try as much as possible to just be patient. That's all we have honey,' Garrett explains.

The next few days, weeks, who knows, are going to drag no matter what we do. I once again focus on my inner strength, staying angry with my parents and pray for my baby sister.

SIXTEEN

Jack

Waking up to watch the sunrise is normally one of my favourite things to do. Today, I have an energy and an enthusiasm that seems abnormal given the circumstances, but I want at it today. I have only one mission and that is to get my girl back in my arms and what happens after that I'm not even thinking about.

I received a call a little while ago from Garrett. He is now in The Netherlands, somewhere in Amsterdam and Melanie is with him. They will stay there until I get Lucie and then we, the three of us, will fly back to the States together. Who knows, Melanie might even come back with us.

I'm up, showered, dressed and my bag is ready when Frank knocks at the door.

'Sleep well?' He asks.

'Yeah, I did. You were right; I needed a good night's sleep and I'm keen to get a move on this morning.'

'We're going to meet Thierry in about an hour so I suggest we get a coffee and some breakfast before that happens, as even I don't know how the rest of the day will pan out after that, but we need to be prepared for you to be hitting the road immediately. Got your bag?'

'Yep, I'm all set. Let's get out of here,' I tell him shutting the door behind me.

We stop at a cafe and order coffee and croissants. I'm not a great lover of pastry but it won't kill me. My stomach feels like it's running on nervous energy. My knee is bouncing and I seem unable to control it.

Fed and watered, we head off about 45 minutes later and make our way to a nondescript office in the centre of the town.

The door is opened by a grey haired, bespectacled man who looks as far removed from what I thought he would look like as you can get.

Frank and Thierry exchange greetings before Frank introduces us and we make our way into the office and each take a seat.

'Jacks,' he says pronouncing with a 's' at the end as if my name were Jacques. 'What you are about to do is the most dangerous of exercises. Do you understand that? For I cannot guarantee your safety or that of your girlfriend. I can only offer the help of my man there and you must understand that I am proceeding with this as a favour to Frank. I am breaking Interpol policy which I am sure you understand, is not the done thing, oui?'

'Yes, I do understand that and I am so grateful for your assistance. My aim is not to destroy or compromise your work or that of your agency. My girl being there is bad luck but nothing to do with your investigation. I just need to get into where she is and I will look after us both and take full responsibility for our lives.'

'Okay, let us get down to business,' he says nodding at my words. 'You will be travelling to Albania, specifically to a place just outside of Elbasan. You will take the ferry from Bari, Italy, to Durres, the nearest port to Elbasan. There is a bus that will take you from the port to Elbasan and should take around an hour. You then take another bus to Covokaster. You will be met by Guillaume at the bus terminal. He has lived in the village for just over 9 months now so he knows his way around and will put you up in a safe house where you two will work on the plan for your girlfriend's extraction. I trust by now you are aware of who these people are and of their capabilities?'

'I am aware, yes. I understand that the men who abducted her were the sons of Sokol Kasovolovnic. Frank tells me that your agency has been investigating the Kasovolovnics for some time and are near to completing. I am hoping that the kidnapping of my girl will help strengthen your case rather than hinder it in any way, Sir.'

'I should warn you Jack, that if you compromise Guillaume or this investigation, we will have you removed from the area and if that means by force, then so be it.'

'I understand Thierry, but I am not some novice here. I am adept at going undercover and I have worked within Europe previously. I speak Italian fluently. I'm sure that is why the passport Garrett and Frank arranged for me is as an Italian businessman travelling. I can maintain that facade without much effort,' I tell him. I can feel myself getting riled up and I know that I need to keep a check on that. *'Don't piss off the man who is getting you to within touching distance of Lucie,'* I tell myself.

'Good, then we understand each other, non?' He doesn't expect me to answer but I nod my consent out of politeness.

‘A car has been arranged for you Jack and the GPS has been set to take you directly to the port of Bari,’ Frank interjects. ‘You will need to obtain your own ticket to the ferry but there are many ferry crossings each day so it shouldn’t be an issue. You do need, however, to ensure that the ferry you catch is via Ventouris Ferries. Once you are aboard the bus from Durres please text your arrival time to the number pre-set for Guillaume and he will meet you at the Terminal for the bus. He has your image so you can trust him to find you.’

It seems set up so the only other thing to establish is where the car is parked so I can be on my way. I stand and so do they.

Firstly, I address Thierry. ‘Thank you Sir, for making the arrangements for me. I will honour my promise to not compromise the ongoing investigation,’ I tell him shaking his hand. The truth is I don’t actually care if I do. Actually, that’s not true, I want these bastards caught and to go to trial but if I fuck it up in my efforts to get my girl, then so be it. Turning to Frank, I shake his hand to give him my profuse thanks. ‘Frank, thank you, seriously thank you for everything. I know you have, along with Thierry, stuck your neck out for me. I wouldn’t be here as soon or have the knowledge of where she is without you so from both Lucie and I, thank you.’

‘Well, my boy, when Garrett called me and explained how much this girl meant to you all, it was my pleasure to be able to do all I could. Now get your butt in gear Jack, you’ve got quite the drive ahead of you. I’ll take you down to the car,’ Frank tells me and I nod again to Thierry before we exit the office.

‘Now son, you have a 12-hour drive ahead of you so make sure you stop to eat and rest. You know that even when you get to Elsaban, it’s all going to be about reconnaissance. Knowledge is power Jack. Intelligence is a higher power. I learnt that the hard way a long time ago when I was a young, hungry agent and thought I knew it all. FBI and CIA are different animals, I know that Jack.

Therefore, my best advice is to think like these bastards, play your part, fit in, be unseen, blend. Then fuck them up Jack.'

I laugh as I shake his hand one last time and get into the car. As soon as I start the engine I hit go on the GPS and get myself ready for a long ass drive.

SEVENTEEN

Lucie

I wake with a start, mid nightmare. I couldn't tell you right now if my sleep time nightmare was better or worse than the nightmare I find myself living during the day but when I wake up I am shaking and covered in a sheen of sweat. Brushing the hair away from my face with my hand, I take a few deep breaths.

I look at my wrists and instantly feel tears burning behind my eyes. Before I can stop them they begin to fall and I cover my face with my hands and cry. Up until now I have felt anger, but what if I can't get out of here? What if Jack can't find me? My parents must be going out of their minds with worry. I can't even think about Mel.

My sister is more than my sibling. I know every day I'm here; she will be in her own personal hell.

It's so odd that I haven't really thought of my brothers at all until now. They love me enough to try and find me but hey, we all know they're not the brightest sparks in the box. Regardless, I think given the opportunity, they'd storm the place and in a bizarre way that makes me smile. I think that when I came along, I was not only the baby of the family, but Melanie thought of me as her baby as I was a girl. She has spent my entire life, mothering me and that was long before our mum actually died. Or didn't die, as the case may be today. Thoughts of my mother come into my head but I brush them out quickly. I'm not ready to go there, to think about the lies and the unnecessary grief we all went through.

Instead, I focus on my body and rub the redness and bruising that was inflicted on my wrists last night. Two hours of pure hell. It was painful and humiliating but I know that was the point of them doing that to me.

Last night, Olga was the one who brought me to my room when they'd got bored with me, made sure I was okay and left. I wasn't okay but my mind was fuzzy with exhaustion and so sleep beckoned me quickly. This morning, she re-enters my room and finding me awake, explains to me that their purpose last night was indeed humiliation.

'There have been explicit instructions that, whilst you are not to be hurt during this time, a deal that even these people won't break, they will be determined to humiliate you in any way they please. The issue of keeping you safe, shouldn't be my priority but now is. It's a complication I do not need Polly but one that I will continue to honour. But, and make no mistake, these people? They are unhinged and dangerous in ways you can't even begin to imagine, so you Polly, you need to be on your guard at all times. Make yourself useful. Do what they instruct and hopefully that in itself will keep you safe. I cannot be with you at all times without becoming suspicious myself and I cannot do that. I will not compromise the reason I am here. You think I'm enjoying this? Huh? You think it doesn't turn my stomach to watch them bring girls here who have been abducted? The things I have seen, I will never unsee, Polly and that is mine to live with. And I will. Long after I get out of this place, I will see it forever. I know you are scared Polly; I'm scared for you. There are times that I am scared for myself. But we must be brave. We have no other choice. Do you understand?' She asks.

'Yes, I get it. Last night…last night, I just wanted out of the pain of being chained like an animal,' I laugh ironically thinking how many groups worldwide spend money and resources freeing animals. I don't disagree with their actions, hell, I donate monthly to one such charity but other than hearing about it on news updates, I don't really think about it. I consider myself quite well informed but until now, I didn't even realise what sex-trafficking was. I mean I knew what it was but that was where my understanding stopped. I certainly didn't realise that you would be treated like a dancing bear, even though that in itself is illegal. How the fuck do these people get away with it?

'Will you get all of these girls out of here?' I ask Olga. Some might think I shouldn't care; should only be concerned with myself but I can't be like that. I can't think about myself getting freed without worrying about the fate of the other girls here too.

'When our mission is complete, yes, our intention is to get the girls out safely but sadly, as I don't know how that will go down, their safety, I can't guarantee that. In the meantime, I need you to ensure that you keep your head above water. I am not a babysitter Polly and whilst I will do everything I can to help you, you must in turn understand that you need to work with me. I can't afford to be exposed. If I am, then you can say goodbye to everybody's safety and that includes both of us.' She tells me as she moves the door to my 'room' forward. 'Get yourself showered and dressed Polly; you are required in the lounge area within the hour.'

Olga leaves the room as I sit on my bed watching her close the door behind her. My hands are shaking and the pain from my wrists continues to bother me. I need to get myself together so I gather my things ready to take to the shower room. Somehow, I have been given some ointment for my wrists. It was here in my room when I got back here last night. I don't know where it came from or who left it here but I'm grateful. I take it with me along with my other toiletries when I head out a few minutes later to take a shower.

Once I am clean and dressed, I make my way back to the club lounge area where I find all the other girls already waiting.

The lovable Blerta is busy screaming at them, she stops when I enter.

'You,' she says pointing at me. 'Come here.'

I walk towards the stage, where she was standing, just as she walks down the steps towards me. We meet almost in the middle and without warning, she smacks me hard across my face.

My hand instinctively goes onto my face, feeling the heat of her slap and the immediate anger I feel. I'm no warrior, but in the real world, if somebody slapped my face, I wouldn't just stand there like I'm doing now without retaliating.

'You're late,' she informs me.

'I didn't know I had to be here at a certain time, I apologise,' I tell her, making sure I keep eye contact. When this is over, I'm setting my sister on her. Then she'll be fucking sorry but, in the meantime, even if I have to bite my tongue, I won't cower to this bitch.

'You do now,' she says turning away and walking back up to the stage.

I am obviously dismissed from her attention and so I turn on my heel to the nearest seat. My hands are still shaking, more so now than before I left my room. Anger is swirling. It's hard to keep a lid on it. I'm not brave or confrontational like Melanie. I always wished I was a bit more like Mel but here that would probably get me killed.

I try to focus on what the bitch Blerta is saying and catch the last bit where she tells us there will be a VIP here tonight. If she said previously who that was, I didn't catch it. I glance at the girls around me who look nervous but I think that's been a constant state of mind since we arrived and not because of the so-called VIP who will be in attendance later this evening. She proceeds to tell us that the club will be closed until 8pm tonight whilst preparations are made and we should go to our normal 'stations' at that time. I assume I'm working the bar and sneak a look over to Liam. He sees me looking at him and nods at me. I take that as my cue to walk over to him as soon as the 'meeting' concludes.

'Morning darl,' Liam says with what looks like a genuine smile, 'you doing okay?'

Wow…somebody is actually being nice to me. I exclude Olga from that as she has a job to do and has made it clear that she is not my babysitter.

'I'm okay,' I tell him looking down at my shoes.

'How are your wrists? Did you get the lotion I left for you?'

'You left it for me? I didn't know where it had come from. Thank you. I really appreciate you doing that,' I tell him, still feeling the shock that it was him.

'You'd be surprised what I can do darl,' he says with a wink.

Fuck, is he coming onto me? Really? Whilst I am in hell?

'You look shocked Pol? Not everything is what it seems.' I'm not sure what to say so I just nod. 'Right Pol, we need to make sure we are set for tonight, so come around here to my side of the bar and let's get sorted.'

Okay, perhaps he's not coming onto me and suddenly, I feel like I'm going to cry again. One person is being nice and I feel like I am falling apart with gratitude.

We work side by side for hours. Liam tells me at one point to take my shoes off if I want to. Oh, it's so lovely to be out of them. Liam passes me a pair of sliders, they're too big but I don't care. At least I don't feel like I'm about to break an ankle with them.

Shortly before 6pm Olga heads towards us at the bar. 'Polly, go and get ready for this evening. There is a dress hanging up in your room that you're going to wear.'

I nod and give a smile of sorts to Liam who smiles and tells me he'll see me again shortly.

Walking into my room I see the dress immediately. I'm not sure it can actually be called a dress, it seems like scraps of fabric to me but I get myself into it, hating every moment as the fabric lays against my skin.

I brush my hair but then stubbornness kicks in and I think fuck it, this will have to do. They don't care how I look. All they care about is keeping me in this cage.

Walking back into the lounge area I see that the evening lights are on and whilst I smirk to myself wondering if these morons think it makes the place look classy, I am yanked from my thoughts as somebody catches my elbow.

Holding my elbow in a tight grip, I turn to see the man himself, Sokol Kasovolovnic. I know his name now, thanks to Liam. He told me that this club belonged to him and that, just as my initial meeting with him led me to believe, he was not a man to be crossed.

'Little girl, don't you look pretty,' he tells me as he runs his fingers down my face. I try to pull away from his touch but his grip on my arm gets tighter. 'Oh, I love it when they fight back,' he says laughing at me. 'Tonight, little girl, you work the bar and then you dance again. I tell you that I want more tonight, so put effort in, yes?'

I nod whilst thinking about all the ways I am going to get this fucker killed. I don't know how it will happen, just know that it will. I want it to be humiliating and painful.

He pushes me away and even though I stumble slightly, I keep upright and make my way over to the way where Liam stands.

'You okay darl?' He asks me. He's always asking me if I'm okay.

'Yeah, I'm okay, despite being manhandled by that animal.'

'Come on kiddo, let's get sorted.'

'Liam, do you know who the VIP is tonight?' I ask curious that there appears to be so much effort going into the arrival of this person.

'One of the old man's business partners. He's been here before, just the once. Bit of a prick but you'd expect that right?'

'Yeah, I wouldn't expect anything less,' I say and for the first time since being here I let a little laugh go. It isn't funny, but I feel I have a connection with Liam. I know instinctively that he's a good guy. I don't know his story, how he ended up here working for these people and I guess part of me doesn't want to know. I'm scared that if I ask, I'll start to see him in a different light and I don't want to do that. I need the comfort that feeling he's a good person brings me.

Liam hands me a tray of candles and tells me to put one on each table and to light them. As I walk around the tables, placing and lighting the candles, I see Blerta and the other girls walk into the lounge.

I spot Carla, the girl from last night, who gives me a half smile. Even if it's not complete, at least it's warm.

Blerta makes her way up the few steps to the middle of the stage and Kasovolovnic joins her, entering from behind the curtain. She smiles at him and it looks genuine. I hate her even more in this moment. I wonder briefly if she sleeps with him. I'm repulsed at the thought.

'Ladies,' begins the smarmy bastard Kasovolovnic. 'Tonight we will have a full house of hand-picked guests and I expect the best behaviour from each of you. If you let me down, you will regret it. The night will finish when my beautiful Blerta tells you. I expect you to comply with any and all requests made to you by our guests,' and on that cheery note he leaves the stage and heads out of the room. Beautiful Blerta? Fuck he must like them rough.

Blerta continues to stand on the stage looking smug. 'Our guests will start arriving soon so get to where you should be,' she tells us before descending the steps and walking out past the bar to the foyer. Not that I have been out that far, but Liam told me that is where the door at the end of the bar leads to. I wonder what it's like. What would happen if I just ran? When Liam told me about the door and what lay behind it, he also said not to bother trying to get through it. There are two guys at the front door who, apparently, wouldn't think twice about putting a bullet in me. My need to run is consuming me. I have several emotions throughout the day and all of them are negative. I'm either in tears, angry or feeling like I might have a heart-attack, but the worst feeling is when I think of Jack. But my need to run is the most overwhelming feeling I experience.

I wish more than anything that I had ignored Mel's text message that night; that I'd opted to call her the next day instead of leaving Jack in the middle of the night and flying back to the UK. Not that I blame Melanie, I don't. Perhaps if I had just been honest with Jack as to why I was living in the States and what kind of people my parents were, what my life had been like growing up but I didn't. I didn't want him to sit in judgement of my family or me. I didn't want to give him a reason not to love me and then by the time I knew his love for me was real, it just felt too late to tell him.

Jack has no family, not blood anyway, just a chosen family consisting of Garrett, Cassie and me. I know I was his family as he was mine. The last time I saw Jack was in the woods and he told me he'd come for me. I believed it then, but I thought I would just be going back to my childhood home and even though I am here now, God knows where, I still believe it. I know he won't stop until he finds me and I pray to God, the universe, that it's soon. I need him. I need him to save me. 'I love you Jack,' I tell him in my head.

I walk back over to the bar as men start entering the club. All of them fit a type; middle aged, slimy looking in ill-fitting suits and repulsive. It's not like any decent human being would want to be here, so all the men here fall into the non-decent category.

The men start to occupy seats at the tables and Liam tells me to go over and start taking orders. I do, remaining polite but standing back from the table just in case any of them try to touch me.

The lounge fills up fast and soon Liam is flat out making drinks and some of the other girls take orders so I can deliver them.

I've just dropped off a tray of drinks to a table when the door opens again and Blerta enters on the arm of a man who I presume is the VIP given her sickly smile.

I make my way to the bar before I take another look. I stop dead in my tracks. I can hear my heart pounding in my ears, despite the music. The VIP is my uncle, Billy Langford.

EIGHTEEN

Jack

This is the longest drive of my life. For business and personal reasons, I've undertaken many long road trips in the past but none of them felt like this. Perhaps it's because everything is so unfamiliar, or perhaps I've never had the urgency to reach a destination like I do now. I have tried to stay within the speed limits, the last fucking thing I need is to get pulled over by either the French or Italian police. I've been on the road now for around 5 hours and decide that I need to stop at the next rest services to use the john and a coffee, maybe something to eat too.

I pull up and decide to shut my eyes for 5 minutes as they feel strained.

I wake up with a start two hours later. Cursing to myself for wasting time but needing to pee now more than ever. I exit the car, feeling the good of being able to stretch out. My back and neck cricks as I straighten up from hours spent slumped behind the steering wheel. The car I am driving is cramped for a tall guy like me. It makes for an uncomfortable journey.

Walking into the rest stop I see several places to grab coffee and after my long-awaited bathroom break, I buy myself coffee, a few bottles of water and snacks.

Sitting back in the car I drink my coffee, thanking the gods for caffeine and for letting me get some sleep. It will power me through the next several hours until I reach the port in Bari. Of all the places I have been to in Europe, Italy is not one of them and I know that this is no sightseeing tour. Enter the country, get to the port and get the hell out of the country. They say that Italy is the most romantic place in the world. If I had Lucie with me, then I'd think a shoe box is the most romantic place.

The ring I bought her, the one I planned on proposing with but woke up the next day to find her gone, is with Garrett and I'm thankful for that. I know he'll keep it safe and I know that once I get my girl home, I can propose to her. Perhaps not how I originally intended but who the fuck cares as long as she says yes. She's mine and I'm hers. 'No' doesn't factor in our lives. I knew within days that she was it for me. And although in the grand scheme of things we haven't been together for that long, what does it matter when your heart knows what you've found? I want the world to know that she is mine. I want her to know that she is and always will be, the most important person in my life. I didn't have that father figure growing up to tell me how to handle romance, but I have observed how Garrett treats Cassie over the years and their love has shown me that real love is not something you take for granted. You cherish it. Protect it. And you never let a day go by where you forget to be grateful for it.

When I finally arrive in the town of Bari I park my car up, careful not to obstruct anything as I am about to abandon it and have no idea how long it will take for the car to be removed. Frank instructed me to ditch it and then catch a bus to take me to the port for my ferry journey. There are several boards up in the port giving the details of the ferry crossing, which appears to not be too long of a journey. Once my tickets are bought, I board the ferry and make my way to the seating area. All you can do during the journey is look out to sea, so I am surprised at how quickly the crossing is and before I know it we are docking in Durras. It takes me a while to find the correct bus that will take me to Elasban but once I'm sitting in my bus seat, I shoot a text to Guillaume to let him know my ETA.

This part of my journey is long, uncomfortable and a bumpy ride. The bus I'm travelling on has definitely seen better years. The seats are ripped and it smells kinda funky on here but that might be something to do with the woman in front of me who's sitting with a chicken in a cage on her lap. Who the fuck takes a chicken on a bus? Two seats across from me, a man sits with a rabbit on his. Nobody seems shocked or bothered by either of them.

As we pull into the bus station my eyes are already out of stalks checking to see if I can spot Guillaume. I disembark a few minutes later and whilst I scan the people around me I feel a hand on my shoulder. I spin to find a man who looks to be in his mid-thirties, wearing black thick-rim glasses with dark hair, greying at his temples. He wears jeans and a thick roll-neck sweater and black gloves.

He gives me a chin-up greeting and holds out his hand to shake mine.

'Guillaume,' he says in a heavy French accent then adds, 'piacere di conoscerti' (a pleasure to meet you in Italian).

I shake his hand with an 'anche tu' (you too).

'Come,' he says leading the way across the bus station forecourt towards a beaten-up old car.

We drive for no more than fifteen minutes before we are out in the countryside where we stop at a small farmhouse.

'This place is safe,' Guillaume says nodding to the house. 'There is also a small flat in the centre of the city, near the castle, for when I need to be there. It is safe also, but for our discussion, it will be better here away from people, non?'

'Yeah man, that works for me.'

We walk into the safe house and it's just like I would expect, like I've been in previously: a simple kitchen, table with just two chairs, a small sofa and a bed. But, as Guillaume mentioned, it is far away from prying eyes which means we can talk and plan with confidence and privacy.

'Would you like some coffee Jacques?' He asks, pronouncing my name in the same way Thierry did.

'Yeah, great, thanks. Going to use the bathroom,' I say.

'It is the door to your right,' Guillaume instructs me, with a point of his finger.

After using the restroom, I come back and take a seat at the table waiting for him to finish making the coffee. He doesn't offer sugar or creamer, just hands me a straight black coffee. I really don't care; hot caffeine is all I need.

'So, tell me what you know about why I am here,' Guillaume asks, taking a sip of his own drink.

'I know that you, Interpol, are watching a sex-trafficking ring, headed up by one Sokol Kasovolovnic. I don't know how many are in his outfit but I know he has some kind of club here and that is where my girlfriend is being held against her will. We believe that Kasovolovnic's sons abducted my girlfriend in the UK and flew her here, with other girls abducted on or around the same day,' I tell him then take a swig of my own coffee. I kept to the basic intel as he probably knows this information already and frankly, I don't actually know much more. I mean I know a few more details but the only reason I am here is to get my girl and get the fuck back home as soon as possible.

'I have a contact at the club, she is one of us and I have got word from her that they do have your girlfriend held there with the other girls. They take many girls but not all survive. These people are ruthless so if a girl causes issues, they simply make her disappear. The club itself is private members only and as such, it is not a place we can just walk into. You must understand that my person and I have been here for nearly one year, one year and we are very close to getting all the information we need in order arrest Kasovolovnic and shut down his operation in its entirety. I understand that this may seem like a long time to have been waiting for us to infiltrate but we need to ensure we have all the players before we attack. Too soon and somebody else, a partner say, can simply get the workers and move to a different location and we have to start again. Sex-trafficking, it is a big problem here in Europe. A problem all over the world, oui? It is my duty to say, that whilst I am very sorry your girlfriend was taken, I cannot allow you to jeopardise our plan. Many hours of time and resources have been put into this operation. It is vital we get all key components. But I will help you, in any way I can, without our mission being compromised.'

'I'm grateful for your help Guillaume. I know how much time and resources go into operations such as yours, but I just want in and out. Get my girl and get the fuck out of here and back to the States as soon as possible. I am happy to follow your instructions to get me inside that club but once I'm inside, I only have one objective and I need you to understand that.'

'I do understand Jacques. I can get you in the club for I, "Signor Giovanni Bianchi" am a member and I may take a guest with me, perhaps, my cousin visiting from Italy?' He laughs.

I raise my cup of coffee which we chink in a cheers motion.

'Let's get to work Jacques. I inform you that we travel around the city for the next couple of days so that you become familiar with where you need to drive away from oui? You will extract your person when we agree the day and time. On that day, a car will be within walking distance of the club and you will take that and travel to a small airfield at Kucovë. From there the pilot is to take you to Holland. There will be no reason for passport checks so it limits information being passed over.'

'Okay, that works. We can map the route, from the city to the airfield, will there be additional support if things get out of hand?' I just need to ensure that I can get some cover here. I'm used to working as part of a team, not that I'm averse to going alone on this but some back up would be good.

'There are various other agents around the city and yes, if necessary, we can bring some out but I'm sure you understand that we would rather not show our full hand until it is necessary?'

'Totally. Fully understood. So, when do we get to take a drive around?' I ask, eager to get this show on the road.

'First, I would suggest dressing a little less American. The club has a strict dress rule, which means we must purchase a suit for you. I suggest we head into town after you take a shower,' he says laughing as he pinches his nose. Yeah, I guess I could do with cleaning up a little, although I didn't realise I smelt bad. Guess you never really can smell yourself?

'There are towels in the cupboard in the shower room, please help yourself.'

I finish the remainder of my coffee and head for a much-needed clean up. It's definitely not the best shower I've ever been in but it's not the worst one either. But at least at the end of it, I'm clean and I won't lie, it's nice to put some fresh clothes on even though they are creased to hell and back.

We set off about half an hour later, just as the sun is setting. Our first stop is to buy the suit I will need. I'm not sure any Italian businessmen, like the one I am to pose as, would ever wear a suit like this, but a suit is a suit at the end of the day. All I need to do is blend in.

Guillaume pulls out a battered map of the city whilst we stop for a beer. I would prefer to do this within the confines of the safe house but I appreciate that he is also trying to give me visual on landmarks to look out for.

The map shows, like many European towns and cities, a maze of streets. From our viewpoint as we sit outside this bar, I can see there is a fair amount of traffic, both car and pedestrian. Some folk are rushing, obviously having finished their working day, whilst others amble along, in no particular hurry. The traffic, whilst fairly heavy, is moving freely. We finish our beer and Guillaume suggests we take a walk in and around the vicinity of the club.

'During the day, the club is officially closed. It re-opens at 5pm each day but the customers, they don't normally arrive before 6pm, after business hours. It is important that we act like any other customer, perhaps like we have finished work for the day oui?' He reasons.

I simply nod, all the while taking in my surroundings more than his words, looking for my own landmarks that will help guide me should I need it. Part of the town is very old and immediately, I see how deceptive getting your bearings could be. As soon as Guillaume informs me that ahead of us is the club, I can feel my urgency to get in there building within me. How can you explain what it feels like to know everything you love and want is mere metres away, but you can't go and get it? Beyond the surrounding walls, caged within, is my reason for living. Walking around and seeing the club, knowing Lucie is somewhere inside leaves me feeling impotent. As we walk around the rear of the club a 'back door' comes into view. I can see that it's metal and I would strongly suspect that it's alarmed up to the hilt. Front door it is then. At this point I'm itching to get moving, get in there, scope it out. Who am I kidding? I just want my fucking girl and to get her back in my arms and the hell out of here to safety. This is not normal behaviour for me; I follow a process and generally that makes me both methodical in my approach and respectful of the team. However, this is extraordinary territory. I'm at a loss to give a shit about the 'how's' and 'why's', thinking only of going in there all guns blazing, finding Lucie and making our escape. That's all I care about. That and making the motherfuckers who took her pay. Scratch that. The motherfuckers who took her and her motherfucking, good for nothing parents. One way or another, they will all pay.

Momentarily I think of Melanie, waiting for us with Garrett in Holland. I know Lucie will want and need her sister and to date, my opinion is that only Melanie actually acts like family. I'm hoping by now she is there and has met with Garrett. Fucking hell, God bless that man. He has contacts everywhere, kind of like the sailor with a girl in every port. I can't even think about Cassie right now. Garrett said she was beside herself over Lucie being taken; I know the feeling. I also know that along with Melanie, Lucie is going to need Cassie more than ever. She'd already been like a mom to her and I'm pretty damn sure, Cassie's maternal feelings for Lucie have tripled in light of recent events.

I tune back into Guillaume in time for me to hear that he proposes we go tonight to scope the club out.

I'm so down with that idea that when he offers we stop for

another beer I find myself saying no, that I'd prefer a coffee. I need a straight head. I'm not planning on doing anything stupid but I do know that sometimes, even the most carefully planned operation, can alter on the spin of a coin. When we walk into the bar, he orders a beer and my coffee and I tell him to give me the keys to the car, that I'm happy to drive back to the safe house tonight so that I can get a lay of the streets ahead of time.

At this point, it's a genuine offer. I have no idea just how tonight is actually about to go down.

NINETEEN

Lucie

'Ah, if it isn't my beautiful niece,' Billy Langford says to me as he stands with Blerta hanging off his arm. 'Don't I get a hello, sweetheart?'

I can't stop myself and don't even think of the consequences as I spit in his face. The moment my saliva lands, Blerta slaps me hard across mine. That woman can certainly pack a punch but I refuse to give her or Billy a reaction.

All my self-defence lessons are pushed back so I don't instinctively take the bitch out. It might be Melanie with the short fuse, I may be viewed as the quiet one, but I can look after myself. It may not be in my nature but I can turn it on when necessary. Perhaps

I'll beat the shit out of Blerta after this has finished and not ask Melanie as planned. The thought makes me smirk. She glares at me. Of course, she does; she's a fucking bitch. THE bitch.

Billy Langford just laughs. Fuck him.

'Pol, come on, don't be a silly girl. I can already see that the lovely Blerta has taken a shine to you. Don't wind her up, kiddo.'

'Fuck you UNCLE Billy,' I say pronouncing 'uncle' with as much sneer as I can muster.

Again, he laughs. I hope when Jack finds me, he blows him out of the stratosphere. Right between his beady little eyes.

'I'll take a whisky, neat, please dear niece,' he tells me. I don't say anything, just turn on my heel and walk the other way towards the bar.

'What the fuck Polly?' Liam shout whispers at me as I walk up to the bar. 'What the fuck just happened?'

'THAT is my uncle. HE is the reason I am here and if they, you or anybody else thinks I'm going to play nice, you can all fuck off.' I am so bloody angry right now; my body feels ready to fight. How dare he turn up when it's his fault that I'm here? That I am living in this hell. He is the last face I remember seeing once they got me on that damned airplane. He was the one who drugged me. Even in my highly emotional state, I know this is bad. Bad for me at least as I'm not sure how I am going to keep myself in check. Adrenaline is pumping hard, spreading heat all around my body. I lock my knees to keep myself upright.

'Well right now darl, get your act together and stop giving them a reason to punish you. Tell me what he wants to drink so you can take it over there to him. I'm not asking you to smile or make nice but toe the fucking party line Polly. You think Blerta won't relish making you her bitch?' He asks me.

I take several deep breaths, closing my eyes, centering myself. When I feel like I can speak normally, I let him know what Langford wants and give him my best fake smile which makes him bark out a laugh.

'That's it darl, game face. All you gotta do is play the game,' he says with a wink as he passes me the order.

Walking back to Langford, tray in hand, each step feels like I'm walking in cement. I have so many questions that I know he can answer but I'm not about to ask them. I wish I could, but even though he could give me the information I want, starting with how my mother is still alive, I have to remember that he's the enemy. My enemy.

'Thank you darling,' he says smiling at me as I place his drink on the table where he sits with Blerta. 'And how are my friends treating you?'

I want to spit in his face again. I want to punch him in the teeth with my bare fist. But I do none of those things, opting instead to shrug my shoulders and say, 'fine'.

'Well, we all know what a woman means when she says she's "fine",' he laughs using air quotes.

The need to punch his teeth down his throat is overwhelming right now. As I go to say something Kasovolovnic walks up to the table. Langford rises to his feet and the two men shake hands then embrace. I feel sick rise in the back of my throat watching these two obvious friends. Kasovolovnic takes a seat at the table and turns to me with that leery smile.

'Get my drink little girl,' he doesn't tell me what he wants but I know before I even turn around that Liam will be on it. Again, I walk back to the bar, again, my legs unsteady under me.

'Here,' is all Liam says as he slides a glass across the bar to me. I take it without speaking and walk back to the centre table where the bastards sit, laughing and joking as if nothing in the world can touch them. I hope that's not true. I hope that somebody blows them both to smithereens.

As I place his drink on the table, I feel his hand cup the back of my thigh. I try to pull away but his grip just gets tighter.

'And what do you think of our new girl, Billy? She is beautiful?' He asks as a question rather than a statement.

'Quite the looker Sol but I guess it runs in the family,' Langford laughs, his eyes locking on me. There's something behind them, something I don't understand but it's probably best if I don't.

'Well, she will put on quite the show for you tonight,' the old man responds.

My skin crawls not just from his hand on my leg but from his comment. I can't be at these fuckers' mercy again tonight; I won't. I'd rather die than feel that humiliation and pain again.

I feel tears of anger and fear beginning to burn the backs of my eyes. At that moment, my friend and saviour Liam calls service.

I tell the men to excuse me and make my way hastily over to the bar. I feel like I am about to have a panic attack; I don't know if it's anger or fear but my chest feels like it's going to collapse and I can't take a breath deep enough to calm me.

'Polly? Polly, look at me,' Liam instructs.

I dare to look up with the tears now swimming in my eyes.

'Polly, calm down. I won't let anything happen to you, okay darl?'

'You can't stop them Liam. The old man has just told Langford that I will put on a show tonight. What does he mean Liam? I can't, I just can't,' I say as the tears begin to fall onto my face.

'Polly, darl, listen to me. I need you to listen okay?'

I nod. I can't even speak. My knees don't even feel strong enough to support me right now so I place my hands in front of me on the bar to steady myself.

'Polly, girls who don't comply get hurt. Do you understand that? They will hurt you Polly and I won't be able to stop them. But if you just do what they say, without fighting back, then you can go back to your room tonight unharmed. Right now, it's your only choice. There are no other alternatives. I know you're frightened but you need to just do what they say. Polly, tell me you understand me?' He gently requests.

Again, I can only nod. My body now feels rigid in fear but there's something else there and I know it's anger. Dad always used to say that nobody should ever go down without a fight. As humans, isn't our natural instinct to fight back when we are in danger? Neanderthal men lit fires to keep wild animals away. I need to light my own fire. These people are worse than wild animals. I look over my shoulder to see that the table of fuckers are laughing together. I don't know if it's at my expense and I shouldn't care if it is.

I turn back to Liam who is leaning on the bar looking at me.

'Okay,' I respond. But it's not okay. He will just keep trying to console me if I don't accept and agree to his words. He is my only friend. Olga told me that she would protect me but fuck it if she isn't doing a lousy job right now. She can go fuck herself too.

I hear the music turn up a notch in the club and look back around to see the first of the girls sauntering onto the stage. My heart breaks for these girls. Will they ever get out of here? What happens to them when they are no longer deemed acceptable to these people? I'm not naive. I know they are not going to be given a pension and told to be on their way and enjoy the rest of their lives. These people wouldn't allow them to be free, free to talk, free to tell whatever authorities about this place and the people who run it. So, what happens to them? I can only think of one option and it makes my blood chill to ice.

The girl onstage looks slightly out of it. Her eyes are blank as she stares at nothing in particular. She dances and strips her clothes from her body. Not that she came out wearing much to start with. The 'theme' here is young girls. School uniform seems to be a popular choice; making these young girls appear even younger obviously gets the sick crowd going. Before the music ends another girl enters stage right. She starts to move as the first song ends and hers begins. And so it goes on.

There has quickly become quite a crowd in tonight. I wonder if they are all associates of Kasovolovnic or just a random selection of perverts? The old man has greeted a few; well they came to the table to shake his hand.

Thankfully, Liam and I are busy so I hope that means that they have forgotten about me. I have been to their table many times to replenish their drinks and Blerta seems to be overly enjoying Langford's company. I wonder if they are lovers? If they are, that's a truly repellent thought, although they deserve each other. If they are, I hope she's a mean bitch to him too.

I look up to the clock above the bar and notice that it's already 10pm. When you don't leave somewhere and don't get to see any natural daylight it's so difficult to keep a handle on night and day. You work when they tell you to and go to bed when they tell you to. Hell, it could be 10am for all I know.

There is no fresh air here, just a recirculated stale odour. I wonder if the customers notice that? Not for the first time I think of where I could be. I presume I am in Europe somewhere given the accents but fuck knows.

'Liam, where are we?'

'In the club, Polly,' he says on a soft laugh.

'No, I mean, where are we? Which country are we in?'

Liam looks down and takes a deep breath. I know he feels our friendship. He's been so lovely to me. He has been my friend but right now he doesn't look like he wants to answer my question.

'Liam? Please?'

'We're in Albania darl,' he says softly.

'Albania?' I repeat.

'Yes. Now no more questions Polly. Go take these drinks to

table seven,' he says turning his back on me.

Albania. That's near Greece right? If I could get away, could I get to Greece? Surely somebody would help me there? I make a decision that no matter what, no matter what it takes, I need to save myself. I need to escape and right now I have no idea how I am going to do that. But if I can get to Greece. I can't even think about the logistics of getting into another country by foot. I could hitchhike but how long would it take me? I don't think Albania is a large country but how would I know which direction to go in if I don't even know where I'm starting from? Okay, calm down, my inner voice tells me. Planning can wait for tonight. Don't obsess. I stop myself from falling down that rabbit hole, instead, I do as Liam requests and take the drinks over to the table. On my walk back to the bar, Kasovolovnic grabs me by the wrist.

I stop dead in my tracks and look down at my feet, my breathing rapid.

I see out of my peripheral vision Blerta rise from her seat. My heart is pounding.

'Gentlemen,' she says walking around towards me, 'please enjoy the show'. As she walks past Langford he slaps her arse and she giggles. Save me, please somebody just save me.

Blerta takes my other wrist and pulls me along towards the stage. I try to resist by pulling backwards but this only makes the bitch laugh. More tears threaten the back of my eyes. God, when did I become such a crybaby?

She all but drags me back up the short stairs of the stage and behind the curtain.

'Do you remember your moves little girl?' She asks me.

I stare blankly at her as she throws her head back and laughs, obviously amusing herself at my discomfort.

She turns to another older lady who I haven't seen before and speaks in a language I don't understand. The other lady nods and takes my hand leading me away from Blerta. I should feel relief that I am away from her but my gut instinct tells me not to. I know what they are going to try to make me do and I won't do it. I won't. They can beat me black and blue but if those fuckers think that I am going to be their dancing animal they are going to have a long wait on their hands. Liam is wrong. I will not comply. I know I can't get out right now, I can't escape without a plan, but I can't just lie down and let these people do this to me.

The older lady takes me to the back and in broken English tells me to undress. I stand stock still and stare at her. She tells me again to undress.

I don't move a muscle. I just stand there and stare at her. From behind me Carla appears. She gives me a weak smile. They converse in their own language and both look at me.

'Get undressed,' Carla gently tells me. I look pleadingly into Carla's eyes. I know that out of everybody I have met so far that there is a kindness to Carla. I don't know if it's because of what she has obviously endured here or whether it's just her resilience that has been broken but she doesn't have the dead eyes of Blerta.

'Please don't make me,' I say quietly in a voice I barely recognise as my own.

Carla reaches out and takes my hand. 'Polly, you have no choice. You must get undressed. They will hurt you if you don't do what they tell you to do. Just do this Polly and it will be over.'

'No. No!' I shout.

I feel footsteps stomping closer from behind me. I don't hear another noise but I feel a pinch to the side of my neck. My hand goes there instinctively as I whirl around to see Blerta with a syringe in her hand. It's empty. Whatever was in there is now in my body and as I acknowledge that thought, whatever it was, it's now beginning to affect me. I don't feel dizzy but I can feel myself smile. Why am I smiling? I feel hands on me, feel my clothing being removed and even though I know they are doing it, I can't seem to be able to stop them. I feel like I am floating. I don't even know if I am still standing. But I feel their hands on me. I want to bat them away but I can't. I don't feel able to move my arms.

I hear voices around me in conversation but it just makes me smile because it's not like I would understand anyway right? That's funny.

I think I am being dressed again. I hope they are taking me back to my room. I do feel tired so I hope that's what they're doing. I can feel myself smile again and I can hear Blerta laughing. Perhaps I said something funny. I don't know, did I speak? I laugh too. It's nice to laugh. I love laughing. I hope I get to go to sleep. I am very tired now. I can feel somebody either side of me and they are walking me. That's nice, they're taking me back to my room.

Something cold slides around my wrist. It doesn't hurt but it feels cold. I hear metal on metal but I don't know what they're doing but then something goes to my other wrist and I can feel my body being supported by something. It doesn't feel bad. It makes me smile. I can hear music. I love music and although I don't know the words to this song, I hum along. Am I singing at the Moon tonight? Oh, I hope Jack comes to see me sing. Jack. My Jack. My forever love. I'm going to ask him to marry me tonight. Just me and him forever. I love him so much. I love Jack. Perhaps I'll ask him after I finish this song.

TWENTY

Billy

'Tonight's entertainment will amuse you Mr Langford,' Kasovolovnic says.

I can't help feeling that I very much doubt his words. I have spent my evening so far catching glimpses of my niece. If her mother could see her right now, I am pretty sure I would be a dead man.

Polly is scared, that much is obvious. What worries me more is the look in her eyes. I know that look. My sister trademarked that look when she was around eight years old.

I was walking home from school one day with a couple of mates when we heard a commotion going on up ahead of us. All we could see, as we ran towards it was a circle of kids and lots of shouting and screaming.

Not knowing what was going on, we pushed our way into the crowd only to find Maree bashing the living shit out of a kid who was at least two years older than her and about a foot bigger.

She was straddled across his chest, beating his face. One blow after another, alternating fists. Scrambling into the middle I picked her up around the waist but she wasn't done. She was still kicking this kid and screaming her head off.

I managed to drag her out of the crowd by holding her in a head lock! All I could think was that our Ma was going to go mad when she saw that Maree's school dress had been ripped.

The crowd started to disperse, kids not even looking back to Maree or even the kid still lying on the ground. The excitement over, it was time for them to go home.

'What the feck was that about?' I asked my sister.

'He said that all girls were bitches,' was her reply as she looked up at me through her eyelashes smiling. And that was when she trademarked her look.

That look told me that no matter what, she wasn't done. Wasn't beat. And you'd be wise to watch your back.

I pray silently to God that Polly won't use the look I saw in her eyes.

This whole thing is a shower of shit already and I swear if anything happens to Polly, Maree would never forgive me. And after that, I would have no say in what Maree would do. But I know it wouldn't be good.

Kasovolovnic is saying something to me but I haven't been listening, too lost in thought but he has a smile on his face and is laughing at something, no doubt his own humour. When this mess is over, I will deal with him myself. I smile at him thinking that actually, perhaps I should let Maree loose on him.

‘She will be out soon,’ he says. I have no idea who he is referring to, but nod in understanding, lest him be aware of any duplicitous actions on my part.

When I look at the stage, I can’t see or hear anything other than the pounding of my blood as it suddenly races around my body after seeing my niece handcuffed to a pole in the centre of the stage.

I look at Kasovolovnic who’s smiling at me, no doubt waiting for my congratulations.

Looking back at Polly she looks odd. It hits me immediately that she is fucking out of it. Drugged. No doubt about it. Her legs are buckling under the weight of her slight frame. She is only being held up by a hook to which the centre chain of the handcuffs is linked through. Although standing on her own feet, she has no idea what is happening to her. The smile on her face is mask-like, her eyes dead.

What the fuck have I done?

TWENTY-ONE

Jack

'What time will we head into the club?' I ask Guillaume. We've been sitting around for a couple of hours now. He has made it clear that we are not going to enter the club until late so that it has more customers. Guillaume has told me that between 10pm and 11pm is the club's busiest time and we could therefore hide in plain sight.

I'm itching to get inside, I need to see my girl. My skin feels like it's on fire waiting for that moment.

Just after 10.30pm Guillaume settles up our tab in the bar. I still haven't drunk anything as I am still planning on driving us back to the safe house. Guillaume has had a fair few drinks but certainly isn't drunk.

'Remember Jacques, this is reconnaissance work only tonight. You can check out the place and then we make plan, oui?' He says for what feels like the thousandth time tonight.

'Sure, I get it. We won't be making any moves without a plan,' I reply.

We park the car near the front entrance of the club. There is no clientele car park, just a doorway from a narrow but short alley directly off a main road.

My heart is hammering hard in my chest, just like it has been most of the day. Obviously, I don't know where Lucie is exactly but I know she's inside. Close. And as I take a deep breath, I know that it could be moments until I see her.

My fear, the one I haven't spoken to Guillaume about, is that she will ruin our cover if she sees me. But my girl is smart. I know with even the smallest of shakes of my head she would know to play along.

Entering the club, I am reminded of a time in Austin when several people had been held hostage in a bar. After the chaos, we had entered the establishment and it looked just like this; cheap, gaudy and with a bad smell; like fresh air is a commodity these people couldn't afford.

A woman behind the counter checks Guillaume's membership card which almost makes me laugh out loud. As if decent, normal people would enter here. He speaks to me in Italian, as we'd agreed and tells me I needed to sign in.

Once inside the club my eyes go in a million different directions all at once before the moment I look at the stage and my world implodes.

To describe what I am looking at in simple terms is my best dream and worst nightmare combined.

The instant relief and gratitude I feel at finding my girl is demolished immediately when I see her, see what they have done to her. Trussed up and vacant.

In a bizarre moment of clarity, I can hear Bruno Mars 'Gorilla' playing. The moment I recognise the song is the moment I pull the gun from the holster attached to my leg and run at the stage.

I can't tell you what happens in the following moments but I can tell you this; nobody is expecting what is about to go down and my girl didn't even know I was there. All I see in the few moments before I run towards her is her body hanging lifelessly on handcuffs attached to a stripper's pole. I see and hear nothing else.

As I run to the stage, presumably with Guillaume hot on my heels, I see a guy to my right jump over the bar, weapon drawn, but not aiming at me. It's immediate carnage. Men jump up from their seats and run towards the exit and girls start screaming. As I leap onto the stage, I hear a gunshot ring out but either the shooter is a shit shot or the bullet isn't meant for me.

'Stand down,' a guy shouts in English. I think his accent is Australian, but I can't be sure. 'Billy, get down! NOW!' Was his next order.

Grabbing my girl around the waist, I hoist her upwards to free the handcuffs from the hook on the pole.

I push my head through her linked arms because no matter what, wherever I am going now, she is coming with me. Never again will I lose sight of Lucie. Her arms hook around the back of my neck, her head falls forward. She is totally out of it so if we are to get out of here, then it's with me carrying her. As I start to move, her forehead bangs against my clavicle over and over. I don't know what they have given her, but it has rendered her pretty much useless in our escape bid.

More shouting continues around us and more shots are fired. As I turn my body around to face the way we had entered, I see a flood of new men in balaclavas entering the room. Guns are aimed and shouting ensues. They are all wearing dark jackets and Guillaume is shouting orders at them. There are now more of them than customers or staff in the room and the atmosphere changes and charges. I knew the moment I saw her on stage that I was about to fuck this whole operation up but right now, with Lucie attached to me, I'm not one bit sorry. Guillaume's plan was always going to take too long anyway! My girl's life was at risk so his plan means nothing to me right now. Girls are lying on the ground, scattered on the floor and stage, cowering. They don't know right now that they are safe. A woman is in the room talking to Guillaume, more shouting than talking and I presume she is his contact, Olga.

I turn on my heel to see the guy who jumped the bar pointing his gun at an older man on the ground on his hands and knees and a big lump of a guy lying dead next to him. My best guess would be the lump had been the old man's bodyguard.

Slumped and dead in the middle of the floor is an older woman.

'Fucking stay where you are Kasovolovnic,' bellows the guy with the gun and the Australian accent. We catch each other's eyes and he nods at me. 'Get her out of here Jack.' I know I've never seen him before so we definitely don't know each other but whoever he is, he had my back. Making my way towards the entrance I stop dead in my tracks when I notice Billy Langford. Just as I am about to open my mouth he beats me to it.

'Jack, get her to the airfield at Kucovë. There is a plane there which I was going to use tonight. We'll meet you there. Now go, Liam will cover you,' he tells me nodding towards the Aussie. I have no fucking idea what is happening right now, who is on whose side, but I know we need to move now. Guillaume is glaring at me and if I were in his shoes, I would probably be doing the same but there is no time for pleasantries. I don't know who else could be here and that means that even though the team here now taking control,

I need to keep my wits about me. Moving to the front entrance with Liam leading the way and Langford right behind us, we leave by the front door. Of all the ways that I saw this going down, walking out the front door was not one of them. Liam continues to cover us as we make our way down the alley and onto the main street which is littered with cars.

'I have a car,' I tell Liam and cock my head left to indicate which direction we need to go. With the hand not holding Lucie's legs, I grab the car keys from my trouser pockets and unlock the passenger door, carefully placing my girl on the seat and shut the door.

Langford puts his hand on my shoulder. 'Our car is there,' he tells me pointing across the road. 'Follow us closely and whatever you do, don't fucking stop boy,' he says and he and Liam take off to get in the parked car.

'Don't think, just drive', I tell myself. Getting behind the wheel I look at Lucie. She is slumped in her seat, only the seatbelt keeping her upright.

'Baby, if you can hear me, I'm getting you out of here darling,' I tell her, chancing a quick kiss to her hair. She doesn't smell like my Lucie. My Lucie smells of lemons. I swear to God, if she has been hurt, I'll rip the fuckers to pieces.

The drive feels long as we are keeping to mainly back roads, no lights save the moon. I can feel my cell ringing in my breast pocket and put my hand in to fish it out.

'Speak,' I answer.

'What the fuck Jack! I've just had Thierry on the phone screaming like a mad man that it's all gone to shit.' Frank. Shit, shit, shit.

'I won't be apologising, Frank. I wasn't going to sit there and watch the woman I love be strung up on stage like a wild animal,' I shout down the phone at him.

'Jesus Jack, is she hurt?' He asks me. I look to my left where

Lucie remains slumped in her seat.

'She's been drugged man, no fucking idea what with but she's out of the game.'

'Where are you now?'

'I don't really know what's happening but Langford was at the club. When it all started going down, he and a guy who obviously works for him got us out of the club and we are now on our way to the airfield at Kucovë. I don't even know the place; I'm tailing their car. I don't know where the plane should be going, I guess back to the UK but I'll get us to the closest place to Holland. Tell Garrett to prepare for our arrival, man,' I say hanging up.

Up ahead I see the car which has Langford and his guy in it brake and indicate left. Following them, we drive a short while on grass before a small plane comes into view.

Both of our cars pull to a stop and Langford exits his and walks towards us. Getting out the car I decide to take charge now.

'Look Langford, I don't know what the fuck is happening right now but I need to get to Holland.'

'Holland? No Jack. Polly needs to go home to her family.'

And there it is. 'Family? I am her fucking family,' I bellow at him. 'And we are going to Holland, or the nearest place this plane can land to it.'

'Jack, her mother,' he says, dragging his hand down his face. 'Her mother is beside herself. She needs her back,' he says in a pleading tone.

'She should have thought of that before she decided that her daughter could be used as a deposit. We are going to Holland. Her sister is there and she is the only one who I'm going to let near Lucie,' I say.

'Who the fuck is Lucie?' Langford asks me in confusion.

'Polly is Lucie. Lucie is the name she chooses to go by. And that's what she will always be known as.'

The other guy walks over to us as we continue our shouting match.

'Liam,' he introduces himself to me, shaking my hand. 'We need to get going, Billy. Jack, I don't know if she needs medical attention but if she was drugged with the same stuff as they've used on other girls, there won't be any long-term damage, just headaches. But we need to get going. I don't know if anybody is on our tail.'

I walk round to the passenger door and undo the seatbelt and loosen it off of Lucie's body. I gently place her bound wrists over my head again, slipping one hand under her knees whilst cradling her back with my other arm. Liam is once again ahead of us and as we reach the top of the stairs to the aircraft, he turns around to guard Lucie's head from the side of the door. I'm both grateful and pissed at another man touching her.

Walking onto the plane, I gently place Lucie on a seat next to the window. I hold her head and place the pillow that was on the seat on the window frame, gently laying her head against it. Leaning down, I kiss her forehead and give thanks for her safety and then buckle her seatbelt.

There are no stewardesses on board so Langford gets each of us a drink himself. Whisky by the smell of it. I take the seat next to Lucie and put my belt on too. Langford excuses himself and walks into the cockpit as Liam sits down on a seat opposite us.

'You work for Langford?' I ask rhetorically but without understanding.

'Hired me a few months back to keep an eye on things in the club. They didn't know I was linked to him but Olga got me in. Here,' he says fishing some pins out of his pocket. 'Get the cuffs off of her,' I thank him. He might work for Langford, but so far, he's been a good guy.

I nod. 'You knew Langford was coming tonight?'

'I had a fair idea it was him. They'd told us earlier in the day that we had a VIP in attendance tonight and the last time they'd told us that, it was Billy. I knew it wouldn't be long between Polly, sorry man, habit you know? Wouldn't be long between Lucie's arrival and Billy being back.'

'You knew about Guillaume too?' I ask him.

He looks blankly at me and shakes his head. 'No, I obviously knew Olga had somebody here in town as her contact but I didn't know who. I recognise him but he's only been in a handful of times before tonight. He does a good job of making himself just fit in,' Liam says smiling ruefully.

'Well he did until I lost my shit,' dark humour in my laugh.

'Yeah well nobody can blame you for that. It was fucking hard for me not to go up there and get her. But cover is everything. I wouldn't have let anything else happen to her and I didn't know they had drugged her until I saw her on stage. She has been working the bar with me all night,' he says huffing out a laugh.

'What's so funny?'

'Tonight, when Billy walked in, she spat in his face, not realising that I was with him and was there to protect her.'

'He's lucky he's still fucking breathing as far as I'm concerned. Where were you when they fucking drugged her?' I can't keep the anger from my voice.

Liam puts his head in his hands and leans his elbows on his knees. Looking up he scrubs his hands over his face. 'Man, if you don't think I'm as fucking angry about it as you then you're mistaken. I kept warning her to cool her jets, that getting angry was going to lead to them punishing her. What else could I do? I couldn't blow my cover…how was I going to protect her if they found out?'

My heart tells me he's a useless fucker but the rational part of my brain, what little is still working, knows he's right and I should be glad she had at least him looking out for her. Although if he's tried it on with her then all bets are off and I'll rip him to pieces.

‘And before your brain goes into overdrive, I didn’t touch her,’ he says calming my inner thoughts.

At that point Langford walks back towards us and takes a seat next to Liam.

‘I won’t lie to you son, I’ve spoken to my sister and even though she is losing her fucking mind, she has agreed to Polly going to Holland,’ he informs me.

‘Lucie. Her name is Lucie,’ is all I can say.

‘Polly, Lucie, whatever. She’s only agreed to it because apparently Melanie is there. You got something to do with that?’ He counters.

‘Right now, the only family Lucie will want around her is her sister. And yes, I arranged for her to be at the meeting point as and when we arrived.’

‘She wants her back you know? Her mum. She wants her back.’

‘That will be Lucie’s choice. Not mine, not yours or her mom’s. Hers and hers alone,’ and it will be. Regardless of what I think, I will do anything to keep my girl happy. And if she wants to see her parents, then so be it.

‘What’s the plan when you arrive in Holland?’ Liam asks me.

‘We stop there, get Lucie checked out and then we go back to the States,’ I tell him as Langford looks at me raising an eyebrow. ‘If that’s what Lucie wants,’ I continue giving him a raised eyebrow of my own.

The plane starts to taxi down the runway and I stretch my arm across Lucie’s chest to protect her from the surge as we take flight.

Once we are in the air and we can remove our belts, I lift the arm rest between myself and Lucie and lay her head gently on my lap, stroking her hair. It feels like an eternity has passed since I have been able to touch her. Never again will I allow another day to pass when I don’t get to touch her.

I look down at Lucie, as she starts to shift. Her eyes are the first to open and in a panic, she starts to scream.

'Lucie, baby, I'm here, I'm here darling,' I tell her stroking my hand down her hair, my other hand rubbing her arm.

'Jack?'

She pushes herself into a sitting position and immediately tries to get to me. My heart is hammering. I pull her onto my lap and cradle her in my arms as she shakes and cries into my neck.

'Baby, I got you, I got you,' I tell her in a soothing tone. I know she's scared. I need to calm her before she sets eyes on Langford. Her body curls into mine and I have never felt a better feeling in my life. My girl is safe and in my arms. I swear to God I will never let her feel a moment of fear again in her life.

'Jack,' she says on a sob. 'I wanted you to save me so badly. I tried to be brave but I was so scared Jack. I needed you so badly.' My girl is shaking in my arms, crying and all I can do, all I want to do is hold her as tightly to me as possible. For her to melt into me and for me to melt around her. Keep her safe forever more.

'It's okay darling, I'm here and I'm not going anywhere and neither are you,' I say quietly just for her ears.

I look at Liam and he gives me a nod. Langford looks on with concern. And so he should. This was his fucking mess that got my girl taken away. I don't care if we are escaping on his fucking plane; he owes us that much at least.

I feel Lucie shift in my arms, her sobbing getting quieter and her breathing beginning to regulate.

'Jack, where are we going?'

'We're going home, baby' I tell her.

'To Cassie and Garrett?' She asks looking up at me.

'Yeah, to Cassie and Garrett. It'll be just Cassie, Garrett, you and me. And Melanie,' I tell her smiling down at her beautiful face.

'Melanie?'

'Yeah baby, she's with Garrett. We are going to where they are first then we're going home.'

'Okay,' is all she says tucking herself back into me.

She falls back to sleep in my arms. Exhausted, emotionally drained but safe. I guess she can sleep now. She wakes up again about half an hour later, lifting her head to look at me. Then she gives me the best present I could ever ask for. She gives me her smile. I lean down and kiss the top of her head.

'Darling, there's something I need to tell you,' I say gently.

She begins to sit up, pulling away from me. I try to hold her to me. I need to explain about Langford. But she moves too quickly and sits up fully, looking across at Liam. She instantly looks shocked to see him. Then she sees Langford. Her eyes widen in shock and her body begins to tremble. I know that look. She's going to lose her mind any minute now. Before I have a chance to speak, I watch her nostrils flare. I need to let her do this.

TWENTY-TWO

Lucie

'What the fuck?' I scream, lunging at that fucker.

I feel Jack grab me from behind, around my waist, hoisting me back towards his chest.

'Luce, baby, stop, you need to listen,' he says in my ear.

'Liam? I don't understand. Why are you here?' Why is Liam sitting next to Langford?

'I work for your uncle,' Liam tells me leaning forward so his forearms rest on his thighs.

'I'm so confused right now. Why do you work for him? Did you know who I was, Liam?' It shouldn't matter but I feel like it does.

'Yes, I knew who you were. When this was set up a few months back, Billy approached me. Directions were clear. Get in there, be part of the club and staff, then when you arrived, ensure you were safe.' Liam lowers his head then pulls back up to reach my eyes. 'I'm sorry I let you down darl. I did my best without blowing my cover. I couldn't afford to get kicked out because if I was gone, who was going to look after you if things got worse? I did what I could honey,' he says softly.

I reach out to his hands and hold them in mine, 'I know you did and I'm grateful that you were there looking out for me even if I didn't know,' I say gently. Letting go of his hands, I move backwards to the safety of Jack's lap and soften as I feel his arms go back around my middle.

'You though…you are something else,' I sneer to Billy. 'What kind of fucking family are you? Actually, scrap that. My own mother has been playing dead for the last eight years so I guess being rotten runs in the family eh?'

'Just listen to him, Lucie' Jacks says in my ear. How is he so calm?

'Listen to what Jack? It's because of him that I was there!' I scream as I struggle to get out of his hold.

'Lucie, we're safe because of him. This plane was for him. Calm down darling and we'll explain. Actually, he can fucking explain because I'm not sure of the story myself at this point.'

I allow Jack's embrace to calm me and look back at Langford, waiting.

'Polly,' Langford starts.

'Her name is Lucie, asshole. Lucie.' Jack says in a low and growly voice.

I rub my palm over his hands that he has around my middle.

'Sorry, Lucie. Listen, I'm sorry kiddo. But you've got to

understand that nothing was going to happen to you,' Langford tells me looking me directly in the eyes.

'Nothing was going to happen to me?' I ask in shock. 'They had me trussed up like a fucking animal! What the fuck is your definition of nothing?' I shout at him.

'Death!' He shouts back. I open my mouth to say something but then stop. 'Look Lucie,' he says running his hand down the back of his head and gripping his neck. 'Yes, I concede it was a deal that should never have been made but our backs were against the wall on this,' he tells me.

'Us? Who is 'us', Billy?' I ask even though the horrible feeling in the pit of my stomach tells me I already know the answer.

'Me and your parents,' he says looking down at the floor.

I move to stand and Jack's grip on me tightens. 'Let me stand Jack.'

Jack removes his arms and allows me to stand and walk to the small aisle on the plane. I pace. I need to. The heat in me is rising fast. I run my hands through my dirty hair and pull on it. My parents. My mum and dad helped him. If I thought that her, them, lying to us about mum being dead wasn't enough to fuck me up, they actually chose to do this to me.

Jack stands and walks towards me putting his arm around my shoulder and bringing me in close to his body.

'Let him tell you the story baby. Just get the facts as to what happened.' He places his hands on either side of my face and brings his forehead down to touch on mine. 'Just listen. Then when we touchdown, we will be on our way to Garrett and Melanie then home. Home and safe. But listen to him. Then you'll know what happened and why. It doesn't have to change a damn thing on how you feel, but when you have all the facts, we can start putting this behind us and move on with our lives.' He gently kisses my forehead then steers me back to our seats. I don't sit on his lap this time, but in the seat next to him. He takes my hand and that simple act alone gives me the strength I need. He's right, I do need the facts.

Billy proceeds to tell his version of events. I don't know this man so have no way of knowing if it's the whole truth. Every now and then Jack's grip on my hand tightens. I may not know my uncle but I know Jack. My pain is his pain. That's what love is.

He proceeds to tell us that it started with the theft of a container and how they stole the wrong one. How the debt was sold to the Kasovolovnic's. How Interpol approached Billy to help track down the Kasovolovnic family and the plan that he and my parents came up with. And now I know the truth; my own family used me as a pawn. My own parents allowed this to happen. They chose getting out of a debt more important than their own flesh and blood.

'And that's about it,' says Billy. 'When you get home, your mum can answer any questions you have left.'

'Home? Mum? Oh, you've got that wrong. The mum who died eight years ago? She's still dead to me. I don't want to see her or my dad ever again.'

'Polly…' Langford says in a pleading voice.

'Lucie. My name is fucking Lucie,' I explode at him. 'I may have been viewed as the weak link in my own family, but don't think for one moment that is who I am. My "family" consists of just four people. Jack, Melanie, Cassie and Garrett. And you can fucking tell them whatever you want because my home is in America with Jack and that's where I'm going.' I can't stop the tears rolling down my face. I'm hurt and so angry. 'And you can tell my "loving parents" that they can go fuck themselves.'

On that note, I stand once again and make my way to the back of the plane in search of a toilet. Entering it I notice that it's actually much bigger than those you get on a commercial airline, which is fortuitous because before I even manage to lock the door, Jack walks in and locks it behind him.

We look at each other for a small beat before more tears start falling and Jack opens his arms taking me into them.

My Jack feels like home. I look up at him as he looks down at me.

'I love you Lucie,' he says smiling softly.

'I love you too, so, so much,' I respond.

And then in the bathroom of a private plane destined for I don't know where, Jack leans down and kisses me. It starts off so gentle and soft but there's a zap when our bodies reconnect and it turns manic. His tongue slides into my mouth and I suck on it. In response his arms around me tighten then move to grip my bum, squeezing hard, pulling my hips in tighter to what is now a rock-hard cock.

'I need you baby,' Jack says breaking the kiss.

'I feel dirty Jack,' but he just laughs as he pulls me in tighter.

'Not that kind of dirty!' I exclaim.

'I don't care, I need you, my body needs you, my fucking soul needs you baby,' and on those words the clothes start getting pulled away from each of our bodies.

Jack pops me up on the counter next to the sink, my bum barely fitting in the space.

Gently Jack runs his fingers through my wet folds as his tongue devours my mouth.

'Fuck me Jack. I need to feel you.'

His lust filled eyes look at me as he places his cock at my entrance and slides in, lifting me slightly. My head rolls back as I feel him fill me and light my soul on fire.

'Fuck, Luce, you feel so fucking good. I was so scared baby. Scared I would never find you,' he says with his forehead against mine. 'I would never have stopped looking for you. Not for a day. Not ever,' he says whilst fucking me slow and deeply.

'I love you. I love you. Only you Jack. Only ever you,' I say, chanting it over and over as he brings my body closer to the edge.

Within mere minutes I can feel my orgasm building. My body feels hot, my stomach tight, I ride him the best I can from the counter, as he leans back so he can rub my clit with his thumb.

'Come for me baby. Come over my cock,' he demands.

The detonation of my orgasm is strong and forceful and I can't breathe through it.

Feeling my body pulse around him, Jack begins to fuck me with abandon, slamming into me hard but holding me from behind to stop me from sliding away.

'Come inside me Jack, I need it,' I tell him, knowing he loves it as much as I do when we lose control of words.

It doesn't take long before Jack's back is arching and I feel him fill me. Perfectly. Ragged breaths are all we can hear as once again our foreheads meet.

Moving, Jack kisses me softly.

'You're mine,' he says gently, 'and I'm yours. Forever Lucie, just me and you baby.'

'Just me and you baby,' I repeat, smiling at him.

Getting cleaned up is slowed by soft kisses and touches and when we leave the bathroom we walk out hand in hand. I have no desire to be anywhere near Billy Langford so I pull on Jack's hands to the seats near the back of the plane. We sit down and buckle in, my head resting on Jack's shoulder.

'Thank you,' I whisper.

'For what?' He says looking at me with concern.

'For finding me. For knowing that I needed you.'

Briefly Jack closes his eyes and when he opens them, I see tears welling in them.

'I can't breathe without you,' he says squeezing my hand tightly.

'Jack, where are we going?'

'The plane will be landing at a private airfield in Holland.

Melanie is with Garrett in Amsterdam. We will get there then make plans to get back to the States. Melanie, she's been beside herself,' he says, 'as has Cassie'.

'Thank you for bringing my sister to me.'

'Don't thank me, this was all on G. I owe Garrett so much but I don't want to discuss it all now. I'll tell you when we get home, darling. I want to just focus on being back together for the rest of this flight. I've texted all the details to Garrett and he has arranged for us to be met at the airfield. I'm not sure if it will be him or a driver but I suspect Garrett will want to collect us and take us back to the apartment. You'll be with Melanie before you know it.'

Liam walks down the aisle towards our seats and takes the one opposite.

'You doing okay darl?' He asks me. His voice is so soft. Not the Liam's voice that I know. I feel myself smiling and nod at him that yes, I am. Jack squeezes my hand tighter; I know he doesn't like Liam. It's coming off him in waves. He is probably at war with his feelings, knowing that Liam looked after me when he couldn't and hating himself for it. He probably hates Liam too. I know this because I would feel the same way. Irrational I know, but love does that to a person.

Liam nods and smiles then gets back up to walk back to his seat. Stopping again to look back over his shoulder and inform us that we will be landing in around fifteen minutes.

'We need to discuss your parents at some point sweetheart,' Jacks whispers to me.

'I don't want to see them Jack,' I tell him feeling the tears coming again. I will not cry. I will not cry over them. 'How could she do that to me? How could she just walk away from me?' The words are out of my mouth before I realise what I've said. 'Jack, I'm sorry. I didn't mean that,' I tell him flustered.

'It's okay darling, I know you didn't. My mom wasn't well. It took me a long time to accept that but I know she wasn't in control of herself. To answer your question, I don't know. I can't understand anybody who would walk away from you.' He gives my hand another gentle squeeze.

'Did you meet them? Meet my parents?'

'Yeah, I met them. I'm not going to lie to you Lucie, I was angry as fuck with them and I don't think I'll ever forgive them for putting you in harm's way,' he says sadly. 'You look like your mom though, I was quite shocked by it, I think. But softer, your face, your whole being is just so much softer.'

'It feels odd that you have spoken to my mum, when I just caught a glimpse of her that day in the woods.' Would I ever talk to her again? I truly don't know.

'That was quite something huh? That was fate darling, tying us back together again. At that point I'd missed you so much darling. I was broken without you. Or at least that's how I felt until, well, you know,' again with the squeeze of my hand. 'Listen darling, when we go home, back to the States, we're not going back to my apartment or yours. Cassie has set us up in a new home, a place I hope you will love as much as I do but if you don't we don't have to stay okay?'

'Where is our new home?'

'Montana. It's beautiful there darling. Open spaces, quaint towns, peace. Nobody will know us and we can start again. Properly,' he says. I can feel him smiling.

'What about Cassie and Garrett? I don't want to not be able to see them Jack. They're our family.' The thought of not seeing them breaks my heart.

'You think those two would let you go?' He laughs. 'You'll see them darling. Cassie found our home and theirs. They love you, us, as much as we love them.'

My heart feels something that it hasn't done in a while. Joy. Happiness. Knowing that wherever we go, we will have Cassie and

Garrett with us. I don't know what to do about my parents, about seeing them again. I haven't even really thought of my brothers. But I don't want to think about any of them right now. I just want to get off this plane and see my sister and Garrett. And be with my Jack.

TWENTY-THREE

Jack

The landing is smooth and I smile down at my girl. Fuck, my heart feels elated. Complete. The plane taxis and when it finally stops, neither Lucie nor I can get off of the aircraft fast enough.

Billy Langford stands by the exit door.

I should thank him for getting us here but if he thinks I'm going to, he's delusional.

Liam stands with him and whilst I understand it, I hate it when he and Lucie embrace to say goodbye.

'I really am so sorry for everything Pol, Lucie, but please, I beg you, don't keep yourself from your mum,' Billy says to Lucie.

'Like she kept herself from me? I had no choice Mr Langford…'

'Lucie, what's with the Mr Langford? I'm your uncle,' he starts to say.

'No, Mr Langford, you're not my uncle because that would mean you are family and I can't imagine doing what you allowed to happen to me to my family. So you can tell my parents, that right now, I'm not interested in what they have to say. That there is no excuse good enough for what I've gone through. I don't know how I will feel in the future, but right now,' Lucie says taking a deep breath, 'right now? I have no interest in seeing them, either of them. Goodbye Mr Langford, I hope with everything in me that I never see your face again. I fucking hope you rot in hell.'

With our fingers entwined, Lucie and I exit the aircraft.

As we descend the steps, the early hours of the morning cold seeps into us. I put my arm around Lucie's shoulder, pulling her into me. Up ahead I can see car lights and even though I'm not sure who is in the car, we head towards it.

Blinded by the lights of the car, we can't see who is inside but we do see both the driver's and passenger's side doors open.

'Polly! Polly!' We hear Melanie's scream for her sister before we can see her face. Then she starts running towards us and Lucie breaks from my embrace to run into her sister's arms.

Crying and hugging ensues, Melanie brushes Lucie's hair off of her face so she can pepper it with kisses.

In the meantime, I can see Garrett walking in our direction too. As he and I meet we embrace each other.

'Well done son. You have her safe,' he tells me.

Still in his embrace, I tell him that I do, that we do.

Lucie pulls back from her sister when she spies Garrett and runs into his waiting arms.

'Darling. Darling, you're going to make this old man cry,' he says into her hair as he wraps her in his arms.

Lucie cries, holding him tightly. Other than me having her in my arms, there is nobody else I would rather see hold my girl. The only person who is missing is Cassie, but we will be with her soon enough.

Letting Lucie free of his embrace, he tugs her hand and tells us all that we're getting out of here.

Melanie puts her arms around me and kisses my cheek. 'Thank you Jack. Thank you for finding her.'

I sling my arm over Melanie's shoulder and kiss her on head, no words unnecessary.

We get into a car, Melanie and Lucie get in the back seat, forgoing seat belts in favour of holding each other close. I turn in my seat and see that Lucie is getting lost in her sister's embrace.

We drive for quite some time although I don't know how long. Garrett and I don't speak; G concentrating on the unfamiliar roads and me, just taking some time to breathe properly. It feels like it's been quite some time since I've been able to do that.

Arriving in central Amsterdam, we get out of the car and enter the apartment that Garrett and Melanie have been staying in.

Melanie walks straight into the bathroom, telling Lucie that she is going to run her a bath. I take a seat on the small sofa letting my head fall back and close my eyes. I feel the dip of the sofa next to me and Lucie snuggles up to me before crawling onto my lap. I circle my arms around her and hold her tight to me, silently vowing to never let her go.

I question how I will ever let her go anywhere on her own ever again, knowing that I'll have to at some point. I can't keep her as a prisoner just to ensure she's safe.

Garrett passes me a beer. 'Lucie, would you like a drink darling?' He asks stroking her hair.

'Just some water please Garrett.'

Bringing her the water, he takes a seat opposite her.

'I know you're tired kiddo,' he says to Lucie, 'but we've got a phone call to make to my wife.'

Lucie nods and Garrett hits the buttons on his phone and puts it on the table between us, hitting the speaker button.

'Hello? Garrett? Do you have her?' Cassie's voice is tearful and shaky and it breaks my heart of hear her like that.

Garrett nods at Lucie.

'Cassie,' she all but whispers.

'Lucie? Lucie! Darlin', tell me it's really you?'

'It's me Cass. Hi.'

'Oh my god, I swear, I've prayed a thousand times for this moment. I'm so glad to hear your voice baby girl.'

Lucie laughs through her own tears. 'So, Cass, I hear we're all moving to Montana?' She says.

'Well, it seems like a good place you know? My sister has a house here that she rents out so that's where you and Jack are going to go and G and I will be renting a place close by. I've bought you a lovely big coat and some new snow boots, cos darlin' we're going to need them. The snow is deep, baby. Oh my god! You're safe!' Cassie is laughing and crying at the same time and so is Lucie. Garrett is openly wiping the tears streaming down his face away, an indulgent smile on his face.

'I don't mind a bit of snow Cass. I just want to come home.' God that warms my heart like nothing else could. Home. Home with me, with us.

Melanie comes out of the bathroom and tells Lucie that her bath is ready.

'Cass, let the girl go. She's going to go and have a bath then we need to get some sleep. Tomorrow is going to be a long day but we'll be home before you know it baby,' Garrett tells his wife.

'Okay, I'll see you very soon. I love you all!' Cassie shouts down the line.

We say our goodbyes and Melanie holds out her hand for Lucie. 'Come on bubs, let's get you into a warm bath,' Melanie says to her sister, wrapping her arm around Lucie's waist. Lucie pulls back from her for a moment, leaning down to kiss me. Her lips feel soft and perfect. Like my girl.

Not five minutes later, Melanie comes back into the room. 'Jack, Lucie wants you to go into the bathroom.' I love that Melanic is using Lucie and not Polly. I get up just as Garrett says that he's going to go to bed and Melanie tells us she is too.

I walk into the bathroom and damn near lose my mind to see Lucie lying back with her eyes shut in a bath filled with bubbles.

I quietly close the door behind me. 'You okay baby?' I ask her gently. I'm not a fool. Even if she says yes, I know it will be some time before she can even begin to process everything that has happened. But I'll be here when she does.

'Will you get in with me Jack?'

I remove my clothes and as Lucie scoots forward, I slip in behind her and pull her body onto my chest, wrapping my arms around her naked body. I lift her arms to take a look at her wrists which have bruising on them.

'Don't, Jack. I don't want to think about it. I just want to feel. I just want to feel you. Feel us, okay?' She whispers.

Leaning forward I kiss her cheek to acknowledge that I heard her. 'I love you,' I whisper in her ear.

'I love you the mostest,' she responds.

'You think you're going to be able to sleep for a bit, sweetheart?'

'I'm so tired but feel wired too. I don't know,' she says.

'Well, we'll try okay and if we can't then no pressure if it doesn't happen darling,' I reassure her.

Holding her tighter to me, I lean down and put my head on her shoulder so that our cheeks are pressed together.

I don't know how long we've been in the bath just holding together for. Lucie keeps leaning forward to let some of the water drain away then running more hot water. Neither of us want to get out.

'What will you do in Montana, Jack? Will you still be an agent?' Lucie asks me.

'I am on a leave of absence, thanks again to Garrett, but honestly, baby? Right now, I don't know. When I left the UK and went to Europe I officially went AWOL and that will cause issues for me with the Bureau, but the truth is I don't think I can continue to be an agent. I don't want to; I just can't be away from you and home again and so I think it's unlikely I could continue with my role anyway. When it's time to talk about the options, we'll do that together okay? Then I'll speak to my boss.'

Lucie nods, squeezing my forearms.

'What about the coffee shop? Is Cassie just going to leave it?'

'Again, I don't know. I know that her friend Maggie has been looking after the place for her.' I have no idea if Cassie plans to sell the place and whilst I should feel bad that she's doing that because of us, I know she wouldn't do it unless she wanted to.

Finally, we get out of the bath and take time drying off, in between just holding each other. Walking into the room we're going to sleep in, it looks like somebody, Melanie probably, has put a pyjama set on the bed for Lucie.

'These are mine from before I left home,' Lucie says smiling as she picks them up and starts to put them on. 'I can't believe Melanie even found them. I don't even know why I never took them with me when I moved to the States.'

I put some boxer briefs on. Not that I don't want to be skin to skin with her but holding her, letting her sleep is what she needs. To sleep safely.

It's not long after we get in bed that I feel Lucie relax against me and I know she's sleeping. I can't. I keep seeing her on that stage, trussed up. I need to talk myself down from the ledge a few times. My anger still evident. I wonder how long it will take for both of us to lay our demons to rest.

I need to let it go. I need to focus on looking after my woman. I need to get us home.

TWENTY-FOUR

Lucie

It feels amazing to wake up wrapped around Jack. I didn't know if that would ever happen again and I will be forever grateful for this.

I hear noise outside our bedroom but have no idea what time it is. Gently removing myself from Jack's embrace, I quietly slip out of bed and through the door, desperate not to wake him.

I know he's been in hell over me and if he is relaxed enough now to sleep, then I want to leave him like that as long as possible.

Wandering to the kitchen of the apartment, I find Melanie at the little table drinking coffee. What's better than waking up next to

Jack? Seeing my sister smile her brightest smile when she sees me.

'You want a coffee, chick?' She says getting up and moving to the coffee maker. 'It's a Nespresso…proper nice. Gonna get one for myself when I get home…well if I go, eh?'

'Coffee, yes please. Why wouldn't you go home?' I stare at her. Why wouldn't she? Where would she go?

'Well firstly, I'm coming home with you lot,' she says over her shoulder.

'You are?' I squeal and jump into her arms as she turns to face me.

'You think you can get rid of me, chicken? I'm not letting you out of my sight.'

'What about Mum and Dad?' I don't know why I am concerned but I don't want Melanie to feel obligated to me.

'Fuck'em Pol, sorry, Lucie. You are my priority as you always should have been.' Lowering her eyes, she breaks the embrace to sort my coffee.

When we are both seated, Mel looks at me with tears in her eyes. 'Guess we've got shit to talk about hey kiddo?'

'I don't want to talk about what happened Mel; not yet anyway.'

'I didn't actually mean that. I mean about me calling you back. Mum being alive. I promise you chick, I didn't know. Well, I did obviously but only a short time before I called you back. But if I thought for one moment…'

'Don't. I don't blame you in anyway and I never will, so there's no reason you should do it to yourself,' I tell her squeezing her hand.

Nodding, she holds my hand tightly.

'I don't know if I can ever forgive myself for what happened to you. God, I wish it had been me that had been taken. Why couldn't it have been me? For fucks sake, I was at home, they wouldn't have had to go to any effort to get me.'

'Perhaps it was because people would miss you Mel? I had a

life elsewhere; people were used to not seeing me. There wasn't anybody who would question why I wasn't around.'

'That actually sounds really logical Pol. Sorry, but that's it. That's the last time I call you that. From now on you are only Lucie,' she laughs.

I laugh too, until I look at her and her face has gone from smiling to hard in a few seconds.

'Mel?'

'I'm telling you now Lucie I will never forgive Mum and Dad. I don't actually know what I'm more angry about, them lying about her being dead? I mean, what the fuck? It's like we're suddenly living in some shitty TV movie. I'm blown away by it. How could they do that to us?'

'I don't know. I don't understand it any more than you do. Perhaps we'll never understand. Do the boys know, Mel?' It's the first time I have asked about my brothers.

'They do now. I thought they might already have known about Mum that is, but they didn't. I had to fight them tooth and nail not to get involved and I only did that because when I spoke to Garrett, who by the way, is the nicest bloody man, anyway, after I spoke to him, I knew the last thing that was needed was our meat heads getting involved.'

I nod in agreement. I'm relieved to hear they didn't know about Mum either. That would have been another betrayal to both me and Mel. 'And you're coming back to the States with us? How long will you stay? I know you have your business and Sammy,' I say winking at her, raising both my eyebrows.

'The gym is in safe hands. As for Sammy…I don't know kiddo. On the face of it, we're just fuck buddies but I think we're exclusive fuck buddies. That's a bit sad right?' She says laughing at herself.

'Perhaps you should speak about being more than that?'

'We'll see. For now, I'm coming with you and everything else will just need to sit on the back burner.'

'Mel, I don't even know where my passport is,' I tell her.

'Firstly, I have your passport because you left it at the house and I thought it would be a good idea to bring it. No idea how we're getting back to the States though.'

'Private plane,' we both whirl round at the sound of Garrett's voice.

'Wow…never been on a private plane,' Mel says smiling. 'When do we leave?'

'In around ninety minutes, girls. Melanie you want to come and get some breakfast with me? We can get some pastries and all eat together. Let Jack sleep a little longer?' Garrett asks.

'Sure, let me just grab a quick shower' Mel says jumping up.

'How you doing darling? Did you sleep?' Garrett says laying a gentle kiss onto my hair.

I look up and smile. 'How did you do it G?' I ask him, using the moniker Jack uses for him.

'Do what?' He says over his shoulder as he sets the coffee machine up for himself.

'How did you get Jack to me so fast? How did you get Melanie? I don't know Garrett, I have so many questions but I know you were the key player in getting me out of there.'

'I'm getting to be an old man Lucie and when you're old you know a few people. You owe people favours; people owe you favours. At some point, one of you is going to call your favour in. I was the first person Jack called when it all happened.' I can hear the pride in his voice. Jack and Garrett's father and son relationship goes beyond surrogacy. It's deeper. It's love without boundaries. 'There's nothing that Jack, Cassie, nor I would do to ensure your safety darling. Wild horses couldn't stop us.'

I smile at him knowing that he is speaking his truth.

'I can't wait to see Cassie,' I tell him, my heart bursting at the thought of it.

'Sweetheart, let me tell you something. A long time ago, for many different reasons, Cassie and I didn't pursue becoming parents. And that was okay with us. We had each other. We were our own team and our own family. Did you know that I was adopted?'

I shake my head no. It's never been mentioned before.

'Well I was and it wasn't good darling. It's not always like in the movies where the new parents come to collect you from the home and you walk off hand in hand into the distance. I was a band-aid kid for my adoptive parents. Their marriage already had too many cracks to speak of and getting a child of six who had spent all his life to date in the orphanage, cos that's what it was in those days, wasn't going to fix them and somehow, they found a way to blame me for their marriage not improving. Now that didn't put me off having kids, but it certainly made me think more about it. But it was never like that with Cassie. We didn't have any cracks. But the truth is, biologically, it wasn't to be. We discussed adopting but then we were selfish with our time for one another and we decided that we would rather stay as we were. We were lucky to get a couple of nephews thanks to Cassie's sister but we never felt like we had missed out. Years later, as you know, Jack came into our life. Jack was covering his own heart with a band-aid. He was, hell he is, the closest thing to having a son. Cassie worries over him like a good mother would do. And then you turned up and turned my woman's world upside. I've never seen her the way she is with you Lucie.'

Tears are burning my eyes and I just let them go. They start to stream down my face as I picture what the reunion between Cassie and I will be like.

'This has changed her, Lucie. Between Jack and Cassie and me of course, you need to be prepared that you will never go anywhere alone again,' he laughs, coming over to once again stroke down my hair as he gently kisses me on the head.

I grab the hand that was on my hair and hold it. Tightly. Looking up at him.

'Now come on sweetheart, no more tears,' he says wiping them away from my face.

'Thank you Garrett,' I tell him with love and honesty and what will be a lifetime's worth of respect.

'Anytime darlin', anytime.'

Melanie re-enters the room, cleaned and dressed pulling her little case behind her.

'I'm ready when you are Garrett. Lucie, I just re-packed the suitcase you had at Dad's house so you have your own stuff,' she says smiling. She says, 'Dad's house' rather than 'home' like she would normally. I'm grateful. I know where my heart thinks of as home and it's no longer there.

'Thanks Mel and thank you for my pj's,' I say laughing.

'Yeah, well don't get too excited chicken cos I didn't wash them before I left which means they haven't been washed for as long as you've been gone,' she says laughing.

'I don't care,' I tell her honestly.

'Okay, darling, we're going to go grab some pastries so we can all have something to eat and we can then discuss what today is going to run like. We'll be back in about a half hour, so you need to wake his lordship and both be ready for when we are back.'

'See you in a bit,' says Melanie.

Nodding at them both I make my way back to the bedroom Jack and I used. As I enter the semi-dark room, I see him and my heart literally skips a beat. The duvet is pushed low, setting just below his hips. His naked torso makes my breath catch. Then something else catches my eye and I smile.

Walking over to the bed, the underside of Jack's bicep is on display fully as his hand is behind his head as he sleeps. Written in a beautiful script I can see the words 'Lucie, forever my love'. Tears well up once again. Where are all these tears coming from? I reach over gently, wanting to run my fingers over the writing but change my mind and lean over him and lay a gentle kiss on the words.

'All true baby,' Jack says sleepily, slowly opening his eyes and smiling at me. No more than a beat later, Jack grabs me, pulls me down and rolls us over so that he's lying on top of me and we are smiling like fools at each other.

'Good morning beautiful girl,' he says kissing my nose.

'Good morning handsome,' I say leaning upwards and kissing his chin.

Then we just grin at each other.

'Ready to go home, baby?' He asks.

'Yes sir, I am. Garrett and Melanie have gone out to get some breakfast pastries but Garrett wants us up and ready for when they get back. We have about twenty minutes or so.'

Getting up and holding out his hand to me, he leads me to the bathroom and turns the shower on, which sits over the bath rather than a cubical.

Jack puts his hand under the spray to check the temperature then motions for me to get in. Stripping quickly out of my pj's I slip under the warm water letting it run down the front of my body. I feel Jack get in behind me.

'Let me wash you sweetheart,' he says gently next to my ear.

He grabs the shower gel as I turn around to face him.

'I love your tattoo. I want one with your name.'

He looks down momentarily before looking and making eye contact again.

'You can have anything you want Lucie.' He takes my face in his hands, the pads of his thumbs gently rub against my cheeks. 'I was never going to give up on you, on us. I was going out of my mind. I knew something wasn't right.'

'My guitar,' I state.

'Your guitar,' he smiles. 'Immediately, that didn't feel right. I knew if you had planned on leaving for good, no way would you have left it. You knew I'd see it. Something to show me you'd be back. Actually, it was more than that; it felt like a clue. I knew that you'd never leave that behind unless you had to. It told me you were in a rush.'

'I think all of that is true. I didn't know what else to do,' I tell him, running my hands up his chest. 'I know that if I'd woken you, I would have to tell you everything. Who my family were, what they were. I was scared I would lose you over it.'

'I always knew there were secrets, stuff you were holding back from telling me but I just assumed that in time, you'd tell me. Why didn't you confide in me?'

'You are the right side of the law Jack. You and Garrett. I didn't want to tarnish myself with telling you all the truth about them. My dad, well, for as long as I can remember, he's been a criminal in one form or another. Not hardcore but a criminal, nonetheless. My uncle too, although I didn't really know him,' I shrug.

'Well, we can discuss everything properly when we get home and when you feel comfortable in doing so. It's too soon right now and I think Melanie needs to be present when we talk about it, okay?'

I nod, relieved that he doesn't seem angry that I did a moonlight flit on him.

Jack starts to wash my body and it feels wonderful to have his hands sweep over me. Then I take my turn to wash him. When we are both rinsed free of any lingering soap I kiss the tattoo.

'I'm going to get one for you.'

'Whatever you want darling,' he says indulgently.

We dry ourselves in the bathroom, then walk hand in hand to the bedroom to get dressed, hearing the front door open as we are nearing ready.

Coming out of the room we find Melanie and Garrett making coffee and putting pastries on the table.

'Wow, these look lovely Mel. You found my favourites,' I tell her giving her a kiss on the cheek. She quickly pulls me into her arms and kisses my head.

'I love you chicken,' she says before letting go and turning away. My sister is not a crier. She's a shouter. Having said that, I didn't know I was such a crier until recently. But regardless of Mel's tough exterior, I know that she hides a heart of gold. We've always been close but now, that closeness has moved to a whole new level. As far as blood family goes, Melanie is the only one I have now. And she is more than enough.

'Right let's eat, people, we need to get moving soon,' Garrett says bringing the coffee to the table and taking a seat.

'We have a plane leaving here at 11am. A friend of a friend's plane so we don't have to go through the normal formalities and we'll be landing at a private airstrip just north of Great Falls. It's a hell of a long flight so we will be stopping to refuel once we are stateside, which will be somewhere in New Hampshire. When we finally get to Montana, Cassie will meet us there.'

I nod my understanding at Garrett then take Melanie's hand.

'You sure you want to come with us Mel? I totally understand if you just want to go home,' I want her to feel like she has a choice even though I desperately want her to stay close to me.

'And miss out on the chance of riding my very own cowboy?' She laughs.

'Oh jeez,' Garrett says shaking his head and Jack and I laugh on.

Gathering our things after we finish eating takes just minutes and we are then on our way to the airfield. The plane looks slightly bigger than the one we arrived on last night and when we enter the cabin space, it has a row of two seats on each side of the plane then directly behind those four, it has the bed type chairs you see on a first-class section, so at least we won't have to sleep sitting up. An older stewardess helps get us comfortable and informs us that we will be taking off shortly. We take our seats and buckle in.

As the plane starts to taxi down the runway, Jack takes my hand in his. I squeeze it in return.

'Ready to go see our new home darling?'

'I am Jack. Let's start our story again'.

TWENTY-FIVE

Jack

Even with a refueling stop, it has been a long-ass flight. At one point, Lucie felt sick but managed to hold it in. I think it was just that nauseous feeling you get when you have breathed in nothing but re-circulated air and plane fumes.

We all managed to sleep at some point, the rest of the time was spent watching movies. Lucie and Melanie shared a game of Scrabble, laughing at each other for making words up. There was a lot of cheating going on but Lucie was happy and relaxed and kept looking over to me, showing me her beautiful smile.

Whilst the plane refuels somewhere in New Hampshire, we are allowed off the aircraft to get some proper fresh air.

The girls link arms and walk up ahead whilst Garrett and I walk slowly behind.

'You ready for a new life, son?' He asks me.

'Yeah. I just want her to be happy and to feel safe G. I want to be able to talk about what's happened and then put it away. I don't ever want her to feel scared ever again.'

'Well, as much as I admire you for that, I think that is probably impossible. You can only do so much to protect her Jack, but we have to remember to let her breathe. If we wrap her up too much, she's going to feel like a prisoner and nobody should ever feel like that. Or in her case, again.'

'You should have seen that place G. I'm glad you never saw her how I found her. I wouldn't want that to be imprinted on your mind. Have you heard from Frank? How pissed is he?' I ask knowing that Garrett would have had to deal with the fallout of my actions at the club.

'Oh, he's pissed Jack, make no mistake. But he gets it. Said he probably would have done the same. Thierry told him that old man Kasovolovnic didn't make it but they intercepted his two sons at the family residence and they will be charged with a litany of crimes including false imprisonment and trafficking. Olga and Guillaume both got out fine and Liam will be helping with the trial. You know man, it is what it is. If that had been Cass, I'd have probably shot everybody in the place so they were lucky you just got what you went for, your girl.'

'I'm sorry if I have caused bad blood for you, but I'm not sorry I did what I did,' I tell him, looping my arm around his shoulder. How will I ever repay this man for what he did to help me get to Lucie?

Before long, the stewardess is calling us over telling us that we will be once again taking off shortly. Back on the plane, we take to the air for the final leg of our journey.

We all choose to stay in our upright seats for the remainder of the flight so that we are all able to chat. I sit nearest the window so that Lucie can sit near to her sister.

Soon we are on our final hour and I am looking out the window when I feel Lucie's body leaning against my arm. I look over to her and smile.

'God, Jack, look at that! It's so beautiful. Look at the snow!' She exclaims as we see the snow-capped mountains and landscape.

'Snow? I fucking hate snow!' Moans Melanie and the rest of us laugh at her statement.

'Too late now darling,' Garrett tells her.

'Oh my god I'm so excited to see Cassie. And I'm excited for you to meet her Mel,' Lucie says to her sister.

'I'm looking forward to meeting her too, chicky.'

In what feels like a matter of moments, the stewardess is checking we all have our seatbelts securely fastened and we begin our descent.

Landing is a bumpy affair with us all doing a little bounce in our seats but the relief is palpable.

Home. We're safe.

When the aircraft finally pulls to a halt, Lucie is out of her seat in a flash. She's literally jumping around the space wanting to get off as soon as possible.

'Patience, young Padawan,' Melanie says laughing as she gathers her personal belongings.

The stewardess sees us off the plane and when we reach the bottom of the steps, Lucie lets out a high pitch squeal and takes off in the direction of an SUV parked up on some grass. We all stop to watch Cassie who is now running full pelt towards Lucie. They seem to catch each other in full flight. If I could capture in a photo what unconditional love looks like, it would be the scene in front of us.

Cassie is holding Lucie's head in her hands, their foreheads pressed together. We start to walk towards them and I feel emotion clog in my throat.

They could be mother and daughter. They are mother and daughter. You certainly don't need to be related by blood to claim those titles.

They both turn to watch us walk up to them. Cassie comes to embrace me and softly cries into my chest. I can't remember what it felt like to have been held by my mom but I know whenever she did hold me like this, I felt loved and safe. This is how I feel now with Cassie.

Cassie and Garrett have proved time and time again that they are my family. And I will spend the rest of my life being their son.

Next Cassie moves to throw her arms around her beloved Garrett, in whose arms she continues to cry as Lucie comes back and wraps her arms around me whilst capturing Melanie's hand in hers.

'Cassie,' Lucie says, 'this is my sister Melanie'.

Now it's Melanie's turn to be hugged and squeezed by Cassie. This woman has enough love for us all.

'Welcome Melanie, I'm so glad you're here. You can stay with Lucie and Jack or we have a couple of guest rooms at the place we are renting that you are welcome to stay in. Your choice darlin',' Cassie tells Melanie.

'I'm not ready to let my sister out of my sight yet, but when they get fed up with me being a third-wheel, expect to find me on the doorstep.'

'Well just know you are welcome darlin'. Right, let's get out of this cold and back to the house,' Cassie tells us leading the way.

The drive takes around forty minutes, Cassie driving with Garrett in the front riding shotgun.

Soon we are pulling into a snow-covered driveway and at the end stands a two-story timber house. It looks like something from a Christmas poster. Lucie squeezes my hand, letting me know she's excited.

Exiting the car, we all make our way up three steps to reach the wrap around veranda. Cassie opens the front door and turns smiling to us.

'Welcome home my darlins'.'

As we enter, the warmth is the first thing to hit us. Looking to our right we can see the source; a beautiful, very large, wood burning stove fire. The house itself is all wood with colourful furniture and rugs. Perfect.

'Oh, I love it Cass! This belongs to your sister? It's beautiful,' Lucie says moving around the space.

'I took the liberty of bringing your clothes up from your apartment and I let your landlord know you wouldn't be back. I hope that's okay with you?'

Lucie nods. She's so busy walking around touching everything, I really don't think she cares. Until she stops dead in her tracks and spins round to face Cassie.

Cassie smiles back at her, obviously aware of what Lucie has just seen. I move towards her and spy it immediately. Lucie's guitar hangs on the wall, waiting for her.

Tears are sliding down Lucie's face. 'Thank you Cass.'

Looking at Cassie, I can see she is dealing with her own tears, simply wiping them away and nodding at Lucie. Words are unnecessary.

'Listen why don't you guys freshen up and we'll, well Garrett can do the same then we'll be back and we can cook dinner here. The house we're in is literally just behind, the other side of the brook.

It actually takes longer to drive there than to walk!' Cassie laughs.

A few hours later we are all back together, dinner is cooking and we are all seated on the couches, listening to each other and the fire crackling. Lucie is snuggled up in my arms, her head leaning on my chest.

No more getting lost, we've finally found home.

EPILOGUE

Lucie

Montana

We've been home for nearly three months now. Waking up to Jack is my most favourite part of each day.

Today, I wake up, rolling over to find Jack watching me. He reaches out to stroke my cheek.

'Good morning beautiful,' he says on a smile.

'Hey handsome,' I say back, reaching out to touch his face.

A tear slides unexpectedly from my eye.

'Hey, no tears baby,' he says wiping it away with this thumb, cupping my cheek and drawing me towards him. Kissing me softly, smiling lovingly. His eyes shine with adoration and it's that which brings tears into my eyes.

'Thank you, Jack,' I tell him earnestly.

'You're welcome, but what am I being thanked for?' He asks.

'For loving me, for never giving up, for knowing I wouldn't leave you if I hadn't needed to. For finding me when I didn't know I was lost then finding me again when I was. For saving my life,' I tell him.

'You gave me life, baby. From the moment we met, you breathed life into my body, into my soul. My life will be forever thanking you for that,' he tells me pulling me close.

'I'm sorry, so sorry, that I never told you my truth, that you had to find out the way you did. I can't say it wasn't my intention to lie to you because it was. I was planning on telling you everything but then I got the message from Mel and I just had to get home. Explaining would have taken too long. You would have insisted on coming with me and I just couldn't let that happen Jack. I didn't know what I was going back to and so I had to go alone. The only thing I could think of that would make you believe I wasn't gone for good was leaving my guitar. I never meant to hurt you, or Cassie and Garrett. I know I did and I'm so sorry,' I say as more and more tears stream down my face.

'Hey, listen to me, you don't need to feel guilty. Getting you back after knowing you'd been taken wipes it all away. I would have moved heaven and earth to get to you,' Jack tells me.

I sniff a laugh, 'you practically did move heaven and earth to get to me,' I say trying to raise a smile.

'You're home, you're safe and those are the only things that matter from here on out. Okay? So no more apologies,' Jack says leaning forward to kiss my forehead.

I close my eyes as his lips touch my skin.

This isn't the first time we've had the same conversation. It's happened probably over a dozen times so far. I am happy and I'm safe but sometimes, when I wake up, the enormity of what we've both been through hits me again and I just need to say what I need to get out. Jack sometimes instigates the conversation but most times, it's been me.

'Do you know what I missed most?' Jack asks with a huge smile on his face. He says the same thing every day.

'I'll go put the coffee on,' I say laughing, swinging my legs out of bed.

'Good idea, then let's put some warm clothes on and take a walk yeah?' He asks getting out of bed too.

'Sounds good honey, but it looks cold out there so I need to find my warmest socks. This London girl still has yet to acclimatise,' I say laughing. I love it here already; I love the peace and the quiet and the overall beauty that surrounds us from every viewpoint. As I wander through the house, with its big windows, it doesn't seem to matter what window you look out of, all you can see is the most stunning vista and whilst some might find the solitude isolating. For me, for us, it's exactly where we need to be. This is our home. It's the place where Jack brought me to recover, where he brought my sister to help me recover. I will never forget that. He could have been selfish but that's not Jack. He knew that I needed Melanie, just like he knew I needed Cassie and Garrett. They found this place for us, well, Cassie did. Garrett called her from Europe to tell her what we needed and she found it. It used to belong to Cassie's sister and initially we were renting it but we fell in love and Jack made her an offer and she accepted. This is us now, our base and our home for as long as we want.

Cassie and Garrett have also moved up here permanently. When I first arrived in the States it was Cassie who gave me a sense of belonging and I guess with everything that has happened in these past months, our bond and my attachment to her has only grown. She is like a mother to me. She cares, she protects. It's her I call every morning and it's her and Garrett who we choose to spend our time with.

We have a permanent room here for Melanie too. She promises to come over as much as possible, knowing I will never go back to England. Who knows she may even move here one day herself?

I don't speak to my brothers a lot. It's been hard on them. They felt pulled with their loyalties and whilst I don't understand it, I love them and I accept that they don't wish to pick a team.

Melanie is different. Melanie would give up her life for me. She never once found her loyalties compromised. She doesn't have a relationship with our mum. As far as Mel is concerned, Maree died all those years ago and my sister is not big on forgiveness.

Mel and I try to talk every couple of days but we rarely speak of our parents. What is there to discuss? Dad dropped a letter from mum off at the gym. It was addressed to both Mel and me. To date the letter remains unopened. Maybe one day we'll read it, when we're together, but for now, it's in her safe, gathering dust. Although she is back at her gym, making a really good business, she no longer has anything to do with the fight nights.

She wants her life to be strictly legit. I get it. She no longer wants to be associated with anybody who could be like the people who took me. She's always protected me; always has and I know she and Jack always will. I have the love of the best four people in the world and I know without a doubt I am the luckiest girl alive.

As for her and Sammy…well they continue to be fuck buddies. I think Sammy would like more but Melanie just isn't ready to fully commit. She told me she thinks he's a bit of a player. I told her that I'd thought the same about Jack. She laughed at that and then started calling Jack Mr Golden Bollocks.

I whistle as I make the coffee but stop when I hear scratching.

'Jack? Jack, you there?' I shout out.

'You okay darling?' He asks me as he wanders into the kitchen. There is a slight smirk on his face and instantly I know something is up.

'What's going on? And don't tell me nothing. I know you. I know your selection of faces so give it up, whatever it is,' I tell him with a laugh in my voice. 'I can hear scratching. Do we have mice?'

'Mice? Up here? Nah. Bears but not mice,' he says barely controlling his grin. 'Let's have a look outside the door, shall we?' Jack says taking my hand and leading me towards the front door of our house.

Jack turns the locks and as he opens the door, a brown ball of fluff runs in.

'Oh my god Jack, a puppy? You got us a puppy?' I say falling to my knees as the puppy comes over to me. I pick him, her, who knows at this point, up and hold the pup to my face so that we are nose to nose.

'Hey baby. Are you ours?' I ask the puppy then look up at Jack only to find him on one knee.

Jack

She's the most beautiful girl in the world and she's mine. I knew it the moment I met her. She really did fill my soul that had previously been filled only with the abandonment that had been in my heart since the day mom left me.

She loves me in a way that only the luckiest of people will ever experience. She is love, kindness, beauty and trust, wrapped up in the most desirable package a man could ask for.

Simply, she is my everything and I am hers. I look up at her as she covers her mouth with her hand, still cradling the puppy in her arms.

'Marry me? I love you today, I loved you yesterday and I will love you until my last breath leaves my body and even then, even then baby, I will continue to love you for eternity.'

The look on her face floors me; steals my breath. Did I ever know it was possible to be loved like this? I wish she'd say something. Instead, she shifts forward on her knees so that we are eye to eye with each other.

Holding onto the puppy with one arm, she reaches out and touches my face, tears rolling down her cheeks.

'Yes, Jack. Yes, I will marry you. In a heartbeat I will marry you,' she tells me.

Smiling, I pluck the puppy from her arms. 'Look at the collar baby,' I instruct her.

She does as I request and sees for the first time, tied to a ribbon on the collar is a diamond ring. A pink square diamond surrounded by smaller diamonds.

'Jack,' she breathes out.

'Take it off the ribbon, baby.'

Again, she does as I request of her; untying the ring from the ribbon and as soon as it's off, I put the puppy down, who quickly scampers away from us.

I pluck the ring from her fingers and gently flatten her left hand out in between us so that I can slip the ring onto her finger.

A perfect fit. Of course, it is.

'How did you get the perfect size?' She asks me, just like I knew she would. Dreading this moment, I take a breath and look down.

'I'd rather not say darling, not right now,' I tell her.

'Tell me Jack, it's okay, I can handle it,' but she knows. She knows that the next words out of my mouth are words I don't wish to speak.

'I got the ring before you left,' I stop, swallowing hard and looking down. 'The day you disappeared was the day I was going to ask you to be my wife.' I watch as the tears flow down her face, part in sadness, part in guilt.

'Don't do that. I didn't tell you so you would feel bad. I just wanted to tell you the truth. As for the ring size, well, I may have checked out your ring size when you were asleep. Does that make me sound creepy? It makes me sound creepy doesn't it?' I say laughing, desperately hoping it will lift the mood.

'No baby. It doesn't make you sound creepy. Stalkerish maybe, but not creepy,' she says laughing, leaning in so her lips find mine.

A simple loving kiss becomes an inferno in seconds. Within moments we are lying on the floor, me on top of her, kissing deeply. Stealing the breath for one another. Feeding air to each other.

Things on the floor are heating up quickly when there is a knock at the door and the puppy barks. We both look at him and laugh.

'You going to protect us Tyson?' Lucie says scooping him off the floor and into her arms where he immediately licks her face.

'Tyson? Like Mike Tyson?' I ask her.

'Why not? Just another protector in my life,' she says laughing.

I reach for the door and open it to find Cassie, Garrett and Melanie standing there, along with Declan and Carmel, just liked I'd arranged. After all, the puppy didn't arrive on his own.

Cassie walks in first, throwing her arms around Lucie followed by Garrett. I watch as Melanie holds back, tears falling onto her cheeks. I reach out to take her hand, drawing her into the house and put my arm around her shoulders, giving her a squeeze.

'Mel,' Lucie cries out throwing her arms around her sister. The five of us watch them, rocking back and forth in each other's arms.

'You're back so soon! I can't believe it,' Lucie exclaims.

'And miss my baby sister getting engaged? Never!' Mel says laughing, smothering Lucie in kisses.

'You knew? Sneaky bitch,' Lucie says laughing, moving around so she can see us all but keeping her arm tucked around her sister. The joy on her face brings me to my knees. I will never tire of seeing my girl happy.

Lucie moves to Declan and I watch as they wrap each other up in a hug. Lucie lifts her arm to pull Carmel into the hug. Yeah, so Declan is a relation of her dad's. She told me that she won't hold that against him. Declan and Carmel have been good friends to Lucie. She loves them and they love her in return. They will always be part of our family.

'Let's celebrate!' Shouts Garrett and we all whoop our acceptance of a great idea.

I move to the kitchen and head out the back door to grab the champagne I've had chilling in the outside store, knowing Lucie won't ever go out there because, well you know, spiders. She can take on a couple of Albanians but spiders are a hard limit for her.

The corks are popped, Lucie has the newly christened Tyson back in her arms.

I cough, taking the stage in front of our loved ones. Our family might be small, but it is most definitely mighty.

'To my beautiful fiancée Lucie. I've always doubted the validity of the word "soulmate", until I met you. You were always destined to be my soulmate, we just needed to find each other sweetheart. You have to be lost in order to be found. And I thank the Universe every day that we found each other. Here's to our marriage and the rest of our life.'

The cheers go up as Lucie and I lock eyes as we clink glasses and take a sip.

‘I love you,’ she mouths to me.

‘I love you,’ I mouth back.

The End

Acknowledgements

Just a bit of background...this story began when I was waiting in the queue at Costa coffee after doing my shopping in Tesco. The barista was my muse for Lucie. I hope to find her so I can hand deliver a copy of this as a thank you.

Now let's start the thanks...

To my amazing boys. Thank you for saying I could do it. That I should do it. Thank you for making me feel like I can do anything. And thank you for loving me the way you do. You two are my world and I love you both endlessly. And no, you can't read it until you are eighteen, so hands off!

My family. Thank you for being so supportive of my dream. For being proud of me even before I finished this. I love you all.

To my beloved Grandparents, I wish you were here for this moment. I will love and miss you forever.

To my beautiful dogs, Dolly and Daisy, who have both, at times, sat either side of me whilst I pounded the keyboard. You are my treasures and my cuddlers.

To the real-life Melanie. The one who encouraged me to write over twenty years ago. I finally did it Chickabelle. Thank you for all of your support. I love you.

To my Neens, the greatest, loudest and pushiest cheerleader I could ask for. Thank you for kicking my arse and pushing me out of my comfort zone. I love you.

The following people read this in its first draft and I will be forever grateful for your time and support. Janey, Liam, Beth, Mel and Jenny. Thank you always.

To Chloe B, who did my first lot of edits. Thank you for getting this off the ground for me.

To my wonderful women's mentor Hayley. Thank you for helping me see the bigger picture, for your support and for helping to build me back up.

To Lou of LS Designs for my amazing cover and format. I will always treasure this cover and your skill. Thank you.

To Sophie, my wonderful editor. Thank you, lovely girl, so, so much. You truly are a star.

To my unofficial Beta's – Jillson and Sam (aka Donnatella). I owe you so much. Thank you both for the time you gave to this and the suggestions you made. See you for the next one? I love you both!

And to my Russ. I have so much to be grateful to you for. Some of it financial, some of it encouragement. But most of all, for the pride I see in your face when you tell people I wrote a book. I bloody, fucking love you.

To our @rantsandbigpants followers…thank you for love! What an amazing bunch you are!!! A special mention to the utterly inspirational women we have met on our RABP journey. I don't want to name names as it's not fair but Caz and Jo (aka @danceyertitsoff & @tit_less_wonder) you two….you are both ridiculous and incredible and we love you for it!!!

And finally, to everyone who buys and reads my baby. My heartfelt thanks to you, always.

Kitty xx

p.s. If you have a dream, follow it. If you think you can't...trust me, you can.

About Kitty

An "introverted extrovert" Kitty is known for her infectious laugh, filthy sense of humour and love of swearing… but she's at her happiest lying on the beach in her happy place, Kefalonia, or in her favourite chair with her kindle and a cappuccino…or a G & T.

Kitty grew up in Essex …(yes, the Essex girl jokes, she's heard 'em all..!) but spent her 'younger' years travelling (and sometimes working) the world; before finally settling back in Essex. She lives with her gorgeous twin sons and ridiculous Border Terrier, Dolly the Dollster.

When Kitty's not working at a well-known makeup brand or writing, she can be found appearing as 50% of the influencer duo "Rants and Big Pants"

She's a loyal friend, multi-tasking mum and voracious reader …but at heart, Kitty will always just be a girl who tucks her vest into her knickers.

Her 'hero' list started with Jackie Collins, Jilly Cooper and of course, JB Fletcher. She adores country music and wishes she could wear cowboy boots all day, every day.

Secrets and Lies is Kitty's first novel.

Connect with me!

Connect of Instagram – authorkittydb
Connect on Facebook Author KittydB
Drop me an email authorkittydb@gmail.com
Join the madness on Rants and Big Pants! @rantsandbigpants

KITTY DB

ROMANCE AUTHOR

Printed in Great Britain
by Amazon

28296948R00203